Deep Blue

Thomas G. Schubert

Wyvren Hearth Publishing

ISBN: 979-8-9927338-0-8 (ebook)

ISBN: 979-8-9927338-1-5 (paperback edition)

ISBN: 979-8-9927338-2-2 (hardback edition)

Visit the author's website at www.thomasgschubert.com

Printed in the United States of America

To everyone who clings onto impossible hope.
You are not alone.

The opposite of Love is not Hate.
No.
Hate is the twin sister of Love.

Both burn brightly within the heart.
Twist the thoughts.
Evaporate all reason and resolve.

Both spark a passion, a hunger, an unquenchable source of warmth and desire.
Empower the afflicted to commit unthinkable acts.

Both threaten to ignite an uncontrollable inferno that will consume everything.

Until nothing is left
but ash.

Prologue

Joaquin woke up and tasted blood. A sickly, coppery taste. He slowly picked his head up from the cold stone floor then set it back down again with a groan.

Everything hurt.

Everything.

He had been dreaming again, dreaming of Elena. They had been in the garden. She had been fawning over her roses, tenderly showing him each and every delicate bud as she rehashed the many years of failures endured before arriving at this moment. The final evening before her perfect roses would bloom.

He could hear the excitement and passion in her voice. He could see the easy joy in her smile.

He loved his wife, completely.

Joaquin moved forward and touched Elena's shoulder. The dream skewed sideways. An unexpected storm billowed dark gray clouds across the sky. He glanced back at their home's entrance a few steps away as heavy raindrops began to land among the flowers. Elena's eyes first looked up at the sky, then back down to her roses. Her children. In the span of two heartbeats the wind picked up, pulling at their clothes. The rain intensified then changed into hail, small pebbles of ice pelting all that lay under its gaze.

Joaquin knew they had to seek shelter. He pulled Elena up the path and mourned the loss of his wife's flowers. Somehow she tugged away from him, slipped her hand out from his grasp and ran back to her babies. He shouted after her, told her it wasn't worth it, but his voice was suddenly drowned out by thunder. Lightning lit the garden in a garish white sheen, revealing an empty space where his wife once stood. Where had his love gone? He shouted again, his hands over his head as he felt the grape-sized hail now stinging his neck, his back. There was no response. He cursed her impetuousness then dove into the rose bushes after Elena. After the heart of his heart.

He would not lose her again.

The bushes swallowed him whole, thrusting his world into a dim haze. Which way had she turned? The thorns pricked his skin, tore at his white silk shirt, gnashed at his forearms and chest. He pressed onward, yelling for her to return to him. The battered rosebuds grew fangs and bit into his calves, chomped bits out of his shoulders and sides.

No! These vile petals and stems would not stop him!

He unsheathed his sword and swung at the monstrous plants, cutting, hacking, carving his way forward. He had to reach Elena. He had to find her! The rose's leaves whipped out at him, razor sharp, slicing deeply into his flesh, flaying his skin into ribbons.

Nothing mattered. Nothing but Elena's safety.

Then, unexpectedly, his sword struck something different. Joaquin knew his fatal mistake before he saw her face. He pulled his weapon back, tried to reverse time and the errant swing but instead witnessed his wife's yellow dress bloom with pure red. Her face grew pale. She looked up at him, the utter betrayal in her eyes destroying his soul.

No. Not his Elena!

He had failed to protect her yet again.

He had no one to blame but himself.

Even after waking, his wife's eyes haunted him, his tears mixing bitterly with the blood in his mouth. Joaquin groaned once more, unsure which was worse, the agony which coursed through his veins while awake or the terror of falling back asleep and failing his love over and over and over again.

His whole existence was utter hell.

After an unknown amount of time, the rough wooden door near Joaquin's head creaked then lurched open. The light from outside his cell hurt his eyes, caused him to shrink backwards into the moldy hay. More pain. A figure appeared and blocked the light, his form filling the doorway.

“You are a pathetic sight, Joaquin.” The man spat out, the thick spittle landing wet on Joaquin’s cheek. “Worse than a lame dog.”

Joaquin responded with a deep growl.

Serpitus.

He wanted nothing more than to wrap his hands around this man’s throat and watch the life drain from his eyes. But his body refused to cooperate. As Joaquin moved to his knees to face his tormentor on his feet the most agonizing pain seared through his skull. His fingers convulsed. His legs locked up. Unconsciousness threatened to overtake him once again.

His growl faded into a whimper.

“Pathetic.”

Serpitus crossed his arms lightly, calmly. He pursed his lips then slipped a dagger out from his belt. It had a gold hilt, inset with rubies. He examined it for a moment before throwing it onto the ground before Joaquin’s face. It clattered loudly against the stone.

“Go ahead, pick it up. I am unarmed. I won’t even fight back. All you have to do is stand, pick up the dagger, and plunge it into my chest.”

Joaquin stared at the length of metal, the light reflecting off its polished edge, the firelight from beyond his cell dancing within its gemstones. How many times had this offer been extended thus far? Six? Twelve? Did it matter? The days and the dreams had become one continuous stream of undeath.

This time it would be different.

Joaquin mustered all of his strength and threw his right arm forward, screaming out from the white-hot pain. He inched his fingers along the stone as sweat exploded on his brow, his fingers slowly closing the gap. He cut the distance in half before his soul groaned out for reprieve from the depths of his core and he stopped.

The dagger was so close.

And impossibly far away.

Serpitus looked down on him in silence. Eventually he bent over, picked up the dagger, and returned it to its sheath.

“Pathetic.” His captor said for a third time before turning to go. Serpitus paused in the doorway, “If you are still alive tomorrow, I will give you another chance. And another, and another. Until you die, or you kill me. I already know the outcome of our little game. Do you?"

After the door slammed shut, Joaquin let out a cry and curled up into a ball, his knees pulled heavy into his chest. As he floundered within the waves of pain a single desire echoed within his mind. A lonely scrap of wreckage in which he desperately clung to within his sea of agony.

I will not die until I have tasted revenge for my Elena.

Part 1

"Where ignorance is bliss,
'tis folly to be wise."
– Thomas Gray

One

The evening air was cool. A light breeze danced through the trees and wandered between the rowhomes, bringing with it the smells of spring flowers, laundry detergent, and car exhaust. Katherine walked at a brisk pace down the sidewalk, not really seeing the neighborhood. Her thoughts churned. As she turned the corner where the faded sign above Haken Brothers Produce invited in potential customers with their half off deal on tomatoes and cabbage, she continued with her internal grumblings.

Robert, her boss, had been in a foul mood all day, snapping at Katherine whenever she had moved too slowly for his liking. No, she had not dilly-dawdled about with the bread for Mrs. Hurst. Someone had put the baking carts back in the wrong order. Someone whose name was probably Lester, though she hadn't said so. Most likely out of thoughtlessness at the end of his shift. Had somewhere more important to be. She had had to pull three carts out before she was able to find the pumpernickel. Yes, she knew Mrs. Hurst came in every Friday for a loaf of pumpernickel. And yes, she normally came in around 11 am, but what you don't get, Robert, is that the bakery had been unusually busy that morning and she had not found the problem until after Mrs. Hurst had been waiting for two minutes. Heaven forbid, Robert, that a single customer would have to wait more than thirty seconds for their baked goods. And heaven forbid, Robert, that that customer would be Mrs. Hurst, who had been loyal to your bakery for over twenty-five years, for nearly as long as Katherine had been alive!

Yes, Robert. Of course, Robert. I'll do better next time, Robert.

Oh, Katherine had wanted to fight back. She had wanted to speak her mind about Robert's callous comments, about the way he thought she had filled the display cases wrong after an hour watching her do so, or about the way her smile was crooked, like she was about to laugh or cry, but the next customer always arrived. Robert was a master of effortlessly shifting his look of irritated patience for her into a welcoming smile for them. She hoped he had felt a little bit of her ire today whenever she had glared at the back of his head.

Katherine stopped at a crosswalk and took a deep breath. No, she was being overdramatic. Robert wasn't all that bad. He wanted what was best for his shop. He just didn't get her. And she was supposed to leave work at work, use these seven minutes of walking to decompress. Or at least that's what Ethan, her brother kept telling her to do. Leave work at work, let the negative thoughts float away like sublimating snow.

The traffic lights changed, the cars moved on, and Katherine crossed the street. Sublimate. That word alone irked her. Who even knew what that word meant, let alone how to use it? Wouldn't snow just melt and make a mess? Is that what she was supposed to do with her thoughts? Let them leak all over? Or did he really mean evaporate? Why couldn't he just say that! Why did he have to constantly use words she didn't understand or describe everything in a weird way? There is a spotlight above your head, Katherine, it is happiness. Let its warm touch illuminate your foul mindset from the day. Let its light wrap you in its calming embrace. Bah! Just because he was a licensed therapist did not mean she needed him to analyze her constantly. It actually should mean the opposite, that he should know without asking that what she needed from him was his support, not more reasons as to why she was failing.

She could hear her brother's response. We only fail because we have not tried hard enough.

Bah!

As Katherine passed by her favorite consignment shop, The Thimble, she internally snarled at her brother's unwanted voice in her head. Why did Ethan refuse to agree with her that thinking over the day's annoyances was a good thing? Wasn't that how you were supposed to process them? He called it mulling. Digging a hole to nowhere. Picking at a mental scab.

How else was she supposed to sublimate her thoughts!

As always, Shandra's arrival that afternoon had helped. Her very presence had a way of cooling off their boss's pretentious attitude in a way Katherine could never recreate. It also was nice to have an ally. During a moment of relative calm she had pulled Shandra into the back and unloaded on her, told her all about the morning, all about Robert's comments and how unfair he had been. Told her all of the things she had wanted to yell straight into Robert's face but couldn't. Shandra had agreed that his attitude seemed a bit harsh, but maybe it wasn't Katherine? Maybe he was just tired. He seemed to be under a lot of stress lately, maybe something was going on at home.

Katherine had begrudgingly agreed to ease up on her boss. But, she had countered, even if Robert was tired he shouldn't treat her like that. Shandra agreed in turn. Give and take, both ways. They quickly hugged and went back to work, Shandra with her unending glow, and Katherine with a little less of a growl. If it wasn't for Shandra, Katherine would have left the bakery months ago. She could always talk Katherine out of her more neurotic moods.

Katherine had only taken the job at Lavigne's Bakery after Christina was born due to its flexible hours and proximity near her home. She hated being away from her daughter every day, but if she had to be, it would only be a few minutes away. Twice now in Christina's nineteen months of life had Katherine received a call from her sister-in-law that had caused her to run the entire way home, flour stained and sweaty, to sweep her blubbering daughter back into her arms.

The first call had been only three weeks into her job at the bakery, Iris asking if anything seemed off with Christina the night before. No, it's nothing Katherine, I've just been unable to soothe her. She's been crying non-stop since you left. That was all it took to spin Katherine's mind out of control. Crying, for two hours? She threw half a sentence explanation to Robert as to why she was leaving then bolted. As she dashed home she went through every possible condition. Influenza, RSV, strep, sepsis, cancer, internal bleeding? Where there other problems she had yet to find? Probably. The internet was full of them! What if her months of research hadn't been enough?

It had turned out to be gas.

The second sprint home occurred two weeks ago. Christina had tripped and fallen face first onto the stairs. As Iris had described it, it was nothing, a simple split lip that would soon be forgotten by the toddler. Iris had only called to keep Katherine in the loop. The amount of blood Katherine found upon arriving justified her unease over her sister-in-law's explanations. Who knew her daughter could bleed that much from her face!

Both times Robert had threatened to dock Katherine's pay for dereliction of duty, and both times Shandra had talked him out of it, using her wonderful words to explain to him the cares of a mother and how much they needed Katherine at the bakery. Shandra really was the only reason Katherine still put up with the place. And the exact reason she would stay there as long as it made sense.

As Katherine turned onto her street, she smiled to herself, realizing she had let go of her annoyance for Robert and replaced it with her love for Shandra. She really was the best.

Take that Ethan!

Alright, that was more than enough thoughts about work. Now, onto the weekend!

Right before the birth of their first son, Ethan and Iris had moved into a rowhome located within one of the many neighborhoods surrounding Philadelphia. They had had these grand plans of fixing up the basement and renting it out for a little extra income, a dream which was finally realized almost two years ago. Unsurprisingly, kids made everything take so much longer than planned. However, instead of reaping in all that extra income, Ethan had graciously offered the space at a discount to his perpetually down-on-her-luck sister.

His words.

Katherine had wanted to live anywhere else, but due to a series of unfortunate circumstances wound up with no other options. At the time she really had been down on her luck. And had only seemed to claw back a few inches of forward progress since then. Went from drowning to treading water, barely.

Even though her brother was a pain most days, she knew he really did care about her.

Where the rowhome's main entrance faced a well-maintained street lined with maple trees, Katherine preferred her entrance in the back. The alley was drivable, just barely, with many of the homeowner's cars parked in at odd angles. Along with navigating around the askew vehicle bumpers, any driver also had to avoid trash cans, three potholes, the occasional broken bottle or stray cat, and when exiting onto the main street, Jerry's blue tent.

Jerry was the drug addict who lived in the corner rowhome. Or, as the Prestons would say, squatted in the rowhome that his grandmother owned. A few months ago, he had broken the home's rear window and instead of fixing it, had erected a few tarps around both the window and most of the sidewalk. Jerry claimed it was only fair since most of the other units had back porches. It only made sense he should be allowed to have one too. Ethan and Mr. Preston had both complained numerous times to the police about the nuisance, only to receive the same tired police response that they'd look into it.

It had yet to be looked into.

Katherine waived to Jerry in his lawn chair as he smoked under his tent, hugged the Preston's porch railing as Timothy pulled his SUV slowly down the alley, scratched Oreo, a stray black and white cat she fed a few times a week, ascended the two steps to her door, pulled out her keys, and entered into chaos.

The pickup.

Junior, Ethan's six-year-old boy was all over the kitchen floor with his blocks, building what looked like a castle. He was halfway through the initial construction, or halfway through demolishing it with the help of a rampaging T-Rex and an out-of-control train. Junior's trains were always out-of-control. Jack, his three-year-old brother was crying on the floor next to him as he kept trying to build a tower over six blocks high, only to have it fall over after five, sometimes due to poor craftsmanship, but more often, due to Junior's out-of-control train. Christina sat with her back against the fridge, her eyes wide as she watched on, gnawing on her favorite board book. Iris was nowhere to be found.

"Iris?" Katherine called out from the kitchen, her stomach instantly growling as the scent of their evening meal, baked chicken, hung in the air.

"I'm over here." A voice called out from the living room. "I had to sit down for a moment."

Stepping carefully over the pile of blocks and children, Katherine found Iris sprawled out on the couch, her eyes closed.

"I'm done. I'm done being a mother, I'm done." She lamented, throwing her hand dramatically over her forehead. "You can take Jack, or Junior, or both of them. I don't care."

Katherine smirked a half-smile in response. "How was Christina today?"

"She was an angel, as always." Iris sat up and sighed. "I swear, girls are so much easier than boys. They just sit there, perfect, listening, attentive. Wonderful little rays of sunshine."

"Have you not heard her recently at 3 am?"

"Oh, I have, but that's your fault, not hers." Iris looked past Katherine and waved at Christina, who was toddling into the living room on unsteady legs. "Isn't that right my little angel, your mom just doesn't know what you like."

Katherine picked up her daughter and gave her a huge smile. "Hey there baby girl! Did you have a good day?"

"Mama!" Christina threw her arms around Katherine's neck and kissed her sloppily on the cheek.

No matter what was going on, Christina's hugs always made it better.

Katherine turned back to her sister-in-law, "Thanks again Iris. Oh, I'll be a little late on rent and child-care this month. I had some unexpected expenses come up, and still waiting on Patrick."

"Again?" Iris sat up some more as Jack bit Junior's foot in the kitchen, causing him to cry out in pain. "Will you two stop it! Jack! Be kind to your brother! Katherine, that's three months now. You can't keep being late like this."

"I know, I know. Won't happen again."

"That's what you said last month."

"And this time it's true."

"It's Patrick, isn't it. Why are you letting him slide?"

Katherine tensed. "He's fine."

Iris shook her head slowly and crossed her arms. "You can't keep letting him use you like this. There is a court order. He has to pay his part of the child support. Jack, enough!"

The crying and fighting from the kitchen continued.

Katherine sighed, "I know, but there's only so much I can do."

"He's not still coming over here, is he? You know what happened last time and how Ethan felt about it. You have to let us know before he shows up."

"No," Katherine shook her head vigorously. "I told him he's not allowed to drop by unannounced. Many times. As I've said, I'll be sure to let you know next time he asks to see Christina and if it absolutely has to be here."

"Good." Iris nodded, "I still don't understand how he could live so far away from your little angel. Now, if she was like Jack, or Junior, maybe. But not your precious Christina. Jack! For the last time! Katherine, he's a bum. That's what he is. What did you ever see in that man."

Christina began to squirm in Katherine's arms, feeding on her mom's anxiety. "Iris, I don't want to get into it now."

"Fine. Let's go back to this unexpected expense. Don't tell me it was for paint again."

Katherine's smirk returned as she turned to go. "Nope, not paint. Christina's hungry."

Iris stood up and followed Katherine into the kitchen, "Canvas? Brushes? Another easel? I know you already have three. I've seen your mess down there. Why would anyone need more than one easel? And how can Christina be safe with everything you have lying around like that? She's going to get hurt one of these days."

"I'll get you the money next week, promise. After the bakery pays me." Katherine didn't wait for a response before disappearing around the doorway and into the basement below.

Upon arriving within her sanctum, Katherine set Christina down in her pack-n-play and fell onto her bed piled with laundry. The boys upstairs continued to yell, thankfully only the muted rumblings of their fight and Iris's loud responses permeated through the floor. Some weeks! At least this one was over. Why did she have to drag herself through work only to be bombarded by Iris's questions and unwanted opinions every night? They were never ending!

Christina moved over to the side of Katherine's bed, "Mommy, food". Katherine ignored her at first, but as her whining grew louder she sat up and sighed.

"I know, baby girl. But some days! Some days you just need to lie down for a moment before you move on to the next thing."

Christina moved her hands to her mouth, indicating with great vigor that she was hungry.

"I know, baby girl, I know. Let's see what we have."

Katherine stepped over a stack of newly purchased canvases and opened the freezer. "Look at that, your mom needs to go shopping again. We've got chicken nuggets, fries, oh, look here, something healthy, peas. And then there is ice cream, more ice cream, half a popsicle."

She looked back at Christina, "At least we have more than rice."

Katherine nodded in agreement with Christina's whines. "All right, chicken nuggets and fries it is. You wouldn't eat the peas even if I cook them. I wouldn't eat them either. Don't even remember why I bought them. Probably out of some misplaced hopes and dreams."

As Katherine threw a random number of frozen items onto a plate then into the microwave, she looked over her room. There was never enough space for everything. With her bed shoved in one corner, the kitchenette in the second, the space under the stairs dedicated to her painting, and the door into the bathroom taking up the fourth corner, everything else was doomed to wallow within piles scattered about. Christina's toys, books, and supplies in one pile on the floor. Important paperwork stashed in a cardboard box on top of the fridge. Her half-finished paintings leaning against the wall next to the bucket of supplies and wad of smocks. Her small dresser piled high with makeup, dirty glasses, coffee cups, pens, and a pacifier. Even the walls were covered with sketches, posters, and paintings she couldn't bear to sell. Which hadn't been much of a problem anyway. She had only sold three pieces in the last year after a dozen of flea markets and festivals. Three paintings that had been commissioned. All three, not her style.

"Do you think I'm doing it wrong?" Katherine asked Christina as she sat down on the edge of a chair filled with art books and handed her daughter a mushy fry. "Do you think my passion alone isn't enough? That they don't see what I see?"

Katherine stared at one of her favorite paintings, a large square canvas filled by a sea of green, teal, blue, and turquoise with an explosion of red and white moments offset slightly from the center. She had painted it a few days after she had broken up with Christina's father. She could still feel the intensity of her rage and sadness piercing the infinite possibilities of the future unknown.

"I think… maybe they don't see it, don't feel it. Maybe I should do something else."

Christina responded with a grunt, a blah-blah of smacking lips, and an extended hand out for more food.

Katherine handed her a chicken nugget this time, "You're right. I agree. It's not my fault they can't feel it. I just have to keep trying. Early bed so I can try?"

Christina chomped on her nugget with her six little teeth, drool sliding slowly down the corner of her mouth then pointed to her pile of toys.

Katherine sighed and nodded. "I know. I'm sorry. You haven't seen me all day and it's Friday. Who doesn't want to party on a Friday. Yes, we'll play before bed. And I can read you about the little engine who could. He makes it to the top of his mountain. So can I."

She spent the next four hours on bonding time before Christina finally fell asleep, her little mouth opening and closing, popping, as she breathed. Katherine stood up quietly from her spot on the floor, yawned, donned her smock and headphones, turned up her favorite techno mix until she could no longer hear the boys above, now tromping all over the floor as Ethan and them played, glanced at Christina once more, smiled, then got to work.

Her current piece was something vibrant, something happy, with oranges and blues streaked across a light gray canvas, but it was missing something, missing its heart. As she stared at the painting and pondered, movement in the corner of her eye caused her to remove her headphones. Christina stirred.

"No, not tonight, not tonight baby girl, I need this." Katherine pleaded as she stared at the ceiling, hoping she didn't have to talk to her brother again about noise after eight. It sounded like they were jumping off the furniture. They probably were.

Then she heard the tapping at her only window. Three sharp clips, one after another.

No.

It was even worse than Christina waking up.

Patrick was here.

Two minutes later she had her ex securely down the stairs without her brother and Iris seeing, her arms folded, and her angry face on.

"You're not supposed to be here!" Katherine hissed.

"Can't I come over and see my daughter?" Patrick asked innocently, an easy smile filling his face.

"No!" Katherine replied, "Not unannounced. You know this!"

"Well then, what if I was here to see you? Would that make it any better? Anymore, exciting?"

"No!" Katherine hated how he still made her thoughts all fuzzy, even after everything he had done. "The only reason I even let you down here is to pay me. You're late."

Instead of answering, Patrick moved past her lightly and stood above Christina. "She's so perfect when she's asleep."

Katherine moved next to him, frowning. "Yea, I do all the work, feed her, clothe her, wipe away her tears, and you get this. Please don't wake her."

"I won't"

She turned towards him, "Patrick, why are you here? And what's in the box?"

Patrick looked from his daughter to the small brown box in his hands, his face shifting from happiness to something else, something dark.

"Kat, I need your help."

"I told you to stop calling me that. And what trouble have you gotten yourself into this time?"

"I need you to deliver this for me."

Katherine glared, "And why would I ever agree to do that? How about you pay your child support like you're supposed to and then come visit us after asking first. How about you do that for me?"

Patrick smiled largely at her again, the darkness evaporating, "And I'll pay you, maybe even throw in a little extra, but only after you help me."

"No deal. We have a court order."

"I know. But look. Here's the thing. I don't get paid until this thing is done."

Katherine scowled. "Then you do it."

He shrugged. "I can't."

"Why not?" Katherine tensed. "Don't tell me… Pat, what's in the package?"

"I don't know."

"You don't know?!" She whisper-yelled. "You brought an unknown thing into my house, into the room with your daughter, and you don't know what it is!"

"Calm down, it's not dangerous."

"How do you know that! You don't know what it is!"

Patrick raised his arms. "Calm down Kat. It's fine. Everything is fine."

She was genuinely mad now, "How do you figure? You show up unannounced, after weeks of not returning my calls, not even caring to see your daughter and ask me to be your little errand girl. How is any of this remotely okay to you?"

"Look. All you have to do is bring this package to the coffee shop on 8th and Walnut tomorrow morning. There will be a man sitting at a table with a chess set. Give him this, move something on the board and say, your move. That's it. That's all you have to do then walk away."

Katherine stared at him, hoping he could feel her wrath, "Patrick, what's with all this cloak and dagger? What have you gotten yourself into? And why can't you do it?"

"Because they know me, I'm a known face."

"Who knows you?"

Patrick set the box down on Katherine's bed, "Look, doesn't matter. I'm trying not to get you involved. You get this package to the man, you make a move on the chessboard, and I get paid. I get paid, you get paid. Simple. Oh, and don't open it."

"Of course I'm not going to open it! And this is the exact opposite of not getting me involved! Have you lost your mind?"

"No. Have you lost yours?"

She hated the way he twisted her words on her. Instead of arguing further she grabbed both him and his box. "No. No, no. Out. Now. I'm not going to play your silly little games. And get this thing out of here."

Christina stirred from Katherine's raised voice.

"Hey," Patrick whispered, spinning out of her grip. "Don't wake our little bug. She looks peaceful."

At that Katherine lost it. She set down the box and grabbed Patrick again, trying her best to shove him up the stairs not caring how much racket she made. Unfortunately, he would not be moved.

"Kat, this is important."

"Don't call me that!" She tugged on his forearm to no avail. "Pay me now and get out."

"Do this and I will."

"Or I'll call the cops and you will."

"You wouldn't do that."

It was then that Katherine looked into Patrick's brown eyes. She shouldn't have done that. He looked desperate. She stopped pulling and bit her lower lip.

"I don't like this."

He put a reassuring hand on her shoulder, "I know Kat, I know."

She threw it off and clenched her jaw. "If I'm doing this, I'm doing it for Christina, not for you."

"I know."

"You're a jerk. Do you know that?"

"I know."

Katherine sighed. "Fine. 8th and Walnut?"

Patrick beamed. "Yes." He then put his hands back on her shoulders. "Have I ever told you how beautiful you are?"

Katherine's nostrils flared. "Oh no! No you don't! Don't try to sweet talk me now. Get out!"

Patrick chuckled. "Thanks Kat, I owe you one."

"You owe me my child support!" She shoved him up the stairs. "And you need to come and see your daughter when she's awake. And tell me in advance next time! You're missing her life."

"I know. Next weekend?"

Katherine sighed heavily. "Sure."

Once Patrick was gone and her door re-locked, Katherine stepped slowly down the stairs hugging herself tight. She was angry at him still, but mostly angry at herself. Why had she agreed to this? She hated being used. And why did some small part of her still want his arms around her?

The brown, unassuming package looked like a viper sitting on the stairs, coiled up and ready to strike.

Two

THE COFFEE SHOP AT 8th and Walnut was an ordinary Starbucks. Nothing sinister, nothing like the seedy place she had pictured in her mind, some hovel hidden in a dark alley where evil men make back room deals. It was a simple Starbucks.

The morning had been a hectic mess. Christina had been slow to get up, grumbling about being awake an hour earlier than normal, and on a Saturday no less. After shooting off a warning text upstairs, Katherine handed off her still winy daughter to a bleary-eyed Iris. She had been sitting at the kitchen table in her sweats and a cup of coffee, the other three members of her family still fast asleep.

"I'm sorry, again," Katherine apologized a third time, "Something came up. A potential art buyer. Last minute, you know their type."

"It's fine," Iris stifled a yawn then smiled at Christina, "I could never have enough time with you, my little angel. Is your mom feeding you enough? Probably not, probably why you're all fussy. Here, let's get you some breakfast."

"Thanks again Iris."

"Oh, I'm fine. Ethan though, you'll need to explain this little adventure to him later."

"Only if he corners me."

"Katherine."

With her daughter handed off, Katherine ignored Iris's weak protest with her phone, searching for the right bus to get to Center City. She hated taking the bus, and doing so on a Saturday morning when half their usual times were not running was less than ideal, but Patrick and his schemes were never ideal.

"Your mom really should get you out in the sun more," Iris continued to talk to Christina as she sat her in her highchair. "You're all pale. That's not good for a little girl. Maybe we will go to the park later. Wouldn't that be nice, my little angel?"

Determining her direction, Katherine kissed her daughter goodbye then slung on her backpack, which now contained the mystery package, and stepped out into the chilly morning.

The bus of choice had been five minutes late. Five minutes that had fueled Katherine's anxiety into overdrive. Would it come? Had she read the app wrong? She couldn't ask anyone standing next to her, no, not the woman in her business suit or the man who needed a bath. If she asked they would know she didn't know and they would judge her for it. No. It was better for her to stand there and wait patiently. She wasn't the only one waiting. It had to come soon. But when? And why was it late? Would it be late coming home too? Why had she let Patrick rope her into this!

When the bus finally did arrive, she sat in the seat closest to the driver, hugging her backpack tight. With every stop and new group of passengers, she glared at each of them, telling them with her eyes that in no uncertain terms was she an easy target. Many ignored her. Some glared back. By the time she was in the city she was tense, exhausted, and wanted to get this over with.

A simple Starbucks.

Katherine paced up and down the street three times before finally entering, moving straight to the counter and ordering an americano. An old boyfriend from college used to drink only americanos. Snobby idiot. She had wanted to fit in, impress him for some silly reason, so she started drinking them as well. Then, after she and the boy had fallen apart due to a vastly different array of interests, she kept with the drink. At least something good had come out of her immaturity.

While the barista worked on her order, Katherine found the nearest wall to prop herself against, not trusting her knees. She scanned the room. It was what you would expect from a Starbucks in the heart of the city on a weekend. A few people waiting for their drinks, two women chatting at a nearby table, and a lone man in the corner reading a book. There was a chessboard set up on the table in front of him.

"Kat", the barista called out and set her drink on the counter.

Katherine grasped the drink like a club, returned to her wall, and sipped on it slowly as she sized up her target. The man had black hair, a clean-cut face, and strong chin. He wore a crisp black suit, black shirt, black shoes, and a bold red tie. He was well built, slim, tan, and sat relaxed, at ease, reading 'Thank You for Being Late' by Thomas Friedman.

Just your typical handsome businessman that you need to deliver a mystery package to because your ex forced you into it.

No big deal.

Katherine took one more sip of her coffee and put on her battle face. She strode purposefully to the chair opposite of the man, set her drink down, fumbled a bit as she pulled out the package from her bag, set it next to the chessboard, moved the queen to E5, looked at the man, who was now looking at her curiously with his blue eyes as she croaked out,

"Your move."

As she picked up her americano and empty bag, the man asked lightly, "Why there?"

Katherine froze, caught in an awkward half-bend over the table. "Why not there?"

The man gestured to the board. "Are you sure that is the move you want to make? Is it the best one?"

The gears in her mind groaned as she understood the question. "I don't know, it looked right."

"Do you know how to play?"

"Yes, but –"

The man moved the queen back into its previous spot. "Then let's try this again. Your move."

Katherine huffed. This wasn't how it was supposed to go! She was supposed to deliver the package and leave, not play chess against the super villain! What if she lost? What if she won? Patrick would have been completely out of his depth with this. He never cared for chess, no matter how many times she tried to teach him. Was that why he asked her to make this delivery?

This guy wanted the right move? Fine.

With her thoughts swirling she sat down, studied the board, and found that black had overextended its pawn line on the left side, a weakness she could exploit. She advanced her knight this time.

"I see." The man responded with his bishop, in which Katherine then moved her queen. They exchanged a few moves and captured each other's queens until it was obvious Katherine had the upper hand. Which meant very little. The board had been set up heavily in her favor to begin.

"Impressive." The man set down his book, smiled ever so slightly, and extended his arm. "Joaquin Morales."

Katherine took his hand, and they shook, his grip firm yet gentle. "Katherine Mason."

"Why don't we start at the true beginning." Joaquin began to rearrange the pieces on the board, "Allow me at least a fighting chance this time."

Katherine looked from Joaquin to the package now forgotten on the table. "Wait. This isn't how it's supposed to go. I give you that, then I leave. That's it."

He didn't look up, "Is that right? Is that how they told you this would go?"

"Yes."

"And how do you want it to go?"

"What?" Katherine was confused. What was she doing? She stood up, the spell broken. "I don't care. My ex told me to bring this to you and I did. Now I am going to leave. It was nice meeting you, Joaquin."

"Ah," Joaquin looked up at her, the board now reset for a new game. "It was your ex who asked you to bring me that. Interesting."

The way in which this man looked at the package then at her, the way in which he sized her up so easily while she remained a tight ball of tension suddenly set her off.

"Look, my ex has a way of getting in with the wrong people. I want no part of it. He owes me money and told me if I gave you this, he'd get paid. Now, goodbye."

As she turned to leave, Joaquin kept talking. "Before you go, humor me, please. If you are the one performing the task, shouldn't you be the one being paid for it? And isn't delivering this to me the exact opposite of having 'no part of it?'"

Katherine turned back, her visible frustration growing as Joaquin repeated what she had said to Patrick the night before. "I already told you. I don't care. Once I walk out of here, this never happened."

"How reliable is your ex?"

"Excuse me?" Katherine sputtered.

Joaquin rephrased the question, "After you leave, how likely are you to receive the funds owed?"

Her face grew dark. "That's none of your business."

"I see. Then maybe you and I could come to a side agreement. Whatever your ex is collecting for these services rendered, services performed by you, I will pay you that directly for a bit more of your time and a few answers."

Katherine hesitated. She had no idea how much Patrick was being paid. "Maybe. What do you want to know?"

"First, would you like to see what's inside?"

Her eyes moved to the brown box then back to Joaquin's face.

"No."

The truth was, she already knew. After Patrick had left, she had stared at the box for a good hour before working up the courage to open it. The contents made no sense. The largest was a mask carved from a hard black wood which gave Katherine the vague idea of a bat with its two sharp teeth and webbed ears. It appeared to be Native American, possibly Cherokee. Then there was a cheap, decorative Catholic cross, complete with a miniature Jesus. It had a tag still on it, purchased for $74.99 from the Cathedral Basilica of Saints Peter and Paul, a church only a handful of blocks from the coffee shop. The most impressive item was a small fabric bag which held a dozen golden Spanish doubloons. After a quick internet search, they dated back to the Middle Ages, the worth totaling up to a few hundred dollars. The final item was a tattered, hand-drawn picture depicting a riot that happened in Philadelphia on June 7th, 1844. On the back of the picture someone had written the following phrase:

'Innocent blood has been spilt.
Innocent blood must be spilt again.
Through the union of these bitter enemies

will my attention be stirred.
Only the one who offers a suitable
sacrifice shall claim my reward.'

No matter which way she tried to puzzle out how the objects were connected, one or two of them made no sense with the others. Maybe Joaquin was a collector of historical items, oddities. But then, why add the cross? Items from Philly? The coins and mask did not fit. Something with religious significance? Did anyone use coins for that kind of stuff, and how would the drawing fit in? She had searched for connections to the phrase on-line and found nothing. Or maybe they were all stolen.

She probably should have listened to Patrick and not opened the box at all.

Joaquin looked intently at Katherine, his blue eyes seeing deeper into her than she preferred. When she did not respond, he nodded slowly to himself then picked up his book.

"It appears I was mistaken." He waved his hand lightly towards the door, "You may go now."

The way in which this man asked her to stay then shooed her off, seemed to care then not care at all irked her even more. Was he trying to get under her skin? If so, it was working.

"Fine." She crossed her arms, "Show me."

This time Joaquin didn't take his eyes off of his book. He turned a page slowly, appearing engrossed in what he was reading. "Play one game with me, a real game, from the beginning."

Internal conflict raged in Katherine's mind. She hadn't played a full game of chess in years, not since her father had passed away. Did this man somehow know this? How would he know? How would he know anything about her? She was a stranger to him as much as he was to her. And why was she still so curious about those items? She wanted no part of this!

"And to help you decide," Joaquin continued, "Let's agree to a number. I will pay you one thousand dollars. Win or lose."

The number caused Katherine's breath to catch in her throat. That was more than she made at the bakery in a week. And this man was willing to hand it over to her for a single game? Why?

"Fine." Katherine sat down angrily and moved her king's pawn forward two squares.

Joaquin made her wait. He finished whatever paragraph he was reading before slowly placing a one-dollar bill in the book to mark his place. Once the book returned to his side, he straightened himself up to the board and leaned towards it and Katherine. After a moment of consideration, he mirrored Katherine's first move.

"What is your ex's name?" Joaquin asked after Katherine moved her queen-side knight forward.

She looked up at Joaquin and shook her head. "Are you trying to distract me now?"

"No. If you need silence I will accept your answers after the game."

After a few more moves, Katherine caught a flaw in her opponent's opening. She was determined to win.

"My ex's name is Patrick Troutman."

Joaquin nodded, considering, "Why are you here and not your ex, why not Patrick? Why are you the one delivering this to me?"

"He asked me to."

"Why?"

"He said he was a known face. Look, that's all I know. He didn't tell me who gave that box to him, why he wanted you to have it, or anything else. That's all I know."

"I see."

After Joaquin's next move, the two players settled heavily into their respective minds, with nothing but the pieces before them mattering. The coffee shop no longer existed, neither did the baristas calling out orders over the commercial folk music and the smell of sugar and caffeine. Only the struggle of two wills played out upon a sixty-four square board.

After another dozen moves for each player, Katherine realized that the flaw she thought she had spied out from Joaquin had instead lured her into a slight overextension. With her overconfidence he had flanked her position masterfully. She tried to correct but he was able to dismantle her best defenses, check-mating her with shocking speed.

Looking over the carnage, Katherine's annoyance with the morning only grew. She had been rusty. She hadn't played in a few years. Her father would be ashamed.

"That was, enjoyable. Thank you." Joaquin picked up the package, not the slightest hint of satisfaction in his victory evident on his face.

He undid the brown wrapping, gently lifting at the folds so as not to rip the paper and slid the shoebox out from its bondage. Once it was free, he shifted the chessboard over and set the box down in its place. After picking up the lid, he withdrew the mask, cross, bag of coins, and picture, one by one, observing each slowly, intensively.

"What does it mean?" Katherine asked.

"I've been dealing with another firm, business related. Their negotiator has a, unique, sense of humor." Joaquin furrowed his eyebrows then sat back. "He believes this is enough evidence to convince me he knows what he knows."

The mystery was gnawing at her insides. "And what does he want you to think he knows?"

Joaquin thought for a moment longer, then let the idea float away. He pulled out his wallet and began counting from a stack of hundreds. Katherine's eyes went wide. Who walked around Philly with that much cash on hand? He handed the one thousand dollars to Katherine, who grabbed it anxiously and shoved it into her backpack.

Katherine stood up, suddenly far past done with this mystery now that she was carrying way too much money to feel comfortable. "Thanks. We done here?"

Joaquin stood up as well, taller than she had expected. "Who taught you that opening?"

The image of her father's smiling face flashed in her mind. "I learned it myself."

"You played a very strong game. You should be proud of your skill."

His compliment after her quick route on the board made her mind tip sideways. "Well, it's been an interesting morning already. I would say I hope your business stuff goes well, but I don't really care about you at all. We're never going to see each other again. Goodbye."

She turned without waiting for a response and stomped out of the coffee shop.

"Patrick, you owe me." Katherine growled out into the air as she moved across the street to avoid passing by any people.

After about a block, Katherine slowed and looked into her backpack, double-checking she hadn't somehow lost the money. Seeing the wad still there, she pulled out her phone. To the best of her memory, she jotted down the first twenty or so moves of their game. She hated losing, no matter the reason. Once she rescued Christina from her sister-in-law, the two of them were going to look up what opening Joaquin had used against her and find out exactly how to defeat it.

Three

After an exhausting bus ride home, Katherine clutching her backpack and staring at any potential thief with hate in her eyes, she ran straight down to her bedroom and stuck the wad of cash in an envelope labeled 'Fun!'. Thinking over it for a moment longer, she took all but a lonely hundred out of the fun envelope and added one each to 'Food', 'Rent', and 'Art Supplies'. She then stuck the remaining six bills in the one labeled 'Christina's College". There had been two hundred in that envelope previously, ten dollars stashed away each month since her daughter was born. And now, a random thirty-minute conversation and chess game had blown all of her previous hard work out of the water.

Feeling slightly less on edge now with the money from Joaquin stashed away, Katherine noticed the house was quieter than it should have been. Moving upstairs she found a note scribbled on the white board on the fridge. 'Went to the park'. She half-thought about sitting for a moment in the uncommonly still house but decided against it. She did not want to give herself more time to let her thoughts swirl. She had already replayed the scene over and over again in her head, what she had said to Joaquin, how stupid she must have sounded, and what she should have said instead. Why had she kept telling him she didn't care? Could he tell she did? Did she? Bah! What did any of this matter anyway? It was all Patrick's fault.

The playground was abuzz with activity, the neighborhood families taking full advantage of the nicest Saturday so far that spring. Dozens of little kids clamored over the play structures, running, swinging, scampering, and laughing with each other while their parents chatted along the edges, commenting about their last snowstorm and how glad they were that the weather had finally turned. Katherine caught sight of Ethan sternly talking with Junior as Jack clung to his dad's leg, whimpering. Not wanting to deal with her brother quite yet, she found Christina. Her daughter was being tailed by Iris as she toddled around, older kids weaving around their slow two-woman parade.

"Hey," Katherine smiled as she joined Iris's side. "Thanks for the last-minute help."

"There you are," Iris smiled sweetly, "I was wondering how long you would disappear this time."

"I told you, just for the morning."

"And I've come to expect your idea of timing isn't all that great." Iris shrugged. "Was Patrick sneaking out of our basement last night?"

Katherine cringed. They had noticed.

"Um… yea, He came over last night to pay what he owes me."

She cringed again. Just like that, she would have to defund Christina's college fund for a few days to cover her lie.

Her sister-in-law crossed her arms, "Katherine. I told you he can't come around like that! Last night! Junior was the one who noticed. You're lucky it wasn't Ethan."

"I'm sorry. And I know."

"Have you been talking to him again?"

"Uh, I kind of have to. He's Christina's dad."

"You know what I mean."

"No." Katherine lowered her voice, "No. Not like that. I'm over him, I told you that."

"Is he why you went running off this morning into the city?"

Katherine's voice got smaller, "Yea."

"Where did he get an art dealer connection? You lying about that too?"

"Work? I don't know. Look, I couldn't really turn him away last night, sorry. But now I have your money. Oh, and if it makes you feel any better, this morning was a complete waste of time."

Iris picked up Christina, hugging her tight. Christina squirmed a bit, babbling that she wanted back down. Iris ignored her.

"This little angel deserves better. I never knew what you saw in that man, and I don't care if you keep messing up your life, but your daughter deserves better."

Katherine fumed. She could take this kind of stuck-up attitude from Ethan. He at least had his life together. But Iris?

"I'm doing the best I can. I didn't choose to be a single mom."

"You kind of did." Iris steamrolled forward, "There is so much more you could be doing with your life, Katherine. So much more. Instead, you choose to work at a run-down bakery and throw paint on a canvas for fun. You need to find a real man, someone who will stick by your side this time, someone who will support you and Christina."

"Ooh, you think I should become a housewife, like you?"

Iris opened her mouth to respond to their tired argument, but instead let Christina down. The two of them took a breath as they watched her wobble, fall on her knees, frown at the ground for its offense, stand back up, then began moving again towards her destination. The stairs. Once there, she bobbed up and down, laughing, holding onto the first step happily.

Iris smoothed the wrinkles on her shirt. "No, what I'm saying is you need stability."

"I have stability. I have a place, I have a job, we have a good life."

"What you have is an ex who is late to pay you, who shows up in the middle of the night, who sends you on dead-end adventures for a hobby that may never pan out. What you have is a lonely Friday night in a dark basement, and a lonely Saturday night to come. What you have is a house of cards about ready to crash down around you."

Katherine growled. "Thanks for the pep talk, Iris."

"When was the last time you went out with some friends? Or had a date?"

"I have a one-year-old! I don't have time for either of those things."

"Yet that lame excuse didn't stop you this morning from dancing when Patrick sang his merry tune in your ear. You know I don't mind watching Christina, even if it's for you to get some much needed down-time. Especially for that."

Katherine was done with this conversation. She turned to go. "Thanks Iris."

"Before you tuck your tail and run, you should go talk with Ethan. He's been annoyed all morning."

"He normally is."

"Enough of that." Iris chided. "No need to be all mopey. This is your fault. Fix it. I'll keep watching your daughter." She turned to Christina and in her sickly-sweet voice said, "Isn't that right, aren't you the best!"

Katherine grumbled to herself and took the long way around the playground. She never really knew if Iris cared in her own, unique way, or if she simply enjoyed meddling. Delaying as long as she could, Katherine arrived at her brother's side just as he was back at his yelling.

"Junior! Take your turn! You can't waltz up the slide when others are trying to go down. We need to respect each other's boundaries and time!"

Junior looked at his dad, frowned, and for once listened. He slid down the remainder of the slide then ran off to the monkey bars, knocking over a younger kid in the process.

"Junior!" Ethan looked at Katherine, his frown emanating displeasure, "I don't like repeating myself. Every five minutes I say the same thing, and every five minutes he's back at it. Junior is still learning. You have no excuse."

"Maybe your son is having a hard time because he's stubborn, like his dad." Katherine suggested.

Ethan's frown sunk further until the edges of his lips nearly touched his chin. "That's not funny."

"It wasn't meant to be. I heard from someone smart that being stubborn is a good thing. Allows you to trust people. A stubborn person won't waver after they've made up their mind."

Ethan eyed his sister, his face softening. "I told you that, didn't I?"

"Yep."

His expression hardened again, "Patrick can't show up unannounced, Okay? Additionally, you can't go off gallivanting around the city and leave Christina with Iris whenever you feel like it. I'm already letting you take advantage of us, with the discount on rent and Iris watching Christina when you work. We aren't your servants."

"I know, I'm sorry." Katherine apologized before she remembered who she was talking to. "I had this last-minute thing, my art, potential buyer. Won't happen again."

"You should only ever apologize when you mean it. I know you don't mean it when it keeps happening."

"I mean it. I do. It won't happen again. Promise."

Ethan sighed. "Katherine, this has been the fourth time this year. We have lives too, you know."

"And that's why I asked Iris if it was okay first. She could have said no, if I was asking for too much, she could have said no."

"You know she won't, you know how she feels about Christina. I wish she would feel some of that for our boys. Typical displacement attachment."

"Sure, whatever you say."

"And she told me she did say no, but you insisted."

Katherine raised up her hands, "Well, sure, she said not really, it wasn't great timing, but when is it ever? And this was important. I could tell she wanted to help."

Ethan sighed again. "Now you're playing the victim, shifting blame. What would dad think of you right now?"

"Oh no," Katherine almost jumped away from that verbal viper. "We are not talking about dad right now. That's not fair."

Ethan continued, "Ever since he died you've been even more erratic, unstable. I don't think you've come to terms with your loss."

'Why do you always want to psychoanalyze me? Why can't you just support me?"

"Because that's not who I am. I know who I am, my true self. This is how I love, by trying to help. I also know my flaws, that I'm enabling you. I don't want to see you continue to ruin your life."

"Iris, now you? It's my life!" Katherine wanted to continue fighting him right there in front of all of the kids, but instead chose to stomp away.

Brothers!

"That didn't look like it went very well." Iris commented as Katherine returned and quickly scooped her daughter up.

"It didn't. He's still Ethan. Sorry for using you, making you watch Christina."

"Oh, it wasn't a bother at all. We had so much fun together, isn't that right my little angel!"

"I'm glad." Katherine began walking away. "See you back at home, or whenever."

After feeding Christina lunch and getting her settled for her nap, Katherine relocated her half-finished painting into her ever-growing pile of half-finished paintings and placed a new canvas on her easel. She stared at her options of colors while Mozart blared in her ears.

Yes, black.

With her widest brush she began to cover the canvas in dark charcoal, her thoughts churning with the rising melody.

What was she doing with her life?

Was there a better way forward than this?

What would her dad have wanted?

Her father, Karl Mason, had passed away three days before Katherine's twenty-fifth birthday. Suddenly, unexpectedly. Doctors had called it a heart attack, though he was as healthy as any man his age could be. Unexplainable. She had been planning to show him her newest art piece, the one that now hung above her bed. It was a small canvas splattered lightly with the seven colors of the rainbow. They had also planned to see the Magic Gardens together, a whole courtyard filled with eclectic sculptures and mosaic tile work on the walls, the floors, the ceiling. But instead of a day filled with her father's smile and perpetual encouragement, Katherine was forced to wrap herself in black and say goodbye.

Her father's death had been hard on the whole family. A titanic shift. He had been the glue that held it all together after Marsha, Katherine's mother had left them when Katherine was seven. Went off with some businessman to New York, said she was done being a housewife and a mother of three brats, that she needed to become her own person again.

Needed to be away from them.

During those next few years her dad had leaned heavily on Laura, Katherine's older sister, between the needs of work, life, and his kids. They had somehow made it through, and at times, even thrived. They never had much, never went on vacations like her friends bragged about or had the gifts her friends discarded, but they had each other. They had good memories and laughter and joy. All thanks to her dad. He had been a perpetual spot of sunshine, no matter what darkness came over the world. Always looking on the bright side. Even after she went off to college, Katherine and her dad chatted nearly every day.

And then, suddenly, he was gone.

A tear rolled down Katherine's cheek. This had been her father's favorite piece from Mozart, his Symphony number 34. Listening to it always made her cry.

Her brush hungrily consumed the white.

It was a few months after her father's death that Katherine had met Patrick. She had eventually worked up the courage to visit the Magic Gardens alone, a kind of way to say her final goodbyes to her dad. There never really were any final goodbyes, not really, but she had been ready to move on, to stop dwelling on the hole in her heart. Once there and wandering around the brilliance that was other people's imagination in tangible forms, broken glass bottle walls, chandeliers of junk, and cryptic phrases cemented in tile, she found herself so lost in thought that she bumped into a stranger. Patrick. She apologized, he waved it off and they intended to go their separate ways, that was, until he began following her and started up a conversation. Something about how nice of a day it was for this kind of a thing, cloudy yet warm, the perfect lighting to view this kind of art. Oh, but he was planning to come back at night, during one of the times where they have the lights on and could see it in a whole new way. She had nodded politely as he kept talking, his enthusiasm eventually pulling her in.

As their morning in the gardens wound down, Patrick had invited her to a Greek food truck he loved nearby. They could eat at the park, keep getting to know each other. She accepted. They laughed through lunch then spent the afternoon walking around the city with no real destination. Simply enjoying the moments as they came. This led to dinner then a memorable night at his place.

Katherine finished covering the canvas with one final, angry stroke. Patrick had been so kind in the beginning, so open to new ideas, so full of life. What had happened? Why had he become so shifty, closed off, so stupid at times? Had he always been that way and she just didn't see it at first? Or was this the natural flow of life? New, shiny things dazzle the eyes, rose colored glasses causing all but the worst of red flags to just appear simply as flags? Or had it been Christina's fault?

Katherine hated that idea. No, she would never blame their falling out on her daughter. Not ever.

No, not Christina's fault in specific, but the pregnancy, the difficulty in raising a baby? Was the idea of being a father too much for him? Patrick had never wandered in his affection while they were dating, though he had always been flighty and a bit unreliable. Did caring for another human or the thought of settling down frighten him that badly?

She had asked him this once, the night of their final fight, the night he threw a chair at her and she had cried till three in the morning. Christina had only been five weeks old. They had both been exhausted and at their wit's end. But by the next morning he was gone. And never really came back. Four years together, gone in a night. Crumbled into dust over a few awful months. Had all their good times and all her love for him not matter to him? Did Christina not matter to him?

Since he had left, Katherine had asked Patrick a few times where he was staying or where he went, first fearing he had found someone else. She asked him why, what had she done wrong? She beat herself up for what she had said, what she didn't say, for the baby weight she couldn't lose, for nothing, for everything, angry at him, angry at herself, angry at how messed up her life had become. The answers really never came, and eventually she stopped asking.

Letting go of someone you loved was never easy. Not knowing why you lost them made it nearly impossible.

After Patrick left, Katherine's life fell apart quite spectacularly. When the rent had come due on their apartment, it was left unpaid. She had called Patrick twice a day for over a month, texting him even more often, avoiding the landlord as much as possible as his polite requests for his rent shifted into demands. They had both agreed that Patrick would support her with her art and in raising Christina, that he was the one with the stable job. But he had walked out. Stopped responding. She ran out of money entirely by the time Christina turned five months old. Eventually broke down and called Ethan for help, who, after scolding her for her life choices, came down and figured out a deal with her landlord, took her and Christina in, and agreed to support her until she was able to land on her feet.

Even though Katherine hated how Ethan treated her like a little kid sister most days, she knew through his actions that he loved her.

Katherine dipped her brush in the red paint and began slashing at the canvas. How had her life withered from all of her hopes and dreams made in art school to, to this? Had she made the wrong choices? Her father's death wasn't her fault. Meeting Patrick had been a joy. They had had good times! They had used birth control. Christina's birth had been an accident. An accident she wouldn't change for the world.

Katherine looked over to her daughter and smiled, her heart swelling with love. Christina's face was pressed against the pack-n-play's bottom, her cheek smushed a bit, her tiny hands opening and closing as she dreamed. Yes, there were still bright moments in the current darkness, bits of joy within the sea of disappointment and brokenness.

Yes. Her father's perpetual advice was still there, still encouraging.

Katherine stood back and looked at her painting. She had carved a thick, jagged canyon right down the middle. Hope spilling through the despair? The pain that she still felt? Something else? A stray thought from that morning floated in from her subconscious.

A man in a black suit and a red tie.

Joaquin Morales.

A man so sure of himself, a man who carried around thousands of dollars without a care. A man who absolutely should look down on someone like her, who probably stepped on hundreds of somebody's like her, who maybe even felt pity for the faceless no ones like her. He probably knew exactly who he was, had everything in his life handed to him, and hated everyone who didn't remain in their proper place. Life was something people like him controlled, not something that controlled him.

Who was Joaquin Morales? What was his story?

Who was someone like her to someone like him? Nothing more than a speck of dust, a bug that appeared then disappeared back to the hole she had come from. Back into her basement.

What had that box been about?

Katherine took off her headphones and pulled out her phone. She called Patrick only to receive his voice mail.

"Yo. Leave a message if you never want me to listen to it. Text me otherwise."

As advised, she wrote two words to her ex.

It's done.

She looked at the simple message for over a minute before adding:

Christina's hungry. When are you going to pay me??

Hesitating for only a moment, Katherine hit the send button then sighed. She hated being so dependent on him still. But what other choice did she have?

Four

SUNDAY MORNING ARRIVED IN all of its glory with a rapping on Katherine's door.

"Katherine", Ethan called through the closed basement door. "Someone is here to see you."

Katherine groggily rolled over and checked the time. 7:18 am. Christina had been up twice that night after Katherine had stayed up too late painting, only falling back to sleep a few hours ago. Who was there to see her at this hour?

"Katherine," Ethan continued, "are you awake?"

"Yea." She groaned, then raised her voice a bit louder. "Yea, I'll be right there."

The shout stirred Christina, but thankfully her daughter rolled over and went back to sleep. Katherine grabbed a bath robe from a pile on the bathroom floor, smelled it to make sure it wasn't noticeably dirty, then slipped it on. A glance in the mirror led her to run a comb through her hair and nothing more. Whoever this was would have to deal with her looking exactly how she should before eight.

Junior and Jack were already up, both glued to the TV, chomping on dry cereal among a mess of forgotten toys scattered across the living room. Katherine found Ethan on the couch, typing away on his laptop as he sipped coffee.

"There you are. He said it was urgent."

"Who said it was urgent?"

Ethan gestured towards his front door. "The man patiently waiting for you at my door."

"Who?"

"He didn't give his name. Said he knows you. Thought he might be one of your buyers."

Annoyed at being awake already and at her brother's attitude, Katherine stepped up to the door and opened it a crack. "Yes?"

Standing alone on her brother's front porch was a muscular man in a loose tie and collared shirt rolled up to his elbows. He looked military with a clean face and crew cut hair.

"Miss. Mason, I need you to come with me."

"Um, why?"

The man folded his massive forearms, "It's important."

"Sure, but why? Who are you and where are you trying to take me?"

The man passed Katherine a business card, "I work for Mr. Morales. There are a few things he would like to discuss with you."

Katherine read the card as she tried to gather her thoughts. The business card was matte black with red lettering: Vamp Industries, Max Smith III, Security. There was a bold red V in the top left corner.

She handed it back, "Well, you can tell Mr. Morales I don't want any part of this. I am not involved."

Max did not take his card back, "I understand Ms. Mason. He thought you might see it that way. He is concerned about your daughter."

Katherine's spine went rigid. "Is this some kind of threat?"

Max waved his hands, "No, no, unrelated. Nothing about the other day. Mr. Morales said he has information for you, something he found out about Patrick Troutman. Wants to help. It'll make more sense after he explains it to you."

"Let me think." She closed the door, then her eyes, then placed her forehead on the wall.

Patrick! What did you do this time!

"What was that about?" Ethan asked, his eyes still on his computer.

"Um, you were right. Art buyer, wants to see my stuff again. You know how their type is, impatient. I guess yesterday wasn't a waste after all."

"That's good news."

"I, um," Katherine swallowed, hating her decision already, "can you watch Christina again?"

At this, Ethan blinked and finally looked towards his sister. "Katherine. No. You promised yesterday!"

"I did, and this is different, it'll only be for a few hours. And she's sleeping still, shouldn't be up for a bit. Once you hear her, just feed her breakfast and I'll be back. Easy."

"You can't keep doing this!"

"I know, I know, but this might be my big break. The one chance I'll ever get. You wouldn't want to live with the regret that you wouldn't help me when I needed you the most."

"Katherine, that was attempted emotional manipulation."

She smiled, seeing a crack in her brother's defenses. "Please?"

Ethan sighed heavily. "Fine. But only this once! We're taking the boys to the Zoo at ten. You have to be back before then."

"Ok, perfect," she dashed downstairs before Ethan could change his mind.

In the semi-dark, Katherine clumsily pulled on the outfit she had worn yesterday. Then, thinking better of it, found a new shirt from a pile on her bed. Joaquin would absolutely remember what she had worn. Did she have time for any makeup? Mascara. Eh, good enough.

Back upstairs, Katherine bounded across the room then through the door. "Thanks Ethan, I owe you one!"

"You owe me a lot more than one. By ten Katherine, Ten!"

"This way Ms. Mason," Max extended out his hand and motioned her to a black SUV parked in front.

Instead of following, Katherine crossed her arms. Why did she have to grab her green shirt? She looked awful in this shirt.

"Not until you tell me where we are going. I've seen this part in the movies. Once I get in that car, I'll disappear."

"No ma'am, we use the other vehicle for that. This is the 'we simply want to talk with you' car."

Katherine looked at Max, then the car, then Max again. "That's not helping."

He sighed. "It's only a few minutes away. And not the evil building. The nice one. We can have you home by ten, as requested, if we don't delay."

Katherine glared at Max, both for overhearing her conversation with her brother and his unwanted sarcasm. Not willing to look any sillier or more paranoid than she already did, she stuck her chin in the air and moved towards the vehicle. Max caught up to Katherine then opened the back door for her. She slid into the vehicle and settled in the seat, then worked to settle her nerves.

The car ride was tense. The silence felt like a weight on Katherine's chest, her thoughts spinning out of control. Was something wrong with her daughter? If so, what? Did they just say that to get her attention, get her in the car? Were they going to murder her? Would she wind up as some face on the evening news?

This just in! Horrible mother abandons her young daughter after trusting the wrong men.

Yep, sounds about right.

Max eventually pulled the vehicle into the loading dock of a glass high-rise building. As he opened Katherine's door, four men in suits appeared from one of the building's side doors. They took up positions in a loose perimeter around the car. Katherine suddenly felt like a fawn caught with her leg in a trap. The silent arrival of Joaquin Morales through the same door did not ease her trepidation.

"This your way of asking for a rematch?" Katherine said first, hoping her stupid courage would cut through her fear.

Joaquin smiled slightly. "It's nice to see you again, Ms. Mason. Green is a good color on you."

The compliment threw Katherine off balance. She crossed her arms, annoyed. "Okay, I'm here. What do you want?"

"I apologize for the abruptness. The past twenty-four hours have been, complicated."

"I need more than that. Complicated, how?"

"Resources, timelines, the balance of power. Information flows. Your delivery to me yesterday has sent off quite the domino effect."

She glared at Max, "I thought you said this wasn't about yesterday."

"I lied." Max replied.

"Please, Ms. Mason," Joaquin interjected, "Remain calm. As requested, you are not involved in that. This is a sideways matter."

Katherine cut to it, "Tell me what you want with my daughter."

Joaquin extended out his hand, "Let's get up to the lab. Dr. Haughman is better at explaining these things then I am."

"Doctor? Lab? Why?"

"This way." Joaquin motioned again for Katherine to follow.

Katherine did not move, "Let's try this again. I'm not going anywhere else until you tell me where we are going and why."

Joaquin nodded, his smile growing, "Most people are too scared at this point to make demands. You have spirit."

"I don't like being in the dark. I don't like being used."

"Then, follow me and I will, illuminate, your understanding."

Katherine huffed once more but finally conceded. The four suits closed in on the two of them, while Max waited by the car. They stopped in front of a bank of elevators, eventually stepping into a large freight car. Instead of the doors sliding open and shut horizontally, a large fabric door closed loudly over the entrance first, then the steel doors locked them inside.

"You mentioned there were other people you've abducted like this? How many other people?"

"Over the last five years? Nine. You are the tenth."

The cab rattled as they moved up. Katherine silently thanked whoever was watching out for her that this mysterious lab wasn't in the basement.

"And what happened to the others?"

"Eventually? Nothing. False positives. Dr. Haughman will explain more."

They exited the freight elevator on the twelfth floor into a half-finished back corridor. Sheetrock was up but the walls weren't painted, the floors still dull concrete, the ceiling open. From the wall, Joaquin grabbed two medical masks from a dispenser, handing one to Katherine before putting one on himself. Once she had her mouth covered, Joaquin stepped forward and waved a badge at a side door. He opened the door and motioned Katherine forward. The four suits remained behind.

The lab space took Katherine by surprise. It was bright, white, clean. The hallway they entered was mostly glass, the whole length looking into rows and rows of benches and casework filled with instruments, vials, whirling machines, and the dozens of men and women in white lab coats operating the space. Beyond the organized chaos, she had a clear view of the city, the morning sun highlighting the Philadelphia skyline.

"This way." Joaquin motioned.

Katherine followed, taking in every bit she could. The interior half of the corridor was a solid wall, filled with larger equipment and freezers. She only knew this because a lab tech pulled something out of one as they passed by, heavy clouds of cold air billowing out. All kinds of utilities remained exposed in the corridor ceiling above, giving her a sense of complication and art. She was amazed how anyone could tuck all that mess of pipes and ductwork into such a small space.

Near the farther end of the building, Joaquin used his badge again and held a glass door open for Katherine. She entered through a small alcove filled with jackets and personal effects, then onto the floor of the lab itself.

Joaquin placed a large hand on her back, the touch causing her to jump slightly, and moved her over to the lab bench at the building's corner, the whole city a backdrop to the tubes, glassware, samples, and hand-written notes. At the bench, a gray-haired man stood hunched over his laptop, punching his thoughts into the machine with his index fingers.

"Dr. Haughman?" Joaquin said, which sent a hand up from the doctor.

"One moment, one moment." He did not look in their direction, instead, continuing his percussion on the keyboard. With a final stroke he stopped, blinked, straightened, and turned in their direction.

"Oh, yes, I was expecting you."

"Doctor, this is Katherine Mason." Joaquin made introductions, "And Katherine, Dr. Haughman."

The doctor shook Katherine's hand with much vigor. "A pleasure, a pleasure. Fascinating times we live in, very fascinating times!"

Katherine blinked in confusion, unsure what to say. Joaquin continued. "I haven't told her much as to why she's here. How about you start at the beginning."

"Ah yes, this could take a moment, have a seat." He pulled out one of the stools under the bench and slid it over to Katherine. Once she was settled, he grabbed another and sat as well. Joaquin remained standing.

"The beginning. Blood!" The doctor smiled, his mask covering his mouth but the mirth in his eyes shining through. "The human body is an amazing organism. Especially our blood."

"Blood?" Katherine asked.

"Yes, blood! You see, we humans have numerous cells, red, white, platelets, markers, antibodies, proteins, sugars, all manner of organic activity swirling through our veins and arteries at every moment, transferring molecules, warding off disease, keeping us alive. I have spent my whole life studying nothing but blood and I'm still finding new things!

"Let's take the common antigen blood groups, for instance. A, B, AB, O, positive, negative, so simple and yet so complex! Did you know there are forty-four systems like this known to date! Which leads me to ask the why, why do we have all of these different markers and types? Why do some of us have more antigens and some of us lack them? What do they do for us? Why? That question always yields the best results, why.

"And that's just if we focus on healthy red blood cells. Life throws us even more options! There are quite a few illnesses which reduce the functionality of these little life preservers. White blood cells are their own ball of mystery of study and complexity. Clotting and platelets, plasma, then, then we can add in the magical transfer of oxygen and other substances through the cell walls of the lungs, the stomach, intestines, brain. The heart and its magnificent ability to beat unceasingly, an organic machine without age until it stops. All of it, fascinating!"

Joaquin coughed lightly. "Doctor, Excuse me for one moment."

Dr. Haughman looked away from Katherine. "Yes?"

"What I meant was the beginning of why she is here. The facts, important pieces, nothing more."

Dr. Haughman blinked and nodded. "Right, right. I'm sorry, my dear, I sometimes get carried away. It's just all so exciting! My life's work, you understand. Alright, specifically, you, why you are here. Ah yes."

The doctor pulled a file out from his overhead lab bench and opened it up to a mass of information crammed into two pages.

"Patrick Troutman. His blood is special."

Katherine blinked. "You have Patrick's blood?"

The doctor looked at Joaquin, who supplied the answer. "He was working for us, was in our system."

"Working for you? No, he couldn't be. He's not a scientist."

Joaquin waved away the question. "In a different department. Not important to this discussion. What is, is the fact we take pride in our employees' health and have them screened when they come and work for us. His blood was flagged as unique, highly uncommon."

"His blood possesses a combination of antigens that are extremely rare." Dr. Haughman added in explanation and showed Katherine the paper. "You see, certain minor adjustments to the blood allow for some extraordinary things, or some truly horrific things. The human body, every system balanced on a knife's edge and in an interconnected weave between every other system."

"Patrick had a good mixture," Joaquin interjected, "his blood was uniquely beneficial and aided us greatly in our research."

Katherine was having trouble following. "And what does any of this, your research and my ex, have to do with Christina?"

Joaquin crossed his arms and sighed. "In order for us to keep working on this life-saving research, we need a source. Your ex was donating blood regularly, once a month, except, he missed last month. We haven't heard from him in about six weeks."

"This doesn't make any sense." Katherine shook her head, "I saw him only a few days ago. Are you sure he was working with you guys? He never mentioned it."

"I'm sure." Joaquin responded. "I know what I'm about to ask is a little, unconventional. We were almost at a breakthrough, Ms. Mason, a scientific discovery in the field of medicine that could revolutionize healthcare treatment. We need a new source. We are asking for your permission to verify if he has passed this unique trait onto your daughter."

Katherine stood up, shocked at what she was hearing, unable to process. "You, you want me to let you harvest my daughter's blood?"

"For science, yes." Dr. Haughman nodded, "We would start by testing your daughter first, confirm she has indeed inherited her father's blood trait, and if so, extract a bit occasionally."

"Why don't you just find Patrick and keep taking his?" Katherine's voice began to grow louder. "I don't want you to hook any kind of machine up to Christina and take her blood, no matter how important it is to your science."

"Well, then, do you know where we can find him?" Joaquin asked.

"I'll give him a call right now."

Katherine pulled her phone out of her pocket. The usual five rings then his generic voicemail prompt about never responding made her angrier than usual.

"Patrick. Hi, it's me, Katherine. You haven't returned my calls yet. Or my texts. I feel like you're avoiding me. Give me a call back. It's kind of urgent."

In addition to the voice message, she sent him a text *'give me a call, NOW.'*. Seeing only her messages to him on the screen and none in recent reply she scrolled up to find when the last time she heard from him. Two weeks ago, another excuse about not paying childcare, and a vague bit about a big score in the future.

"How much were you paying Patrick for this blood donation?" Katherine asked suddenly. Patrick would never agree to something like this for free.

Joaquin answered. "I'll have to check with accounting, but I would say in the range of a few thousand every month. Again, his blood was very rare and well worth the cost."

"A few thousand?" Now Katherine was even more angry at Patrick. And he said he didn't have the money to even pay for his daughter's lunches?

"The answer is no." Katherine shook her head and stood up. "No. You may not use my daughter for your experiments. Find Patrick. Use him."

Both Dr. Haughman and Joaquin looked disappointed.

"Are you sure?" Joaquin asked. "The amount of compensation for your cooperation could be, negotiated."

The idea of not having to worry about money tempted Katherine. But then she weighed it against the idea of using her daughter, selling her out, harvesting her body for that stability.

"No. Not a chance."

"Alright." Joaquin nodded. "I can respect that. Thank you for hearing us out. And thank you Doctor for your time."

"Of course! Sometimes a bit of an interruption knocks the dust loose, leads to new discoveries!"

As Dr. Haughman went back to his work and Katherine and Joaquin left the lab, an uneasy silence fell between the two of them. The whirling of machines and coughing of freezer compressors only sharpened the grating atmosphere. The four suits rejoined them in the back hallway and took their positions within the freight elevator, a box of protection around their human cargo.

Once off the elevator, Joaquin turned towards Katherine. He handed her a business card. "If you change your mind. My number is on the back."

Katherine took it and read it: Vamp Industries, Joaquin Morales, Chief Operations Officer, Senior Strategy Analyst.

Katherine stuck the card in her back pocket. "I won't. That is, change my mind."

"I understand." Joaquin extended out his hand. "It was a pleasure, again."

Katherine shook in response. "Yea, sure."

"Maybe our paths will cross again someday. You intrigue me."

"Yea, maybe." Katherine bit her lower lip. She shouldn't ask.

"Does this have anything to do with that poem, phrase thing on the back of that picture? The one in the box?"

Joaquin smiled lightly, his eyes locking with hers, "No, as I stated earlier, unrelated. You should reconsider our offer, it would be very helpful, for both of us, if you accepted."

Katherine swallowed, "I'm sure."

Joaquin held his gaze for a moment longer then turned back towards the elevator doors, "I understand."

Without any further farewells, once the elevator opened, Joaquin stepped out and moved through a side doorway, deeper into the building. Katherine was corralled by the suits in the other direction towards Max and the waiting SUV.

For the whole ride home Katherine tried to process what had just happened, the insanity of it all, but the only thing she could think about were Joaquin's deep blue eyes and how when he looked at her like that, her mind went blank.

Five

KATHERINE WOKE FROM A slit of inevitable morning sunshine attacking her through a crack in her blinds. She rolled out of bed, took a shower, put on the first thing that was anything but green, picked up Christina, tromped upstairs, threw her in her highchair next to Jack yelling about not having enough milk in his cereal and Junior at the counter helping himself to a cookie. Iris sat at the table, ignoring them both with her phone. Katherine waved goodbye and was through the door before Iris even looked up.

There was no need to wake up before 6:17 am, but not a minute could be spared if she was to arrive at the bakery on time.

Out on the back porch Katherine found Oreo waiting with his tail swaying in the air. She rewarded his patience with a few scratches under his chin. As she did, a sleek, orange tabby rubbed itself between her legs. She picked up the newcomer and looked for a collar, unsuccessfully.

"Where did you come from little guy?"

"First time I've seen him around." Mrs. Preston commented as she watered her flower boxes. "Another stray. Oreo probably told him that you'll provide a meal if he's sweet enough."

"Morning Mrs. Preston." Katherine smiled and set down the tabby, "Any word yet on getting Jerry evicted?"

The seventy-year-old woman looked over at the tarp tent and sighed. "No, and I don't see why ever not. Lord Jesus willing, the police will finally understand how much of a nuisance that man is to the neighborhood and do it this week. I've been having Timothy phone them almost daily. The smells!"

"Well, maybe today will be all our lucky day." Katherine moved past, only to be stopped by the usual Monday morning question she was hoping to avoid.

"Did you make it to church yesterday?"

"Not this week, Mrs. Preston. Christina needed the sleep." She hated using her daughter in this perpetual dodge against all things religious, but over the past few months she found it to be the best defense.

Even so, Mrs. Preston sighed again, this time in disappointment for Katherine. "While I have given up on Jerry, some souls will never be saved, there's still hope with you. And Christina! She needs the Lord in her life. Will do you both good. Ethan and Iris and the boys as well. You tell them that, alright?"

"Oh, I agree Iris needs some help." Katherine smirked at her own joke, "We'll go next week?"

"The Lord doesn't like when you make promises you don't keep."

"Enjoy the morning Mrs. Preston." And Katherine kept on walking, feeling her neighbor's judgement all the way to the end of the alley and around Jerry's blue monstrosity.

After the brisk walk, Katherine silently stepped in the back door of Lavigne's Bakery five minutes past seven and let the smells of baking bread lift her spirits.

"You're late." Lester commented from his spot on the counter, his large fists kneading dough effortlessly.

"Ssshhh," She put her finger over her lips, slipped on her apron, grabbed a bit of flour from a bin, and dusted her shoulder.

Life wasn't about how busy you were, but about how busy you appeared.

"You know, Robert doesn't like it when you're late. Says it puts him in a sour mood. Feels like you don't care."

"I do care, thank you very much.", Katherine nodded to the baker and stepped over to the racks to inspect his morning work. "These look great."

Lester shook his scarred face. "Flattery doesn't work on me girl. I'm too old for that. But thank you."

"Katherine, is that you?" Robert called out from the front counter.

"Yea, it's me."

"You're late."

Katherine moved to the front of the shop and put on her best smile. "No, I was taking inventory of where we were at so far. As you have told me, can't let inventory run low during the morning rush."

Robert looked from her floured shoulder to her face and frowned, his white mustache twitching. "I didn't hear you."

"Another thing you've been saying, I make too much racket in the back. Been trying to work on that too."

He grumbled and opened his mouth to say more, but shifted his frown to a smile and turned towards the door as a customer stepped in. "Welcome to Lavigne's. Ah, Mr. Orvel, how are you this morning? How was your weekend? Fishing, right?"

Zero points for Robert, One for Katherine.

Lavigne's Bakery was a simple space, with an antique charm. With well-worn wooden floors that squeaked slightly when you walked, a smattering of decorations and photos from the fifties in France, and chalk signs hung on the back wall describing what could be purchased at what price and any specials for the week. The long room was split with a large counter built of lit display cases showing off as many baked goods as possible. The whole front facade was glass storefront, with the name of the shop displayed on the windows in bold lettering. Seven people could wait inside comfortably, while Robert insisted there never be more than five or else it was chaos.

Lester typically arrived in the early morning hours and began the baking, completing the first round of goods by the time Robert arrived to fill the displays. Katherine only overlapped with Lester for two hours and found him to be an odd character. She knew only a little about him. He wasn't a talker. He had done a few tours in the Iraq war, lost a buddy at some point, face scarred from that time. He didn't seem to have a family, and Katherine wasn't sure about his friends or outside hobbies. He had been working for Robert since he returned to the States and left the army, over ten years past now. At times he was a stickler for the rules, hovering to the point of annoyance over the pettiest of things, and other times he would easily bend when she expected a solid wall of resistance. To Katherine's point of view, Lester did his job without a fuss then disappeared with as minimal chit-chat as possible.

He was, in many ways, the exact opposite of her boss.

The owner of Lavigne's Bakery, Robert Lavigne, began at the bakery under his father's tutelage and had either worked or run the business for nearly sixty years. He loved to talk and knew all of his customers by name, as well as their kids, grandkids, upcoming weddings, anniversaries, places of employment, heartaches, and dreams. He knew when they came into the shop and what they enjoyed and, most importantly, how to get them to buy a little more through a nudge or a joke or a bit of understanding. Everyone seemed to know Robert and love him. Why couldn't she?

With her boss distracted by Mr. Orvel's arrival, Katherine made herself busy with the morning chores. Checking in with Lester to see if he needed a hand with the bread or deliveries, back to the front to wait on customers with Robert, over to the side counter to prep the bags scheduled for pick-up, then onto cleaning wherever whenever she had a moment to spare. She took over the counter alone during the midmorning lull as Lester left and Robert moved into the back. A half an hour before noon and the lunch rush, Katherine's best friend arrived.

"Hola, mi amor." Shandra appeared next to Katherine, beaming, "This weekend was beyond loco! Do I have a story to tell you."

Katherine smiled at Shandra's joy, "Oh, and I have a few to tell you, but you go first."

Shandra was shorter than Katherine, with black hair and a small nose ring. "So, you know Miguel, my brother. He's been working on this huge case for the past few years down in south Philly, gangs, drugs, weapons, some human trafficking. Took months to get in with the right players, then months to set up the right meetings, and on and on and on. He's been building up evidence for a while, cutting through all this red tape at headquarters, required paperwork, chain of custody, all of it. Then, Saturday night, something happened, something spooked the whole lot of them. By Sunday morning? Their whole operation vanished. Gone. Like it never existed. All the bit players, the grease men and low life labor? No clue where the leaders went. Last night Miguel was swearing up a storm at mi padre's house, about the brass trying to stick it on Miguel, told him he made a mistake. He kept going on and on about all of his hard work now gone up in flames due to some bureaucratic hard ass not allowing him to move faster. It's a mess."

From Shandra's many stories, Katherine knew her half-brother had been a detective for over twenty years. He knew the city better than almost anyone else.

"Did he say what happened? What spooked them?"

Shandra shrugged, "He thinks someone tipped them off, some rata, maybe even someone in his department. Miguel's pissed mostly, because now, instead of being out on the street he'll be stuck to a desk for a few weeks, maybe more, wrapping up everything he's collected so far, archiving, tagging, and labeling. More red tape, more busy work. Creating a paper trail for the next time they come back, if they come back, something to cross-reference."

"Well, at least it's not all lost."

"But the bad guys are still out there! Hard to feel good when he was so close to getting them locked up and, poof, gone."

Shandra demonstrated an exaggerated explosion with her hands high in the air. Her expression of annoyance was quickly replaced with a smile as two new customers stepped inside.

"Hola! Good morning!" Shandra almost bounced with excitement, "Welcome to Lavigne's! How are you two doing this fine Monday morning?"

The elderly man smiled openly as he looked up at the signs. "Fine, fine," He squinted through his glasses.

"Shandra," Robert popped his head out from the back, "Can I get your help for a moment?"

"Sure!" She turned towards Katherine, "They're all yours."

Katherine stepped up to the register and towards the unknown faces. Robert wanted her to be more personal. "Welcome to Lavigne's, Mr.?"

The elderly man focused on her, "Weiss. And whom do I have the pleasure to speaking with?"

"Good to meet you, Mr. Weiss. My name is Katherine. How may I help you?"

The man took off his glasses, "Yes, I seem to have put on the wrong pair this morning. My apologies. Do you have butter croissants?"

"Yes, we do. We are a French bakery, after all." Her smile faded when her joke fell flat. "How many would you like?"

"A dozen, please."

As she began filling a bag, she looked over at the second customer, a broad-shouldered man wearing a bowler's hat and round sunglasses. The size of him made the elderly man look tiny in comparison.

"I'll be right with you."

"Oh, no bother." Mr. Weiss chuckled and waved his hand. "He's with me."

Katherine looked from the older man to the one in the black jacket and felt she was missing something. "Okay, no worries."

"How much would that be?"

"Sixteen dollars."

"Fair, fair." He pulled out his wallet and dug into it for his card as Katherine set the bag down. "I've heard so many good things about this place, decided today was the day to try it out."

"I'll be sure to tell Mr. Lavigne that his reputation is growing."

"So many good things," Mr. Weiss continued as if Katherine hadn't said anything. "I do have one question. The best bread is made from the best ingredients. Do you know where Mr. Lavigne sources his butter?"

"Yes, actually, I do. Local creamery, Seven Stars Farm, a few miles out of the city."

"Ah yes, they have an excellent operation. Very happy cows. Do you know the secret to happy cows?"

"Good grass?" Katherine guessed, "And lots of space?"

"No. Other happy cows." Mr. Weiss chuckled to himself. "They're like yeast, you add one happy cow into the herd and the feeling permeates through the whole lot. Simple as that."

Katherine handed over the bag once he paid. "Interesting fact. Here you go. Enjoy your morning, Mr. Weiss."

Mr. Weiss pulled out a croissant, smelled it, then broke it in two. "Are these kosher?"

"I," She had never been asked that. "I do not know."

The old man chuckled and bit into the bread. He smiled as he chewed, "Very good, worth the cost. You see, things like bread, kosher, it all depends. All depends on if you would expect milk or cheese to be in the recipe. Buttered croissant? Butter. Don't eat it with meat, thus, kosher. See, easy."

"I see." She did not.

"I like you." Mr. Weiss commented as he put the remainder of the roll in his bag and turned to go. "I think I'll be back again soon. As long as your bread remains this good. Yes, we'll chat again very soon."

Katherine couldn't help but smile as the old man left the shop, the man in the hat following. Robert's customers were some of the craziest people, but also the sweetest people in all of Philadelphia. Something about this place attracted them. She never knew what kind of conversations she would have at any moment.

A middle-aged woman Katherine knew filled the gap Mr. Weiss left, "Good morning Mrs. Jones. Two loaves of French bread again?"

After a twenty-minute flurry of customers, Shandra returning to help after Mrs. Jones left, another gap suitable for conversation arrived.

"So, how was your weekend?" Shandra asked as she wiped down the counter, "You said you had a story? Your brother still being a pain?"

Katherine nodded. "He is, but this isn't about that. Patrick showed up."

"Oh no," Shandra brought one hand to her mouth. "He didn't."

"No, it was fine. I shooed him away. I was hoping he came around to finally pay me, but no, like always he needed something from me."

"What was it this time?"

"He had me deliver something to someone, a box of artifacts? Old stuff, to some rich guy in a coffee shop."

Shandra cocked her head to one side. "That's odd. Artifacts? Patrick working for a museum now?"

"I don't know what he's doing."

"So, you didn't do it? Did you? Deliver these artifacts?"

Katherine hesitated. "I did."

Shandra stared at her. "Girl! Ay-ay-ay! I keep telling you, he's going to keep taking advantage of you if you keep saying sí, sí. You can't keep rolling over every time he smiles at you."

"I know, but he said he would pay me if I did this. And I need the money."

"Did you make him pay you first."

"Um... no."

"Girl!"

"I know, I know!" Katherine crossed her arms. "Sure, I rolled over. But it wasn't all that bad. After I delivered the package the rich guy I gave it to paid me a little extra for my troubles."

"That's more like it, getting men to pay you for the things you do for them!"

"But then it got weird."

Shandra was enthralled. "How so?"

"Well, yesterday, some security guard arrived at my door. Told me to come with him. So, I go..."

"No."

"... and he me to Joaquin, the rich guy..."

"No!"

"... and he takes me up to a lab, some research facility and goes on to tell me that Patrick was donating blood for science or something..."

"Patrick? Science?"

"I know, right? But then he says, Joaquin, that Patrick's blood is special and so might be Christina's. Wants to test her for it."

"You said no, right?"

"This time I did! I'm not letting anyone with needles around my daughter."

"Good." Shandra smiled widely. "Your story was so much better than mine! How come you have such a fascinating life? Mine is work, family, my brother, and sleep."

Katherine smiled in return, "I would trade my excitement for your family in a heartbeat."

Shandra's smile turned sad, "You have Ethan, he's great!"

"He is, in his own way." Another customer stepped into the bakery, ending their chit chat. Katherine looked up, maintaining her grin. "Welcome to Lavigne's. How may I help you today Mrs. Kibbler?"

Upon arriving home for the evening, Katherine found two police cars parked in front of her rowhomes.

"The city! Finally here to take down Jerry's tent." Katherine said to herself as she stepped into her alley.

She scratched Oreo and the orange tabby, then stepped into her house. "Iris!"

"In here Katherine."

It was when Katherine found two policemen standing in the living room with her brother and Iris that she knew something was off. Instinctively, she grabbed Christina off of Iris's lap.

"Iris, Ethan, What's this about?"

"Ms. Mason?" The taller policeman asked.

"Yes, that is me."

She could feel the bad news coming. She did not want to hear the next part but had nowhere to run. Instead, she held her daughter tight.

"We're here in regard to one Patrick Troutman. You were one of his emergency contacts."

"Sure, what about Patrick?"

"I'm sorry I have to be the one to tell you this. He's dead. We found his body last night."

Six

THE REST OF KATHERINE'S evening was absolute emotional carnage.

The second policemen apologized for the intrusion and stated they needed answers as quickly as possible with the way the case was evolving. Katherine didn't understand. What case? Iris interjected with her perfect motherly tone, pulled Christina out of Katherine's numb arms, and took her to be upstairs with the boys. Ethan asked if his presence was needed further, no, nodded, then told the two men to take as long as they required before following his wife.

Once Katherine was alone with the two police, they held nothing back.

Bureau of Criminal Investigation

- TRANSCRIPT -
Interview Date: March 23, 2017
Case #: 50-258-A4
Offense: [BLANK]
Interview of: Katherine Mason (KM)
Interviewed by: Officer Kingly Levingston (O1); Officer Jake Johnson (O2)
Overview: On the date stated above, officers Kingly Levingston and Jake Johnson interviewed Katherine Mason within her home in regard to the death of her former domestic partner, Patrick Troutman. She was not under investigation or suspicions at this time. Also present was her brother, Ethan Mason (EM)

Begin recording: 4:13 pm

O1: Ma'am, I am going to record our conversation… if that is alright with you.

KM: Yea, sure.

O1: All we'll need to do here is ask a few questions, Ms. Mason. Answer as truthfully as you can. You are not required to answer any you do not want to. Okay? Ma'am, I need you to verbalize your affirmative. Head shaking is good, but I need the words too.

KM: Okay, yes.

O1: Great. Here we go, easy one to start. When did you last see Patrick Troutman?

KM: Friday night.

O1: What was the situation? Where, why?

KM: He came over here, uninvited, wanted to see Christina. I asked him for child support, he said he would get it to me soon, then he left.

O1: About what time of the evening was this conversation?

KM: About 9:30, maybe 10:30. Somewhere around there.

O2: He didn't stay the night?

KM: No.

O2: Why not?

KM: He has his own place to live.

O2: Why?

KM: He has his own place. Is that really any of your business?

O2: Did he normally come over uninvited?

KM: Sometimes.

O2: And was that a problem? Him coming over unannounced? With you two being separated and all?

KM: It was fine with me. Less so with my brother. They had a fight last time he was here. I didn't mind, I want him to see his daughter. Wanted him to. Past tense now, I guess.

O2: Was there a fight this Friday when he showed up unannounced?

KM: No.

O2: Your brother mentioned before you arrived that things between you and him and he and him were, tense. Patrick didn't argue with you or with Ethan?

KM: No. Are you accusing me or my brother of something?

O1: No, we're just getting details. Understanding the situation. We'll move on. Where did Patrick Troutman work?

KM: With family.

O1: Okay, sure. What was the name of the company?

KM: I don't know.

O2: What do you mean you don't know?

KM: He was into security. Corporate stuff. With an uncle. It was sensitive, didn't want me to know much about it.

O2: Corporate stuff? Such as?

KM: I don't know. Camera systems? Campus hardening? Threat assessments? He would sometimes be out late into the night, or over weekends, one time he was away for two weeks with no communication. Whenever I would push, he would get offended I didn't trust him, so, I trusted him.

O1: How long were you two together?

KM: Almost four years.

O1: And within that time, you had no idea what he was doing? Where he went during the day?

KM: I knew where he was, he'd tell me that. Mostly around the city. Sometimes to other cities. Salt Lake, Atlanta, Chicago. He'd send me photos of the airports, bought me small gifts.

O1: Did he ever mention the name of a Waya Kipp?

KM: No.

O1: What about a Khaleem Truce?

KM: No.

O2: Why did you two split up? I saw you had a daughter. Is she his?

KM: She is and, it's complicated. And still personal.

O1: Excuse my partner. we're simply trying to get some background on the type of man he was.

KM: He was a good man! I had a great life with him. He made me laugh. Until he left.

O2: So, he left you. It wasn't mutual. Why?

KM: A difference of opinions? Maybe I pushed too hard. I wanted stability, wanted him to be home in the evenings so we could raise our daughter together. He refused to leave the company, not with how he felt about his uncle, all the opportunities he had provided him over the years. Didn't want to betray him. And it stabilized after I became pregnant, work hours. Patrick talked to his uncle and the hours were more consistent then, but not always.

O1: So, Patrick left you because you wanted him to quit his job?

KM: No, not really. I don't know why he left. I asked him a few times. The only thing I got out of him was that he wasn't able to do it. Raise Christina. I don't know why. He wouldn't open up to me.

O1: That's okay Ms. Mason, we're not here to accuse you of anything. Do you remember his uncle's name?

KM: No.

O2: No?

KM: No.

O2: Let me get this straight. Your boyfriend, who you were with for four years, was working for an uncle you did not know, for a company with no name, and you trusted him?

KM: Mostly, yes.

O2: Mostly?

[pause]

KM: I followed him one day, about a year into our relationship. Followed Patrick. I was angry he wouldn't tell me where he was going, what he was doing all day. I thought he was having an affair or something. I was paranoid. All day, he was driving around town, going into places, coming out, boxes, really boring stuff. I followed him twice more that year. Same thing.

O1: Did he know you were following him?

KM: No, I don't think so.

O2: Did you ever tell him you had followed him?

KM: No.

O1: Did he leave anything around the house, anything from work, do you have anything that might have a name, or an address?

KM: I can look, but I don't think so. He hasn't lived with me since Christina was born, and I moved since then too. I don't think I kept any of his. And he always came home in his hoodie and jeans, never carried anything on him. He wanted to keep work at work and home at home.

O1: When you followed him, did he stop in an office or building you were unfamiliar with?

KM: All of the places he stopped at were unfamiliar.

O2: Did he stop somewhere to begin his day and then end it?

KM: No, not that I could tell. Look, I didn't follow him the whole day. And he told me most of his heavy work came in spurts. He'd get a call and plans would change. I learned to be okay with the occasional disruption.

O1: Who would call him?

KM: His boss, his uncle.

O2: This is the same uncle with no name? What did they talk about?

KM: I only heard the one side. It was a lot of, uh-huh, sure, understood.

O1: What did his uncle come up as on Patrick's phone?

KM: It simply said 'Boss'.

O2: Not uncle?

KM: No, boss.

O1: And he would jump whenever his boss would call? If he was in the shower?

O2: If you two were getting close, frisky?

O1: Jake.

O2: You know what I mean. Ms. Mason?

KM: Sure? He always had his phone on him and would always take his bosses calls. Or call him back right away. It was annoying at times. So yes, I would say so. Obviously you think his work got him killed, or else you wouldn't be asking these things. What do you think he was doing?

O2: Nothing. We're gathering background. Did you ever meet this uncle? Have dinner with him?

KM: No. I mentioned it a few times early on to Patrick, wanted to meet all of his family. But after Marge, his mom, and meeting his dad… let's say, Patrick's parents are, unique. The topic of meeting the rest of his family kind of fell off after that. He was uncomfortable when we talked about family, and I didn't want to push.

O2: Sounds like a great relationship.

KM: You haven't told me yet where you found him, or when.

[the sound of a door opening somewhere]

EM: Don't mind me. Just grabbing some food.

O1: That's fine, Mr. Mason. We're actually just wrapping up.

KM: So? Where did you find him?

[both officers are heard clearing their throats]

O1: Mr. Mason, if you wouldn't mind, this will only take a few more minutes.

EM: Of course. However, Junior would not stop complaining till he had some goldfish. We're going through a minor sustenance attachment cycle. Quite normal.

KM: Thanks for that bit of information Ethan.

EM: There, that's all I needed. You say a few more minutes?

O1: About five more, yes.

EM: Excellent. Jack is also getting restless, feeling a bit threatened by your presence. I probably shouldn't have said that. You two, keep doing your duty. Okay, I'm gone again.

[pause in the conversation as feet are heard scuffling and a door closes]

KM: How did you find Patrick?

O1: Do you want to know the details? Or general conditions?

KM: I can stomach the details. Tell me what you know.

O1: His body was found dumped in an alley across town. We were notified of him early Sunday morning. He died sometime Saturday night. Right now, you are the last one who we know had contact with him when he was alive.

KM: That was almost two days ago! Why are you only telling me that he's dead now?

O1: It took us some time to identify the body.

KM: Why? Tell me why, damn it!

[pause]

O2: His throat was slashed. A lot of damage in that area, his face, his chest.

KM: [gasp] Did he suffer?

O1: We don't know ma'am. It could have been an instant death. [Snapping sound] Coroner is still identifying the exact cause. Whatever happened, he's at peace now.

KM: [soft crying] Thank you, for telling me.

O2: Where were you after seeing him on Friday night? Did you go out? Do anything?

KM: No, I went to sleep. I don't have a car, and Christina was sleeping.
O1: Your brother has a car?
KM: Yes, but I don't like driving it. Do I need a lawyer?
O1: No, no, Ms. Mason. You are fine. And I think that will be enough for tonight. I can see you're still in shock. Please, if you remember any more details, anything odd about the last time you saw him, anything that seemed out of character. Or about where Patrick worked or his employer, don't hesitate to call me.
KM: I will. But, can't you guys pull that kind of stuff from tax records? Paystubs?
O2: That takes time. Warrants. It's best if we can handle these things quickly, right after the incident. Holes like your boyfriend has lead to questions, which, if left unanswered for too long, lead us to start assuming things.
KM: Things like he got what was coming to him? You can say it, I can see it in your eyes. You think he's a criminal.
O1: Ma'am, what my partner is trying to say is, there are a few details about your ex that aren't adding up. That's all.
KM: He, he was a good man. Sure, he had his flaws, but don't we all?
O1: We do. I'm sorry for your loss, Ms. Mason.

End of recording: 4:34 pm

Once the police left, Ethan and his family reemerged. Katherine clung to Christina until it was bedtime, bouncing between mental states as Iris attempted to console her, eventually opening up a bottle of wine. By nine, Christina was asleep, and Katherine was tipsy enough to do something stupid. With a bit of protest from her brother, she told him she was going to simply walk and think for a bit.

No, Ethan, I won't do anything stupid.

While Katherine let her feet move and her anger burn, she made three phone calls.

The first was to the bakery, recording a message for Robert in the morning, telling him the news and that she would still be in, but that the situation was still fresh. She would let him know if anything changed.

The second was to the number on Joaquin's business card. Instead of getting him directly, she was greeted by a live assistant. In that moment she let loose, gave the poor girl a piece of her mind, told her under no uncertain terms would she give up until she had a meeting set up with Joaquin. As soon as possible.

No, I will not hold! Do not hang up on me! Oh, you have to use the other line to get him?

Fine.

But if you even try to hang up on me, so help me I will find you and make your life miserable! I know where you live!

Elevator music.

She probably shouldn't have said that.

Footsteps ever onward into the night.

Yes? Yes I'm still here! Sorry about the other thing. Oh? Tomorrow morning? Same coffee shop as before? Sure. That'll work. What time? 8am. Thanks. And sorry again, and for the yelling.

Click.

Her third call was back to the bakery, updating Robert that, in fact, she would not be in tomorrow.

Sorry.

Drained emotionally, physically, and mentally, Katherine returned home. She found her brother and Iris still up. He had canceled his morning appointments and might have to cancel the rest for the day. Told the office that his sister was more important. The move struck Katherine hard. Ethan put almost nothing before his clients.

Iris opened another bottle of wine and the evening became a blur. Sometime in the early morning after Iris had gone up to bed, Katherine sat at the kitchen table with her brother, silent, the two of them staring at nothing. When she eventually stood up, muttering that she probably needed sleep, swaying slightly, Ethan did the unexpected. He did not say a word. All he did was hug his little sister.

In that moment of unexpected tenderness, Katherine desperately wanted to but found that she was too numb to cry.

Seven

Having earned nearly no sleep the previous evening, her head still pounding from the wine, Katherine was a ball of nerves and steam when she stomped into Starbucks at 7:37 am. Her plan was to be there first, to be sitting in Joaquin's seat, waiting for him. Let him come to her.

Unfortunately, Joaquin was already there, this time reading 'The Order of Time' by Carlo Rovelli. Without bothering with coffee Katherine plopped down across from him and folded her arms in anger.

"You knew." She began, glaring with all her might.

Joaquin looked up to her, raised a single finger to indicate he needed a moment, then went back to his book.

"Oh no."

Katherine nearly launched herself over the table, knocking over a few chess pieces, and snatched the book out of his hands. She threw it down next to the chessboard, pieces scattering everywhere, and went back to her angry crossed arms half slouch. The few people around them turned to stare.

"You knew." She repeated.

Joaquin was unphased. He merely folded his leg over the other and placed his hands on his knee.

"You're early."

"You knew." Katherine repeated for a third time, emphasizing each word with as much venom as she could muster.

"I know a lot of things. To which are you referring this morning?"

"About Patrick. You knew he was already dead. That's why you had me up in your lab on Sunday, asking about Christina. Only reason for that is because you knew he was already dead."

"Patrick Troutman is dead? I am sorry to hear of his passing."

"No! That's not good enough!" Katherine bit off the ending, becoming acutely aware of how she looked and how loud she was being. "Tell me the truth."

Joaquin suddenly looked very sad. "You are correct. I knew before we spoke on Sunday."

The reality of her ex's death hit Katherine harder the second time around. She went very still, "Why didn't you tell me?"

"It was a business decision. I needed your head clear for what I was about to ask, needed you undistracted. Ultimately a poor decision on my part. I apologize." Joaquin looked at his watch. "And with that, I must apologize again. I need to be going."

"No!" Katherine stood up with him, the easy apologies grating on her. It was only 7:39 am. "Your secretary said we would meet at 8. And you haven't told me anything but lies. Do you know who killed him? Was it you?"

The accusation hung in the air between them like an unpinned grenade.

Joaquin looked her in the eyes. "No. Ms. Mason. I did not kill Patrick."

She believed him. "Then, do you know who did?"

Joaquin ignored her follow-up question, his face unreadable, "Ms. Mason, what I came to do has been done. I broke your trust by obscuring the truth. I apologized. Now we move on in life, separately."

"That's not good enough." Katherine growled, moving in front of Joaquin, blocking his way. "I need to know more. What was my ex doing working for you? He worked for his uncle. Security."

"That's confidential." He responded, picking up his book, a wide brimmed black hat, and sunglasses.

"The police are asking."

"They tend to ask questions when murders occur. We have been cooperating." He then put on his hat, glasses, and moved past her.

Katherine followed after him, "I won't stop digging."

"Digging, into what, exactly?"

"Into what he was doing for you. Why the police are asking questions. Why he was murdered. Who murdered him. You might be able to buy them off, but you can't buy me. You know more then you're telling me still."

"Oh?" Joaquin's lips rose into a half smile. "You think so?"

"Yes."

"And you still think I'm a reliable source? Even after I've admitted to my flaws?"

Katherine thought for half a moment. "Yes."

"Then how about dinner, tonight. 8 pm?"

She blinked at the unexpected question. "What?"

"You said I couldn't buy you. I would like to try. Are you free tonight for dinner?"

The shift in the conversation had Katherine stammering. "Um, sure?"

"Excellent. I'll have Max pick you up at 7:30. Wear something elegant, yet comfortable. Something that is you. Maybe something green."

And with that Joaquin continued walking, leaving Katherine with her mouth open, unsure what had just happened and what she had agreed to.

Iris smiled to Katherine in the mirror, "I don't know why you're fretting so much, you're beautiful."

Katherine didn't feel it. The dark blue dress showed off her shoulders and clung to her waist. She felt too exposed with the open neckline, even with her long brown hair hanging loose. Was this her? Was this too much? Would she impress him? Why was she trying to impress him?

"I've been eating too much ice cream." Katherine poked her own belly.

Iris snorted. "You? Fat? Ha! I could barely fit into this dress after Junior was born and had absolutely no chance after Jack. But you? The baby weight melted off your bones."

"You think?" Katherine turned and continued her examination. She needed to get back in shape. Do some crunches or something. Squats. Yoga. Baby lifts.

"Yes. Look at you, now look at these extra, we'll say, fifteen pounds on my hips." Iris patted her midsection lightly. "You, me."

"Yea, I guess."

"You're the envy of all other mothers at the park. I've seen how their husbands look at you."

"Ew. No."

Iris laughed. "And with that neck of yours, we should do something classic, oh, I know." She opened a few drawers in her dresser then fished out a string of pearls. "Perfect."

"You don't think that'll be too much?"

"Absolutely not. He's some big-wig CEO or something, correct?"

"Something like that. He's rich."

"And this is the first time anyone as shown this much interest in your artwork?"

The lie was still working. At this point Joaquin being an art dealer made more sense than the veiled and foggy truth. Whatever it was. "Yes. He wanted to discuss things further."

"Then you're not only selling him your art, but you. Who you are. The artist behind the work."

That line was far too close to what Joaquin had said earlier. That he wanted to buy her.

"No, I don't want to be used like that."

"Of course not!" Iris fake pouted as she put the pearls around Katherine's neck, then smiled with her teeth. "But if I were you, and some swanky man wanted to buy my art, and wanted to have dinner with me at his place, I would use all of my, talents, to make sure he remembered me."

"Iris!"

Her sister-in-law laughed. "I'm only joking! Your ex died yesterday. There. I properly soured the mood. You're selling your art, nothing more. But, if you do enjoy yourself, I won't judge."

"I will not be enjoying myself. This is a business thing only."

Iris shrugged and went back to her dresser, finding two pearl earrings that dangled off golden chains. "I know that if I wasn't married to your brother, and I was being courted by a millionaire I would try every avenue. You never know what the right evening could lead into. You're broke."

Katherine glared at her sister-in-law, “I am very aware of that, thank you very much.”

“And you need a man, or at least a better source of income.”

“I will not use my body to feed my daughter!”

Iris’s smirk only widened, “What did you say he looked like?”

“I didn’t say.”

“But you’re blushing.”

“That’s because you won’t stop!”

“mmhmm.”

“He’s… he’s not unattractive.”

“And neither are you. But if you want to be stubborn and waste this opportunity, keep it strictly business...” Iris left the rest unsaid as she turned Katherine back towards the mirror.

“This isn’t me.”

“Trust me. This is right. You look gorgeous. Shoes?”

“I’ll wear mine.”

“Which ones?”

Katherine pointed to the pair of black flats on the bedroom floor next to her clothes. “Those.”

“Those? With this dress?”

“Yes. He said to wear something comfortable. I’ll suffer and put on all of this, blech, but I won’t kill my feet for a man.”

“How tall is he?”

“On the taller side, I come up to about his chin.”

“Then you can wear heals and see into his eyes. Easier to kiss him that way too.”

“Nope. Sticking with the flats. And not doing any kissing tonight either.”

Iris smiled. “Fine, business. But you do want to sell your art, right?”

Max arrived at 7:30 on the dot. Katherine kissed Christina goodbye as she babbled on the floor next to her cousins, told Iris one more time that it was strictly business after her look suggested otherwise, and stepped out into the night.

"Ms. Mason." Max's face was expressionless, holding the door open once again for her. "I was not expecting we would see each other again so soon."

"Joaquin has some explaining to do." Katherine held her face even, not willing to give away how nervous she was feeling. "Where are we going tonight?"

"To one of Mr. Morales's residences. He has a penthouse downtown, about fifteen minutes from here."

"Of course he has a penthouse. One of many residences." Katherine climbed into the car and smoothed her dress. When Max stepped into the driver's seat she asked, "Does Mr. Morales have dinners with women like this often?"

"No. Not often. There was one a while ago, seven, eight years ago? No, it's been at least seven years since he's invited anyone else up like this."

That was not the answer Katherine had expected. Was there something wrong with him? What had made her change his habits?

"Did he tell you to say that? You can tell me the truth."

"He did not. And I did."

The drive into City Center did nothing to still the butterflies in Katherine's stomach. They only seemed to flutter faster with the passing minutes. What was she doing? This was crazy! Patrick's mutilated body was found in some alley three days ago and now she was having dinner with his boss's, boss's, boss. Or maybe even more bosses beyond that. A powerful man who knew about his death before the police. Was she doing this to honor his memory, to figure out what happened to her baby girl's dad? Or for her daughter's safety? Or for something else? What did she want out of this? And why did Iris's annoying bad advice keep looping in her head? This had nothing to do with her art! Or her selling herself for her art! Or her selling herself for any other reason! Or him being attracted to her! Stupid Iris and her stupid bad advice!

"Do you trust your boss?" Katherine suddenly asked Max.

"I do." Max replied.

“Has he ever lied to you? How long have you worked for him? He ever given you a reason not to trust him?”

“Ma’am, I’ll be honest with you. In the past fifteen years? No, he has not. I’ve never caught him in an outright lie, not once. But he does tend to skirt around the truth. Feign, dance, distract. He always has his reasons. Best you make him stick with simple, short answers. He likes to talk, you’ll see. You get him to respond with a simple no or yes. Best advice I can give.”

“Thank you Max.”

Before she knew it, they had pulled up in front of a gleaming high-rise made of glass and steel. Max stepped out of the car and opened Katherine’s door.

“If you head on inside, tell the receptionist your name and she’ll take you from there.”

“Okay.”

Katherine stepped forward and laughed lightly on the fact of how different she was to the man she was about to see. She, a single mother, one who lived in the basement of her brother’s home and worked in a bakery. Joaquin, a wealthy businessman, one who lived with a view of the city, in a building with its own wait staff. She knew in her bones she was well out of her depth in this.

Katherine swallowed hard. Nothing to do now except pretend she belonged. Easy.

Once inside, the receptionist nodded and smiled when Katherine introduced herself and led her to a bank of elevators.

“Oh, those are for the normal residences.” He said when she slowed. He then took her through a door to a smaller private lobby where the elegance of the first seemed faded and drab.

“This is Mr. Morales’s private elevator.” He waved a card in front of the reader and the doors opened. “It’ll take you straight up. Do you have need of any further assistance?”

“Um, no. Thank you.” Katherine stepped into the car and couldn’t help but stare at the receptionist until the doors closed.

“What am I doing?” Katherine fell into the elevator wall as the car rose, resisting the urge to put her hands over her face and ruin her makeup. The butterflies were now an angry swarm of killer piranhas.

"No!" She glared at her own reflection within the door's silver surface. "I belong here. This is fine."

When the car doors reopened, all belief in herself was shattered in an instant.

What she stepped out into was something straight out of a dream. Straight in front of her was a modern yet cozy living room twice as large as her basement apartment with an unobstructed two-story view of the city in all its evening grandeur. Potted plants flanked couches and armchairs that probably cost more than her brother's minivan. A vibrant red rug lay below the furniture over black marble floors. The whole wall on her left was filled with bookshelves that had to hold over three thousand books, with the occasional trinket or decoration scattered within. On her right was a black slate fireplace, complete with a low burning fire adding to the room's ambiance. Past the fireplace and within the building's windowed corner, a sixteen-person dining room table sat below a modern silver chandelier. Two seats at one of the table's corners were set for dining, the full array of accoutrements laid out in perfect form. Low jazz music played in the background from nowhere and everywhere.

"Welcome." Joaquin appeared from a door set within the bookcase wall, his smile easy, his steps light. He was still wearing his black suit, black shirt, and red tie. "Can I take anything for you? A handbag, jacket?"

"No, I'll be fine." Katherine clutched her purse, not wanting to lose access to her phone or pepper spray. "You have an extraordinary house."

"Thank you." Joaquin moved towards the table. "The chef has informed me the appetizers will be ready momentarily. Would you like some wine?"

Of course he has a chef. He probably has a butler and a fully stocked harem too. "Sure. That would be great."

"Do you have a preference?"

"Whatever you want to drink is fine."

Joaquin moved over to a wine cooler, bent down, and considered his options. "I'm partial to a deep red. We are having lamb tonight, so I will go with a mature Rioja. This one comes from Northern Spain. La Rioja Alta, 2005. Does that sound acceptable to you?"

"Sure."

Katherine knew very little about wine and what she did know came from college. At that time, and even now, all it had to do was taste good and get her tipsy. She sat down, hoping she had chosen the correct seat between her two options.

As Joaquin uncorked the bottle and began pouring two glasses, a white-haired man with an apron stepped into the room and placed a platter of stuffed mushrooms, cheese and rye bread bites, and roasted vegetable skewers down on the corner of the table. A second waiter followed close behind with a cheeseboard filled with over twenty different varieties. A third chef then added a basket of freshly baked bread slices and a crock of butter.

“Thank you, Frans.” Joaquin nodded to his staff then handed Katherine her glass. “And thank you, Katherine, for your company this evening. Please, eat, enjoy.”

The options were overwhelming. Not wanting to appear snobbish or ungrateful, Katherine took a bit of each onto her plate. And with her first bite of mushroom, she knew she was in trouble. It was absolutely delicious. A sip of wine to clear her thoughts only added to the problem. It was the best wine she had ever tasted. Leagues better than the cheap bottles Iris had pulled out last night.

Joaquin followed Katherine’s example and took a bit of everything. The two of them ate slowly in silence, each watching the other, neither willing to break the spell just yet. Both sizing up the opposition. Or at least that was what Katherine was doing. Joaquin was probably thinking of her as a mouse and him the cat. Just toying with her, playing with her, wondering what game he should play next with his prey.

Maybe he would grow bored and try to swallow her whole.

He needed to learn that she was no one’s play-thing.

“Now that we’re here, alone,” Katherine began after another sip of wine. “I need answers. Do you know who killed Patrick?”

“Straight into the heart of it.” Joaquin’s slight smile grew, “It is customary we enjoy our dinner before we dive into murders and revenge.”

“I’m a bit impatient. Also, I never learned how to follow the rules.”

Joaquin stood up and moved over to the window. “Alright, we shall discuss on your terms. But first, have you made a decision about your daughter?”

“I did before and it hasn’t changed. The answer is no.”

“That is, unfortunate.”

Katherine set down her glass and stood up as well. She would not allow this man to talk down to her, even if she only made it up to his shoulders.

“Is that how it’s going to be? You want to make this an exchange of services? My daughter’s body for justice for her father?”

Joaquin turned around, a bit hurt. “No, that is not why I invited you. As I told you before, you intrigue me.” Pause. “Your late ex-fiancée was employed in the logistics division of Hydro-Tech LLC. Shipping and receiving. Not even two years.”

“Two years?” Katherine thought back to when Christina was born. Patrick had changed jobs?

“When, exactly?”

Joaquin pulled out his phone from an inner jacket pocket. After a moment he responded. “August 12th.”

“Christina was born in September. Why would Patrick start working for you then?” She asked, more to herself then Joaquin.

“He was hired in August, and his bloodwork came back in October. He joined our pilot research program in October and has been donating blood for about a year and a half. We estimate we have six more months of testing before we can reach any solid, initial results.”

“Well, Christina isn’t your replacement. No matter how much you’re willing to pay.”

“I understand.” Joaquin nodded then swept the idea away like a bad smell. “It was a long shot regardless. How are you holding up? From your loss?”

“I’m fine.” The personal question skipped off Katherine’s mental defenses. “Do you know who killed him?”

“Yes.”

Katherine blinked. “Yes?”

“Yes.” Joaquin repeated. “He was killed due to the actions of the man who gave him that box.”

"Waya Kipp?"

It was Joaquin's turn to blink. "You told me you did not know who gave Patrick the box."

Her guess at one of the two names mentioned by the police paid off. Katherine pressed on her momentary advantage. "I learned of him later, after our meeting. From the police. I dug a bit and found that Waya is leadership of some consulting firm in Tennessee. Nothing to do with security. And no way they were related, unless Patrick dad's brother was adopted. What do you think Patrick was doing working for him?"

"A good question." Joaquin thought for a moment before continuing on. "Do you know if your ex kept any records, any place he might have stashed a paper trail that could be used to piece this puzzle together?"

"Nothing at our place, he cleaned everything out when he left, and I got rid of anything else that reminded me of him when I moved. He had a truck. His work vehicle. I don't know where it is. It might be at his mom's place."

"I see. Katherine, this is also a long shot, but if you were able to find anything that linked Patrick to Waya, a paper trail, POs, e-mails, pay stubs, anything like that, maybe I could help more."

"Help, how?"

"I have a large legal team at my disposal. We do not rest idle when one of our employees is killed. Currently, though, we have no leverage."

A new idea came to Katherine, one which caused her to panic. "Was it my fault?"

"Was what your fault?"

"Patrick's death. Did he die because I gave you that box? Should I have told him no?"

Joaquin's eyes shifted from concern to compassion. "No, no Katherine. His death was not your fault. Not in the slightest."

Instead, Katherine picked up her glass and took a large gulp of wine. "I don't believe you."

"His fate was sealed far before you delivered that package to me."

"Are you sure?"

"I am."

And suddenly she was crying. All of the emotions of the past twenty-four hours broke through the flood gates, and she found herself hugging herself, sobbing. Joaquin moved quickly to her side and pulled her into his arms.

"That's alright," he said as he patted her back every so gently. "It's going to be okay."

Katherine pushed him away, anger replacing sorrow. "How can you say that? You barely know me. You don't know anything about me or my life or anything. You just want to use me or use my daughter for your stupid research. You see me as some tool or toy you can play with. I will not be used."

"I wasn't thinking that at all." Joaquin stepped back, folding his arms. "I can see you are strong. You will be okay."

"Oh, I'm strong? You think so? And that's, based on, what?"

"I can tell."

"Oh, you can, can you?" Katherine took another large gulp of wine, finishing off the glass, then raised her voice, "Tell me Joaquin. How hard has your life been? Did your mother leave your father when you were seven? Did you have to stuff cardboard in the bottom of your shoes so that they would last longer? Did you ever pretend with your brother and sister that rice was more than just lumpy white mush, pretend it was a hamburger or a salad because you were eating it and some chicken broth for the twelfth day in a row? Or did you grow up on red wine from Northern Spain and had to really suffer at times with the lesser vintages from the South?"

"Katherine, I –"

"Oh, no, I'm just getting started. Did you then have your dad die on you right when you thought you were figuring your life out? Have the only person who truly loved you yanked out from under you because of some stupid heart problem? Then did you find the man of your dreams, only to have that dream become a nightmare within a few short years? Wake up one day and find him aloof, distant, almost hating you when he finds out you're pregnant? Did you have him leave you and force you to raise your daughter all on your own then go and get himself killed? Have the police laugh at you, tell you you were an idiot to love him? Do you have to figure out how to feed your daughter every day and hate yourself when all you have is money for rice?

"No, I don't think so. I can tell. You grew up rich. Pampered. Taught by the most amazing teachers to do the most amazing things. You probably know nothing but a life of luxury and ease. Wait staff making you amazing food. Living in amazing houses. Driving amazing cars. Using other people. Trying to use me. You think I'll be okay because that's what people like me do, we survive. Either that, or we die. And what does that matter to someone like you? You'll just find some other girl to flirt with and mess with their heart and break, steal their children away, crush them between your teeth then move on to the next, and the next, and the next."

Katherine had tears streaming down her face, her whole chest heaving with the effort from yelling.

Joaquin sighed sadly. "Katherine. I am sorry for your loss."

This was the exact wrong thing to say. The apology only fueled Katherine's anger. "You're sorry? You're sorry? We don't ever say sorry unless we mean it. What are you sorry for, Joaquin?"

"I am sorry that life has been so hard on you. It shouldn't be this way."

Katherine could tell he was trying to be genuine. A little bit of the wind left her sails. "Fine. You can be sorry for that. But you cannot be sorry for me. Never be sorry for me."

"Of course. I will always admit my mistakes. I said the wrong things. It will not happen again."

She bit off a laugh, "You're a man, of course you're going to say more idiotic things to me. That's what men do."

Katherine then wiped her face, smearing her make up. She then cursed under her breath. She wasn't used to wearing make-up anymore. This was all Iris's fault!

Joaquin picked up one of the napkins on the table and handed it to Katherine, who took it graciously.

"Great, now I'm a mess." She laughed bitterly after she blew her nose. "Do you have a bathroom?"

"I do. It's this way."

"Thank you." Katherine grabbed her purse and hoped she remembered enough on how to fix her face. "I'm probably the worse date you've ever had."

"No, not at all. Your honesty is refreshing."

"Now you're just saying that."

"I'm not. It is."

Katherine could tell he meant it.

Before stepping into the bathroom, she turned to Joaquin. "Why am I here?"

"You had a few questions. This is a better place and time to answer them."

"And that's it, no other reason?"

"Honestly, selfishly, I wanted to get to know you better."

"There it is. Joaquin, stop beating around the bush! You wanted to use me. You thought I'd be an easy lay, dazzled by your decadence.."

"No," Joaquin shook his head. "Not at all. Katherine, I don't do this often. I don't make a habit of dinners with beautiful women. You can ask my staff."

"Paid actors."

"Katherine, I am telling the truth."

She wanted to believe him. "Then what, what about me fascinates you? Is it my unique style of make-up? Or the way I yell at you and accuse you of murder?"

"It's your mind, your spirit. They are rare, you are special."

"And this doesn't?" She motioned at her body and her blue dress.

"You are lovely to look at, yes. That is not my goal. It maybe someday, but not tonight."

"Oh, so all it takes to catch the eye of the great Joaquin Morales is to play chess with him and lose?"

"Something like that." Joaquin smiled. "Honestly? Standing up to me and not backing down. Treating me as an equal. How about you clean up and we can continue this conversation over dinner. I would hurt Franz's feelings if we did not eat what he prepared. He is an excellent chef."

"Fine." Katherine nodded then closed the bathroom door.

The room was pristine and spotless with a rose marble sink and floor and white tile walls. Looking at herself in the mirror, the image of her tear-streaked face and smeared makeup made her grimace. She bit off a laugh, backed away, then sank slowly onto the floor. She was a mess! Why had she said all of that to Joaquin? Why did he still seem to like her?

Who was this man?

EIGHT

"WAIT, MEJOR AMIGA, BACK up!" The shock on Shandra's face was clear. "Patrick croaked, and to celebrate, you went on a date with Mr. Moneybags?"

"Mm hmm." Katherine nodded, a little ashamed of herself.

"Talk about celebrating the loss of a pain in your neck. How was it? Did you guys...?" Shandra asked with a glint in her eyes.

"No!" Katherine jumped back, waiving her arms. "No, no. No. We did not."

"Did he want to, and did you turn him down? That's smart, you know. Or... was it awful?"

Katherine thought back to her evening with Joaquin as she leaned on the bakery counter, the part of the night after she fixed her makeup. To their laughter together. To his smile, his eyes. To the way he weaved words in the air like candy, to his thoughts, his passion. It had been almost 11 pm before she left his place, and only due to work in the morning for both of them.

A dreamy smile fell on Katherine's lips, "No, it wasn't awful. He had really, really good food. I need my own chef now."

"Doesn't everyone?" Shandra was giddy. "Are you going to see him again? Tell me I'm now best friends with the richest future wife in Philly."

Katherine blinked, then shook off her cloud of daydreams, "No, it's not like that. Well, maybe. Possibly. Still a long shot. Anyway, I don't know. He didn't say. I left last night and now here we are. Back to real life."

Shandra threw Katherine another one of her shocked faces, "Girl! You're telling me you spent your whole night with the guy and he didn't ask you out on a second date? No more amazing time to look forward to up in his apartment? Ay! That's not good at all!"

"Well, last night wasn't really a date. It was more, business. I think. I don't know. I had three glasses of wine. I was enjoying myself, wasn't thinking much past the moment. I left, he didn't say anything more, and now I'm here."

"Then call him!"

"And what, leave a message on his business phone with his secretary?"

"You don't have his personal number?"

"No."

"Girl!" Shandra began to pace. "You are the absolute worst at this. You at least have to get his number!"

Katherine was blushing. "As I said, it wasn't like that. He invited me there to talk about his research and my daughter's involvement and I was there trying to understand Patrick's death. Why does everyone keep thinking it was a date?"

"It was at his house?"

"Yes."

"Over dinner?"

"Yes."

'Just the two of you, no lawyers, or secretaries to take meeting minutes? No people up on screens over zoom calls watching you two gab on and on about mushy, gooey, romantic stuff?"

"No, to both the romantic gabbing and the other people."

"Girl!"

"Fine! I'm an idiot!" Katherine laughed at herself as a customer walked in. "But I'm not calling him. Welcome to Lavigne's Mrs. Baker. The usual?"

"Yes darling." Mrs. Baker slung her oversized handbag onto the counter and sighed, "Harry's doing it again. I think he knows. Keeps telling me it's the best bread I've ever baked for him. Won't stop raving over the sandwiches. Why did I ever tell him I made this bread myself?"

"You could come clean." Katherine suggested as she placed two loaves into a paper bag.

"I can't do that! He'll never trust my cooking again. This is the first thing he's liked that I've made for him in thirty years of marriage!"

After helping the string of customers, Shandra gave Katherine the death-eye stare. “You’re going to be like that?”

Katherine hated it when Shandra did this. She thought she was right, and she wouldn’t let it go. The problem was, she normally was right. It wasn’t fair. Why did she get to have such a useful superpower? All Katherine could do was say the alphabet backwards. One of your generic, run-of-the-mill superpowers.

“Be like what?”

“Be all elusive, all, come chase me! Girl, this is a billionaire we’re talking about. He doesn’t play games. You take your best shot, or they forget about you. You’ve already made like thirty-seven mistakes. How many more do you think you can survive?”

“We played chess again.”

“What?” Shandra smirked, amused, “chess?”

“Yes, chess. You said he doesn’t play games. We played chess, last night, again. He beat me, horribly beat me again, but yea, you’re wrong. He does play games.”

“Ei! That’s not what I meant girl, and you know it.”

Katherine smirked in return. “Fine. I’ll call him. But I have a few things I need to do first.”

“What’s more important than hooking a billionaire?”

“Plenty.”

“Such as?”

Robert stepped out from the back and stopped short of his destination. He looked suspiciously from Katherine to Shandra. “What are you two ladies yapping on about?”

“Katherine is going to marry a billionaire.” Shandra answered plainly, moving over to her boss, and taking the tray of bread from his hands.

“Oh, when is the wedding? Am I invited? Are you catering the baked goods from here?”

“Soon, you will be, and yes, absolutely.” Shandra smiled sweetly at the both of them, “Katherine just has a few, calls, to make.”

Robert folded his arms. “Calls after work. Katherine, there’s another tray in the back. Since you’re not a billionaire yet, go get it.”

"Yes Robert." Katherine smiled thinly then shook her head at Shandra. Her friend gave her a goofball expression in return.

Even with her constant poking, Shandra was the best.

Katherine unbuckled Christina from the car seat and took a deep breath. The drive out to Norristown was as stressful as always. In addition, I-76 and I-476 had been backed up that evening which gave her thoughts ample time to churn.

She had borrowed Ethan's minivan from her less than enthusiastic brother to visit Patrick's mother. Knew this couldn't wait. Not with the cops snooping around and Joaquin being less than informative. Her billionaire wanted to help, but only if she helped him first. So be it. Not only that, if she didn't keep searching for answers while things were fresh, Christina would grow up not knowing why her father died.

She couldn't have that.

Patrick had always been closed lipped about his job since they had started dating then living together. Exactly as she had told the police. At first Katherine found it mysterious, her boyfriend worked in security! But she eventually grew annoyed at his secrecy. If it wasn't that interesting, he should tell her about it. What did he do all day? Where did he go? What did he see? She didn't like having this gaping hole of time about the person she loved with no details to fill it in. After following Patrick, she had had a little more to go on, some vague details to paint her mental picture of his day. She also felt like an awful person, not trusting him.

Maybe she had good reason not to trust him.

Security. That's what he said. That's what he always said. Maybe he had been involved with something illegal. Something she should have worried about more. Maybe after Patrick had left her and Christina, she should have been more direct in figuring out why. Maybe it hadn't been her. Maybe it been something else? If so, what? Why? She had let all these questions go unanswered, so many times. No longer. She would not let him get away with it any longer.

Even if he was no longer around to respond.

Of all the people in Patrick's life he seemed to trust, his mother was in the top three.

Mrs. Troutman lived in a run-down neighborhood in a single-story house with a small yard enclosed in by a chain link fence. Mr. Kibbles was already barking at Katherine's approach in his yippy way, hopping up and down with his whole body. Katherine always repressed the urge to kick the little brown Pomeranian. All he did was yip and pee. Christina remained very quiet on Katherine's hip as she knocked on the front door, both of her eyes staring at the dog, looks of excitement and fear flashing back and forth on her face. It took three more knocks before Katherine heard a call from the rear of the house. Within another minute the front door opened.

"Hello Katherine," Marge nodded as her eyes swept past her face, "There's my pretty little Christina!" Both of Marge's hands went to Christina's cheeks, pinching them firmly. Christina's expression settled on mild fear. "Katherine, come in, come in."

Of Patrick's two parents, Katherine preferred Marge by a wide margin. Even with her bad hip and smoking habit, she always tried her best to play with Christina and respectfully stepped outside for a drag. She had also been on Patrick's case for months now, calling Katherine nearly weekly to let her know she wasn't going to let her son skate off his duties to support his daughter, not a chance. He would not be like his old man. Raising a kid by yourself was hard work, she knew!

"Hi Marge, how are you holding up?" Katherine asked as she stepped into a disaster.

Marge also had a bit of a hording habit. Every available seat was filled with garage sale finds, from boxes of clothing to old electronics to kid's toys. She specifically had a thing for fake flowers. Dozens of clear totes filled with flowers of every color imaginable stood stacked against the back wall. Red and green for Christmas. Pink and blue for Easter. Orange and black for Halloween. Marge never took them out, never used them for their stated purposes, no, they remained in their boxes. But she had them all, just in case.

"Oh, fine, fine. Thanks for coming out all this way. Sit anywhere you'd like."

Scanning the room, Katherine decided to shift a box full of puzzles to the floor. After it landed with a muted crash, she sat down on the corner of the chair, her back against a stack of mirrors. She then set Christina on her lap, keeping a close eye on her daughter's wandering hands.

"Has anyone else come out to see you?"

Marge attempted to sit on the couch, eventually giving up in repositioning a pile of dresses enough to find the cushions beneath and simply plopped down among the lot.

"Oh, a few friends. Maggie and Barbara made me a lasagna. Ate it last night. Broke open a bottle of scotch to pair with it. I'm sure it tasted good. Don't remember. Both were gone this morning. But that's enough about me, how are you doing? No one can be doing so well losing a, an almost husband, for good this time."

Marge also had insisted on calling Katherine and Patrick husband and wife after a year of living together. Easier to explain to her friends. Less questions that way.

Marge was who she was.

"I'm surviving. Still in shock I guess. I just wanted to come over, cheer you up, make sure you were doing alright."

"I'm fine! Patrick was a wild one, always knew he would kick it before me. He hadn't come to see me in months, so it's not like I've lost much. Like his father in that regard. Way I see it, can't hurt losing something you never had."

That wasn't true. Sometimes those things hurt the most. But Marge would never admit it.

"Let Christina play!" Marge smiled at her granddaughter. "There are some toys right there I dug out. I'm sure she'll love them."

Katherine cautiously set her daughter down in front of a box of mismatched blocks. She kept having to redirect Christina's attention back to the blocks as Marge and her continued talking. There were just so many more interesting things to play with mom!

"You sure you're doing alright? You been taking your pills?"

Marge waved away the question. "Of course! It takes more than this to knock me down."

"The police came by my place two nights ago. Did they make it out here yet?"

"Yea, they came by Monday night, told me about my son's death."

"Did they have any questions for you?"

"Yes, they did."

"What kind?"

"Oh, the usual. About who he was, who he worked for, what he might have been doing that night, stuff like that."

"What did you tell them, about who he worked for."

"Why, the truth. His uncle. Something in the city. He never really told me much anyhow. Stopped talking to me about real things after college. Became so vague and aloof."

"Is his truck here?"

"No, why would his truck be here?"

Katherine shrugged, trying not to appear too interested. "No reason. Thought I might have left something in it. Wanted to check."

"Patrick hasn't been around here for months. I told you that." Marge scowled, "Good-for-nothing son of mine. Not for months. Then he went and died. Did you hear? He went and got himself killed. That idiot."

"Yes, I heard." Katherine nodded. "Marge, are you sure you took your pills?"

Marge screwed up her face, "I can't quite remember. Lasagna, scotch, morning. Oh, I'm sure I took my pills in there sometime. I always do."

"Can I grab a glass of water?"

"Oh, I'm a terrible host," Marge moved to get up. "Not offering you anything."

Katherine stood faster. "That's fine Marge, I can grab it. I know where you keep the glasses."

The most important thing about visiting Marge was knowing whether she had taken her pills or not. She suffered from a few mental problems, memory issues in which her alcoholism wasn't helping. On the kitchen counter sat a pill box with letters for the days of the week. Today's box, Wed, had three little pills still in it. That would make the next few things easier, and harder.

Katherine returned with a glass of water and sat back down, pulling an unconnected extension cord out of Christina's hands.

"I'm having an awful time remembering Patrick's uncle's name. What was it again?"

Marge was looking down at Christina, her eyes a bit unfocused. "She's getting so big! How old is she now? Year and a half?"

"Nineteen months. Marge, did Patrick leave anything from work lying around? I wanted to get the stuff back to his uncle. What was his name again? Help clean up these last few loose ends for you."

"No, Patrick hasn't been around for months." Marge repeated, a glazed look covering her face before she snapped back to the present, "you're not letting Christina play! Let her explore, it'll be good for her."

"She's fine with the blocks."

"Oh, but I bought her so many other toys." Marge slowly stood up, moving over to a pile of kitchen appliances. "I'm sure they're in here. There was this doll, one with yellow hair. And another one with brown hair, like her. She should have them. I bought them for her."

"Thank you Marge, but my place is already full of toys you've already found. Christina's fine with what we have."

"Nonsense. A girl needs her dolls. Ah, here they are."

They were sad little things, one a ragdoll with a missing eye and a tear at her armpit, the other a plastic baby doll with a stained dress.

"Give these to her, see if she likes them."

Katherine took the two dolls from Marge and placed them down at Christina's feet. Her daughter stopped, looked at them, then went back to the extension cord. Katherine forced herself not to think about where the dolls might had been before Marge's place. They were sanitary, right?

"Thank you Marge. She loves them both. Anyway, did Patrick ever mention anything to you? Anything about a Waya Kipp or Khaleem Truce? Maybe a Joaquin Morales or Vamp Industries?"

Marge stopped. "Where did you hear those names?"

"From the police." Katherine responded honestly. Mostly.

Marge sighed then returned slowly to her pile of dresses before responding. "They asked me some of those names too. The first two? No idea who they are." She scowled, "What are the other two? Some company?

What does any of this matter to you? Why aren't you letting the police handle it?"

Maybe Katherine had pushed too hard. "I'm trying to understand how Patrick died, that's all. I don't want Christina to grow up not knowing."

"You tell her this. Her father was an idiot. Like his father. He worked for the wrong people, wanted the wrong things, did the wrong things. His only talent was to show up, mess things up for everyone else then disappear. That's exactly what his father did, knocked me up then gave up. I tried to raise Patrick right, tried to keep him away from his fate, but fate and family curses can bind us tighter than all of our hopes and dreams. You tell your precious little girl that she doesn't have to be an idiot like her father or her father's father. She can be more."

"I will." Katherine could see the deep pain in Marge's eyes.

"Patrick wasn't around here for months. Didn't come and see his old mum for months. It's not right."

"I know." Katherine didn't know what to do or say, so she sat there and let the stale air eat the silence.

"I told the police about the family curse you know, told them Patrick probably died due to it."

Katherine rolled her eyes. She was hoping they could slide right past that one. Marge always got animated when she talked about Patricks' families supposed curse.

"Good thinking."

"Have I told you about it?"

Katherine nodded. "You have. A few dozen times."

"Yes, yes. And it's all true! I did my research, confirmed it all."

"I'm sure you did."

Marge was huffing now, waggling her fingers in the air. "Patrick? Deadbeat even with his brains, couldn't hold onto you. Got himself killed in an alley. Cursed. Patrick's father? Deadbeat, drifting in and out of life, waste of human space. Maybe cursed, but he didn't need much to help him fail. His father? His first wife died giving birth to Patrick's dad. His second wife? Cancer, young age, before they even knew much about cancer. His third wife? Car accident. Thirty years searching for love, married for six. Three funerals. Cursed."

Katherine nudged Christina away from the box of vases. They all looked about ready to break, "That doesn't sound like a curse to me Marge, just bad luck."

"That's not how it works." She snapped back.

"Oh? Was there some witchcraft in Patrick family's past? Some wrong done by one of his ancestors?"

"I don't know. I tried. I tried so hard." Marge was almost crying now. "I've researched and looked, asked around, spent good money on astrologers, mediums, physics, you name it. I didn't want to see Patrick end up like his dad. I failed. Katherine, I'm sorry, I failed."

This was a bad idea, coming to see Marge. There was nothing here.

Katherine stood up. "I think you might have forgotten to take your pills. Let me go get them."

Marge was sobbing now. "Every last one of his father's father's fathers ran into bad luck. Everyone I could find. Cursed! World War I, economic ruin, there was even his distant grandfather who died in a riot in Philly back in the 1800s. Freak accident, got blown up by a cannon. Cursed."

That last part stopped Katherine halfway to the kitchen. She turned around. "What was that?"

"Patrick was cursed." Marge coughed out, wiping her eyes. "I don't want it to happen to Christina. She's too young, too lovable."

"No, not that, I got that. The part before that, about the cannon?"

"Patrick's family has been in the city for generations. There were riots here, sometime ago, and his great-great-great-great-whatever grandfather got blown up by a cannon."

Katherine pulled out her phone and flipped to the picture of the picture in the box she had delivered to Joaquin. "This riot?"

Marge squinted. "I think so. 1844? Yes, that sounds right."

A cold wave washed through Katherine. No, this was a coincidence. It couldn't be related. What did this mean?

"This crazy man told me about that one, private investigator, two years ago. Told me about Patrick's dad's family line and going back to that riot."

Katherine stood up again, half listening. "Marge, I think we need to go. Something came up. Let me get you your pills."

"Oh," Marge looked disappointed. "Okay." She struggled to stand again. "It was good to see Christina. She's getting so big. I wished Patrick cared about her like he should have. The last time I saw him care about anything was over a damn box. He should have cared about you, about little Christina here. No."

For a second time in only a minute, a wave of icy dread swept through Katherine.

"A box? What kind of box?" Katherine was not a current fan of Patrick's boxes.

"A little thing. It had a padlock on it. He said it was important."

"A box from work?" Katherine looked around the clutter, "From something else? Where is this box Marge?"

Marge smacked her lips. "I remember the private investigator, slimy man he was, remember him because he came over a few days after Patrick went all crazy."

"You're not making sense Marge."

"Yes I am! You listen here! Two years ago, a little before Christina was born, Patrick came over one night with this crazed look in his eyes. I thought he was afraid of becoming a father, what with how he was talking about how he had done the wrong thing, how he couldn't look you in the eyes anymore. Kept going on about how he was evil, how having Christina was evil."

"Evil?" Katherine hadn't heard any of this before. Marge liked to embellish the truth. This felt very different.

"He was raving and going on about how he was going to die for his sins one day. Then he handed me this box. A little thing. It had a padlock on it. I told him he was talking crazy, that he still had a chance to make it right, to not piss away his life like his father did. That together we could break the curse. That he could build a stable life, with you. Raise his daughter. Finally bloom."

"Marge, where is this box now?"

"The police were asking questions."

Katherine stiffened, "You gave it to them?"

"They were asking about Patrick, about my baby. He died. Did you know?"

Marge was quickly slipping away. The look of pain in her eyes had shifted to something glassy, distant. Gone.

"I did. Marge, where is the box? Do the police have it?"

"Box?" Marge blinked back into the present.

"The little one, with a padlock on it. From his work? Patrick gave it to you when Christina was born?"

"Oh, that box. Patrick told me to keep it safe. Told me not to tell anyone about it. That it was important if he was to die one day. I told him not to be so dramatic, but he made me take it. Made me swear I wouldn't tell anyone about it."

Katherine could feel her heart pounding. "Did you tell the police about this box?"

Marge scowled. "Now why would I do that? I just told you. Patrick told me not to tell anyone about it. If there is one thing I do, I keep my word."

"Marge, where is this box now?"

"Do you not have a drink? Look at me, I'm an awful host." Marge began picking her way through the singular path available between the fake flowers and overwhelming junk towards the kitchen, "what can I get for you? Can I get Christina a snack?"

"I already have a drink Marge, you got me water Marge, It's right here." She motioned to the glass resting on the stack of newspapers.

Marge blinked. "Oh, then do you want something to eat? My friends brought over some lasagna. I was going to eat it tonight. Maybe open up a bottle of scotch."

Katherine frowned, suddenly very sad to see the confusion on Marge's face as she searched for the lasagna in vain. "That's alright Marge. I won't be here long. I just came here to get the box Patrick left you. The little one, with the padlock on it. The one you told no one else about. Where did you put it?"

"It's in his closet, high shelf. I think."

"Okay Marge, you stay here. I'm going to go grab the box."

Katherine picked up Christina, who was annoyed at losing her grasp on a random assortment of plastic plates. Katherine also picked up the brown-haired ragdoll and two blocks from the pile and they moved into

Patrick's childhood bedroom. The bed, the desk, and most of the floor was covered with junk. Katherine set her daughter down amidst the chaos.

"Don't grab anything too dangerous baby girl."

Christina babbled happily in response.

Katherine's heart sank after opening the closet door. Not an inch of space remained unpacked. It might take her hours to find this thing. If it was even in here. If it even existed. If Marge hadn't handed it over to the police and forgot she had.

"Marge," Katherine shouted out into the front room. "What does this box of Patrick's look like?"

"Box? Which box?

"The one with the padlock on it. From his work."

"Oh, that one. He was acting all strange. It's a little thing."

"What color?"

"Metal. Grey-brown metal. Like one of those old money boxes."

Katherine added an old ladle and a set of serving spoons to Christina's pile of toys, hoping something new would keep her busy. She then dove in.

Fifteen minutes later, success.

"Is this the box?" Katherine stepped back into the living room, her daughter in one arm, clutching the ragdoll, the money box in the other.

Marge blinked for a moment then nodded. "Hey, that's the box Patrick gave me that one night. Strange night. Did he tell you about it?"

"Yes, yes he did. Do you know what the code is?"

"Code?"

"For the padlock."

"No. But he said it was important. That it would help if he was to die. I thought he was being melodramatic. That night. He got drunk and told me stories about gray men and mind readers. Kept going on about how the world was run by some shadow council, that we are all just puppets. Pawns the angels and demons move around the board, use and discard."

Patrick drank? Since when? He always avoided the stuff, said he didn't want to end up like his parents. What else did she not know about her ex?

"I'm sorry Marge, but we're going to have to go. Do you want to give Christina a kiss?"

Marge gave Christina a huge hug and kiss on the top of her head.

"Thank you for bringing her over. Oh, and she found the doll I bought for her! I'm glad she likes it. You two are always welcome, you hear?"

"I know."

"Maggie and Barbara were going to bring me over a lasagna. You sure you can't stay?"

Katherine swallowed. Patrick had always told her not to worry about his mother, that she could take care of herself. Katherine had fought and argued, hated herself for choosing not to step over Patrick's opinion, no matter how wrong he was. But now? She could see plainly that things were not going well. And Patrick could no longer argue, or help. Or do anything.

"I can't. I'm sorry. Marge, Is there anyone I can call for you?"

"No, Maggie and Barbara will be over soon. I'm fine! Always have been fine. Don't worry about me."

"Marge, you didn't take your pills today. I'm going to get them for you."

"I didn't?"

Katherine stood in the middle of the living room and watched quietly as Marge swallowed all three pills.

"Once I'm gone, I'll call the doctor and make sure he knows you took your medication today. And see if I can get you some extra help. Alright?"

Marge waved her hand. "I don't need help. I'm fine. I'm fine."

"I'll let the doctor know you're fine then." Katherine smiled then set her jaw firm.

She wasn't going to turn a blind eye any longer. She was going to get Patrick's mother the care she deserved.

Nine

Storm clouds rolled in on the drive back home, causing traffic to be even more nerve-fraying. By the time Katherine pulled into the alley, barely dodging Jerry's tent and its deluge of water, and swung into the spot between her brother and Mrs. Preston's porch, she was completely exhausted. Taking a moment to calm herself, she pulled her knuckles off of the steering wheel and sank deeply into the driver's seat.

She hated driving.

"Home safely, baby girl." Katherine turned and found Christina fast asleep in her car seat. Katherine smiled. "At least one of us enjoyed that drive."

With as swift a transition as possible, Katherine hopped out of the van, pulled open the side door, water already dripping down her back, unstrapped her daughter, cradled her sleeping head in her arms and dashed to the back door. Christina stirred a little as Katherine juggled her keys, but within a few moments she was safe again in her pack-n-play, snoring. With a second trip back out into the pouring rain, Katherine grabbed the box and ragdoll then locked the van. After reentering the house, she set the box on the kitchen counter and moved into the living room, finding Ethan alone on his laptop.

"I'm back." She placed the keys into his outstretched hand, his eyes remaining on his screen.

"How was the drive? How was Marge?" He asked after adding a bit more information into his patient's chart.

"Uneventful, just traffic. And rain. And Marge is Marge. How's your evening?"

"Oh, quiet. Boys and Iris are off at a birthday party. They left me here to catch up a bit on work. Oh, there's some leftovers from dinner in the fridge. If you want any. Shepherd's pie. With sweet potatoes this time. And kale. Healthy. Iris woke up this morning complaining about dying soon and not being in shape. So, I get to suffer."

"Thanks. I'm not hungry."

Ethan closed his laptop and followed Katherine into the kitchen. "I'm being inconsiderate. Complaining about nothing. How are you holding up?"

"I'm fine."

"You were out late last night."

"Business." Katherine grabbed the money box and moved towards her basement door. "Nothing more."

Ethan frowned. "Are you sure?"

"That it was just business? Yes."

"You know what I mean." She could hear her brother's concern. "About you. Losing a loved one impacts all of us differently. It can take time to process."

Katherine sighed. "Ethan, I'm tired. And I'm holing up. As best I can be expected. And I lost Patrick almost two years ago. His death is tragic, but also … a little relieving. I'm conflicted. Can I have the space to do some processing?"

"Absolutely." Ethan nodded and backed away. "I'll be in the living room if you need anything."

"Thanks, big brother."

"Anytime, little sister."

Katherine hated Patrick's boxes.

With a burning, white-hot passion.

More than she hated anything in the whole wide world. And if anyone asked in that exact moment, she hated them even more than her mother.

And that was hard to do.

With this new box she had tried every combination possible. Patrick's birthday. Christina's birthday. Her birthday. Their birthday months combined, the date of their first date. The date he left her. Random numbers. Twisting and turning the dial hundreds of times over the past hour to no avail. After throwing the box across her bed in disgust, she moved upstairs and reheated some of Iris's healthy shepherd's pie as she stewed in her frustration.

As she ate at the table, listening to the rain and letting her emotions rage, Ethan reappeared. She quickly told him about the box in order to stay firmly off the subject of feelings and grief and asked him what she should do about it. He did not have any bolt-cutters. Nor did he have any hacksaws or blow torches. She could get a locksmith, but was it really her property? Had Patrick told her about it, had Marge given it to her, or had she stolen it?

Katherine returned to her basement with the remainder of her dinner, now annoyed at her brother as well.

She hated Patrick's boxes, her mother, driving, feeling so insecure about everything, Patrick's going and getting himself killed, his abandonment of her and Christina, his lies to her, the secrets he kept in stupid boxes, her crooked smile and too wide teeth, and her brother, mildly. In that order.

And probably some other stuff that wasn't as important right now. Like cherry pie. Whoever liked cherry pie was a psychopath. Patrick had liked cherry pie. She should have trusted her gut with him. That was a clear sign if she had ever seen one before. But then, his damn smile.

Katherine found Christina awake as she descended, allowing her needs to distract Katherine from her current brooding mood and problem with boxes for a few hours. After they picked through the better parts of the leftovers together, (really, who ate kale?), Christina played with her blocks and the new ragdoll as Katherine researched more about these riots in Philly.

The Navalists riots had occurred in the city in the summer of 1844. Katherine was shocked and appalled at how similar the story mirrored current events. For the nearly two decades prior, Irish Catholics had been immigrating into the city, looking for a better life then the ones they left in their motherland. Being poor and without connections or capital when they arrived, these immigrants began to compete with other established groups for the low paying jobs in the area.

The second and third generation American Protestants, the 'Navalists' who worked these entry level jobs did not appreciate this new flood of competition nor the religious disintegration. They quickly began to persuade established shop owners that the Irish were uneducated, thieves, pestilence, and generally bad for business. Their racism led to job postings declaring things such as "Irish need not apply", or taverns to hang signs like "No dogs or Irish allowed".

Eventually the Navalist's anti-Irish Catholic rhetoric became deadly. After the Navalist groups began spreading the false rumor that the Irish Catholics were trying to remove the Bible from public schools, a hate fueled rally turned riot in May of that year led to the destruction of two Catholic churches, St. Michel's, and St. Augustine's.

Escalation insured.

A second riot erupted in July after the Navalists discovered that the Irish belonging to a church in Southwark, St. Philip Neri, had begun to arm themselves for protection. The Navalists were enraged that the state governor had allowed these 'dogs' to form their own militia and stockpile weapons. The Navalists demanded the church surrender their weapon's cache or be destroyed. The governor, owning his part in creating this situation, activated the state militia to help defend the church against any potential problems. The Germantown Blues were called into action. In an attempt to dissuade the Navalists, cannons were brought out.

Why did men always think bigger guns would solve their problems?

As the Navalist's anger swelled and the crowd grew unruly, many throwing bottles and bricks at the militia, the order to fire was given.

Muskets erupted and smoke filled the street. The Navalist's fell back but not in total retreat.

On a nearby wharf a cannon meant to protect the river and the militia was commandeered by the Navalists. The Navalists filled it with nails, rocks, broken glass, knives, and whatever else they could find on hand. They then wheeled their direct response to the front of the church and fired.

The violence raged for days. The Navalists eventually gave up. The church was saved, but at a steep cost.

After the riots were quelled, at least fifteen people were found to be killed and over fifty injured. Additionally, the riots marked the Catholic Church's end in its efforts to influence the public school system. Instead, they began to create their own set of schools. Seventeen Catholic Schools were founded by 1860, with over seven thousand in the country today.

Quite a few of Katherine's friends in college had gone to Catholic School. She was amazed at how hatred from almost two hundred years ago could ripple through and affect her life today.

As Katherine read on, she had to read the list of casualties of the militia three times. It was right there.

Sargent Guyer was killed instantly by the Navalist's cannon. Privates Ent, Ashworth, Osborne, Cox were wounded. Corporal Troutman was hit badly in the hand and groin, succumbing to his wounds within a day.

Troutman.

Katherine scanned article after article to confirm Marge's crazy investigator's story, that this man was related to Patrick. She found that Corporal Henry Troutman had been married to an Elizabeth Miller. They had lived in the back room of her parents' home when the civil unrest began. She tried to follow and find if they had any children before Henry's death but was unable to navigate the web of genealogies. Was Patrick really a descendant of Henry? Was it true?

Giving up digging into the past for now, Katherine returned her full attention to Christina, who was growing bored of her toys. They read some books about talking clouds and unicorns. The plink, plink, plink of the rain continued, thunder booming out infrequently as true twilight descended. The sound eventually soothed Katherine's mood. She always liked the rain, how it smelled, how it sounded. It felt like home. She could remember curling up into her blankets as a kid, her father's strong arms around her as the power went out due to the storms. How he would laugh at her and her sibling's fright and tell them stories late into the night. She now wrapped her arms around her daughter, kissing her head, holding her close as the rain sang on.

Christina in her arms felt like home.

It was about the time Katherine was putting Christina back in bed, her huge yawns splitting her face, that she noticed the water on the floor. It started out as a little trickle, an innocent, liquid intruder trailing out from underneath her refrigerator. Katherine stared at the unexpected snake for a moment before grabbing a towel from the bathroom and using it to eradicate the threat. Then another one appeared, this one from under her stove, then another, out from the wall near her art supplies.

Katherine dashed upstairs, panic setting in, "Ethan?"

He was in the kitchen with his rain jacket on, "Hey, kids want me to be their chauffeur. Iris convinced them to ask because she refuses to walk home in this. Can we talk when I get back?"

"No. There's water. In your basement."

Ethan blinked, "Water?"

"Water."

The two of them ran downstairs to find the situation deteriorating rapidly. There was now about a quarter of an inch of water across the floor, the liquid soaking boxes, canvases, and toys with indiscretion. Katherine shrieked and pulled her box of important papers from the floor back to the top of the fridge, a glob of liquid following.

"Where is this all coming from?" Ethan stood on the last step, watching his sister splash about, saving what she could. "It's not raining that hard. This has never happened before."

"I don't care why. What do we do?"

"We have to stop where it's coming from. Where is it coming from?"

"It started under my stove."

Ethan splashed in after his sister, the standing water now half an inch deep, and pulled Katherine's stove away from the wall. "Nothing. Are you sure?"

"Did a water line break?" Katherine pulled a half-finished pile of art out of the water and threw it on top of her bed to join a pile of laundry. "It's getting worse."

Ethan moved into Katherine's bathroom and yanked open the utility closet's door and fiddled with the pipes. "That fix it?"

"I don't know! Everything is all wet!"

"It is coming through the walls?" Ethan wondered, looking at the length of Katherine's apartment. "From the Preston's?"

"Why would it come from there?"

"I don't know, I'll be right back." Ethan awkwardly scaled Katherine's stairs and left her alone with the mess.

Within a minute he stuck his head through the doorway upstairs, panting. "The Preston's basement is worse."

"Worse?" Katherine now had Christina on her hip, her daughter crying, still flinging a few last items onto the mound that used to be her bed. Everything was ruined!

"We think it's coming from Jerry's."

"What's coming from Jerry's?"

"The water!"

Katherine raced outside, not even caring about the light rain still coming down. She found Mr. Preston hammering on Jerry's back door, the blue tent flap thrown aside. Mrs. Preston remained dry on her back porch, wringing her hands. Oreo and the orange cat sat under her flowerpots, looking onto the scene with mild curiosity.

"Jerry, open up!" Mr. Preston shouted, his hunched back moving up and down with his shouts. "Something's wrong."

Ethan gaped for only a moment before taking charge. He stepped under the tarp and began to pull at the makeshift plywood boarded up over Jerry's kitchen window. The shoddy work took no time at all for him to rip lose. He then propped Jerry's lawn chair up to the sill and stepped up and over.

"He can't do that." Mrs. Preston called out from her porch, "Timothy, tell Ethan to stop that, he's breaking and entering."

"Barbara, he's going to fix the problem." Mr. Preston leaned against the locked door, wheezing. "Jerry's not home. Or passed out."

"He should wait for the police. This isn't right."

"There are six inches of water in our basement, Barbara. That isn't right either!"

"What would the Lord think of this?"

"I'm sure he would walk on that water then rip open Jerry's front door." Mr. Preston grumbled.

"Timothy! Really!"

"Enough of your yapping. Ethan is fixing it."

A few moments later, Ethan unlocked the back door and reemerged, soaked from head to foot.

"I found the problem. The water meter is ripped out, along with most of the pipes. I can't shut off the water."

"What do you mean you can't shut off the water?" Mrs. Preston asked while Mr. Preston asked, "Are you sure?"

"Yes. The shutoff in my house is right after the water meter. With no meter, or shutoff, or pipes, water is pouring straight into the basement from the pipe. It's three feet high down there."

"Oh my." Mrs. Preston gasped. "How did that happen?"

"I bet Jerry took it." Mr. Preston growled.

"Why would he take it? Why would he need a water meter?" Katherine asked.

"Scrap the copper, sell the meter. He needs to support his habit somehow."

"That makes no sense." Katherine replied.

"Does anything a drug addict do make any sense?" Ethan motioned to the blue tarp around him. "We need to get a hold of the city, have them shut if off at the street."

"How do we do that?"

"I already called 9-1-1." Mrs. Preston offered.

"No, that's for medical emergencies. 3-1-1." Ethan already had his phone out, then cursed. "It's all wet. Katherine, can you call?"

"Yea."

She pulled out her phone and dialed the number. Within a few moments she was talking to a city operator, describing the problem, a water line break. She was reassured a team would be out there shortly. After she hung up, she headed back down to her apartment with Christina, now finding over two inches of water on the floor.

What else could she save?

After another few minutes of impromptu puddle stomping and interior redecorating with one arm, Ethan yelled down to his sister. "They're here."

Katherine returned to the alley to find Ethan having a very heated discussion with a broad-shouldered man in a city uniform. Three vans were shoe-horned within the alley and a dozen men stood around waiting for something. Out past their alley, numerous police cars flashed their blue and red lights, painting everything in an inhuman glow. The arrival of the city brigade had caused half the neighborhood to stir and come out to watch on in curiosity. The police attempted to keep the onlookers back, some whom Katherine knew, some she did not.

"Why do you need in my house! The problem is in there!" Ethan continued to argue.

The broad-shouldered man folded his arms, annoyed, "Protocol sir, we need to assess the damage."

"Why? I thought you were here to shut off the water!"

"We are. Team's already on it. Rest of the guys need into the affected units. For insurance purposes. In case you sue. Photos only."

"That doesn't make any sense." Ethan threw his arms in the air.

"Why would we sue?" Katherine wondered out loud. Christina squirmed and buried her face into her mother's shoulder.

The city worker turned towards her, "Ma'am, not my call. Standard protocol during an event like this. If you two would step over here, we could discuss this further."

"I will not have anyone entering my house." Ethan said and he and Katherine were directed a few steps away from their back door. As they turned, the official signaled towards his crew. Without warning, six men charged into Ethan's home.

"I said no!" Ethan took a lunging spin back towards his door, only to be held back by the broad-shouldered man.

"Hey!" Katherine shouted as well; her left arm grabbed by another. She tried to shake it off, surprised at who she found on the other end.

"We need to go." Max whisper in her ear. "You aren't safe here."

Katherine pulled back and found Joaquin's driver staring at her, a City of Philadelphia baseball cap hiding his crew-cut hair.

"What are you doing here?"

"Get out of my house!" Ethan flailed and kicked. His arms were restrained tightly behind his back.

Max did not answer. He pulled Katherine and Christina along, through the vans and city workers, then put her arm around her in the crowd. “We can’t talk here.”

“Why not? What is happening?” Katherine broke free of Max after they were clear. “You being here doesn’t make any sense. None of this makes any sense.”

Max pointed to his black SUV. “Get in. We need to go, now.”

She could tell he was on edge, looking for someone, or something among the chaos. “What about Ethan? The Preston’s?”

“They’ll be fine.”

“How do you know?

Max calmly opened the passenger door, motioning her forward, “Trust me, you and your daughter’s life depends on it.”

The look in his eyes was all the more convincing she needed, “Okay.”

Katherine jumped into the car and before she could ask what to do with her daughter, Max was in the driver’s seat pulling them away from the flashing lights. She slid hard into a car seat as the car spun around, then nearly slammed into the side door as Max picked up speed. Christina began to cry.

“Easy!” She shouted to Max as she worked to strap her daughter in and the car continued to jerk around, “Is that really necessary?”

“Sorry about the driving, Ms. Mason,” Max said as they skited around another corner. “I need to shake a tail. And make a phone call.”

“Shake a tail? Max, what is happening?” Katherine moved down into her daughter’s face working to soothe her. It only did so much.

“Sir?” Max answered to the voice in his ear.

“Yes … Yes, I have them. … Yes. Yes, we’ll be clear shortly. … I saw two Golems, a Gypsy, and possibly a Yona. Seems like everyone has come out for this one.

“Yes, I’ll let you break the news to her. We’re fifteen minutes out, twenty if this tail remains persistent. … Gypsy, more than likely. … Understood.”

Katherine moved away from her now screaming daughter and looked behind them, trying to find the vehicle that was supposably following. She saw nothing but parked cars as Max hung another corner, slamming

Katherine's head into the window. She groaned as they swung yet again, this time into a narrow street, then back out going the other direction.

"You should buckle up." Max informed her.

"You think?" She moaned and found the belt.

After five more blocks of hairpin maneuvers, Max looked back at the two of them. "Should be clear now, going to chance the highway. Sorry again about the ride."

"What is going on Max?!" Katherine yelled, both to be heard over her daughter and from her anger. "This is not okay!"

"I agree Mrs. Mason. Mr. Morales will explain."

Oh, Joaquin better have a really, really good explanation.

TEN

MAX DID NOT DRIVE anywhere where Katherine expected. They were not headed towards Joaquin's home nor the building where the lab was located. This time, they drove to the south of the city. All the way to the Delaware river.

Soon, Katherine found herself staring out at thousands of shipping containers. To calm her fears, she thought of them as oversized building blocks stacked along the asphalt fields. Ready for some giant toddler to come and mess them all up. It was a mental trick she had done when she was a child, take something unfamiliar and scary and turn it into something silly. She imagined that the infrequent pools of light from the lone streetlamps as fireflies amid the pitch black of the inky night. They drove through two security gates, both unmanned, the large chain link arms swinging up slowly as their car approached, then back down as they passed through. The gates? Butterfly wings. The barbed wire? Vines growing on top of a brick wall in a garden.

She knew it was childish. But it helped.

Katherine asked only twice more where they were going, receiving the same answer both times.

Somewhere safe.

This didn't feel safe.

Christina eventually calmed down then fell asleep during the drive, the peacefulness of her daughter's expression both easing Katherine's nerves a notch and raising her trepidation. Why had she brought her daughter along? Was this some kind of trap, some kind of planned kidnapping after she had refused to let them have Christina's blood for their experiments? Was the flooding an accident? Or was that too, part of the plan? It had to be. She felt like a terrible mother, allowing these men to steal her only child. But what other choice could she have made? Everything had happened so fast.

The car eventually pulled into a dimly lit warehouse, a cavernous space devoid of anything but steel columns and air. The lights overhead mimicked the grid pattern of the space, cold and foreboding. The large dock door automatically began closing after the SUV entered. Katherine thought of it as one great white tooth crunching down on them, belonging to some dragon or something, devouring them. Wait, that wasn't a calming image. The drawbridge to a castle? Drawbridges went up. Never mind. Her mind was onto more important things now. She saw him as they slowed.

Joaquin.

When the SUV stopped, Katherine unbuckled Christina, causing her to fuss. Max told her she was safe in the car. She glared at him. There was absolutely no world in which she was going to leave her daughter behind.

With her bleary-eyed daughter curled up in her arms, Katherine strode over to Joaquin, fury plain on her face. He was the picture of ease, leaning against one of the columns, his arms crossed as if he often stood in abandoned warehouses and felt right at home in the dusk.

"What is going on?" Katherine asked, biting off each word. "Why am I here?"

Joaquin spread his arms out wide. "Thank you for coming."

Behind them, Max was busy pulling a few items out of the back of the car. A folding table, chairs, a pack-n-play.

Katherine turned back towards her captor. "I didn't have much of an option. Max literally drug me off the street. I don't even think Ethan knows where I went."

"Ethan, Iris, and their boys are fine."

"How do you know that?"

"I have eyes." Joaquin sighed. "You are right to be mad at me. Things tonight were a bit, touch-and-go for a moment. They've settled back down." He sighed again, his whole demeanor shifting like a great weight landed on his shoulders. "I brought you here because I have a fair bit more apologizing to do. You asked me not to apologize unless I truly meant it. I do. The frustration you're feeling from this current knot of problems was set into motion by me. I am sorry."

Katherine didn't know what to say, so she just stood there, annoyed.

Joaquin continued on. "Come, sit. Let your daughter lay down."

Katherine looked disparagingly at the makeshift conference room slash nursery.

"I prefer to stand."

"Suit yourself."

Joaquin moved over to one of the folding chairs and sat down, looking just as comfortable and at ease as when he had sat on his couch at home. As the silence stretched, Katherine knew she was being silly. Relenting her stubbornness, she laid her daughter down slowly in the pack-n-play.

"It's okay baby girl," Katherine patted her daughter's back, "It's okay."

Katherine stood over Christina and soothed her daughter till she was settled, making Joaquin wait. She then joined Joaquin on the other side of the table, sitting back, her arms crossed.

"You can keep apologizing, but first, why a warehouse?"

"We are here," He motioned to the space around him, "because it is one of the safest places for us to be right now. Emptiness, it's good for a great many things. No one can catch us unaware."

"Sure. Then right into my next question, what happened tonight? Why do you think I am in danger? Beyond you two, who else was planning to kidnap and murder me?"

"I need to give you a bit of background before answering your question. It'll help you understand this evening within the right context."

"Fine. History. Go."

Joaquin folded his fingers. "There are a great many factions within the city that play for power. Companies, institutions, individuals. Each has carved out a place for themselves, their little kingdom to rule over, so to speak. The minions within these fiefdoms toil daily either at expanding their territory and influence or defending what is currently under their domain. Politically, economically, culturally, religiously, power shifting and flowing back and forth, waxing and waning.

"Your ex, and now you, have unfortunately stumbled into the mix of a volatile little skirmish between four warring factions."

"Oh, so this is a business thing?" Katherine shook her head, even more annoyed. "Of course it is."

"Isn't everything in life about business? I want something, you want something. We trade, exchange, negotiate the terms, be it information, time, emotional reassurance, our bodies, you name it. Some individuals hold vast quantities of resources and swing their mallet to great effect. Others have very little, yet multiply, twist their daggers to reap a crop a hundredfold. These are the few, the cunning, the brave, the lucky. Then there are the rest of humanity, the masses. They squander what little they have, are taken advantage of, amount to nothing, and die."

"How very poetic of you." Katherine frowned. "You tell that to all your clients before you cheat them?"

"No."

"Is that how you see the world? Is that how you saw our dinner last night? Just another business transaction? The exchange of information and time?"

"No."

"Your father recite that stupid bit of knowledge to you as you went to sleep at night? How you are so much smarter than everyone else? How you'll crush the masses under your foot? Oh, there may be a few dead bodies, but that's the price of doing business!"

"No. He did not."

Katherine grew tired of his non-answers. "Then why are you telling it to me?"

"Because I know you would understand."

"You presume a lot, Joaquin."

"And I am normally right."

Katherine glowered at him, not backing down from his eyes.

"What did Patrick stumble into?"

Joaquin smiled lightly then blinked, breaking the stare. He opened his left hand and looked at his palm.

"I, the first player in this game, represent a large corporation, Vamp Industries. We have arms in pharmaceuticals, healthcare, bioengineering, and some highly classified government contracts. Just alone in our research branch, with each PI, principal investigator within a lab block, there are dozens of technical assistants and hundreds of contractors supplying and supporting everything from managing our facilities, sourcing our raw products, and shipping our goods. Everything has to run in perfect motion, the most complex timepiece with springs and gears, inputs, outputs, buttons, knobs, levers, and doodads.

"My primary job is to find the dirt within all these moving parts, find where the grease has run dry and correct the problems before the machine shutters. Most of my work is done in the office, confirming shipping dates, negotiating deals between vendors, a lot of boring stuff you wouldn't need to suffer through me detailing.

"Every once in a while, I have to deal with bad actors. We call them threats. They wish to break the process, or at least rip out a part of its heart. Waya Kipp is one of these bad actors. We fondly call him, the Medicine Man. He is faction number two."

"The man who you say killed my ex? The crazy guy who you've been negotiating with through boxes of junk?"

"Yes. Do you remember the tribal bat mask? It was a traditional Cherokee ceremonial mask. As I mentioned before, Waya has a flair for the dramatic. It was his way of him saying, this is from me, for you."

"Why a bat?"

"For my boss. A way of calling him out. Many refer to him as the Bat."

"You're starting to sound like a whole bunch of kids with silly nicknames. Or maybe you're all crazy and think of yourselves as superheroes. Super villains? Corporate suits by day, murderers by night."

Joaquin's smile turned sad. "Do boys ever really grow up? Or do they simply find faster, better, and more shiny toys to play with? Higher stakes to wager and greater risks to take?"

"In my experience, no."

"And you would be correct. Adults are simply big kids who have learned how to see past the instant pleasures of the right now and plan a bit for the future, have learned how to hold a modicum of restraint over their emotions. There is a time and a place for everything. Everything, Ms. Mason. A mature adult simply knows when, and where, and to what degree."

Joaquin smiled shifted again, this time a little feline, predatory. "Ah, your presence and comments tend to make me digress. Back to our history lesson?

"Waya, the Medicine Man, has had an ongoing dispute with Vamp Industries. An intellectual rivalry. It's far more complicated than that, but for your purposes, we'll keep it there. Patrick was working for him. He was a double agent, a man who worked for the Medicine Man, who worked for me, feeding the Medicine Man information."

This somehow didn't shock Katherine. "Patrick was a corporate spy?"

"Yes. As I told you, he worked in shipping and receiving for almost two years. Within that capacity, he knew when things came in, from where they came, and in what quantities. He fed this information to Waya who has now used it to bolster his case against my company. I do blame myself for this oversight in security, but there are a great many ants within my anthill. I can't watch them all.

"Ah, but Patrick wasn't a stupid man either. He knew what he was doing would eventually get him into trouble or get him killed. He did the smart thing and stashed away a cache of information against Waya. Made himself a dead man's chest. The box you found in his mother's home."

"You know about that?"

"Yes. This is the first item in specific I will apologize for. I learned of its existence and general whereabouts a few days ago. We tried to recover it from his mother, but she was, less than cooperative. She said she knew nothing about it, had no idea what we were talking about. Waya's men tried the same. We've both been watching her house since then, waiting for the right time to make our move, hoping the other team slipped up and let us gain an advantage. But then, I tipped you off, suggested you do a little digging. Knock the contents loose to enable an easier acquisition.

"I underestimated you. You found it much faster than I had planned. I am sorry."

"Then, those men, tonight, the ones who ran into my house?" Katherine knew they hadn't been from the city! "They were yours?"

"They were Waya's. The Medicine Man also moved more quickly than I anticipated, flooded your neighbor's house, created an opening for himself from an opening I created and stole the evidence. Easy to blame an addict for irrational things."

"That box, was on my bed, under everything… " Katherine jumped up before she knew what she was doing, "I need to get back, there was water everywhere! All my stuff, my paintings!"

"Are most likely all destroyed."

"No." The news hit Katherine like a sledgehammer straight into her face. "No. This can't be happening."

Joaquin stood up, moved around the table, and put a hand on Katherine's shoulder. She threw it off. "Stuff can be replaced. I am sorry about your artwork. I can see they meant a lot to you."

Katherine steeled herself. What was done, was done. She turned back to Joaquin, fire in her eyes.

"We need to tell the police."

"That won't do anything."

"Why not? Waya's men, breaking and entering? Destruction of property? Impersonating city officials? Ethan was there, he'll want to press charges too."

"That ball is already rolling, Waya has it covered. The minor offenses will be handled through small claims court, the complaint already created and processed. Compensation has already been earmarked, enough to give you and Ethan the peace of mind to stop asking questions."

"How do you know this?"

"I've seen Waya cover his tracks before. A little money to grease a palm, a little story to make sense of the situation and most of the affected people shrug and walk away."

Katherine balled her hands into fists.

"Oh, he's an idiot if he thinks I'm going to stay silent. I'm going to find this Medicine Man guy and make sure he pays for killing Patrick."

Joaquin shook his head. "Katherine. Please, stop."

She did not like the tone of his voice. "Why? I thought you said he was your enemy too. He should pay for what he's done."

"And he will. But not from you. All you'll be able to do is make a little bit of noise and lose. You're like a rabbit fighting against a bear. Rabbits don't win."

It irked her being called a rabbit. "Then why are you telling me all of this? Whose side are you on?"

"I am on my own side. I don't want to see you hurt. In our short time together, I have grown fond of you. That is why I brought you and your daughter here, to apologize, to warn you, and to protect you if other moves tonight were made. Thankfully, they were not. To help you see that this is far beyond your abilities. Please, take the money Waya offers, forget about these things. Mourn Patrick for as long as you need to but please, move on."

Katherine did not like the finality in his request. She could hear the unspoken underneath. "If I do as you ask, will I, will I be able to see you again?"

Joaquin shook his head. "No."

Katherine's head and heart raged against each other. She knew logically this should come as a relief, that never seeing Joaquin again would be for the best. With everything he had done, how he had turned her life upside down, lied to her, and yanked her around, it was best they parted ways. But her heart stubbornly hated the idea. She hated the thought of losing him so soon. Why was she always attracted to the wrong men!

"Then I can't do that."

"Katherine, sometimes things are not meant to be. Timing, situations, bad luck. That is life." A deep sadness entered Joaquin's eyes. "Sometimes life acts upon us without any regard for our wishes. Sometimes other people do the same. It's less a question of finding out how you gain control, and more a question of what you will do with what little control you have."

Katherine wiped hot tears suddenly in her eyes. She changed the subject. "You mentioned there were four factions to this stupid game of yours. Who are the other two?"

Joaquin nodded and stepped back. "The other two are currently observers. You might have heard Max mention Golems and Gypsies. Codenames. They have been sitting on the sidelines, watching my little spat with Waya but will attack if they smell blood in the water. Any weakness from either side and both observers will become a serious threat."

"Great, more problems. Who are they? What companies?"

"It's best if you don't know."

“Then why tell me this much?”

“So that you understand the delicate position you are in. Waya has the dead man’s chest and no longer needs you but knows of you. I want to see you unharmed. The Golems and Gypsies will hurt you or your family to gain even a hair of an advantage. I am sorry, again, but you are powerless amongst titans. It’s best if you forget about all of this, forget about me, and live your life.”

Katherine looked down at her daughter. No matter what her heart wanted, she couldn’t put her in danger.

“And if I don’t give up? Will you protect me? Will you protect Christina?”

“I can only help you so much. Tip the scales so far. It would not be advised.”

Katherine sighed.

“Fine.”

Joaquin’s facial expression did not change, but she could tell he was relieved. “Thank you. And one last time, I am sorry. For everything. Once we get the all clear, Max will take you home. I, unfortunately, cannot stay any longer. The night has more needs.”

In seeing him turn to go, presumably out of her life forever, she hated her next question.

“What about your research? What if…” Was she really considering this? ”What if I think it over again, let you maybe have a little bit of Christina’s blood, for the right price that is! Can we see what happens next? Between us?”

Joaquin slowed then turned back towards her. “Hm, yes, I almost forgot. That was the last item I must apologize for. We’ve already tested your daughter’s blood. I cannot use her.”

This information caused Katherine’s own blood to run cold. “You. What?”

Joaquin motioned over towards Max. “It was relatively easy. Harmless. When Iris was watching her at the park today while you were at work, she had a bit of a slip. Scraped her knee. Max was nearby and rushed over to help. As he cleaned the wound, he took a sample for processing.”

Katherine quickly moved towards her sleeping daughter, lifting her dress to expose her knees. A large bandage covered the right one.

She glared at Max, "You, you touched my daughter? You stole her blood? Without my consent!"

The driver was unphased. Joaquin spoke for him, "Max helped me clean up a loose end. A question that needed to be answered. There are now no lingering remnants. We can have a clean break."

She felt the urge to punch him, "You should have asked."

"I did."

"And I said no."

Katherine stomped away a few feet letting her anger radiate. When she turned back and found Joaquin still smiling, she snapped.

Katherine screamed and rushed him, her fist out. "You!"

Joaquin caught her first swing easily, then grunted as her other fist plowed into his side.

"Never do that again!" She swung a few more times, pelting him with blows. "Never, ever, touch my daughter."

Joaquin did little to defend himself. Max simply stood and watched. After a few more moments, Katherine's rage evaporated. She leaned into him, panting. Joaquin wrapped his arms around her, his chin resting on the top of her head. This time she did not push him away.

"Goodbye, Katherine."

"Goodbye." She mumbled with her face buried in his chest. Tonight, he smelled like the rain.

After they released, Joaquin turned and left, saying nothing more. Katherine stood next to Max and her daughter, alone, her heart feeling as empty as the space around her.

Part 2

The enemy
... of my enemy
... of my enemy
... is my?

Eleven

THE NEXT TWO MONTHS of Katherine's life were bursts of intense activity mixed within long stretches of utter normality.

Beginning with her return home, she found Ethan wound up tight. As soon as Christina was back to sleep, her pack-n-play set up in the living room, he took turns with Iris, bombarding Katherine with questions.

Where did she vanish into the night? Why did she have to leave right then? Why not arrange for this meeting with her art dealer some other time? Who did this guy think he was, needing to see her at a moment's notice? Did she not explain to him what was happening at her house? Why did she take Christina? That seemed highly unusual. Why would an art dealer want to meet her daughter?

Katherine's lack of sleep combined with everything else over the last few days in no way helped her constitution, mood, or responses. Combined with everyone's frayed nerves over the flood, questions soon turned into shouts and accusations. Was she safe? She met this guy through Patrick. Was she being sucked into his chaos, even after his death? We never liked Patrick, not with his shifty eyes or how he wouldn't really answer a question. Did you pick this up from him? You have a problem with our direct questions? We're family, you need to let us in.

In turn, Katherine launched a guided missile barrage of her own.

Iris, why did you let some stranger touch my daughter? Oh, it happened at the park. She fell? You let a stranger help? Why didn't you tell me about it sooner? I found the bandage. I should know about these things.

Iris counterattacked.

You freak out about every little thing Katherine, think the world is falling apart if your little angel even coughs once.

Oh, I freak out about everything? That is not true! I am a perfectly stable mother!

Yes a stable mother drags her daughter with her across town at bedtime! When it makes sense she does!

Katherine fumed. It was her life, why did her brother constantly need to poke his finger into her business? Oh, he cared? That didn't give him the right!

They were just trying to help? Yea, Iris? Is that right? Help? Like all that great advice you gave me before my meeting with the art dealer? All that advice about throwing myself at him for a deal? Selling my body to him?

That comment finally raised Ethan's haunches.

You gave what advice to my sister?

It was innocent, playful! I wanted to make the mood light. She's always so glum, so much stuck in her own head. At least I didn't let a pack of stray men roam through my house, ransack my sister's apartment, my wife's sanctuary. Who knows what they stole.

That was not my fault! They entered without my consent! And I will be suing the city! If they only had come out to deal with Jerry when I informed them of the nuisance the first fifteen times, none of this would have happened.

Still. I wouldn't have let them in. I would have come and picked up my wife, who was left standing in the rain with her two kids after making all kinds of excuses as to why you were late. It was embarrassing. You should have called.

My phone broke!

Katherine excused herself as the shouting continued and went downstairs to survey the damage. It was worse than she feared. The intruders had thrown everything off her bed, off the walls, dug through drawers and cabinets in their mad search for the lockbox. The most heartbreaking item ruined was her rainbow painting that reminded her of her father. It had landed face-down in the mess, now soaked through. In the better spots, the colors were off and in the worst places, the canvas warped, and the paint cracked. Her other paintings were in varied conditions, from untouched, thankfully, to water damaged and broken frames. One had even received a puncture.

Everything else could be replaced. Her art could not.

Still on her easel under the stairs, knocked sideways, Katherine found the piece she had begun that week, the black abyss with the red streak cutting through the center. Her thoughts bitterly went back to Joaquin. She had known him less than a week, why was she so upset about losing him? Her future with him felt the same as her apartment, destroyed, unable to be repaired. There had been a connection there, something more than a simple attraction. She had begun to hope again, if only for a single day.

She was such an idiot! What would a man like that ever find in someone like her? She had nothing to offer him and somehow she had fooled herself into thinking she had a chance. To think that he might have liked her, for some insane reason, to think that he wanted her for something more than as a tool for his own purposes.

Everything was business to him. Even love.

What a terribly lonely thought.

In that moment Katherine felt drained to the core. She shuffled upstairs and found Ethan and Iris had moved their argument to the second floor, leaving her the relative quiet of the living room and the couch. She fell asleep listening to her daughter's slow breathing and let her mind float.

If only her life was as simple as it was for Christina. Food, sleep, cry, play, repeat. All within a basket of love. Pure, rich, deep love from her mother. And love from her aunt, and her uncle, and cousins, mostly. When they weren't ripping toys out of her hands or knocking her down. Love mattered!

Oh, baby girl! I will always be here for you. No matter what.

The next morning arrived without a care. With her head throbbing, coffee in her hands, and Christina happily playing with Jack for once, Katherine called the bakery and told Robert of her continued problems at home. He was not happy. He was never happy with her calling off. Oh, a flood this time? After a death? What's next? A fire? Riots? She hoped not.

Ethan sat next to Katherine on Iris's phone, bitterly having called off work to deal with the damage. He quickly connected with a city operator who knew about their plight. Within two hours Ethan's sour mood was flipped on its head with promises of compensation for the misunderstanding and contractors to arrive that very day to begin the restoration. By that afternoon, Katherine was standing in the alley with Christina at her hip, scratching Oreo's neck with her free hand as she oversaw four men carry her salvageable belongings into a moving van as temporary storage. Once Katherine's apartment was cleaned out, the team did the same for the Prestons. Katherine was provided a hotel room for the duration of the repairs, which took two weeks.

Patrick's funeral was on Saturday. Katherine wore a black dress borrowed from Iris and sat in the back with Christina, listening to Marge speak briefly about her son at the gravesite. It was a small affair, with only six people attending on a overcast, windy spring day. Beyond his mother, the other attendees were all Patrick's friends whom Katherine already knew. She had hoped stupidly that someone from Patrick's work, maybe even Waya himself would show up, but also found his absence relieving. She was supposed to be moving on from the quagmire Patrick had waded into. Easier to do that when an opportunity to mettle did not fall in her lap.

Time moved on.

Back to work on Monday. Shandra was all gasps and exclamations of wonder as Katherine spoke of the flood and her fallout with Joaquin. Katherine then spent the week apologizing to loyal customers over her absence, Robert's idea, and shared some personal tidbits from her week with them, also Robert's idea. Give them something to remember. Listen to their woes, build trust. Strengthen those bonds of community, Katherine, you can't just be all smiles and sass, Katherine. Shandra smirked as she listen to her complain about their boss's advice, then agreed with him. He knew what he was talking about.

Over the next month the drama with Shandra's brother's investigation intensified. Various members of the gang he had been under cover with began to show up around the city, dead. At first it was considered an odd coincidence, people like them wound up dead for many different reasons. But when the third body appeared after a week, Miguel was reassigned from filling boxes of evidence and filing reports to the street once again.

After a few weeks of navigating the underbelly, Miguel was able to reconnect with a part of his old crew. He learned more about the night they disappeared, that they had been tipped off, not by someone internal and higher up, but by a new player in town, someone foreign, someone looking to carve out their own turf. Crazy Steve thought the whole situation was messed up. Who had the balls to put out such a large hit when they didn't even know the city. Rival outfits had joined in on the strike, groups they had been on good terms with now cutting them up like a prized pig. Indigo had heard that there was movement, retaliation planned, soon, and that Miguel should either keep his head down for now or pick up a gun.

Shandra confessed that her brother worried about her too much. Said she had to keep telling him that that kind of arms war would never make it all the way to her apartment or the bakery. Her neighborhood was safe. And he was great at his job, he was there to protect her. The craziest things that ever happened to people like them were flooded basements.

Katherine held her tongue. Right.

Once the basement was repaired and improved with a sump pump, hardwood flooring, cabinetry with twice the storage as before, and all new appliances, Katherine's items were returned. Mostly. She was beyond infuriated at the storage company when she learned that all of her artwork had been somehow mysteriously lost. How was that possible? The pot-bellied man didn't know. She called the company's main office for almost a week before she learned someone told her they might have thought they were trash and threw them away, maybe. No. Her artwork, trash? How dare they! That night she poured all her anger into a new piece, one with bold strokes of orange, red, and yellow, a fire, her rage against the world and how little control she had while living within it. Stupid Joaquin and his stupid words! She hung the finished piece up where her rainbow painting had been, only to move it to a different wall the next day. She then tried to recreate a few of the lost pieces, only to grow angry again at the imperfection of her memory. Eventually she threw all the bad copies away. They weren't the same.

Her walls remained blank. A reminder that sometimes things were lost that could never be replaced.

The compensation payments for the city's mismanagement came informally, dumped into Ethan and Katherine's bank accounts without notice. Simply twenty-nine thousand dollars appearing for Katherine and fifty-eight thousand for Ethan's family. Ethan called the bank instantly, wondering over the suspected error, only to be told, no sir, this was a legitimate transfer. I'm sorry, we cannot track who it came from.

Then things got weird. Weird for Ethan, Iris, and the Prestons at least. They didn't know what Katherine knew. Ethan tried to contact the helpful receptionist with the city he had talked to prior. She had left for another opportunity. The restoration company went out of business, their homes their final projects. The storage company was bought up by another, their original name erased from the internet. A letter for the payment finally came, a sad, typed single page letter detailing the deposits. Fourteen thousand, five hundred dollars to each member of each family. Keep this for your records.

Ethan thought it an odd coincidence that the amount was five hundred under the IRS gift tax limit for the year. Katherine told her brother not to worry so much, that coincidences were only that and they should move on. Sure, keep some back for taxes if you want, just in case. But let's look at this as a happy accident. You and Iris can finally go on that vacation you've been talking about! See, Jerry isn't so bad of a neighbor after all. And the Blue Monster is now gone. It's all worked out for the best. Ethan still tried to grumble about the money and it not feeling right, but Iris's excitement over finally seeing Europe eventually overruled his anxiety.

Katherine took Christina's portion of the blood money and set up an official 529 college savings account. Allow interest and time to do its thing. She used her half to finance Marge's care. After a few dozen calls over a handful of weeks, she convinced her daughter's grandmother to allow a caregiver into her home twice a week. Someone to help with the meals, medications, cleaning, someone she could talk to. It wouldn't last forever, she barely had enough for a full year, but it was something. Part of her hated not using any of the money for herself but the other part felt keeping it was wrong.

Better to use a sour situation to help others.

Not the worst outcome.

Weeks went by. The Preston's returned from a trip to Florida. Ethan and Iris argued over the details of theirs. The trees filled out their leaves. Katherine continued to feed Oreo in the evening. She became unreasonably sad after she realized the orange tabby she had decided to name Lynx hadn't shown up since the night of the flood. Maybe all the activity had scared him off. She met a few new moms at the playground, planning to plan a play date with them sometime soon.

Christina continued to grow and learn new things, added at least three new words into her vocabulary each day. Her daughter brought so much joy and laughter into Katherine's life. There were many nights where she would lie awake and know that if she didn't have Christina, she wouldn't have been able to keep moving forward. In those moments, she was determined to become the best mom, the best version of Katherine she could be, for Christina. All she needed to do was improve a little every day. Even just one percent improvement each and every day would add to great things in the long run.

May's arrival came with a new focus, a new task in parenting that they could conquer together.

Potty training.

Katherine broke their first weekend down into fifteen-minute chunks of time. A well-defined battle plan. On the potty, off the potty, nothing, nothing again? Treat for a good job! Many accidents. Frustration, encouragement, then uncertainty going into the week. Iris was supposed to follow the plan.

Iris did not follow the plan.

Oh, Junior was too much. The end of the year for first grade was too draining. And Jack, he was a terror this week. He needed extra attention. And every fifteen minutes till she goes? That seems excessive. Besides, wasn't teaching her before two a little ambitious? Jack was barely potty trained at four. Must be your first kid syndrome. Maybe slow it down a bit Katherine?

Second weekend, second skirmish in the grand battle. Many explosions. Many tears on both sides. Why was this not working? You were doing so well last weekend! Baby girl!

Monday.

I don't care, Iris. Do whatever you want.

Third weekend.

We need a break baby girl. We need a break. This is exhausting.

This whole life thing, it's exhausting.

Twelve

THE TRIP UP TO Trenton was spur of the moment. Out of character for Katherine. One moment she was lying on her bed, staring at the ceiling and wondering why anyone chose to be a parent with all the mess and heartache that went along with it. Christina was great! And a handful! And sleeping soundly. Jack and Junior in comparison were yelling at each other, their shouts easily heard through the floor. What was wrong with Iris? Why had she chosen to have two? Ah, but there was something special about having a big family. The holidays, the little and large moments of laughter together. The feeling of belonging. The head and heart knowledge that no matter how much she screwed up, Ethan would be there for her. That she could call up Laura at any time and vent to her.

Family was great.

In the next moment Katherine was franticly researching train timetables and finding the earliest she could be in Trenton the next morning.

Her grandfather lived in Trenton. Retirement home a few miles south of the city. She hadn't made it up there since last Thanksgiving when she had tagged along with Ethan and Laura. She always gave him one reason or another, ignoring the real reason. Mostly said it was a money thing. But now?

He was family. She should go visit him. Forgive the past, move on. It would be good to see him, good to catch up with him, lay new roads. Maybe it could be a bit of a reset for both of them, a challenge, a fresh start. Something to get herself out of her rut.

And for this trip she didn't have to drive.

All she had to do was steer clear of a few red button topics.

Easy.

The next morning turned out to be a sunny one, unseasonably warm and humid for late May. Katherine packed her backpack full of the essentials for Christina, extra diapers, two changes of clothes, wipes, food, two toys, her ragdoll from Marge, and a blanket, then stuffed a few granola bars and a water bottle in the remaining crevices for herself. Christina was strapped onto Katherine's chest, and off they went.

Or at least all the way upstairs before the first roadblock appeared.

"What do you mean you're going to visit Butch?" Ethan asked after commenting on his sister's equipment and receiving her reason for the supplies.

"Why not?" She smiled innocently and tried to slip out the back door, only to have Ethan put out an arm.

"Because it is a bad idea." Ethan played his role of big brother too well sometimes. "You know why."

"I do. But he's family."

"And sometimes even family doesn't get a free pass."

"Maybe it's been long enough. Maybe it's time we forgive and build new bridges."

"That's not something you should decide alone."

"Why not?"

"Katherine, we all agreed after dad's funeral. We'd see him once a year, together, for the holidays. All three of us. You, Me, and Laura. No more, no less. It's worked splendid for the past five years. Why are you trying to upset the apple cart now?"

"Maybe I realized life is too short and it doesn't matter what he did."

Ethan guffawed. "Doesn't matter? Yes it does!"

"It'll be fine. He'll be fine. Besides, I've already called him, and he knows I'm coming. So, I'm going. Now, are you going to hold me your prisoner? Or are you going to let me leave to see my grandpa?"

Ethan glared at his sister then stepped aside. "I'm lodging my formal complaint. I'm going to call Laura as well. Katherine, we should have discussed this first."

Katherine shrugged. "I'm not known for doing the smart thing, remember? I think you said that to me a few times when I started dating Patrick."

"And we both see how well that turned out." Ethan said before stopping himself.

It was Katherine's turn to glare. "I'll tell him you said hi."

Ethan stepped aside. Done. First roadblock scaled, if not very gracefully. Onto the second.

Public transit with a toddler.

Katherine took a bus into 30th St. Station then stood on the platform, waiting to grab the Trenton line out. Two strangers gave Christina a smile, and another commented how precious she was and asked for her name. Katherine thanked the older lady then pretended to be busy with a backpack strap, not wanting to make small talk. It was only a little rude. Why did strangers feel the urge to talk to kids? It was weird. The train eventually rolled in, doors open, she slipped through the crowd and into a seat with only a bit of finagling with her backpack and carrier.

Then came the discovery of a dirty diaper. Already? Baby girl!

It was such a mom thing to do, changing her daughter on the seat of a train. No one was judging her, right? Whatever. If they were, they could judge away. What else was she supposed to do? Try to change her in the train station bathroom a half an hour from now? That would be even more of a disaster!

Katherine breathed in, breathed out, hugged her daughter close after she was clean then relaxed for a moment. Christina spent the rest of the trip goggling out the window, watching the scenery pass by. The world through the eyes of an almost two-year-old. Everything was new. Everything was magic.

When they arrived in Trenton, Katherine called for an Uber. The driver talked about how their kids were finishing up college, how they are excited for their next stage in life. A little worried for them. Then onto reminiscing a little over the stage she was in. Katherine listened on, starting out the window at the grey buildings, wondering if this visit was still a good idea.

She worried too much.

She worried about worrying too much.

Second hurdle complete. Onto the main event.

Her grandpa's retirement home was a large scale complex, with over five hundred private living units spread across campus. Some were single story homes. Most were apartment style residences. A full wing was dedicated to nursing care units. Her grandfather, in his 80s but still in good shape lived in one of the ground floor units. Katherine went right up to his screen door, smiling at the small garden of herbs he kept on the porch, and knocked.

Within a few moments, her grandfather opened the door.

"This is quite the surprise!" He smiled widely, his wrinkly face the picture of happiness. "I shouldn't be seeing you for another few months!"

"I decided to break protocol." Katherine smiled back. "I always was the troubled kid."

"Troubled kid? More like the one with the spine. You still living with Ethan?"

"Yep."

"How's he doing?"

"He's the same. Still thinks he knows best."

Her grandpa laughed. "Same thing since he was ten! As stubborn as your father."

'As stubborn as you,' was what Katherine wanted to say. Instead, she remained positive, "He's kind too. He let me have a place to stay, helped me and Christina out when we needed it."

"Of course. Come in, come in. We don't need to talk out here the whole time. This way you can get Christina off your shoulders."

She followed him in silently, sat down on his couch, and set her daughter free. Her grandpa kept his living room clean and orderly, with the couch, his large reading chair, a coffee table, television on the wall, and a few plants. He always liked to keep his place tidy, a regiment learned from his time in the army. Everything had a place, or it did not belong.

"Don't eat the dirt, baby girl." Katherine pointed at the potted plant then made a frowning face at her daughter, who looked back at her and babbled an affirmative. "Dirt!" She then went right for the largest potted plant. Katherine sighed and worked to distract her with her ragdoll.

"She's getting so big." Her grandpa commented as he slowly sat back down in his recliner.

"She is. Sometimes when I go to bed then wake up, she's three inches taller."

Once resettled in his armchair, Katherine's grandpa chuckled in response. "They'll do that. Your dad's sister did that when she was three, grew a whole head taller after she was walking. I still don't know how we kept up. How are you doing, by the way, being a single mother?"

"Oh, it has its moments."

"You still working at that bakery place?"

"Yep."

"And Ethan's wife watching Christina while you're there still? She still, you know?"

Katherine nodded. "Yep, she is. And yes. She's still Iris."

Butch nodded. "Horrible decision, Ethan marrying that one."

Katherine shook her head as she danced with the ragdoll, finally getting Christina's attention with the toy. "He seems happy, and Iris is a big help. With Christina."

"You know, your dad should have taught you two better. Laura too."

Katherine sighed, feeling the tension already in her shoulders, "Can we not begin by talking about dad or Iris like that?"

Her grandpa stiffened. "Like what?"

"It, just… never mind." Katherine let the silence stale for only a moment. "I wish I could be around Christina more often. I hate leaving for work every day, but I would also hate being stuck in the house all day."

"It still surprises me you weren't more careful about it."

Katherine's eyes narrowed, "About what?"

Her grandfather gestured towards Christina, who had abandoned the doll and had a handful of dirt. Katherine quickly reached for her daughter and shook her fist above the plant, getting most of it back where it belonged.

"You two weren't married. There isn't stability here for a girl to thrive. You of all people should understand, with your mother."

Katherine graded her teeth. Why had she come here? Was this visit really worth it? Maybe Ethan was right. Nope, nope, she would make this pleasant. Lay new roads.

"I know. I messed up. Things sometimes happen."

Her grandpa nodded, "That they do. When we don't have a plan, things tend to explode. 'Nam will teach you that. I've told you plenty what no plan did to that place. Disaster."

"Yes you have." Katherine sighed again, "But a family is not the military. Life isn't about orders. And I'm learning. Being a parent. Wasn't the worst thing to happen either, just not planned. I couldn't imagine my life now without Christina. She's really the only one I have, with Patrick leaving me, then dying."

"Awful stuff, that is. How are you holding up?"

"Better, better than a month ago. Still a bit rough. Did you hear my basement flooded a few days after Patrick died?"

Her grandpa looked interested. "No, tell me what happened."

Katherine filled him in on her last few months, remaining on the positive side, told her grandfather about the flood, her job, how Christina's been doing, all she's been learning. She then asked about what he's been up to, how he spends his time. He's in a bridge club now, read a few books. Still exercises every day, just a bit different now that he's older. Went to a reunion with some of his old squad but then decided to sell his car. Nowhere to go anyway. Not with how he's been disowned by the family.

And after fifteen minutes of neutral conversation Katherine thought they had found some stable ground.

Butch grumbled, "It's your father's fault. Poisoned all you kids against me."

"It's not that, it's..." She had agreed to herself before coming here not to talk about this. Talking never helped, "Look, I don't want to rehash the past. I want to make some new memories, some good memories. Can you do that, for me? For Christina?"

He grumbled some more, "How can I do that with this huge elephant in the room? You still don't trust me. Tell me Katherine, why are you really here if not to work this out?"

She felt small under his gaze. No. She would not talk about it.

"To see you. That's all."

"That is all?"

"Yes." Katherine stood up and turned Christina away from disappearing down the back hallway. "I wanted to see how you were doing. Family is important."

She cringed at her words as she watched her grandpa's expression harden. She shouldn't have spoken her mind. That was the exact wrong thing to say.

Butch snorted twice and crossed his arms. "Sure it is. Sure it is. Family is important. You live an hour away and it's always excuses, excuses about money, excuses with Christina. Using your own kid against me. Actions speak louder than words, Katherine. Much louder."

"I'm here now."

"Yes you are. I'll ask you again. Why?"

Why did he have to be this way? Why couldn't he let it go? Why couldn't she? Why did they have to dive into the same argument rehashed over and over for the last five years? Why had she come without reinforcements?

"Fine. You want to get into it? Let me have it."

Her grandpa appeared to be reconsidering, then spit it out.

"You're all doing nothing but ruining your own lives. All of you. Ethan with his whacko job talking to broken people, running his house like a zoo. Laura, traveling around to wherever her heart desires, no roots, no anything. And you, with a kid, no career, no partner, living in your brother's basement. It's a disgrace."

Katherine felt like someone had punched her in the gut, she spoke softly, hurt.

"I'm trying my best."

"And your father, he was worse. It was his own damn fault that he died."

"It was not!" Katherine shrieked, scaring Christina.

"I told him he needed to take better care of himself, that he had been working that construction job for far too many years, put in too many long hours. It took a toll on his body. Worked himself to death."

"And what else was he supposed to do? He was alone with three kids. And he eventually became a foreman, told others where to hang the drywall instead of doing it himself."

"Still, he was working stupid hours. The stress was worse for him than the labor! He was drinking more again, not as much as when you guys were little, but still. It all added up to an early grave."

Katherine picked up Christina, who was now wining about not being able to eat dirt for the fifth time. She dug out a cracker for her to munch on.

"That's not fair."

Butch crossed his arms, "It's the truth."

"If you thought my dad worked too much, where were you when my mom disappeared? Oh right, you were off peddling your schemes. What were they all? Auto repair shop? And when that fell through, auto parts store? And when that didn't make enough money, wasn't exciting enough, classic car refurbishing? Is that when you stole money from us or was it for your self-storage lots that only needed a bit more liquid to really take off?"

"Bad luck on bad luck. And I did not steal a penny from your father. He lent it to me."

"That was my college fund! It was supposed to be a two-year loan! We never saw that money again!"

"Repayment was contingent on me making money out of the business. Couldn't much do that when the police seized half the containers and word got around that I couldn't keep a tight lid on that kind of stuff."

"You needed to find better clients! Not fences and thieves!"

"Is that what your father told you?"

"Is it not true?"

"How was I supposed to know they were storing stolen stuff? Should I have put that on the application? All types of people wanted, except not you grubby thieves. You think that would have fixed it?"

"Why do you constantly sit there and think you know what's best for us? Why do you constantly judge us for our mistakes then brush yours aside? Dad was trying his best! His best! He had an impossible situation and he loved us. He was there."

Katherine was nearly shouting at her grandfather. Feeling the heat in her voice, she huffed at him, wiped her slobbery hand on her jeans and found another cracker. "I can forgive you for your really, really bad business luck. I have forgiven you about the money. But all this other stuff?

All the hate towards dad? All the hate towards Ethan and Laura and me? Where is all of this still coming from?"

"None of you listen to me. None of you see the trainwreck that you keep doing to your own lives. Laura I'll give a free pass. She had it harder than you and Ethan, had to see her mother leave when she was older. That messes up people."

"Oh," Katherine's voice rose an octave, "She gets a free pass but I don't? You don't think I wasn't old enough to remember her and dad shouting at each other night after night? You think I wasn't also there pulling the blankets over dad after he passed out again on the couch? You don't think I cried myself to sleep for years thinking I'd become an orphan because I thought he was going to die at work or from the men who kept showing up on our doorstep demanding money? You give Laura a free pass but not me?"

Katherine brushed a few crumbs from her lap onto the floor. Her own small form of protest.

"I didn't come here to talk about the past. I came here to see how you were doing. To rebuild some bridges."

Butch's frown almost engulfed his whole face. "It'd be easier to do that if I could see my grandkids and my great grandkids more than once a year. Ungrateful brats, that's what you all are."

"We're the ungrateful ones? You yelled at Ethan about all of this during our dad's funeral! You never apologized!"

"I was right!"

"You were not!" Katherine took a deep breath and found another cracker for Christina as she wiggled in her arms. "You were not. Our father died naturally. Freak accident. Ethan is not in a dead-end career for whack jobs and idiots. Iris is fine. Laura is not wasting her life. I'm not ungrateful nor ruining my life. I've made mistakes, as have you. I own mine. Do you own yours?"

Katherine had had enough. She stood up.

"I wanted to see you. I wanted you to be able to see Christina. This was a mistake."

"Fine." Butch took another sip of water then waved his hand around. "No no, sit down. Sit down. I surrender. You're right. I'm being abrasive. Come, sit. Sit."

Katherine eyed her grandfather and slowly returned to her chair. After she set Christina down, she did not stop her from walking over to the potted plant, taking another small fistful of dirt and sprinkling it on the carpet. "Dirt!" Her daughter was mesmerized by the way some of the clumps fell to the ground and some stuck to her hands.

"Can you not let her do that?" Butch pointed to Christina.

"Sorry." Katherine winced at her own rudeness then wiped her daughter's hand off with a wipe from her bag. Christina squirmed on Katherine's lap until she was handed another cracker.

The silence stretched.

"We have to go soon." Katherine spoke, "Did you want to say anything else?"

"No, just... talk."

"So..." Katherine began again after the second wall of silence staled. "Who all is in your bridge club?"

"Frank. Steve. Henry." Her grandfather named in staccato precision.

"Are they nice?"

"Sure. Except Henry died. Last week. Have to find a replacement."

"Oh, I'm sorry."

"Happens to the best of us." Butch shook his head and wrinkled his face as if he was fighting a bad smell.

"Look... Katherine... I'm sorry."

Katherine felt the air leave her lungs. Butch was where Ethan got his stupid rule about saying sorry, about only saying it when you meant it. When was the last time Butch had ever said those words to anyone?

"Okay, about what?"

"Now don't look at me like that." Butch sighed and went on, "I'm... you know.... Because I wasn't there for you. For you and your dad. You're right. I've made a lot of mistakes in my life. A lot of mistakes. I'm glad to hear you're facing yours. It's hard. I'm a stubborn old bastard and sometimes I don't know how to apologize."

She turned away, unsure she could hold it together, "It's fine."

"Katherine." He said in all sincerity. "I love you. You know that, right?"

What was happening? He was a military man. They did not have feelings.

"I love you too grandpa." She was now crying, silent tears streaming down her cheeks. "I… why can't we just be a normal family, for once?"

"I don't know. I'm sorry." Butch never apologized. Never! What was happening? "Please, stay. If only for a few more minutes. Let me help you make one of those good memories you wanted."

Katherine sniffed, barely pulling herself back together. "Okay."

Thirteen

"Good morning Mr. Weiss," Katherine forced a smile as the elderly man stepped up to the bakery counter. "The usual? Two dozen croissants?"

"Good morning. Yes, yes." Mr. Weiss nodded irritably, his mind on something else for a moment before he refocused on Katherine, visibly relaxing. "Yes, the usual."

"Mr. Weiss!" Robert raised his arms and smiled. "How good to see you. You're here early today. How is the wife? The grandkids?"

The old man chuckled, "Oh, Robert, you know, you know. The first thinks I have the energy of a twenty-year old, do this dear, do that dear, why are you moving so slowly dear? But she is lovely, lovely still. More beautiful than the day I married her. And the others, the others do have the energy of twenty-year olds! Michael graduated from Yale, my boy. Was up there for the ceremony this past weekend. He's going far, going places. Molecular Biology. Already has an internship for the summer and half a dozen promising prospects. California, Boston, even an option here in Philadelphia."

Robert nodded along as if he knew exactly what it was like to have a grandson graduating from an ivy League school. "If he knows what's good for him, he'll keep his eyes off the East Coast. Too many new ideas on the east. Too many odd ideas."

"Here you go, Mr. Weiss." Katherine handed him the bag of croissants. "Can I get you anything else?"

"No, not today." He paid for his goods and gave them all a warm smile, "Always a pleasure. Until next week?"

"Enjoy the sunshine, Mr. Weiss." Robert waved him off.

After Mr. Weiss and his silent, broad-shouldered bodyguard left, Katherine's boss turned towards her. "You forgot to ask him how he was doing."

She dropped her smile, "He's here for bread, not for an interrogation."

"People want to feel wanted. Has he not returned every week since first finding my place? That's the added touch of the relationship. Always does the charm."

"Or maybe it's your baking? Maybe both?" She threw him the undeserved compliment, hoping it would get him off her back. She didn't feel like fighting.

"Yes, that too. All of it is important." Robert turned towards Katherine, looking her in the eyes. "What am I doing? I'm being insensitive. You don't need to hear all of this from me again. Margret would say I'm not seeing the tree through the forests. You've had a difficult couple of months, would be difficult for anyone. Go take five in the back. I'll hold the counter."

"Thanks." Katherine smiled weakly then slipped into the rear.

Without comment Katherine sat on a stool at the table where Lester was busy working. She propped her elbows on the table and rested her chin on her hands, unfocusing for a moment as she watched him kneed.

Knuckles into dough. Over and over, pounding, rhythmic. Something solid she could fall into that wasn't her sea of emotions. Why did they have to be so overpowering? Why couldn't she just let them go and be okay again?

"I lost my grandfather, a few years back." Lester said unexpectedly as he began to divide up the unbaked bread into pans. "It can be hard. Disorienting. A solid pillar in your life, removed."

"I don't want to talk about it." Katherine snapped back, standing up suddenly and moving away from her co-worker.

Lester shrugged. "Okay."

The undeserved tension created by Katherine's sour mood heavily grated on her. She tried to let it go, but instead, the pressure combined with Lester's crack of caring caused her to turn back around.

And unload.

"I don't even know why I'm feeling like this. I didn't even know him that well. My grandfather. He wasn't around when my dad was alive, was always too busy with his projects, his businesses. Always trying to turn a profit. He worked late into the evenings, over weekends, worked through planned family events, holidays, did anything he had to to get ahead. And did any of it matter? No. He went bankrupt right before retirement. None of us knew how he was able to afford the place he got, maybe my dad did. But my grandpa was too stubborn to ask for help, too stubborn to admit he was wrong, too stubborn to have anyone believe he was weak.

"You know, I hadn't seen him for almost half a year? Yep. I saw him every Thanksgiving with my brother and sister, like a strike team going in, saying hi, then leaving with minimal damage. That was my relationship with him after my dad died. Duty. Agitation. Anger. A lot of anger. I hated him for not showing any remorse at my dad's funeral. For everything he said that day. He just stood there, all serious like he always was, the model military man. Not a shred of emotion over his son passing away. Oh, you'd like him. He was a little like you. Serious to a fault. You want a hug? Too bad! Then he got into an argument with Ethan, right there at the funeral. Started ranting about how he was ruining his life and would end up just like his pops. It didn't go well. Didn't go well at all. So, I went to see him once a year, because he hurt us all. I went to see him, because he was family.

"I went to see him two weeks ago because he was family! And he apologized to me! He told me he was sorry and that he loved me.

"He… he told me he loved me."

Katherine's anger instantly evaporated to a flood of tears, barely able to get her words out between her sobs.

"And then he went and died! Died in his sleep! Two days after I went to see him! It was like he had been waiting for me, waiting to see me one more time before he let go of life, gave up, stopped caring forever. Or maybe I broke him? Maybe I said something wrong, caused him to give up. Am I bad luck? Does my presence kill people? Or maybe he knew it was time. Maybe I knew it was time? Why did I go see him? We only went once a year. Always. Agreed to it. We had agreed."

She looked at Lester and realized he had stopped moving. She coughed out a bitter laugh. "I'm sorry. You don't need all of this. You don't need any of this."

Lester eased his shoulders and nodded slowly. "You're fine. You're not alone."

Katherine laughed again, choking back another flood of emotion and words. "Thank you."

"Of course."

She didn't know how he did it, but somehow his few words had made her feel so much better. In that moment she had the massive urge to run up and hug him. Would he want to be hugged? Did her grandpa really want that hug? Had she let time pass for too long and now would never know? Lester was up to his elbows in flour, and never looked like the hugging type. Her grandpa never looked like the hugging type.

Without overthinking it any longer, she dashed around the table and grabbed his side, burying her face into his massive shoulder.

"Thank you."

He moved oddly, causing Katherine to back away in panic, but it was simply to free his arm. He wrapped it around Katherine and gently pulled her back into his side. They remained like that, her squeezing him with all her might and sobbing, him patting her gently on the back.

"Katherine." Robert poked his head out from the front, paused at the sight, then continued, "Someone is here to see you."

"Okay." Katherine wiped her eyes sloppily then stepped away from Lester. She was a mess of flour now too.

"Thank you."

Lester nodded. "Again, you're not alone. You never need to feel alone."

Katherine held back a new set of tears, these ones of joy, and returned to the front of the bakery, only to stop dead within the doorway.

Joaquin stood with all his calm demeanor in the waiting area.

In a moment of panic, Katherine turned instantly around, hoping he hadn't seen her yet. He probably had. She was a mess! What was he doing here? No, she couldn't deal with him, not right now. Not after spilling her guts out to Lester. Not with all these emotions still swarming her in all directions. Not after he assaulted her daughter, that was probably too harsh, but still! He took her blood and tested it after she told him no!

Not after she finally stopped dreaming about him.

"Lester." Katherine's plan was stupid. She didn't care. "There is a man in the waiting area. Go, um, make him disappear."

Lester raised his left eyebrow. "Come again?"

"I don't know! You're big, muscular. Imposing. Go out there and tell him something. Tell him the building is on fire. Or something. That he needs to leave and never come back."

"Katherine, are you okay? You're not making any sense."

"Katherine?" Robert poked his head into the back again. "I saw you come out, then you left. Where did you go?"

Katherine crossed her arms. "Tell that man I don't want to see him."

"Can you tell me why?"

"Because I don't!" Katherine shouted then cringed. Joaquin was sure to have heard that.

She looked at Lester then Robert, embarrassed and annoyed. "Fine. Fine! If neither of you men want to help me, I'll do it myself."

With all the anger she could muster, Katherine strode past Robert and right up to the counter.

"Welcome to Lavigne's Bakery. How can I help you?"

Joaquin smiled lightly and stepped up to the register opposite her. He wore his usual: black suit, black shirt, and red tie which today also included his large-brimmed hat and sunglasses. She could smell his sweet and musty cologne. He was still way too good looking for his own good.

"Can we talk?"

"We are talking, Joaquin. You told me I would never see you again, Joaquin."

"Somewhere more private?"

"You always enjoyed talking to me in a coffee shop. How is a bakery any different?"

He slowly took off his sunglasses. "Katherine."

The way he looked at her made her weak in the knees. This was not fair! He should not be able to do that with just his eyes!

"Fine." She stepped back and took her gaze off of him, pretending, rather poorly, that she was indifferent. "I'll need to ask my boss first."

Joaquin turned to Robert. "May I have a moment of Ms. Mason's time?"

The fact he asked for her, the fact he didn't let her do it herself was infuriating!

"We've been a bit slower this morning, that would be fine. Just, not too long Katherine. I don't pay you to chat with customers."

"You don't?" Katherine shot out sarcastically as she lifted the small flap separating the waiting area from the space behind the counter. She then cringed. Why had she said that to her boss? Joaquin was scrambling her already scrambled mind! She set the flap down with a minor bang then stepped up to Joaquin's side.

"Now, where would you feel more comfortable? Someplace public. With people. Lots of sunshine. I'm sorry but I'm not a fan of empty warehouses at the moment."

"Can we walk?"

"Oh, inventive idea. Takes a billionaire to come up with something so inventive, so new!" Katherine strode out of the bakery's front door with purpose, forcing Joaquin to follow after her.

Joaquin quickly fell into stride next to her, his sunglasses back on. "You seem annoyed."

"Oh, I have no idea why I would be annoyed, no idea at all. You, disappearing from my life after I barely got to know you, you, off to your rich man club, doing what rich men do after playing with the hearts of lonely and vulnerable poor people. No idea why that would annoy me. Disregarding anything I asked. Nope, I should be thrilled to see you. Maybe even be on my knees for you. Would you like it if I got onto my knees for you?"

Joaquin did not take the bait. "You're hurt. What happened."

Katherine's mind sharpened. Did he know? Is that why he was here?

"It doesn't matter."

"It does to me."

His sincerity brought back her ire. "Oh, so whatever is bothering me matters to you now? I'm so sorry I couldn't have been enough for you before. Guess I need to be a bleeding heart for you to care."

She stopped abruptly, forcing Joaquin also to stop and turn towards her. She put her hands on her hips, "Joaquin, what do you want?"

He thought for a moment. She was unable to see exactly what he was processing due to his sunglasses. "Things have changed."

"Obviously. Or else you wouldn't be here. Out with it. Why?"

"Waya wants to talk. He wants to talk with you."

"Why?" Katherine asked again, annoyed even more now that he confirmed this surprise visit had to do with business.

Of course it did. Everything was business to this man.

"Him and I have reached an, impasse. During negotiations he has continually thrown out impossible requests. Speaking to you, in person, seems to be the first I can potentially fulfill."

"Sure, but, why me?"

"He said he has an associate that hasn't seen you in a very long time. One Karl Mason. He said you would recognize the name."

Katherine's mouth popped open.

Her father.

"That's, not possible."

"I did not think so either. The funeral records to your father's death are clean. There does not appear to be tampering.

"But."

The way he said that single word changed everything.

Katherine was instantly teleported to the memory of the funeral, to her grandpa and Ethan fighting, to her father's body, his still face, his peaceful face. Like he was only sleeping.

"My father is dead. Why would Waya say he wasn't?"

"I don't know. He likes to tug at our feelings. It's probably nothing. He did ask for you by name. He mentioned your father by name. Either he's playing a very sick game, or he has a plan."

"No." Katherine whispered, a feeling of dread and anticipation welling up inside her soul. Her father, alive? Could it be true?

"The meeting is tomorrow. We would need to fly out to Denver tonight, immediately. Waya is not one to give much time for considerations or countermoves. I am asking you to join me and meet with Waya and your father, if he is there. I will be with you the whole time. You will not go into whatever he has planned alone."

"No." Katherine responded, louder this time, then began walking back towards the bakery. "No!" She added when Joaquin caught up.

Her father was dead!

"I would not be here unless this was the only option."

"Yea, I know." She snarled at him. "No", She said for a fourth time, picking up speed.

"You would be compensated for the time, for the hassle. Fifty-thousand dollars."

Katherine stopped again, and not because of the outrageous offer. "Joaquin, what do you think of me?"

He paused. "In what way?"

With the response, her mind wandered into dangerous areas. She shut the mental door hard to those thoughts. "As a businesswoman. As a spokeswoman for your company in this matter."

"I think you would do admirably."

She snorted. "Spoken like a man with his back up against a wall. You need me. That's the only reason you're here."

"Waya told us it was the only option to continue talks. To bring you."

"Why me?"

"He must know we had dinner together. He likes to needle people."

"Right. This is all about you. It's always all about you. You don't care about me as a person."

"That's not true, I – "

Katherine cut him off, "You pursued me when it made business sense, then disappeared when it made business sense. You only care about what I can give to you. You only care about what value you can squeeze out of me."

"Why are you angry at my –"

"Two hundred thousand dollars."

"Done."

Katherine blinked. She had thrown out an absolutely insane number to keep her advantage then end the conversation for good. To show him that he only cared as far as his money allowed. He was not supposed to say yes to that number without hesitation!

What was she thinking? He was a billionaire! That was like his pocket change! Her number should have been so much higher!

And that amount of money would change her life.

He held out his hand as she looked at him in shock. "Max will pick you up in two hours. I would advise you to dress for travel, but do bring a dress for tonight. The blue one looked wonderful on you. I want to show you the town, show you my personal appreciation for doing this."

Katherine shook his extended hand, her head spinning. "Wait, two hours?"

"I'll head back to the bakery with you, explain to your boss that you will be out of town for a few days. Should be a simple matter. Do you need childcare arranged for Christina?" Joaquin nodded as if it was already done and started walking.

"I'll ask Iris." Katherine had to do the following this time.

Her father, was alive?

"This is a bad idea." Ethan had his arms crossed. His serious face was locked in.

Katherine mirrored her brother's stance, her face even harder than his, "Why?"

Why did her brother have to be home from work for lunch! When was he ever home from work in the middle of the day? Katherine was supposed to stop in quickly, convince Iris to watch Christina for a few days, explain to her the size of the art deal she was about to land, and have it be a win-win-win. But instead, she had barged in on them having a quiet lunch together, the boys at summer camp for the day, Christina napping.

And in all honesty, she didn't think it was a good idea either! Their father couldn't be alive. He couldn't. And since he wasn't, why had she been hand-picked to be the liaison between two warring companies? What did she have to offer that any of the hundreds of lawyers could not? Was Joaquin right, that she was simply being used as a pawn to get under his skin?

She hated being used.

Ethan continued arguing, "What you're telling us doesn't make sense. You're saying this art collector, dealer, entrepreneur, looked at your work in the spring, abducted you for an impromptu meeting when my house was underwater, disappeared after he learned your pieces were lost in the damages, and now reappears a few months later urging you to fly across the country? For what reason?"

Katherine's lies were becoming problematic. She should have changed up her story. "He, he wants me to look at some talent out in Denver, inspiration? Maybe he'll have me commission a few new pieces? I don't know, it's art! It doesn't always make sense."

"Why you?"

"Why not me?"

She refused to tell him anything more, not until she had proof. Not until she saw their father for herself.

"I think what Ethan is trying to say," Iris added in, "is why does this art guy value your opinion now? Before today and he asked you to fly off with him, did you think he had any interest in your art at all?"

"No." Katherine admitted truthfully, begrudgingly.

"Are you sure you're going to Denver?" Ethan asked.

"Yes!" Katherine defended, feeling squished between her two landlords. "Why would he lie about that?"

"I don't know," Ethan shrugged, "maybe to abduct you again? This time without your daughter? Maybe it was too messy for him to make both you and your child disappear."

"What, are you saying you think he's some human trafficker or something?"

"I don't know, is he?"

"I don't believe you!" Katherine began to yell. "This is the first good thing that has happened for me in the past few months and you're trying to tell me it's just another cover for more trouble! Don't you want me to be happy?"

"Katherine," Iris moved in front of her husband before he could respond. "I think, what Ethan means to say, is, he cares about you. He doesn't want to see you hurt."

"Thanks for the interpretation Iris." Ethan bit off.

Katherine fumed, "Don't you both not get it? I am already hurting! Life sucks! Things are so far out of whack and I'm barely holding on. This is a chance for me to have a single win. Something to balance out all this other crap!"

Ethan's expression softened, "Katherine. Do you need to talk to someone?"

Katherine's eyes bulged, "What are you… No! Every time you suggest that! I don't want professional help! I know I'm messed up! I know what's wrong with me! I just need to get some traction in life again. I feel like I've fallen down a mountain and am half-buried in rubble. This could be the best way for me to dig myself out."

Ethan was not moved. "Flying to Denver. With a stranger. An art collector with no name. On a moment's notice?"

"Maybe you're just jealous. Maybe you want to go instead of me."

Ethan's nostrils flared. "Classic misdirection! I can get you to in to talk with Sherly. She's one of my best associates. Deals with women's problems all day long."

"I don't want to talk to Sherly!" Katherine yelled at her brother, panting when she took a breath. "I don't want to talk to anyone." She continued, a bit quieter. "What I want is for you to be supportive of me. And if you can't do that, can you at least watch Christina while I'm gone? Can you do that at least for me?"

"We can watch her, can't we Ethan?" Iris interjected.

"No, we cannot do that." Ethan glared at both of them. "I will not enable her chaos any longer."

"Ethan." Iris said his name lightly, pleadingly.

Katherine's brother looked from his wife to his sister then slammed his hands on the table.

"Fine."

He stood up, grabbed his baseball hat, and shoved it hard onto his head. "Fine! I voiced my legitimate concerns and neither of you care. Figures, you never listen to my good advice. I came to spend a quiet moment with my wife and enjoy a rare opportunity, get away from the drama of work. But who am I to think I can have any of that. No, not with my little sister always causing even more drama. I'm going back to the office to drown out my own problems by listening to other people's problems for the afternoon."

And with that Ethan stomped out the back door.

Iris looked hurt but did not follow. Instead, she turned towards Katherine. "I'm sorry for him. He's been extra grumpy since your grandpa died. Been beating himself up for not joining you."

Katherine shrugged and sat down at the kitchen table, defeated. "It's fine. He's right. I am being erratic. Always have been."

"Now, don't you go and beat yourself up too. I will watch Christina for as long as you need. How long will you be gone?"

"Two days?" She forgot to ask. "Maybe three. A few." Was this really a good idea? No, she would not back down now, not after how Ethan had acted. "I'm not really sure. I'll let you know if it's longer than two days."

"Okay. You go and enjoy yourself. Forget about everything else that's happened for a few days. I think it will be good for you."

"Thanks Iris." She squeezed her hand. "Oh, do you have any dresses I could borrow?"

"To impress your buyer?" A twinkle entered Iris's eyes., "I might. How did the first one go over?"

"I think he liked it."

"Then come, follow me. I have a few more that might look even more stunning on you."

Fourteen

Max drove Katherine and her overstuffed suitcase to the airport, skipping the terminal entirely and driving straight out onto the tarmac. He pulled up in front of a hanger housing a medium size private jet that had a dozen people swarming around it, getting it ready for takeoff.

"This one?" Katherine asked Max, intimidated by the ease with which he treated driving around planes as an everyday occurrence.

"This one. Joaquin's larger jet is out of service for maintenance." Max was not joking.

"Larger jet?" Katherine swallowed and stared. Who was this guy that owned two jets? "Okay, sure, that's too bad. I guess we'll take the smaller one."

"Take-off is in five minutes. Best you get on board. I'll bring up your luggage."

"Okay."

Katherine stumbled a bit getting out of the car. She looked around quickly and found no one even looking in her direction. Steeling herself to appear authentic, she held her head high and walked confidently over to the steps. Once inside the plane, she found the two pilots on her left going through their pre-flight checklist. To her right, instead of the usual rows upon rows of bucket seats, she found six recliners clustered around two tables and a lounge couch. Joaquin was already on board.

"Katherine, welcome." He stood up, smiling warmly. "I'm glad you agreed to this rather unusual arrangement."

"I still don't know what I'm getting myself into."

"Come, sit. I'll fill you in on as many details as you need, as many as I am allowed to share. Once we're in the air I can also get you a drink if you would like."

"Sure." Katherine sat down opposite her host. The chair was made of white leather and was firm yet plush. It had to be the most comfortable thing she had ever sat in. And it was on an airplane!

"Three minutes, Sir." The flight attendant noted as she moved from the front of the plane to a space in the rear. Max stepped onto the plane and settled himself at the table behind Joaquin, facing away from the two of them.

"Is anyone else coming?" Katherine wondered out loud.

"No, not this time." Joaquin buckled in. "Should be a little over three hours to Denver, depending on wind speeds. Just in time for dinner. I made reservations for us at one of my favorite spots in the city, allow ourselves a bit of enjoyment before the work begins tomorrow."

"Sure, which is, us, talking to Waya, and my dad?"

"Yes."

"Do you…" Katherine paused and rephrased her question, "Is it even possible to think he could be alive?"

Joaquin put his fingers to his lips and thought. "Possible, yes. Probable, no."

"How would it be possible?'

The plane began to taxi off onto the runway.

"There are a great deal of, options, available to someone like Waya. Expensive, both in terms of time and capital. My assumption is that he lied about your father simply as a hook for you to come. If so, it worked."

"Why lie about something absurd like that?"

"Waya is very good at reading people, knowing what to say to make them act."

Katherine didn't follow, "He's never met me."

"He's met Patrick." Joaquin continued over her next question before she asked it, "We speculate your involvement tomorrow is directly related to your ex's history with Waya. They worked together for a great many years. They were close. Which, admittedly, is a fact I find most intriguing. Vamp Industries has an extensive background check process in place, even for those who work in shipping and receiving. Patrick and Waya's connection was not uncovered until after his death. Either Waya planted that bit of information for us to find when he wanted it found, or he has been far more methodical in covering his tracks than I previously appreciated."

"Why would Patrick lie to me about where he worked? Why would he tell me for three years that his boss was his uncle? I still am having a hard time believing that part, let alone all the rest of it."

"We will be taking off momentarily," The pilot announced over the intercom, "please make yourselves comfortable."

Joaquin nodded to Katherine, "Yes, I read what you told the police. However, it's true. We dug into Patrick's phone and the number he had saved as 'Boss' is directly connected to Waya. We were also able to link Patrick's movements in the last two weeks of his life. They line up perfectly with Waya's known locations."

Katherine blinked. "Wait, you read the police report?"

"Yes."

"And you hacked Patrick's phone?"

"Yes. We had to tie off any loops, close any possibilities."

With much less acceleration and noise than Katherine expected, the jet sped up rapidly and was soon in the air. After it seemed to level out, Joaquin unbuckled himself and moved over to the mini bar.

"Drink?"

"Yes, please."

"What would you like?"

"I don't know, surprise me." Katherine paused for a moment hearing her own words then barked out a laugh. "Surprise me? I'm an idiot! I'm on a plane with a stranger who steals police records and hacks dead guy's phones for profit. What am I doing here?"

Joaquin looked over at Katherine with a mild curiosity. "I would hardly call us strangers. We shared a meal together. Food bonds people."

"Okay, fine. An almost stranger who I know nearly nothing about. A man who owns at least two jets and can fly halfway across the country at the drop of a hat. I am way, way out of my depth here! I live in the basement of a rowhome in Philly! The basement of my brother's house! And for some reason two mega companies are playing a lovely game of tug of war with me as the rope. It makes no sense! This is the kind of stupid stuff you only read about in books!"

"Yes, and soulmates and true loves are fantastical myths manufactured by the greeting card companies and Hollywood. You could never find another person who knows you so well, someone who could nearly hear your thoughts and anticipate your needs before you have them. Someone who makes you feel alive and cared for, who makes you smile at their very memory and even the bad days with them are good."

Katherine thought again about Patrick. Her mood darkened more. "Love rots. It's all just initial attraction, fascination for something new and shiny until it chips and shows its true self. Gold paint over cheap plastic."

"True gold may be hard to find and is easily intimidated, but when you do find it, you know it's pure."

Joaquin set a drink with a lime on the rim in front of Katherine. "Moscow Mule. Half strength, in case flying and alcohol doesn't mix well with you. But I am willing to bet that a little bit of spirit will help you through your current mental anguish."

Katherine took a large gulp. It was way too good. Everything Joaquin had was way too good. "Nothing lasts forever. People eventually disappoint you and hurt you. Break your heart and leave."

"Most do. But there are some out there, some good people who truly do care. The best of us."

Katherine took another mouthful. "Oh, and I'd assume you consider yourself one of these golden people? The best of us?"

Joaquin's smile turned sad as he took a sip of his drink, something smokey brown in ice. "No, Katherine. No. I am one of the worst of humanity. I am the kind of man who knows what he wants and takes it. Without reservations. I know when to be patient and when to seize the moment. I don't play by the rules. I will do what must be done, even if it hurts the people I love. I live in the world of kill or be killed. I am not prey."

Katherine took a third gulp, finishing her drink. She could already feel it in her belly. "Okay killer, what is it that you want?"

"Right now? I want to calm your fears, about our trip, and about tomorrow. I want to have this meeting with Waya and leave with a clear path forward. I want to get to know you better, to understand, who is Katherine Mason?"

She snorted. "Me? Complicated. A mess. Broken goods."

Joaquin's smile returned to happiness, his eyes shining with mirth. "Oh, I doubt that is all. May I ask you the same question in turn? What do you want?"

Katherine held his gaze for a moment before looking out the window. Everything looked so small and insignificant from this high up. A whole world that could fit in the palm of her hand.

"I don't know."

"Mmmm. Try again."

Katherine looked back at Joaquin. She could see the depth of his interest. "Honestly? I want some stability. I want to feel like I have both of my feet on solid ground. I want to provide a good home for Christina, to be able to provide her the life I never had."

"You feel like you're drowning?"

"Yes."

Joaquin nodded. "I have felt that in my life as well. That overwhelming feeling of grasping for a handhold and every time you reach out, the rock breaks beneath your fingers and you collapse into the open air. A very long time ago I felt trapped in a deep, black dungeon. Moldy hay on the ground, rats scurrying over my limp body, my captor taunting me. Believe me, I understand."

How could this man in his suit, sitting on his private jet ever feel a whiff of what she was feeling?

"Sure. Something like that."

She looked back out the window. Maybe if she could somehow fly away from her problems. Never return. Maybe if she could find a different perspective, distance herself so they would become like all the cars and people down there. Living their lives. Whole families, whole neighborhoods no larger than a piece of ice in her empty glass. Melting away into nothing.

Joaquin could tell the moment had passed. He cleared his throat. "Back to business?"

Katherine nodded and returned her attention to the cabin, "Yea, sure."

"Aright. Background. Things between our two companies have, heated up, in the last week. For a few months now Waya's company has been sizing up Vamp Industries. Over the weekend he's taken his knives out, legally speaking. Not a good look for us if he draws blood. If he does, then the real sharks begin to circle. We've been able to keep him at the table, but most of his terms of surrender have been non-starters."

Katherine followed along as best she could. "What does he want? Besides wanting to talk to me?"

"There is a piece of real estate he wishes to obtain from Vamp industries. He might mention it tomorrow. The Cathedral Basilica of Saints Peter and Paul."

"You own a church? And that was why the crucifix was in the box!"

"Indeed."

"So, if the bat mask is your boss and the miniature Jesus is what he wants. What about the Spanish coins?"

"They might have been a threat, or perhaps an offer. Not important to tomorrow."

Katherine raised her eyebrow, "How is a bag of coins a threat?"

Joaquin shook his head, ignoring the question. "Back to the main topic, my company is unable to part with the Basilica, for both historic and political reasons. We have owned the building for nearly a century and wish to keep it under our control. Not many know we are the true owners, so I would suggest you keep that bit of information to yourself."

"Is this building more important to you then whatever damage he's threatening to cause?"

"Yes." He pointed towards the empty glass in her hand. "Do you want another one?"

This was a bad idea.

"Sure, maybe one more."

When would be the next time she flew on a private jet with a billionaire making her mixed drinks?

As Joaquin was fulfilling her order, she continued, "Why does he want your church?"

"He doesn't. He wants what's inside the Basilica."

"What is inside the Basilica?"

"That is confidential. What you need to know for tomorrow is he cannot have it under any circumstances. Not the building outright, nor access to the building for any length of time."

Katherine didn't follow. "It's a church? Right? Isn't anyone able to just, walk in? What would I find if I walked into this Cathedral for Two Dead Guys?"

"A beautiful building, a holy sanctuary."

"And not what Waya wants?"

"No." Joaquin set the second drink in front of Katherine. "This one is full strength. Take your time."

She took a proper sip and the alcohol hit her tongue, causing her eyes to widen. It was strong! But not in a bad way. She really shouldn't be drinking this much on an empty stomach!

"Then where are you hiding this thing he wants? Oh, don't tell me it's in the basement? In some secret catacombs under the floor?"

When Joaquin didn't respond quick enough, Katherine laughed. "It is! Oh, this is great. Is it some death laser? A nuclear bomb? Some long-lost scrolls that discount the whole Bible and could send the world into anarchy and atheism? Oh, the horrors! What would Mrs. Preston do?"

"No," Max turned towards them and commented from the other table, "We keep the death laser in our volcano and the nuclear bombs in our silos in the desert, obviously."

Katherine giggled. "And the scrolls?"

"Deep sea research lab."

"That was my second guess!"

"Max." Joaquin raised an eyebrow at his employee. "When did you learn about the volcano?"

"I've always known about it." Max shrugged to his boss then winked at Katherine. She laughed.

"Back to tomorrow?" Joaquin suggested after the moment faded.

"Yep," Katherine settled herself then giggled again.

Really, this was Joaquin's fault, giving her drinks! Making her feel like she could be herself around him. Why did she say these things out loud? Why didn't she keep them in her head?

"Serious talk. Back to serious." She took a deep breath, "Does he want anything else? Anything else besides what you've buried under your Basilica?"

Joaquin nodded, "He has asked for a few more, unique artifacts from Vamp Industries' collection. Also, non-starters. He seems to know exactly what to ask for, what we cannot concede, then uses it against us in the next round of negotiations. A common tactic, if not a bit infuriating."

"Okay, what can I offer him then? If he asks?"

"Katherine, I don't want you to get the wrong impression. You will be there to listen. Nothing more, nothing less."

Katherine bristled at this, "Joaquin, Waya asked for me by name. I can't help you if I don't know anything. And you can't tell me you're going to tell me everything then leave out all the interesting stuff."

Joaquin sighed. "Waya is known for running his mouth. He will most likely tell us a fantastic tale of how he was wronged, how we are trying to take over the world with our death lasers. Most of what he says will seem insanity. Listen to me closely when I say this. He is a master of manipulation, a savant at reading people and knowing what will happen next. I could try and prepare you for tomorrow, but any of the mucky details will only complicate our meeting, distract you from the goal. The goal of tomorrow is for you to remain at my side and listen. That's it."

"What if he separates us? Gives me an ultimatum? Tells me I need to decide right there or else he's done? How do you want me to deal with that if I'm in the dark?"

"You need to trust me. Katherine. Do you trust me?"

"Yes. As far as I can throw you."

Joaquin was not impressed by her answer. He frowned, "Which isn't very far."

Katherine put her arms in the air, "I barely know you! I'm here to talk face-to-face with the guy who killed my baby girl's father. And really, I am only here to see if my dad is in Denver, and for the money. That's it."

"And if Waya offers you a million dollars to betray me?"

"Is this like, a suitcase he's handing me, or a promise that he'll pay me, pinky swear?"

"Would you take it if it was a suitcase?"

She thought for a moment. Was a million dollars that much more than two-hundred thousand? It was.

"I don't know. That's not a fair question. Why is Waya suing you?"

"Officially, he claims we wronged him, stole some of his work. Unofficially? He's looking for power, for something he can't claim without a lot of noise."

"Oh, you called him the Medicine Man. I get it now. He's the mad scientist and you are the evil corporation gobbling up all the good stuff. He used to be good but has thrown away his morals to take you down."

Joaquin's smile turned into a smirk. "Not quite."

Katherine kept going, "Oh! Am I the caped superhero? Swooping in to save the day? And at the end of this movie, I team up with you, the misunderstood sidekick to take him down?"

At this Joaquin laughed, "I'm the side kick?"

"Of course you are! You feed me all the intel, come out into the field and bumble around a bit. You're the eye candy. I save you at the last moment and the credits roll."

"Makes sense to me." Max added. "You are very nice to look at."

"So is she!" Joaquin gestured towards Katherine in mock annoyance.

"Eh, not my type," Max turned back around, smiling. "You can have her."

For the remainder of the plane trip, Katherine continued to bombard Joaquin with questions and sarcasm, eventually leading them into more personal items.

Joaquin was the only child of a corporate mogul, his father away on business most of his childhood, his mother estranged from the family due to, drama. He was raised by the help, and by the age of five spent most of his time at boarding school. A few years after he graduated from college, the University of California, his father passed away and left him sole heir to the estate. He returned to Philadelphia for the funeral and to work out a deal with the board of his father's company, securing for himself an honorary position. He played around for a few years, saw the world, then became serious and returned to Philly a second time, taking on the responsibilities he now held.

He did not date much, was never married. No children, no significant others. Max was his closest friend, which Max agreed with. They had their work and that was enough.

"Do you ever get lonely?" Katherine asked.

Joaquin nodded, "Yes. But it is far better for me to love myself, for me to learn and grow and not rush into something I'll regret. Life is long and when the time is right, when the right opportunity comes along, I will know. I see too many people making rash decisions due to momentary emotions and ruining their futures."

"Do you think that is what I did? Fell for a guy who worked for some super genius villain, had a kid with him, then got dumped?"

"With how you look when we talk about him? No. I believe you loved Patrick, that you love part of him still. You did not make a mistake. He did. I see that too in life, good people being hurt by bad people, honest people being used by villains."

"Do you think I'm a good person? Do you think Patrick was a villain?"

"You, yes. Patrick? I am not sure. He could also have been a good man, used by a super genius villain. Influence and corruption can spread from one polluted source into many lives."

"Am I a good person, but also an idiot? Allowing myself to be used by an evil man like you?"

Joaquin shrugged. "I am not evil. I am simply, not good. I am gray through and through. Out for myself and myself alone. I have done too many bad things in my life to ever be considered righteous again."

"So, you're that billionaire who murders ten-thousand children in China with one of your prototype vaccines and then gives a few million dollars to a save the children's fund to ease your conscious? Wonderful."

"Not, quite… but essentially, yes."

"Well, at least you're being honest."

"As honest as a single person can be in admitting their own failures and flaws. I have made many, many mistakes. I will continue to do so. Such is the plight of human nature."

"You sure like to flow into philosophy all the time. Are you doing this to impress me? Or is this the real you?"

Joaquin smiled easily, "Katherine, I am being me."

She gave him a side eyed look in return. "Alright. Well, that's what they all say before their secret identity is revealed. If you aren't a super villain, are you a cyborg programed to spout only the most ridiculous things? Are you a werewolf? Oh, I know! You're a sexy vampire!"

"No, no, yes."

Katherine punched the air in success. "I knew it!"

Joaquin laughed with his eyes.

When they touched down in Denver, it was the first time Katherine was sad to get off a plane. A black SUV was waiting for them at the hangar. No security, no delays.

Being rich was awesome!

They stopped by the hotel first to freshen up and let Katherine change into something more formal. Joaquin asked if she had an outfit and offered to go out shopping with her to find one if need be. She was flattered but thought she was prepared. The hotel room she was given was near the top floor, opposite Joaquin's. When she stepped in, she gasped at the space. There was a whole table with eight chairs in the first room, a lounge with couches and chairs in the next, then a king-sized bed in a third connected room. The bathroom felt almost as big as her whole apartment, with a walk-in shower that could easily fit four people, a jacuzzi tub, and two sinks set into a massive counter. This room for one evening probably cost more than her brother's monthly mortgage!

She had some time before dinner, but unfortunately not enough to try out the tub. She changed into a flowing green dress with a low neckline and settled a golden fish necklace at her throat. She kept her hair down, laid lightly around her shoulders. Confident. Comfortable. Once she was ready she met Joaquin in the lobby. Max was conspicuously absent, which didn't bother Katherine in the slightest. Instead of his usual black suit, Joaquin was in a dark charcoal one with an orange tie. He looked as handsome as always.

"Ready?", He asked, holding out his elbow for her to take.

She took his arm in her hand. It felt toned under his jacket. "Of course."

The restaurant was only a few minutes away. They chose to walk. The evening held a dry heat, the sun low in the sky feeling so much larger than it did in Philly. They strolled along the walking mall among the crowds, arm in arm, laughing lightly with each other. The place Joaquin had chosen was a high-end steakhouse with a grand assortment of options Katherine had never heard of before. As the waiter rattled off the various specials and their pairings, Joaquin stepped her through the choices, noting that anything she chose would be excellent. When he saw her stumble he took charge, ordering for both of them. A little bit of everything.

With wine and appetizers, the evening became almost magical. Food was served and Katherine tried whatever was set before her. Asparagus fried lightly, artichoke salad with cheese, a whole assortment of cheese and meat cutlery, then onto prime rib steaks and an arugula salad. Whenever Katherine felt like she was reaching her limit the servings would slow down, the two of them would talk and laugh, and a new dish would arrive at just the right time.

Joaquin was even more delightful as the evening progressed than during their first dinner together. They danced around many topics, from how it was to work at a bakery to places Katherine would like to visit to what it was like not worrying about money and what each other did in their limited spare time. She told him about how Christina got her name, that Andrew Wyeth was her dad's favorite artist and their visit to the Brandywine River Museum when she was eleven had changed her life. After seeing the painting of the girl settled on the grass she wanted to invoke that kind of wonder and longing in others, wanted to learn to paint and make others feel something too. Joaquin knew exactly which painting she was talking about, he seemed to know everything! They stayed away from sports, neither of them liking them, but when she got him started on books, she knew she had found his passion. If felt like he had read everything in print, from the classics all the way up to the hot off the shelf summer sizzlers. She would not consider herself a reader, but the way he spoke about it, the way his eyes glimmered when he described how an author phrased something or a satisfying twist to a plot, she felt compelled to start reading more.

They topped off dinner with coffee and chocolate mousse. Katherine was extra giddy after the two drinks on the plane then three glasses of wine over dinner. She felt like she was laughing louder than she should be, but also didn't care because everything felt so alive and wonderful in that moment, like all of the weight from the past few months had been lifted and she could see clearly again.

Being next to Joaquin felt right. It felt like they belonged together.

For the first time in a long time, she felt truly happy.

They walked back to the hotel arm in arm, Katherine leaning on Joaquin's shoulder a bit. She wanted him to put his arm around her, to snuggle up into his side. Then, annoyingly, Iris's words began playing over and over in her head as they stepped into the elevator. She should make the most of the evening, she should seduce him. Enjoy herself without limit. No, she was not like that. He would not want her like that. Yes, he was absolutely charming, and she wanted nothing more than for him to wrap her in his arms and kiss her as the cab ascended. Being so close to someone, alone with someone like him, it was impossible not to want more. Did he want more? Was this a one-way attraction? Was she reading into things too much? Should she move towards him? Would he reject her? Would that ruin an otherwise perfect evening?

The elevator doors opened.

The moment ended.

Joaquin smiled warmly and wished Katherine a good night and sweet dreams then stepped into his room. She stood looking at the door for a time, her thoughts in disarray. No, no, he saw her as a business partner. As a tool to use then discard. Nothing more. This was all in her head. He did not want to kiss her. He did not want to make love to her. He was a billionaire, and she was nothing.

This was all in her head.

She had loved the evening with him, loved her time with him, his words, his laughter, his smile. His deep blue eyes. She would leave it at that. Want for nothing more than that. A happy memory of a perfect evening.

She would leave it at that.

Without knowing what she was doing, Katherine knocked on his hotel door. After a moment it opened up and he was standing there, his jacket off, tossed onto the back of a nearby chair, his tie loose. She could see a bit more of his neck, see him in a way that felt relaxed and intimate.

"Katherine." He said her name, not as a question, not an accusation, not in surprise or disdain.

He said her name and it felt right.

Continuing to fall into this insanity, she stepped into the room and kissed him.

He felt cold, his lips to hers. He felt warm, his breath in her mouth.

He tasted right.

It was but a moment, a brief, wonderful moment of pure connection. He and her sank into each other's bodies and Katherine's whole world felt complete.

Then he pulled her back.

"Katherine… I…" This time when he said her name she could feel the uncertainty. It caused her to pause.

"What is it?", She asked, breathless from the intensity of it all, holding onto him, her doubts doubling themselves by the second, multiplying like deadly cancer in her mind.

"We, we shouldn't."

She stepped back, leaned against the wall and closed her eyes. Her doubts assailed her from every side. The room felt like it was spinning.

"Why not? Am I not good enough for you?"

Joaquin returned to her, this time wrapping her in his arms, embracing her fully.

"It's not you." He whispered in her ear. "I'm sorry, you have done nothing wrong."

She pushed him away to look at him in the eyes, "Then what?"

"I…" He left the single word hanging in the air.

Reality shattered her perfect evening. She coughed out a laugh. "You're gay, aren't you. That's why, that's why! Max? Why am I so stupid! I should have seen it."

She turned to run away, to hide her face, and cry herself to sleep. Joaquin's hand on her shoulder made her stop.

"No, I am not gay."

She turned. "Then what?"

"I, I'm not ready. Katherine, Katherine. Please hear me. You are absolutely beautiful, your hair, your laughter, your mind. You are everything

I would ever want in a woman. You have filled my heart with so much joy tonight. But, I cannot go any farther. Please, it's nothing you've done wrong. I'm … I'm not ready."

"Okay." She sniffed away the coming flood of emotions. "Okay, I get it. It's fine."

"Katherine." He said her name with more care and compassion than she had ever heard from another human being.

Her response was stoic, "It's fine. I get it. Goodnight."

"Katherine."

She trudged across the hall, the stars and glory of the evening shattered husks around her feet. How could she be so stupid! Why, why had she not let it be!

Without caring about anything, she threw herself down on the king-sized bed, fully clothed. And cried. She sobbed until she ran dry. Cried for the loss of Patrick, both over the loss of his love and his presence. Cried for her grandpa, for the love and time lost over past hurts. And cried for the hole in her heart where her father's love had been. He had loved her more than any other man in the whole world. Loved her unconditionally.

And he was gone. He had to be gone. He could not still be alive. She would hate him so much if he was alive and had not told her, left her alone for so long without a single word. And she would do anything to see his face again, to hear his voice.

Katherine's thoughts moved onto her daughter, to Christina. She missed her dearly, even if it hadn't been a single day since they were apart. She wanted nothing more in that moment than to wrap her arms around her daughter and sing her to sleep.

Instead, Katherine wrapped her arms around herself and hummed Mozart's 34th symphony until sleep finally, stubbornly arrived.

FIFTEEN

A PHONE CALL WOKE Katherine up.

She had been dreaming about her father. He had been reanimated as one of those zombies, lumbering, stupid, his face contorted. An old record player was blaring out Mozart but sounded like it was underwater. A dark shadow filled the sky, a presence she could feel, crushing her. She began running with Christina in her arms, running but getting nowhere. Ethan was reprimanding her, telling her she needed to stop and tie her shoes. Iris was suggesting she show a little more leg. Her grandpa was scowling at her as he threw grenades at the enemy. Shandra encouraged her, Vamos! Vamos! You can go faster! Patrick didn't say anything.

She ran.

The phone kept ringing.

Blinking away sleep, she turned over, the fish necklace pulling away painfully from her skin. She picked up the receiver and muttered out a, "hello?"

"Ms. Mason?"

"Yes?"

"Good morning. I hope you had a pleasant evening. Mr. Morales would humbly request your presence in forty-five minutes in the lobby."

She looked at the clock. It was 7:15 am. She had maybe found five hours of sleep. And not very good sleep either.

"Yea. Sure. Whatever."

Her head hurt. She drank too much yesterday. She used to be able to drink that much in college and bounce out of bed.

Getting old was a problem!

The voice on the other end continued, "Then can I tell him you will be joining him?"

"Yea." She groaned and sat up. Her dress was a mess of wrinkles and broken dreams. She had kicked off only one shoe, the other alone, sad by itself on the ground. "Yea, I'll be down."

Fifty-two minutes later, Katherine exited the elevator. She hated riding down alone in that stupid box. Hated her thoughts from the night before. What had happened? Why had she been so stupid?

She found Joaquin in the lobby, back in his black suit, black shirt, and red tie.

"Good morning Katherine." Joaquin smiled warmly. "Breakfast?"

"Morning." She stated, as wooden as possible. "Sure."

She folded her arms, attempting to radiate her annoyance. He either didn't feel it or chose to ignore it.

Men!

Walking together that morning was a wholly different experience. Instead of the joy and butterflies Katherine had experienced not even twelve hours earlier, the glaring morning sun indiscriminately glared down on her. It set the world into the harsh reality it was. They were there for a job. They were two people, two very different people who had remained two. Separate. Alone.

The gap of air between them felt like an uncrossable chasm to Katherine.

And she wanted it to stay that way.

At the café, Joaquin ordered a bagel and lox, not even bothering to take off his sunglasses and hat, while Katherine asked for an over easy egg and croissant. She pecked at the bread through the silence, knowing full well that Lester made better rolls. She would have to compliment him more when she got back.

Eventually, the expected moment arrived.

"I'm sorry." Joaquin began, only to have Katherine cut him off instantly.

"No, no. We are not doing that. I was an idiot, you stopped me. Nothing happened. Let's move on."

I fell for you. You were utterly charming. You rejected me. I'm hurting.

"Let me explain." Joaquin overrode her wishes, continuing despite her darkening face. "I have a medical condition."

That was not what she had expected to hear next. "A what?"

"A medical condition. It's, personal. A bit sensitive. But it causes moments like last night to be, more, difficult than it would be for normal people."

All of Katherine's built-up wrath, ready to release full force collapsed. "What kind of a condition? Does it prevent…?"

He shook his head. "No, no. I can perform just fine. Better than fine. It's, again, complicated. I can't speak on it more than that. But please, know that you are lovely. Your mind, your heart, I feel at ease with you. I feel I can talk to you, open up. I just couldn't go where you wanted to last night."

Katherine beat herself up a bit more internally for beating herself up last night. "Nothing happened. It's fine. Let's move on."

"Okay."

"Now at least it makes a little more sense why."

He put his hand on hers. "Thank you for understanding."

She blushed. "I thought you hated me."

Joaquin laughed. "The absolute opposite! It has been years since I've met anyone like you. Someone I feel this way about. I have learned to be a private person, to keep things too close to my chest, not disclose, not share. Part of my upbringing, part of my job. It seeps into other areas of my life. I am trying to be honest with you. It's still not easy."

"Thank you for telling me."

"I wanted to tell you this last night, but the moment went by so quickly. I was not expecting that."

Katherine looked at Joaquin's face, his eyes. "You weren't?"

"I had a wonderful evening with you. I wanted to, but I didn't think you did. I wanted to remain respectful, being here on business and all."

Business!

He continued. "I wasn't prepared for that, that's all. I had put it out of my mind already. Then the moment came and went. It's been a while since I've had a moment like that. Then, I felt even if I came over to apologize it would have landed badly. I am glad you understand this morning."

"You should have come over." Katherine said quietly, looking back down at their intertwined fingers. "You should have explained it to me last night."

"Then I am sorry for assuming the wrong thing multiple times."

In that moment, with the look in his eyes she wanted him to reach over the table and kiss her. She ached for him to pick her up and bring her back up to the hotel room, for the two of them to continue where they had left off so poorly the night before. She knew she was being a giddy schoolgirl, but this man!

Instead, he moved on.

"The meeting today."

Katherine cleared her throat and sat back, pulling her hand away from his. He casually returned his hands to his lap. "Yes. Business. Serious. Meeting."

"Waya has provided the details. He has a building, here, downtown. Six blocks away. We'll meet there." Joaquin looked at his watch, "In about an hour."

"An hour?" Katherine's nerves rattled into hyperdrive. "I still don't know anything. Am I dressed properly? You'll be there with me?"

"Yes. The whole time. And if I'm not, take this." Joaquin passed a small box over the table to Katherine. Inside was a delicate diamond necklace with matching stud earrings. "It's a radio. Two ways. The earrings use bone conduction. You'll be able to hear me even when they're not in your ear, and I'll be able to hear you and Waya through the piece here."

She looked at the gemstones curiously. They looked like ordinary stones.

"Just in case?" Katherine's fears were not being helped by this new twist.

"Just in case. I like to be prepared, and Waya likes to surprise. And as I've said before, he's a master at manipulation. He will tell us things that are outright lies in order to get a reaction. He will weave the truth with fantasy until you don't know which is which. Don't trust him. If he separates us, all you need to do is listen. That is all. You're not negotiating with him. You are not offering him anything. Take whatever he gives and bring it to me."

Sixteen

Max joined Katherine and Joaquin at the café at 8:30 am on the dot. The three of them then walked the six blocks to one of the many office buildings in the area. At first glance it didn't look like a super villain's evil lair, but when did they ever advertise themselves like that? It was a generic office building with windows and conference rooms. Katherine could see half a dozen employees milling around their desks, discussing various matters.

Minions plotting world destruction?

Or maybe unsuspecting victims, brain-washed into doing their master's bidding. The Medicine Man, drugging his employees with a vitriol cocktail of mind-control serum. He's in there now, laughing away, plotting his next move. His claws clutched around some armchair, watching from on high as Katherine enters. She'll step up to his throne, bowing, kissing his feet as they rest upon his tiger rug. Then, at the moment of triumph, he'll pull a lever and she'll pummel eighteen stories and two basement levels, straight into his pit of spikes.

And die.

Once inside the totally normal office building, Joaquin stepped up to the receptionist and announced that they were there to see Waya Kipp. The totally-not-a-robot receptionist with her perfect smile and hair stood up and brought them to the bank of elevators, noting that Waya was expecting them. They were brought up to the fifteenth floor and asked to relax in a small waiting area. Within, there were five corporate chairs, a potted plant, and a hideous print of lifeless shapes alone on the wall to keep them company. The white walls everywhere else were worse.

"Are you doing okay?" Joaquin whispered over to Katherine.

She nodded, not trusting her voice.

"This should only take a moment. Standard. Waya likes to make his guests sweat for a few minutes before pulling them in, thinks the extra time with your thoughts will weaken you."

"It's working." Katherine whispered in response, feeling trapped.

"Breathe." Joaquin said, grasping her hand for only a moment. "Breathe."

After an eternity, which was technically only three minutes, a generic looking man in a suit stepped out of a set of double doors. "Katherine Mason?"

"Yes?" Katherine stood up. Joaquin stood up with her.

"This way please." The suit motioned for her to follow. When Joaquin stepped forward as well, the suit put his hand out. "No. Just Katherine Mason."

"This was not the agreement." Joaquin protested.

"There was no agreement. Waya would like to talk with Katherine and no one else. Or you can leave now, and he will declare war. Your choice."

Joaquin turned towards Katherine. "You okay?"

"Yea, sure, just talking, right?" Katherine smiled weakly.

She was not okay in the slightest.

"You'll do wonderful." Joaquin put his hand on her shoulder and squeezed. He then reached into his jacket pocket and pulled out a bag. The bag of Spanish coins.

"Give him these."

"Why?"

"He'll understand." Joaquin handed her the bag then sat back down.

"This way Miss Mason." The suit moved forward, through the doorway and into a hallway lined with windows on one side and more geometric shapes in frames on the other.

"Remember, you're not alone." Katherine heard Joaquin's voice faintly in her head. It was the weirdest sensation, "I can hear everything you hear."

"This way." The suit turned and opened another series of doors. They returned to the windowless interior of the building. The next door gave Katherine pause.

"You want me to go, in there?" She pointed at the huge slab of metal which swung open slowly only after the suit swiped his badge, punched in a code, and looked into a retinal scanner.

"We are entering a SCIF. Please hand me any cell phones or electronic devices you may have on your person."

Pure panic settled between Katherine's shoulder blades. "Why? What is a SCIF?"

"It is a space built to render communications in, or out, ineffective."

"This was expected Katherine," Joaquin whispered in her head. "We have these too. Our communication will still work."

Katherine looked again at the thick metal door then to the man's outstretched hand. She slowly took out her phone and handed it to him, where he placed it in a bag, zippered it up, then set that bag in a nearby cubby. She wanted to ask Joaquin how he knew it would work, how he could be so sure, but hadn't the faintest idea how to phase it without drawing suspicion.

"This stops all communication? Fascinating."

"Quite. This way."

Stepping over the door's threshold felt like entering into the lion's den. The suit closed the door behind them. With a loud bang the door secured itself and a light near the top of the door changed from red to green.

Not good. Not good at all.

"Nothing can get in here? How do they build these spaces?" Katherine asked as they walked, clutching the bag of coins. Beyond the door, she saw no change to the office décor.

"It's a mixture of different layers of passive shielding in the walls."

"I'm still here Katherine. Breathe." Joaquin's voice was like a candle coming to life in a dark cave. "I'm still able to hear everything."

They walked down another corridor and into a small vestibule holding nothing but a bench between two doors. The suit did not follow her in.

"When I close this door, the one opposite of you will click. Proceed forward."

"Okay."

When the door behind her shut with a series of electronic clicks and the light above it went green, after a pause, the one in front of her clicked in the same way and the light went red. She opened it slowly and stepped forward.

The space beyond was small and felt smaller, with dark gray walls, black ceiling, and black carpet. In the center, a round wooden table held four white high-backed chairs. In the chair opposite of Katherine's entrance sat a man. He was of average looks, older, with a lined, weather-beaten face. He had a long braid of gray streaked hair over his shoulder and wore a collared shirt with a beaded necklace.

This man was not her father.

"Welcome, please, sit." The man smiled openly and indicated to the three empty chairs around the table.

Katherine chose the one opposite of the man.

"Ah, an adversary." He rumbled out, his voice low and gravely. "A question to be answered."

"A what?" Katherine asked, already feeling unsure of herself.

"Your choice radiates your intentions. You sit on my left? You consider me a friend, an equal. To my right? An advisor, one who seeks an audience. The chair opposite me? You are here to do business."

"Sure."

Which seat she chose mattered? Did it matter how she placed her hands? Should she put the coins on the table or in her lap? Was she breathing too fast? Was she blinking too many times? Should she say something more? No. All she had to do was listen. She waited and sweated.

The man eventually continued, "It is a pleasure to finally meet you, Katherine Mason. My name is Waya Kipp. Patrick Troutman had spoken at great length about you, on many occasions."

"You knew Patrick?"

"Yes. We walked the same path together for a great many years. We shared the same ideals. I was saddened when I heard of his passing."

"Saddened? You killed him."

The accusation hung in the air. Katherine was shocked she had said it so blatantly. She decided to lean into her bravado, steeling her face to show this man he could not push her around.

Waya did not visibly react.

"Ah, you are a hasty one. Before we even finish introductions you are invoking the blood debt of an innocent man. Or, at least, innocent in your eyes. Before we get to that question, I have one of my own. Would you like to see your father?"

Katherine tensed, her hasty mask already cracking. "He's dead."

Waya nodded. "He is."

She didn't follow. "Then, why did you ask if I wanted to see him? Are you going to summon his spirit or something?"

Waya's smile widened. "No. More. I am here to offer you a gift no one else can provide. Healing for your family. A childhood with your parents in love, together. Make it so the divorce between your parents never happened. Make it so your father's health remained strong, so that he never would have weathered and died. In essence, give you the life you should have had. To that end, you will help me."

Katherine scoffed, "How do you plan to do all of that?"

"Katherine, there are a great many things about this world you do not understand. We, you, I, humanity have been born blind, our eyes conditioned from youth not to see beyond what they want us to see. See the power hidden in plain sight. Possibilities that extend far beyond your imagination."

"And you think resurrecting the dead and rewriting history is an option to you?" Katherine asked. "Joaquin warned me about you, that you'll lie to me. I am here to hear what you want from Vamp Industries. I am here to listen to your offer. Nothing else. Oh, and give you these."

She threw the bag of coins across the table. They skidded with a satisfying clink.

He looked from her to the bag. "Ah, I anticipated these headwinds. This will be enlightening, for both of us."

Katherine crossed her arms. "My father is dead. You lied to me about him being here. You killed Patrick. Why should I trust anything you have to say?"

Waya sighed and opened the bag, examining each coin as if it was the first time he had seen anything like it. "You are correct. I have used deception to bring you to me. Everything I say in this room will be the truth."

"Tell me what you want from Vamp Industries, then let me leave."

"We are sitting inside a Faraday cage. Do you know what that is?"

"No."

"While a SCIF is built to block most communications, it is not perfect. The finer pieces of technology, such as your necklace remain active, remain a problem."

She unconsciously clutched the diamond around her throat.

Waya slowly motioned to the walls around them, "Surrounding us on all sides is an active copper sphere, built specifically to create a null space where absolutely no electromagnetic radiation can leave, or enter. You sit in the most secure space to have a candid conversation within all of Denver. Possibly the whole nation, though my rivals have deeper pockets and we both know, money can always craft a better shield."

Had she heard Joaquin's voice since entering this room?

"Yes, I see the understanding in your eyes. Joaquin cannot hear us. You and I can speak freely."

"I don't know what you're talking about."

"Katherine, If I have bound myself through honor to remain truthful, please extend me a likewise courtesy and do the same."

In that moment she decided she didn't like this man. He knew too much.

Waya nodded as if she had agreed to his request and went back to examining the coins, "Very well. I will tell you a story, then we shall move onto why you are here, what exactly you will do for me, and what I will do for you.

"I am a medicine man of the Cherokee nation. We are a people with a long history, a proud people, a people who lived in this land, lived in the land your ancestors named America long before the white man came to our shores. We were strong and treated the white man with respect when they were weak. We made many treaties with their kind, traded with them, lived in harmony with them until they grew powerful, grew greedy and vile. They used treachery to steal our land and kill us. The white men today are still trying to kill us, erase our history, our culture. They lack the wisdom and humility to teach future generations about their ancestors' errors, about the Trail of Tears or the Treaty of New Echota.

"Ah, but we are not guiltless, my people. We have reaped what we have sown. You, my daughter, are destined today to hear about the origins of disease and medicine.

"In the old days, the animals and plants, the beasts, birds, fish, and insects could talk, and they lived together in peace and harmony. Then, my people grew. They became abundant and proud. They began to spread over the whole earth and encroach on the animal's land. To make matters worse, my ancestors fashioned bows, spears, knives, blowguns, hooks, and all manner of weaponry to slaughter the animals and use their flesh for food, their skins for blankets and clothing. Even the smallest of creatures, such as the frogs and worms were not spared. They were trampled upon by my ancestors out of pure contempt.

"After this injustice had gone on for a time, the animals met in council to decide how to respond. The bears met first, with the great White Bear presiding as chief. They lamented over the loss of their friends. War was declared. Then came the question of which tools they should use to wage this war. Man used the bow to terrible effect, made from a staff of locust wood and the string from the bear's entrails. So, one of their number sacrificed themselves to make a bow for the group. The first arrow shot went off target as the bear's long claws caught the string. Some suggested they trim their claws to use the bow properly. When this was done, the second arrow flew straight and true. However, Chief White Bear objected to this, saying they could not make such a sacrifice. What good was it to win their war against man if they could no longer climb trees, no longer hunt, and eventually starved? The bears argued for a time and eventually decided that man's tools were not meant for them. They left the council with no solution. It is due to the bear's contempt for Man as to why no hunter asks for the bear's pardon before killing him.

"The next animal to hold council was the deer. Their chief, Little Deer was wise and knew they were not able to wage war on Man, for he was too strong. He also saw the bear's folly and decided on a compromise. Asked that when a Man went to hunt, he must first honor the deer's spirit by asking for their pardon. If the hunter was to ask for the Little Deer's blessing in the hunt, all would be well. But if he failed to ask, Little Deer would follow the trail of blood of one of his slain brethren, come upon the hunter while he slept, and strike him with rheumatism, swelling his joints and causing him to never be able to hunt again. This is why all hunters ask for the deer's pardon before going out on a hunt.

"The next council held was that of the fish and reptiles. They were a cunning group, determined to punish man's offenses by making them dream about snakes coiling around their bodies, striking fear into their hearts whenever they attempted to gain a moment's rest.

"Finally, the birds, insects, and smaller animals held their council with Grubworm as chief. They were determined to end the matter, that if at least seven votes were cast against Man, they would be guilty and be put to death. It did not take long to reach seven, with the frogs, squirrels, mosquitos, grouse, ducks, and all other beasts clamoring to have their say over the offences handed down to them by Man. Grubworm grew vindictive. He decided to craft disease after disease as punishment, so many in fact that my ancestors would have no chance to survive.

"The plants, who were friendly to man, caught wind of the Grubworm's evil plan. Every tree, shrub, and herb, down to the grass and moss agreed to furnish a cure for each and every one of the new diseases and proclaimed, 'we shall be here for whenever Man has need of us.' Thus, came medicine, and medicine men, who use the kind gift given by the plants to furnish the remedies against the injustice done by the animals."

At the end of his story, Waya pulled the strings to the bag of coins, set them off to the side, and folded his hands.

Katherine had listened quietly, intrigued. When Waya ended, she had no idea what any of it meant.

"Okay?"

"The sons of the first Man, Kanati, are known as the Little Men, or the Thunder Boys. They play in the clouds and live in the Sky Vault. When you hear the heavens clap and the rains come, the Thunder Boys are on the move."

"I don't get it. What does any of this have to do with Vamp Industries or what you want with them?"

"Which story do you believe is true?"

"Um, neither? They're folklore, fantasy. Stories to explain why the world is the way it is."

"Oh? Or are these stories mirrors to the truth, names and places changed, the underlining events remaining pure? What can we truly know as truth without experiencing it ourselves? If a bear was to speak to you, would you believe it when it happened? Would you tell anyone about it? Would they think you crazy?"

"Oh, they would absolutely think I was crazy if I told them a bear talked to me."

"What if Ethan told you a bear talked to him. You would believe him?"

"Maybe."

"What about Iris?"

"Absolutely not. Hey, how do you know my brother and his wife's names?"

He ignored her question, "Then it is not the story, but the credibility of the storyteller which validates the tale?"

"No, maybe? I don't know. Possibly. Some people you can trust."

"Do you trust Joaquin?"

There it was. The point. "I do. Enough. He hasn't caused me to distrust him."

"Even after he forcibly took your daughter's blood for testing?"

"How do you know about that?"

Waya shrugged. "He has ears, I have ears. The birds have ears."

He was getting under her skin, "Yes. Even after that. He told me about it, and we moved on."

"Do you trust me?"

Katherine worked hard to keep her face still. "No."

"How do I earn your trust?"

"Did you kill Patrick?"

"No. I did not. Joaquin's boss did."

"That's a lie."

"Because the truth from an untrustworthy source is less truthful? Or because you don't want to believe the truth?"

She worked to keep control of the conversation. "What proof do you have?"

"Ask Joaquin. He'll confirm."

"Why would he do that? He said you killed him."

"Knowing Joaquin, he crafted his words in a way to mislead you. I'll assume he blamed me for Patrick's death, which is not untrue, but also, unhelpful. Blame can be passed onto many parties. But, blame is different from literally holding the knife. Yes, a portion of my actions are to blame. So are Joaquin's. So are Patrick's. So, are yours. I will own my part in his death. Yes. I asked Patrick to do things for me in which ultimately led to his death. However, it was Joaquin's boss who spilt his blood."

Katherine's head spun with this new information. "Okay, so, let's say I believe you. You lied about my father. That is unforgivable."

"I did not. Help me and you can see him again."

"That's not possible." She balled her hands into fists. "You can't bring people back from the dead."

"I can't, correct. My medicine does not allow that. But I know of another source, another option."

"You're talking crazy!"

"Am I?"

Katherine did not like all of this dancing. "Can we get to the point? What do you want from Vamp Industries? Did you drag me across the country just to tell me some stories about bears and deer?"

'No. It was for what I am going to tell you next."

"Okay, out with it."

"Katherine. In this world, there are places that hold great power. We call them ley-lines. They are born out of moments of great conflict or loss, massive turning points in personal or national history in which rip the literal fabric of our world. You may think of them as folds, or creases from our physical realm into the spiritual realms."

"That sounds ominous."

"They are as dangerous as they are powerful. Some are constant sources of energy, wellsprings in which their holders can draw power out from without end. Others are highly tuned tools, useful for one purpose and one purpose alone. Still others are like a great cache of weapons, locked, yet with the right key can be opened, providing access to a burst of unworldly power. Enough to change the very flow of history. Enough to do everything I have promised I will do for you."

"You're insane." Katherine stood up, done with this conversation. She moved towards the door and tried to open it. It was locked. She scanned the walls. There was no button, fire alarm, emergency escape, nothing to get her away from this man and his lies.

"Vamp industries holds a ley-line like this in their possession. I have deciphered the key."

She turned back towards Waya. "Let me guess. The ley-line-thing is below the Basilica of Saints Peter and Paul."

"Correct."

He said it in such a way that made her want to believe him. There was no way any of this was true!

"Joaquin told me you can't go there. He won't let you."

Waya put his hands out, palms down, onto the table. "Katherine. All I need for you to do is invite Joaquin to an art exhibit."

"What? Why? When?"

"It's the premier gala showing off an array of new, young, talented artists. One of them is you."

Katherine's breath caught in her throat. "Me?"

"Yes, you. In three weeks' time, a gallery I own in the City of Brotherly Love will be showing your work. Your full collection, restored from that quite unfortunate bit of water damage."

"You have my paintings?" The constant twists in this conversation kept her so far off balance!

"Yes. Another one of those minor inconveniences, stealing your art. An offence in which you will be generously compensated for once you see your work in full display with Joaquin at your side."

"Why? Why did you steal my art? Why do you want me to bring him there? Is that when you're going to attack the Basilica?"

"Yes."

Katherine opened her mouth and no sound came out. What was going on!

Waya continued as if she wasn't gaping at him. "You'll get the invitation in a week's time. And that is all you need to do. Have him in the building, have him completely distracted at 10:00 pm and I will do the rest."

"And if I say no?"

Waya began to stand up, "You won't."

"Okay. No."

Waya smiled. Slick. Confident. "Katherine. I have met with the Thunder Boys. While the plants provide me with the great miracle that is medicine, the Little Men have gifted me with power beyond your understanding. I can see the paths before us, the trails within the dark forest of Fate in which you are most likely to tread without intervention, and those that require a bit more of a nudge. This meeting here? You in Denver? Your glorious evening last night with Joaquin? Those were my hands in Fate, events orchestrated by my foresight. You will continue to walk down my intended path. I have seen it."

She hated being told what to do! "No! I don't care about my art, or about seeing my dead father again. I won't help you."

"You do care, you care very deeply about what people think about you. That is why you will do this. Once I unlock the ley-line, I promise you that your family will be whole again. I will rewrite your past with such completeness that you won't even remember this conversation. It will never have happened. Instead, you will have everything you ever wanted. Fame, family, love. Your mother, your father, Patrick. The perfect life. All of it."

"Stop saying that! You can't bring people back from the dead! You can't change the past!"

Waya turned to go. "Yes, I can. With your help. Do not pick the wrong side."

Katherine danced around the table as Waya moved towards the door. She grabbed his shoulder with all of her strength and tried to turn him around. He barely shifted. "What am I supposed to tell Joaquin? When he asks me what we talked about?"

"Tell him whatever you would like."

"Fine. I'll tell him you want me to lead him into a trap."

"I expect you to do exactly that."

She stepped back and put her hands on her hips, still unable to find a foothold in this conversation. "I'll tell him you want him distracted so you can take over his church and we don't go to this stupid gala. This was all for nothing. Pointless. Good job. You lost."

"You will bring him to my gala. I have seen it."

He reached for the handle. Katherine slipped in front of him and shoved her back up against the door, forcing him to stay in the room. "You're not making any sense!"

Waya frowned. "Please, Ms. Mason. Move."

"No! Not until you tell me what this was all about!"

"I have. And you weren't listening. I have spoken the truth in its entirety. Do you require one more nudge? Very well. If you still don't believe me, ask Joaquin again if he is a vampire."

Katherine blinked, then laughed. This man was absolutely crazy! "A... what?"

"You heard me. And that will be all Ms. Mason. Until we meet again."

Katherine stared at the door after Waya left, far more confused than she had ever felt in her life.

SEVENTEEN

KATHERINE PACED BACK AND forth within the cabin of the plane, unable to catch her breath, frustrated at how small this cabin was. Why couldn't they have used the larger jet!

After another minute of her mind rolling over itself, exploding into tiny bits of shrapnel only to do it over and over again, she turned back to Joaquin and locked him in a death glare.

"You're a fucking vampire??"

Joaquin nodded, not a hint of a smile on his face, "Yes."

Katherine went back to her pacing, her mind refusing this to be true. It couldn't be true. This made no sense! Vampires weren't real! And they sure didn't have eyes like Joaquin's!

"I can see you're distressed."

Katherine stopped pacing and returned to her glaring. "Distressed? Distressed was three stops ago. I am livid! Are you lying to me? Are you and Waya in some kind of billionaire mess-with-people club? Do you extract great pleasure from watching my brain slowly disintegrate?"

"No, and no. No club. Hard truths are no less true, simply more difficult to swallow. And you asked earlier. I was honest then too."

That sounded way too close to what Waya had kept saying.

"I was joking! You were joking! I thought you were joking! Bah!" she growled at Joaquin and went back to her pacing.

After leaving Waya's building, Joaquin had been apologetic over the gaps in his back-up plan, the inoperability of the microphone and headphone jewelry. Sometimes even the best laid plans went sideways. She had used her irritability over being left alone with Waya as a cover for some time to think, time to digest everything she had heard. None of it made any sense! With the main reason of the visit done, they had checked out of the hotel and drove back to the airport, Katherine remaining tight lipped the whole time. It wasn't until they were airborne that she asked her first question.

'Are you a vampire?'

She had expected Joaquin to laugh at the absurdity of the question like he had done before and say no, or at the very least deny it. Joaquin would ask, why would she ask that again? She would say, Waya really was as crazy as he seemed! They could have a drink and she could have relaxed again. They could have enjoyed the trip back to Philly in comfort. They could have talked a little bit about business then Max could have stepped into the cockpit or somewhere, and they could have had some time in private to discuss, other things.

Why had she needed to get that annoying little bug out of her ear first? Why not just deal with the rest of the meeting and forget about that obviously insane part altogether?

But… she had asked. And he had said yes.

Katherine threw up her hands, "How is this possible?"

"The short answer? It is. The long answer is a lesson in history. Which do you prefer?"

"We have time, give me the long one."

"Alright, sit down? Do you want a drink?"

Katherine plopped into the way-too-comfortable airplane chair. "No drink. My head is already spinning just fine."

"Alright." Joaquin leaned back, his fingertips together. "Earth, humanity, what you see is not all there is. There is a spiritual realm as well, a place where a great war between the forces of heaven and hell has stretched on since eternity. A war for power, for dominance. Why? I do not know. I have never received an answer as to why they war, only that they do.

"At some point in the past, Earth, humanity became a battlefield. Since neither side wished to lay complete waste to the beauty in which resided here, they remained subtle in their efforts. The forces of heaven created, expounded, provided super-human abilities for their hired and coerced minions to use. The forces of hell corrupted, twisted, and defiled. I am one such creation."

"You're a vampire?" Katherine asked again, still not believing it.

"Yes."

"A real, blood sucking vampire?"

"Yes."

The scene in the lab came to Katherine's mind. "You wanted my daughter's blood? You wanted my daughter's blood!!"

Joaquin put up his hands. "Yes, but no. It's more complicated than that."

"Then explain. And it better be good, because I'm suddenly getting evil, child murderer vibes from you."

Joaquin stretched out his hands in an attempt to look open and honest. She imagined it as him trying to wrap her up in his evil claws. She had wanted him to touch her! She had kissed him!

"Blood is not homogeneous. That is, different blood is better, or worse for us. Lines of families, certain combinations of traits and genes can create superb attributes… hmmm, let me back up a bit. Let's start with what I am. Whatever you think you know about vampires could be true. It could be false. There are a lot of misconceptions out there. Some created on purpose to confuse. Some that even we don't know how they became a thing."

"Do you kill people?"

"At times, yes."

"By biting their necks and sucking out their blood?"

"At times, yes."

A chill ran down Katherine's spine. They were holding hands last night! They were almost… last night!

"Can you turn into a bat?"

"No, I do not."

"But your boss? Is he a vampire too? Would only make sense. That's why it was a bat mask!"

"He is, and he prefers that form when shapeshifting, yes."

"Can you not shapeshift too? Why not? Don't you want to fly around at night?"

"Have you ever seen a bat in the city? Even at night they are a bit too conspicuous for my tastes. I prefer to blend into my surroundings. Being a man in a suit is far less memorable."

"I read in some book that you sparkle in the sun. I haven't seen you sparkling."

Joaquin laughed at that one. "That is one of the more idiotic ideas about vampires. I do not sparkle. The sun burns."

"I've seen you walk outside. You haven't burst into flames."

"I could, if I wasn't properly protected."

"Protected?"

Joaquin pinched his skin. A thin layer of, something, pulled up. "I constantly wear a protective layer of UV nanoskin during the day. It absorbs and redirects the more harmful effects to my person. If I was to go out at noon without it, I would shrivel up like a grape in about five minutes."

"Nanoskin?"

"Yes, one of the many technologies Vamp Industries has perfected. Many years ago, in fact. Back in the thirties. Also, one of the reasons Serpitus, my boss, asked me to start the company. He wanted to find solutions to the problems the arcane cannot solve. While we have access to a much greater library of methods in comparison to the average person, demons are wholly uninventive, and angels, too pompous to care. Men writhe in the mud and thus, are much more ingenious."

"Vamp Industries? Vampire Industries?" Katherine laughed again, "You don't think that's a bit too tongue-and-cheek?"

"Again, I prefer to hide in plain sight. Many have called our company a soul-sucking entity that can burn in hell. I find it comical how close they are to the truth."

This was too ridiculous to be true! "Is Waya some vampire too? Was I in that jail cell with another monster like you?"

Joaquin frowned, "Monster? Some call me that. I am what I am. And as for Waya, he is a Medicine Man."

"You've said that before. And now you have to explain. Does he have some superpowers too?"

"Did he mention the Thunder Boys, or the Little Men?"

"Yea, he seemed to have a bit of a hard on for them."

"Always the talker, Waya. Loves his stories. A long time ago, many centuries in fact, far before the birth of America, two angels decided to use the Cherokee people as their own. They taught them medicine, hunting, language, and in return, the people paid them homage. To a select few, they gave them the ability to see into the future, see people's motivations and the paths in which they may walk. Waya has been gifted with these traits. He can see where what will be will become what is. You can think of him as a puppeteer, pulling the right strings to shape the world towards his wants."

"He knows what I am going to do?"

"He does, in part."

"And that is why he told me about you being a vampire?"

"I would suspect so, yes. He possibly wants you to hate me. Has it worked?"

What she hated was that she was being manipulated and constantly left in the dark. "Maybe. Depends."

"On?"

"On if I believe any of your answers. Or his. This is all complete insanity!"

Joaquin nodded. "And no further from the truth than the statement, I am alive. What is truth? What is alive? What is life? Are they all rigidly defined, or do they have some soft edges, some places that even they themselves can't see."

Katherine scowled. "Stop with that fluffy stuff. Focus on keeping me from stabbing you in the heart with a wooden stake."

"You could try. I can bleed, but that would do little else."

"If I tied a crucifix onto it? If I dipped it in holy water?"

"Am I that much of a threat that you're trying to kill me now? What else did you discuss with Waya?"

Katherine shook her head. "Oh no, we're not done with you yet. You helped your boss start Vamp Industries in the thirties? How old are you?"

"A little over 900 years."

Katherine blinked then laughed. "900! You look good for your age!"

"Thank you."

"Where were you born?"

"Spain, in the 1100s. I was one of the great Spanish knights."

"Then what happened then to make you into, into what you are now?"

Joaquin sighed deeply.

"Have you ever loved someone? I mean, truly loved someone? With every last fiber of your soul? Loved them so strongly that when you were with them the colors of the world were brighter? Whatever you ate or drank with them became the most pleasurable thing to have ever crossed your lips? You could talk and laugh and just be and moments of nothing were pure ecstasy? Have you ever loved like that?"

Katherine thought, then shook her head. "No."

"Well, I have. When I was thirty-six I met a woman, Elena. My soulmate. It was like the creator had painted the two of us together. We fit perfectly, in every way. She had hair like the sun, golden, her eyes as blue as the clearest of lakes. Her hips, her legs, her shoulders. Oh, her laugh made me shutter with desire and her stare alone made my heart race! And she was my equal. My beloved. My whole world and more. We could talk for hours, debate the intrigues of the royal families or the infighting of the church, rumors over our household staff, new clothing styles, even the right way to shoe a horse. Everything was a joy. Being in the same room with her was enough, being intwined with her was an intoxicating drug I never wanted to sober up from. Never.

"But then..." A single tear fell from Joaquin's left eye.

Katherine felt the urge to extend her hands out to comfort him but held back. "What happened?"

"Loss is the most mysterious of emotions. It's not the pain of something done to the heart, but the pain of the heart being without. Before I met Elena, I felt my life was complete, felt I was a healthy man who knew where he was going. I was respected by my men, loved by my serfs, my slaves. But then... but then, while we were together, everything actually made sense. We took on the world together, fought together, lost sometimes, won constantly, and I thought it would never end. But then it did. Serpitus came. He was jealous. He was power hungry. He was cruel. He came in with a vengeance, full of malice and spite. He was the one who transformed me, the one who gave me this curse of undeath. And for that gift, he killed my Elena. Right in front of my own eyes."

A stream of tears was now silently trailing down Joaquin's cheeks.

"He made me watch the life in her eyes fade away."

Katherine had no idea what to do. She felt stunned, shaken. "I'm sorry."

Joaquin nodded, ancient memories swirling for a moment before he wiped his face clean and regained his composure. "Loss. It's the pain of having no more future with what you once had, the pain of memory. Before I met Elena, I was a strong and capable man. After Elena was gone? I was but a husk. Her memory haunted me for decades… and in all honesty it still does to this day.

"At first I was enraged, hellbent on enacting my revenge on Serpitus. This was before I understood the full reasons for his cruel act. In order for me to survive the change and become a full-blooded vampire, the subject, I, needed the will to live. You see, this curse changes your very nature, turns you inside out and rips your soul to shreds. Hatred is a powerful reason to keep on living. It's the Siamese Twin to love in fact. Hatred, just like love, drives a person to incredible lengths, causes them to have but one goal, one mission. And while Serpitus could not control my love for Elena, he could absolutely control my hatred for him.

"Those first few months without my beloved were agony incarnate. After my Elena and my household were slaughtered at his hands, he captured me, brought me to his estate and locked me up. While my body fought to consume itself, I had nothing to occupy my days. My mind churned and my heart grieved. For weeks on end I couldn't get up off the floor, couldn't think straight, couldn't bear another moment without her by my side. I would fall asleep and she would be in my dreams. I would wake up and she would be gone. I contemplated ending myself more than once, more than a hundred times, searched aimlessly within my insanity for a reason to keep on living. A reason Serpitus aptly provided.

"He came into my chambers every day, to check up on me, to see how I was progressing. For the first few weeks he brought with him a dagger. One like this."

Joaquin reached behind his back and pulled out an ornate dagger. It had a silver hilt filled with sapphires, the largest about the size of a quarter. The blade was about four inches long, straight, with a wrapping of silver thread entwisting the steel up to the tip.

"He would hold his dagger out for me and mock me, tell me how weak I was, how pathetic I was, how I was foaming at the mouth, how I writhed in pain, how I kept screaming at every last twitch. He would tell me all I needed to do was take the dagger from his hands and kill him with it. He wouldn't even bother to defend himself. Ah, but I was too weak, the curse had too firm a grip on me. I couldn't even stumble to my feet. After a few minutes of taunting, he would laugh and promise me another visit. Tomorrow. And so, I willed myself to survive, till tomorrow, then till the tomorrow after that, and after that.

"Eventually I forced myself to stand. Eventually, I had hardened my grief into the blazing inferno of revenge. I thought I was cunning, appeared weaker than I was for a few days, appeared the lamb before my day to become the lion arrived. Ah, but Serpitus saw through my guise. It was like he could read my mind. The day I planned to strike, he came in with not one dagger, but two. He held onto this one's equal, a golden dagger encrusted with rubies and threw the silver dagger at my feet. He mocked me, told me to pick up the dagger and show him if I was a man, or a maggot. Words, words are words, yet they can pierce the heart and prod the ego.

"I did. I picked up the dagger and attacked. It was pitiful. Absolutely. My first thrust went wide, my follow-up slash met nothing but air. Serpitus knocked the blade from my hand, looked at me with pity, threw the dagger's scabbard at me, then left.

"Left me with the blade to do with it what I would.

"That night. That was the hardest night of my life. I stared at these sapphires for what felt like an eternity, stared into them, and wept for my Elena. Wept for the shambles that my life had become. Wept for how wretched I had become. I had been a Spanish Knight! One of the best! Wept at the pain and the reality that I was ready to end it all and now could. Wept until the tears ran dry.

"Yet. I survived.

"Loss, it never really leaves you. The memory of Elena is still in my mind, her love, her face, her everything.

"I eventually came to a deep peace that night that life is filled with loss, and loss defines the importance of life. The best lives are lived in the most intense of ways and lead to the deepest of loss. I would have it no other way.

"Serpitus came back the next day, and I would say was, surprised, that I was still alive. I had passed his first of many tests. Most do not. As the months turned to years my tether slacked. I was eventually able to leave the manor, then the country, then roam freely out on missions for him. While I traveled I have always carried this dagger with me, for two reasons. The first is so that the next time I see Serpitus I can kill him with it. The second is to remind myself that everyone has a choice in life. Our actions are our own. I chose to survive. I chose to do what I do. My life is mine and mine alone."

Joaquin slid the dagger back into his belt and folded his arms. "That is my story, that is how I came to be so damnably cursed."

Katherine blinked away her own tears. "I'm so sorry. I didn't know."

Joaquin's face was stone. "You still don't know the worst of it. I have lived for over 900 years, and due to my curse can never truly love again. To be a vampire is to be a creature who runs on pure instinct, pure adrenaline. Every moment of every day I must restrain my deepest nature, my urge to kill, to feed. And love, physical love with another unlocks. It opens the heart and opens the mind. And in that act of complete surrender, in that act of making love I am doomed to lose control.

"After Elena died and I wandered the world for a time under Serpitus's bidding, I eventually found another woman. Another who touched my heart in a way I had not felt for a long time. I felt hope. Liliana. She had raven's hair and a smile that made me forget my name. And I killed her."

"No." Katherine shook her head in horror.

"Yes." Joaquin sighed. "I loved her, and I destroyed her. She died in my arms after I was satisfied, after I bit her and watched my toxins steel her life away. That was my second worst night on this earth, cradling her pale body, reviling in the sweetness of my kill and shouting out in bitter agony over what I had done.

"A man who cannot control himself is just a beast.

"There were three others throughout the years, three other women whom I have killed out of loving too deeply. Each time I thought I could control it. I was wrong. Each deserved better. Each one I told myself would be the last. Yet, you can only deny Fate for so long."

"And that is why you pushed me away last night?"

Joaquin nodded slowly. "Yes. It was not so hard last night, not yet, to say no to you. But I feel… I know it will become impossible with you too soon. There is this pull I feel towards you, Katherine. Magnetic. You are amazing, truly. Your mind, your thoughts, your presence, your whole being. And I refuse to let something this beautiful end in tragedy. It's better I remain at arm's length then do something I will regret."

"I understand." She had no idea what he was going through. "It's alright."

Nothing was alright.

Joaquin sighed, "I have lived a long life. I have done many good things in my life, and I have done many, many evil things. I apologize a thousand times for my trespass with your daughter."

Katherine unconsciously stiffened. "What would you have tried to do with her if she would have been a match?"

"Blood, every person's blood is unique. When a vampire, when I consume human blood, I am supercharged for a time. Heightened reflexes, strength, a greater depth of sight, sometimes flight, shape shifting, sometimes more. My abilities depend on the type of blood consumed. Some people have exquisite blood. Patrick was one of them. A bit of his blood and I could lift a car without pause. I could punch through a wall. I could take a bullet to my chest and feel no pain."

"Is that why Waya killed him?" Katherine asked, "Because he learned he was valuable to you? He wanted to hurt you?"

"No. Serpitus killed Patrick."

When Katherine did not think her world could be any more turned upside down, it flipped again.

Waya had been telling the truth about that too.

Joaquin continued, "After Waya sent me the box you delivered, the threat of what he knew sent Serpitus into a rage. He summoned Patrick, extracted as much information out of him as possible then drank straight from his veins. Killed him and gorged himself, flew straight towards where Waya should have been. Waya was not there. Serpitus was even more outraged at being thwarted that he thew his wrath at a rival faction, the Gypsies, destroying a vital piece of their operation. Petty, rash. But that is what Serpitus is.

"After he returned to his normal self, he demanded that I find a new source of this special blood now that Patrick was no longer an option. I obliged, and I doctored the test results. Your daughter is extraordinary, like her father. I couldn't have it, couldn't see her used and destroyed like so many others. She will not be used by Serpitus. You have my word."

Katherine didn't know what to say. "Thank you."

Joaquin nodded gravely. "My purposes for blood research are much different from Serpitus's. He wants to understand the differences that various strains provide in power, formulate the most potent elixirs we can and use them to destroy our rivals. I, instead, want to unlock the mysteries of my kind and find a way to reverse my curse. I want to become human once again, to love fully once again. Then, allow myself the rest I have denied myself for so long. I want to rest, to grow old, and finally? Die."

EIGHTEEN

"YOU WANT TO DIE?" Katherine was shocked by the frankness of his statement. "I don't want that at all. Can vampires not die?"

Joaquin waved away the comment. "No, we can die, just not naturally. Let me rephrase. I am tired. I wish to accomplish my life's goal then find rest once again as a normal human. Before that can happen, I need to see Serpitus suffer for the near millennium of pain he has caused me. I need to see justice served. I will stop at nothing for my ultimate revenge. Then, and only after that, I want to find a quiet place, find someone to enjoy my last days with, and age naturally."

"Do you think you will find a cure?"

"I do not know. I have been searching for close to six hundred years. I have looked in the heavens above and the depths of hell below. I have made deals with both sides, been betrayed by both sides. I am hopeful that we will find something through technology. There have been a few breakthroughs and many setbacks. However, if I am nothing else, I am patient."

"You said before… are you really six months out?" Part of herself hated herself for even suggesting the next question again, "Would Christina's blood really help you find it?"

Joaquin shook his head. "Maybe. Maybe not. That number was thrown out to let you know we are close. However, Dr. Haughman is always six months out. As for your daughter, we can find another donor. Our kingdom is always on the lookout for exceptional sources of blood."

"Kingdom? How many vampires are there?"

"A few hundred worldwide. Serpitus commands around a third. There are five other autonomous factions, a group in South America, one in

Europe, Africa, the Far East, and the Indies and Australia. New members make it through the change occasionally. Old members die. We are not the most numerous aberrations in the world."

Katherine was just getting her mind wrapped around vampires and mind readers being a thing. She broke into a cold sweat at the thought of there being more things out there.

"What other aberrations are there?"

"Oh, most you've heard of. The myths never truly die. Werewolves, clairvoyants, mages, green men, wise men, nymphs, zombies, necromancers controlling the zombies, warlocks, giants, dragons, succubus, the list goes on for a bit. Heaven prefers to enhance, make their legions strong, peerless, beautiful. Hell likes to corrupt and twist."

"Dragons? Are there dragons in Philly?"

Joaquin chuckled, "No, not here. Philly is controlled by three groups. I mentioned them to you earlier. Each of us is in loose agreement over the segments we have under our thumb."

"Yea, but when you mentioned them, I thought they were organizations of people, businesses, not cults of monsters."

"We are both. The vampires, Serpitus through myself and a few others control the local government, the police, basic services. We don't put our fingers on the scale, but we keep a feel for the pulse. It allows us to adjust as needed, if ever needed. The Golems hold sway over the businesses, the cash flows, and the goods and services. Then the Gypsies rule over the people, the marketing campaigns, the gangs, the religious organizations, aid organizations, food distribution. We, monsters, as you call us, squabble at times, but it's normally minor. That is, until Serpitus's unprovoked attack on the Gypsies shook this balance."

"And Waya?"

"He's a minor pawn trying to weasel his way in where he doesn't belong. A disrupter looking to upend our three-legged stool. An outsider. He has some leverage, so my job as of late has been to keep him distracted."

"Leverage? Over a pack of vampires?"

"The correct term is council. Council of vampires."

"Oh, I'm sorry. I'm not up on my vampire knowledge."

Joaquin smiled lightly, “Understandable. As for leverage, he does. Some of it is personal. The Spanish coins I had you return? He knows who I am. My history. He knows of Elena, knows of a great many things of my past. He could disrupt, quite a few of my threads, if he were to tug. I would greatly prefer he does not tug.”

“And you can’t just kill him?”

What was she suggesting? How could she ask such a thing?

“I might be able to, but then his minions would scatter. Become bugs eating away at everything. I either need to root out the whole nest, or I need to keep him at the table. Speaking of tables, you still have not disclosed what you two discussed.”

The shift in subject forced Katherine to grapple with an answer. “He was weird. Told some stories about his culture, tried to keep me guessing. At least that’s what I thought it was. I don’t know anymore.”

Katherine paused. Should she tell him? Would telling him eliminate her chances of ever seeing her father again? Why was she even considering helping Waya? Why did she want to help Joaquin?

“He wants me to lure you into a trap.”

“Oh?” Joaquin’s eyes glimmered, “What kind of trap?”

“He stole my paintings, said he was going to display them at a gala. He asked me to take you to see them. Keep you distracted.”

“I see. I would imagine that is when he plans to move.”

“Yes. He wants access to your, ley-line, thing.” She felt a bit silly saying it out loud.

Joaquin leaned back. “Ah, yes. He told you about that too.”

“He mentioned it. Said it had power, that there were different kinds. What is it?”

“Each ley-line is a tear in reality, remnants from the celestial conflict. I’ve heard they are created after the death of an angel or demon. Their corpses, though we can’t see, leave impressions on the world, places and objects of power.”

“And you have one of these below the basilica?”

“Yes. From our best information, there are five ley-lines in Philly. The golems control two, both created during the conflicts which birthed our nation. The Gypsies hold a recent one, created as a result of the M.O.V.E.

bombings. It was a period of unrest for the city, another moment of conflict in which Serpitus overextended himself. He wanted the Gypsies out, said they had no place here. Instead, he created for them the most impressive of footholds. We cannot repeat this mistake with Waya."

"And you and your boss have the other two?"

"Yes."

"The one under the Basilica and another?"

"Another." Joaquin did not say more.

Katherine moved on, "For the one under the Basilica, he said he has the key for it, to unlock it."

Joaquin nodded, "Yes, that is his greatest piece of leverage."

"Is it like he described? A treasure chest of power? You have it but you can't use it?"

"It is. Some ley-lines are dormant until they are activated. Spiritual beings, they do not think like us, their world and their interactions within it are as foreign to a human as a human's ways are to a bacterium. With our ley-line, there was a riddle given by the fallen angel or demon, a sacrifice that must be offered for its power to be claimed. We have spent untold amounts of effort to figure it out, without success. If Waya thinks he has the solution, we have a problem."

Katherine thought back to the box, "The picture, and the poem on the back."

"Correct."

"Couldn't he unlock it for you? You two share whatever's inside?"

Joaquin looked hard at Katherine and her question. "We don't like to share." His smile quickly returned, "Sharing also seems impossible. '*Only the one who offers a suitable sacrifice shall claim my reward.*' We don't trust him, and he does not trust us. We don't know what the key is, and he does not have access to our ley-line. Stalemate. If he has declared he is going to move against us, we can use it to our advantage. Lure out the key."

"Joaquin," Max moved over to the two of them. "We're about an hour out."

"Thank you Max."

"Is Max," Katherine looked at Max, "are you a vampire too?"

"I am not." He smiled slightly then returned to his seat.

Joaquin took out his phone. "I offered it to him, the chance to let him join our council. He's pondering the options. There's a lot to be said for remaining human."

"I love my wife." Max commented, turning towards the two of them. "And my kids. The upside isn't worth the risks."

"And I stand by you fully, good friend." Joaquin turned back to Katherine. "We have one more problem to work through."

Katherine suddenly tensed, feeling very small under his gaze. "Um… what kind of problem?"

"With you now knowing more than most, you have become an asset. A target. While you are under my protection, I'm sure our trip has not gone unnoticed. I am certain others will contact you."

"Others?"

"The other factions in the city, the Golems or the Gypsies. Or both. I will keep you safe, but I cannot keep you isolated."

"Why would they want to talk to me? I still don't know anything, not really."

"Leverage, each of us is always looking for leverage. When a new player joins the fold of knowledge, no matter how minor, each faction will try to get their claws into you."

"Is my family in danger?" Katherine tensed again. What did she keep getting herself into?

"Not anymore than usual. You currently aren't worth the mess to clean up."

"Geez, thanks."

"No disrespect, a simple truth. However, more than ever I need you to trust me."

Katherine was not sure how to respond. "I'm sorry, but this is a lot to take in."

Nothing changed with Joaquin's face, but he looked disappointed. "I understand. Think of it as seeing the world a little bit more clearly. What else did Waya say? Did he offer you anything to help him? You haven't mentioned anything about your father. I'll assume he wasn't there?"

Katherine stood up and moved over to the bar, "My father wasn't there, no." Why did she want to keep secret the absurd reward Waya promised her? “He lied to me about him, told me it was the only way I would come talk to him. Nothing else.”

Joaquin’s face shifted again, “I see.”

Katherine filled the silence with the clinking of ice into her glass and the pouring out of the most expensive looking bottle.

“What should I plan to do about this gala?” She asked when she sat back down.

Joaquin folded his fingers, thinking. “For now, nothing. When you get the invitation, let me know where and when it is, and we’ll figure it out from there. I can feel things moving in the shadows, I simply can’t see the full picture yet. I’m hoping time will help. Are you sure he said nothing else? Any small detail might matter.”

Katherine took a large gulp, almost coughing at the intensity of the drink. She needed to get off this topic till she had more time to think. Waya had offered her a new life, a total restart with her father and mother. Joaquin? What did he offer? Katherine glanced back at Max, hoping he wouldn’t listen to her next question. He would.

“What about us?”

“What about us?” Joaquin repeated.

“Was all of that, last night, this morning, was all of this, fake? Can you even feel emotions as a vampire? Were you using me? Leading me on?”

Joaquin’s eyes softened. “Katherine, no. Not at all. I am not manipulating you. Last night was genuine. I feel everything, maybe even at a deeper level than you do. Not from my condition, but from my experiences in life. I know what feels right, what feels wrong. You, to me, feel right.”

Katherine blushed. “Thank you.”

“Are you free next Saturday?”

“Am I, free?”

“Yes,” Joaquin pulled out his phone again and looked at something. “We’re already at, Thursday for the week. I have many, many items to attend to when we return. Apologies. Then you have work again, which I should try not to disrupt further. Yes, dinner, next Saturday. My place. We can go over the details Waya sends over, if they arrive by then, and continue getting to know one another. Would you like that?”

"I, um," Should she want to spend more time with him? This had to change everything. Why did she want to say yes?

"Can I have a few days to think about it?"

Joaquin looked saddened but then nodded. "Yes. That would be fine. A few days to process. I understand."

"It's not that I don't want to!" She blurted out, "It's more, I don't know. Everything feels like it's upside down. I need a few days to reorient myself."

"No, I understand. No further explanations needed."

A bit of stale air settled between them. Katherine growled internally at herself for asking the question about their future then ruining the moment. She always did this! She took another large sip of her drink, then took another. At least it was smooth going down.

"What's your number?", She asked suddenly.

"My phone number?" Joaquin looked up from his phone and refocused on her.

"Yes. I have your receptionist's number, or your office number, but not yours. It's awkward going through your secretary to get a hold of you."

"Ah," he did something on his phone, then hers buzzed. "There you go."

"You had mine?" Then Katherine laughed. "Of course you had mine."

Joaquin shrugged shyly. "I hope you don't mind."

"Oh no," Katherine smirked then quieted down. "I understand."

Nineteen

Stepping off of the plane felt like exiting a dream. Joaquin did not join Katherine for the drive home, their farewells stiff and stunted. Like something massive had been slammed between them. Was it her? Was it him? What would happen next? What did she want to happen next? He was still the same charming man, but was he?

She had to remind herself… he wasn't a man at all.

The drive back to her house felt like deja-vu in reverse. Max remained silent and Katherine let her thoughts churn. She felt like every shadow had teeth. How did everyone not know about this stuff? How was the world infested by monsters and it had somehow remained secret? But then, were real monsters any worse than the political and corporate monsters who she had thought already ran the world? Would real monsters be better? At least they wouldn't be faking it.

Then came the doubts. Honestly, what proof did she have that Waya and Joaquin were telling the truth? A billionaire and businessman's word? That's it? She should have asked Joaquin for proof! Asked him to see his teeth, or something. That little bit of skin film could have been there for hundreds of reasons. He could have planned to use it to explain everything, a prop to validate his insane lies. Why would he lie about this? There had to be a saner reason to all of this than Joaquin being a vampire fighting against a mind reader to unlock some object that could rewrite the past, that the city was carved up and controlled by the legions of a spiritual war and no one knew.

Exiting the SUV and lugging her suitcase up the steps while Max drove away felt like being shipwrecked on an island that used to be her home.

Everything was now in tatters. And she was the only one who knew. The only one who saw how bad the storm had wrecked everything.

Katherine stepped inside to the usual scene for the early evening. Junior was on the floor making vrooming noises, his cars and trains scattered everywhere. A fantastical train track setup spanned across the coffee table, were supported by Duplos as they ran down to the floor, then went through a mountain range of clothes baskets and heaps of laundry before splitting off to a fully working depot. Jack happily hopped around the scene, a plane in his hands, zooming through the skies above. Christina bounced along, giggling at Jack's noises, who then made even louder noises to cause her to giggle more.

Upon seeing her mother, Christina's face brightened even more, "Ma'ma!'

Katherine was barely able to get her suitcase past the door swing and shut it without completely toppling a half-built village. "Hey baby girl!"

Iris looked up from her phone, lounging with half a foot on the couch. She sat up and smiled.

"Hey there, how was it?"

Katherine turned to Iris, "It was, good."

Oh no. What was her cover story? What could she tell Iris and Ethan? Why hadn't she planned for this before she stepped through the front door?

"Tell me about it! Did you wow the billionaire collector?"

"I, um. He wowed me."

"Oh yea? Details!"

"I, um. I have a gallery in three weeks. With my art."

Katherine cringed visibly after speaking, unsure if even that could be said. Was she going to it? It fit so perfectly with the lies she had been telling her brother and Iris... had Waya known this? Did he plan for her to say this to them, more spiderwebs to trap her, to force her to go? She hated feeling like a puppet!

"That's wonderful!" Iris frowned, "What's wrong? Is that not a good thing?"

"It is, it is. I'm just tired." Katherine sighed then stepped over the children's masterpiece and picked up Christina. "Oh! I missed you!"

Christina's toothy grin was the best thing ever.

"Ma'ma!"

"She did wonderful, as usual," Iris smiled, then looked at her sons and scowled. "Jack, don't even think about that. Your plane stays in the sky. It does not crash into the village! Think of the children!"

Katherine hugged her daughter, filled her nose with the smell of her, fresh diapers and lilac laundry detergent. Feeling Christina begin to squirm, she loosened her grip and flopped onto the couch next to Iris, Christina happily in her lap.

"I don't know Iris. I don't know how to feel."

"About the gallery? I thought this was why you went? I thought this was your dream!"

"It was, it is. I, I thought it would feel different. Be different. Maybe I'm still in shock. Yea. I'm still in shock."

"It's great news!" Iris gave Katherine a sideways hug, "Three weeks? Where at? Can we come?"

She absolutely wanted them to see her work this way! Was it safe?

"We'll see. I'll get details in a bit. They're still setting it up. And it's exclusive. Might not be able to get you tickets."

"Oooh, so exclusive that your brother and his wife can't even get through the door? That's fancy! What art are you going to show? All your old stuff was trashed, right? Have you made some more stuff since then?"

"Um, they found my old stuff actually. The investor. He was able to track it down after the restoration company tried to trash it. The things billionaires can do."

"That's even better news. It seems like things are finally taking a turn for the better!" Iris gave Katherine another hug then turned towards her warring sons. "Jack, don't wreck the track on purpose, I put a lot of time into it! Junior, don't you even think about hitting your brother again!"

Katherine sank deeper into the couch, wrapping her arms around her daughter. "It was crazy, the trip. I can't say much about it other than that. Not what I was expecting at all."

"Was that billionaire man with you, the one you keep talking about?"

"Yea, he was there. And I haven't talked about him, much."

Iris smirked, "And you impressed him, I'd take it? To get a gallery with your work? Good job!"

Katherine looked at her sister-in-law and scowled. "No, not like that! And he's not even the one who's promoting this gallery. It's some other collector. They're rivals? It's complicated."

"Oh, he brought you to a rival collector and you let the rival guy buy your work? That's shrewd! But hey, if the first guy won't take your advances, play the men off of each other! Good for business! Good for you!"

"I hate business." Katherine grumbled.

She also hated lying. And not being able to talk about what she really wanted to talk about. About vampires and dark secrets. About a man with blue eyes who she shouldn't trust but couldn't get out of her head. About how she wanted to run as fast as she could away from this mess and as fast as she could into Joaquin's arms, do anything for him. Yet, she had to keep reminding herself what he truly was. Joaquin hadn't specifically forbidden her from talking about it. But not to Iris. Or Ethan. No, no. Not them.

Iris continued on, not hearing any of Katherine's thoughts. "Sometimes we have to do the wrong thing to get the right results. Sometimes we need to suck up our pride and grovel a little bit. It sounds like you did what needed to be done."

"Sure." Katherine pouted, "And I don't like it."

Iris shrugged. "That's just how the world works sometimes."

"I hate how the world works."

"As do I. But, it's where we live." Iris stood up. "You look famished. You have anything downstairs?"

"Does ice cream count? Then no, not really. I need to go shopping again."

"How about you stay up here for dinner. I'll have Ethan pick up pizza. Give you some time to unwind and you can tell me and Ethan all about your trip. And we can have wine!"

Did she have the mental capacity to tell half-truths for an entire evening while drinking more? She was sure to get some wires crossed after two glasses. Did she care?

"Sure. That sounds great."

Iris's smile widened. "Yey! Simply making it to the end of the day is a good enough reason for wine! And we have more to celebrate today! You're getting your own gallery show, yey!"

The evening was normal. In every way. Once Ethan arrived with the pizza, they ate, played with the kids, and chatted lightly. Katherine was on the floor for most of it with Christina always within arm's reach. After a bit of whining, Ethan became a troll for the trains to drive away from, then laid down like a mountain that should not move. Daddy, stop talking! Mountains do not eat pizza! Katherine's brother did not apologize for his gruffness before the trip but enjoyed hearing about Katherine's upcoming opportunity. Iris tried her best to pull out all the juicy details from Katherine's time with Joaquin, feeling like she was hiding something, which she was, only to become more absurd with her guesses after the kids were shipped to bed and the wine disappeared. You had dinner together? And what else? You had separate rooms? Did he join you or did you join him? Is he a good kisser? I see you're blushing!

Before too long everyone was calling it a night, Ethan due to work in the morning, Iris from barely being able to stand, and Katherine from pure exhaustion.

No squad of SWAT team banged on their door, arresting Katherine for harboring state secrets.

No fires or floods were started, no neighborhood evacuations called to flush her out of the relative safety of her home and kidnap her again.

Work on Friday was normal. In every way. Robert was glad to have her back in the bakery, extra cheerful and a bit out of character, but not in a bad way. Lester was as solemn as usual, baking their bread and leaving for the weekend with nothing more than an extra nod and thin smile for Katherine. Shandra wanted to know all about her trip to Denver, going quiet when Katherine was less than forthcoming. She knew this was going to be the hardest person to keep in the dark, but Katherine still hadn't decided if withholding the truth would be better than sharing the insanity.

Shandra tried to spark up the conversation a few times with news from Miguel, the gangs, and their drama, but that only sent Katherine into a deeper spiral downwards. vampires, attacking gangs ruled by Gypsies. Shandra's brother in the middle of it with no clue about the truth. How was that fair? Thankfully, the Friday busyness of the bakery kept her required dodging to a minimum.

None of the customers pulled Katherine aside, asking her to sell her soul for a shred of mercy.

No apocalyptic news stories flashed across the media landscape, declaring hell had broken lose and demons walked among us.

The weekend was normal. In every way. Katherine took Christina to the park and only felt she needed to look behind her shoulder every two minutes. She painted some and let her thoughts bleed into the techno music flooding into her ears, her thoughts as jumbled as the beat. She went shopping for food, choosing a healthy balance of produce and frozen junk. She repaid her brother and Iris for their constant support by watching Jack and Junior for an evening while they had a night out. The kids and her built the largest tower ever then ate ice cream while watching Cars. She fed Oreo and to her surprise, the orange tabby, Lynx returned! Hey there guy, where have you been off to? Any exciting stories? She chatted with Mrs. Preston about how Jerry hadn't been seen for weeks, not since the city condemned his rowhome. Mr. Preston thought he had heard someone rummaging around in the place over the weekend, but there was no sign of entry. Maybe Jerry? Maybe ghosts?

Where ghosts real too?

Through it all, while talking to the moms at the playground, while trying to fall asleep, while laughing at Jack's attempt to draw a picture of his dad or Junior's even worse attempt, Katherine's fears ran in a thick cord throughout her mind, remaining in the back of her consciousness constantly. And nothing happened. She felt like a spring wound too tightly, waiting for the world to explode on her again.

And nothing happened.

She desperately wanted to call Joaquin but had no idea what to say. She wanted to trust him, but also hated the fact he was the cause of all of this. She wanted to see him again, to magically return to the evening in

Denver before she knew what she knew. She wanted to do that evening over, to be more understanding of his limitations. Maybe fall asleep in his arms instead. Cuddle up to his side. She wanted to do that evening over and wrench the secret out of him before the meeting with Waya. She wanted to ask Waya more questions. Was he the good guy? Was Joaquin the bad guy? Was it reversed? Was there a good side to any of this? Did she want to be part of any of this?

The next week began. Katherine went back to work. The intense feelings from her trip to Denver slowly began to fade. The shock from all this new information slowly began to fade. The fear that she would be jumped at any moment slowly began to fade.

She could live life like it was normal again!

Except for the building anticipation of seeing Joaquin again on Saturday. And the day of her art exhibit inching ever closer. And the nagging worry that even if she perfectly ignored it all, a hungry shadow with teeth would eventually catch up to her and try to devour her whole.

Her instincts were right. The shadow arrived on Wednesday.

Twenty

The evening air was warm. A heavy blanket of haze hung on the trees and over the houses, the summer's humidity thick and sticky. Katherine walked slowly down the sidewalk, not really seeing the neighborhood around her as her thoughts churned. As she turned the corner where Haken Brothers Produce detailed deals on sweet corn, blueberries, and chicken, a familiar face began to walk at her side.

Mr. Weiss smiled warmly at Katherine. "Katherine, is it? From Lavigne's Bakery, correct?"

Katherine shoved her thoughts into the back of her mind and returned to the present. "Yea. Hello Mr. Weiss."

She felt someone else behind them and turned. Two broad shouldered men in bowler hats and sunglasses followed three steps behind, their faces unreadable.

"They're with me. Unimportant. The perils of being an important man, you know."

"Sure." She stopped at a crosswalk, hoping Mr. Weiss would turn in a different direction. Unfortunately, when the light turned green, he followed along.

"This weather is really troubling. We should not be having these kinds of temperatures already. Never had these kinds of temperatures when I was growing up. The politicians think they understand more than the scientists and the common people suffer. The plight of history."

"Sure."

Katherine wasn't sure if she was supposed to be polite with a customer outside of work or if she was allowed to tell him she wasn't interested in his thoughts. Maybe if she simply remained with one-word answers he would get the hint.

"Do you know much about history? Katherine?"

"Some."

"It's a tragedy when the youngest generation does not appreciate history. An absolute tragedy. My family is one of history. I can trace my ancestors all the way back to the kings of old. I'm Jewish, you might have guessed. My father and mother were forced to flee Germany before World War II began. I was a baby. Now? Now I see the young and old alike forget so quickly why a little ignorance, hatred, and intolerance led to such an awful thing as war."

"Uh huh." On her list of the worst ten things to do after work, Katherine was sure being lectured by a customer was in her top seven, at least. As they passed by The Thimble, she decided to end, whatever this was, before he started up again. "Look, Mr. Weiss, I'm tired. And I don't hate anyone. I love hearing your stories about your wife and your sons, about all they're doing. At the bakery. I have a lot on my mind right now."

Mr. Weiss's face changed somehow, darkened. "Another trait of young people, disrespecting their elders. I see how you look and talk to Robert. You should treat him better."

"Okay, thank you for the advice Mr. Weiss." She turned towards a side street she usually didn't take hoping he wouldn't follow. "I'll see you tomorrow for your croissants?"

"No, I don't think so, not tomorrow."

"Okay then." She began walking away, only to have him continue.

"There was another reason World War II happened, one they don't talk about openly. It was sparked due to another, larger war. An eternal war between, spiritual forces."

Katherine slowed as her mind went into overdrive. She glanced at this short man with his two bodyguards in a whole new light.

"I don't know what you're talking about." Katherine quickened her pace, only for Mr. Weiss to catch up with more vigor than he had ever displayed before.

"I've heard the whispers. The key to a quite remarkable cache has been found. The treasure trove will be opened, soon. I've watched you for a while, waiting. I first wanted to see what kind of a person you are. You do not impress me."

"Oh, thanks."

Was it better for her to go home? Or maybe it was better for her to lead this man away from her home. No. She needed to stay in plain sight. Stay with other people. At the next intersection she turned towards the park.

Mr. Weiss and his strongmen followed, "There are two forces swirling around you, one more powerful than you can imagine, and one a fly who thinks of himself as an eagle. But, flies can bite and enrage larger animals to do rash things. I'd rather not have an enraged tiger tearing up my city. Wouldn't you agree?"

"Your city?" Maybe she could keep him talking, get him to give up something that Joaquin could use. Was he part of the Gypsies? Or the Golems? Or someone else? How many someone else's were there?

"Yes, partly. I share it with two others. Joaquin and his ilk. The others, unimportant to this current discussion. Katherine, where do you see yourself fitting in?"

She shook her head. "I don't."

Mr. Weiss almost looked fatherly, "That's no longer an option for you. We all have a role to play, our part in this larger game. You like chess, your father taught you how to play. We'll use that as an example. You see, I prefer to listen, let others move the pieces around the board. But sometimes I need to recruit more pawns."

Katherine's mind was flashing red lights, a siren blaring. Warning, warning, warning!

"Chess? You want me to play against me sometime?"

Mr. Weiss laughed, actually laughed.

"Oh, no my dear, no. Not at all. I want you under my thumb."

"I don't... I don't follow."

The elderly man stopped laughing instantly, "I'd like to know which way the wind will blow. To that end, I need ears to hear for me, eyes to see for me. Nothing needs to change! I will come into the bakery and buy my croissants. While I do, you will inform me of anything and everything you hear and see from our, other friends. Understood?"

Katherine stopped and put her hands on her hips, no longer playing dumb, "And why would I do that?"

"Because I can protect you. Because you are a small fish in a very, very big ocean filled with sharks. You need friends."

"I have friends."

"Oh, you do, do you? Let me enlighten you a bit. Vamp Industries is not a friend. He is using you. He will discard you at the drop of a hat. That is what their kind does. Has he not done so already once? His kind are vile, evil, manipulative, and wholly predictable. They run on instinct and rage. They are simple creatures really. In the end, they devour all."

Katherine frowned, "Joaquin is different."

Mr. Weiss's eyebrows shot up. "Oh, he is? Is he now. You trust him? Did you tell him everything? About what our little fly offered you in exchange for your cooperation? Did you tell him about the Medicine Man's offer to restore your family, your father, and your life to its, pristine condition?"

"How do you –"

He cut her off with a raised hand. "I will keep to my usual schedule. I will let you have a week to think over my proposition. I know you'll make the right choice."

And with that, Mr. Weiss turned and walked away, leaving Katherine standing in the middle of the sidewalk, unsure how she had survived.

Katherine nearly dropped her phone when it began to ring.

She answered it. "Joaquin?"

"Hello Katherine, it's good to hear from you."

She had called him twenty minutes ago, had been pacing around the park for twenty minutes. Panicking. Her heart was racing. She should have been home by now but couldn't function in the state she was in.

"Joaquin! Someone came. He wants me to work for him, pass him along information. What do I do? Do I start packing? Where do I stay? Do I hide out for a while? Will Christina be safe?"

"Slow down, who came? What happened?"

"This older man, Mr. Weiss. He's been buying bread from the bakery for a few months. He caught me on my walk home and just went off. Started telling me things he shouldn't know about. How does he know I like to play chess?"

"Katherine, what did he look like?"

"Older, short, white hair, Jewish. Had these two bodyguards behind him."

"Okay, That's good. They don't like to get their hands dirty. He's harmless."

"Well, he didn't feel harmless! And that felt dirty to me! Who is he? Who does he work for?"

"He's part of the Golems. Businessmen. All talk, deals. Did he offer you anything? Did you take any money from him?"

"No! He wanted me to be his pawn. What is going on?"

"Exactly what I told you would happen, happened. Another faction has contacted you. This was expected."

"He didn't contact me. He tried to recruit me. He knows about you. He knows about Waya! What do I do? Do I need to leave the city?"

"No. You're safe."

"I don't feel safe!"

"You are."

Katherine continued pacing, kids playing happily in the background, directly mocking her anxiety. "That was not okay!"

"You're fine. Katherine, breathe. The Golems made themselves known to you. They told you what they want. The next time they will give you their price. You keep me informed and we'll take care of it."

"This isn't okay!" Katherine whispered with all her might into the phone. "I don't want this!"

"I know. And I'm sorry, but this is what it is. As I warned you they're feeling you out. That's all."

"I don't want to be felt out! I want to have a normal life again!"

"What is normal? My life is extraordinary, and normal at the same time. Each person lives their own unique experience, and we all share in this bond of humanity together."

"I don't want your philosophical mush right now! What do I do?"

"Are you home?"

"No."

"Then go home. Be with Christina. Relax. You did exactly as you were supposed to do. You listened. You contacted me. I will handle it from here."

Katherine wanted to throw her phone at him. "I don't believe you."

Joaquin paused. "Say that again?"

"I don't trust you yet."

Another pause, "Okay. Katherine, I hear you. How do we get there?"

"Prove to me everything you're telling me is true."

"It is."

She screamed in frustration. A few nearby parents looked at her oddly then politely turned their conversations in other directions.

"I have no proof! Waya talked a lot of words, no proof. You could be lying about this whole thing for the fun of it. Ooooo, I'm Mr. 900-year-old man. Ooooo, I'm so scary and brooding and of course I'm some monster that kills people. Mr. Weiss threatened me with his two thugs blocking off my escape but looks like your ordinary grandpa. Did you pay him to say those things? Next are you going to tell me he's really a merman? Show me little flaps of skin that I'm supposed to believe are gills? I have no proof with any of this! I still don't know that you all aren't playing tricks with my mind!"

Joaquin paused again. "What do you need?"

"I need proof!"

"What kind?"

"I don't know! Something that is real. Something that isn't your word against how I know life really works. Show me what it means to be a vampire! Bring me to your boss, he can turn into a bat, right? Have him transform! Fly around! Do something I can see!"

The pause this time was long enough for Katherine to think the call was dropped. "Hello?"

"Are you free tonight?" Joaquin finally responded.

"I can be."

Her heart began to race even faster at the thought of seeing him again so soon. Did she really just suggest they go meet with the man who murdered Joaquin's wife? What was she thinking suggesting that!

"Max will pick you up at nine."

"And where are we going? To see your boss? I still don't much like your surprise late-night excursions."

"No. I'm going to take you to church."

The Cathedral Basilica of Saints Peter and Paul was a highly impressive building. When Katherine arrived at night it was all lit up, its stone columns, facades, and statues highlighted to radiate their splendor. Even from a distance she had to look up to see it all, its architecture designed specifically to make her look up towards the heavens. And standing silently on the steps was a supposed vampire, a creature of hell. Joaquin. She could already feel her breath quickening at the sight of him. Why did he make her feel this way? Even after all that he had told her? Was she the heretic or was he? Or were they both?

"Katherine, welcome." Joaquin smiled lightly and stepped towards her. "How have you been?"

She steeled herself. He would not get to her. Not tonight. "Honestly, a mess. Thanks to you."

"That is expected with what I forced you to process. And I'm glad you still do not believe me at my word alone."

Katherine glared at him, "Oh, you're glad I'm yelling at you? You're glad I'm forcing you to back up your wild claims?"

"I am. Those who believe quickly are easily manipulated. Those who believe after careful consideration are much more unshakable."

"I'm happy I could please you then." She hmphed. "What are you here to show me to 'make me believe'?"

"A cannon."

Katherine paused, then laughed. "A cannon? Is that some kind of religious book? Or like, a literal boom boom cannon?

"The boom boom kind."

"You brought me here, to show me a hunk of metal... and you think that's going to convince me? Don't tell me your magical ley-line is a cannon."

"It is."

"Of course it is."

Of course he oozed nothing but a confidence that made her feel at ease. Why did he have to be so good at this?

"Fine." She crossed her arms, resisting his pull. "Lead the way."

Joaquin held the front doors to the church open for Katherine. She stepped in and did her best not to stare. The interior was gorgeous, with a high vaulted ceiling, hundreds of pews flanked by columns, resting on a marble checkered floor of dark green and light beige. The copper dome she had seen on the outside of the church was settled over the focal point of the room, the negative space haloing where the priest would address the crowd. Chandeliers hung from the ceiling, their low light giving the whole space a presence of peace, holiness, and grandeur.

"You sure you own this?" Katherine whispered over to Joaquin as they stepped down the center aisle, their footsteps ringing into the air.

"Yes."

"I don't know, that doesn't seem right for some reason."

"Don't think of it as ownership, more as stewardship. We keep artifacts such as this cathedral in pristine condition, so that all can enjoy."

"And so that you can sell trinkets, make back your investment, eh?"

Joaquin looked where she was pointing, towards the gift shop. "No. That place makes little to no profit. It's there to help the people unburden their souls."

Katherine crossed her arms again, "How?"

"People often feel burdened by guilt, by shame, by remorse. Sometimes a free gift, stepping into a place like this, a kind word from a priest is enough. Sometimes they aren't. The gift shop gives the public an opportunity to buy something small, a way they can purchase their own forgiveness."

"Is everything in life so deep to you? Even a simple gift shop has to have some higher meaning? Some hidden purpose? Maybe if I buy the right things in the right order angels will sing in heaven for me too?"

Joaquin frowned. "I seem to be annoying you."

"No," She shook her head, feeling on edge. Frayed.

This wasn't his fault.

This was all his fault.

"No, I just. Forget it. Your magical cannon that is going to make me believe, it's in the catacombs below, right? Which way?"

"This way. And for clarity, the ley-line is not the cannon, per say. It is centered around the cannon."

"Sure, whatever. I'll take your word for it."

Joaquin quieted, accepting her mood, "You'll understand when you see. This way."

At the front of the nave, Joaquin turned towards the left and entered through a side door. This went into a chapel, smaller than the main cathedral, but still impressive in size. Joaquin moved to the front, passed through a series of doors which eventually led to a narrow set of stairs going down. They rapidly left the airiness of the holy spaces above for the church's cramped basement below.

After a few dozen steps and two turns, Joaquin and Katherine came to an unassuming door. Joaquin punched in a code at the door's key panel, the keypad well hidden within the side wall. The door clicked and they stepped through. This led them to a spiral staircase made of industrial metal, twisting further into the earth. After a dozen rotations, they stepped in front of another door, this one similar to the massive metal one Katherine had passed through in Denver. Joaquin swiped a card at this door, entered another code, and placed his hand on a pad. The door hissed and swung open.

On the other side of the door stood two men, flanking yet another door. The men were dressed in all black and carried a large array of weaponry on their persons, the largest of which was a rifle strapped to their backs. Joaquin nodded to them both in turn and moved through the otherwise bare room.

The two men barely acknowledged their presence. It was creepy. Katherine waited till they were through the next door, this one made of an odd metal similar to gold, before looking back. "Who were they?"

"Brothers. Another fact about vampires, we don't need to eat, or sleep. These two are newer within our ranks and are tasked as part of a group which guards the ley-line. It's a thankless job, but one in which must be done."

"They just stand there? All day long?"

Joaquin nodded, "Yes. It helps them learn that time matters little to a vampire. After enough two-week rotations down here, life begins to feel like a very long, single day."

"Two weeks? Just standing in that room?"

"Yes. It's peaceful. They have the company of each other, they have their thoughts, and they have their job. What more could you want?"

"I don't know, excitement?"

Joaquin laughed. "Life is not exciting, not usually. Everyone's lives are filled with hours, days of nothing. Yours, for instance, standing at a counter, filling orders for customers, sleeping, eating, being. We choose to remember the good parts. The rest of our time, merely bridges between memories."

"I guess."

"Constant excitement can wear on the soul. Everyone needs a break, space, time to process, to think. Why not while standing deep within the earth, protecting one of our most valuable assets? Here we are."

Through one more door, this one solid glass, Joaquin led Katherine into a large, round room. The ceiling was domed, carved straight out of the bedrock. In the center of the room was a round pedestal, and on the pedestal sat a cannon.

"This, is our ley-line."

Katherine was less than impressed, "A cannon. A literal cannon. In some special room in the ground under a church. And you think this is what is going to convince me you're telling the truth about everything? Or did you think adding in the two guys outside of this room and that story about them standing there for two weeks would push me over the edge? Come on."

"Katherine. This cannon is a door into the celestial realm, a closed door, for now, but one which holds great power. Power beyond your comprehension."

"Yes, it can rewrite history, change everything. You're beginning to sound like Waya. He was crazy."

"He was not. Touch it."

She looked at Joaquin sideways, "Touch it?"

"Touch it. This is why we are here. One touch will convince you I am telling the truth. There are very few places in the world like this, very few places where you will feel what you are about to feel. While I could show you my power, show you the shape of a vampire and my strength, I prefer for you to believe through these feelings."

Katherine looked from Joaquin to the cannon and swallowed. Well, she had gone this far already, why not only a few steps more?

When her fingers lightly brushed the cannon's surface, her world exploded.

She was no longer Katherine Mason. She was somewhere else, someone else. She was in the heart of a riot. Men pushed into her on all sides, sweaty, swearing, waiving torches and muskets, yelling over and over how they didn't want their kind here. She pushed herself through the sea of bodies and found herself in the front of the mob, staring straight at a church. It wasn't the cathedral they had left but a smaller church, somewhere else. And in front of the church a few dozen men hid behind makeshift barricades, their muskets aimed at the crowd. Aimed at her.

She could feel the hatred for these men in her veins. They were protecting the Irish, those Catholic bastards! They were protecting the enemy. They did not belong here. They had no place here. They were destroying her great country. They would ruin Philadelphia.

They had to die.

She swore then threw her brick at the men, nearly hit one in the head. She shouted again with the men around her, felt the mob rush forward. The defenders of the church pushed back. Guns went off.

It was utter pandemonium.

She felt more alive than ever before in her entire life.

As she dove for cover and found a nearby barrel to hide behind as the musket fire peppered into the crowd, someone behind her yelled from the top of a building, or the top of a wall. He stood in front of a cannon, shouted how he would make these potato farmers pay! He put a torch to the cannon's bunt and thunder exploded into existence. Katherine threw her hands in front of her face as the barricade before her shattered and men screamed. She could see blood in the street, from both sides.

Katherine scampered out from behind her cover, charged the enemy, and bellowed out in victory!

A voice, disconnected from the violence sang sorrowfully in Katherine's ears.

'Innocent blood has been spilt.
Innocent blood must be spilt again.
Through the union of these bitter enemies
will my attention be stirred.
Only the one who offers a suitable
sacrifice shall claim my reward.'

And then she was Katherine again.

She took her shaky finger off of the cannon and stumbled backwards, Joaquin catching her in his arms.

"Do you believe me now?"

"I…" Katherine's head was swimming.

"Careful now," He spoke softly, "It can be disorienting."

Katherine pushed away from him and took a few uneasy steps. "What was that?"

"That, is our ley-line." Joaquin's eyes suddenly shone with a glow she had not seen from him before. "Power beyond understanding. All we have to do is unlock it."

"And Waya has the key."

"By solving the riddle…" Something had changed in Katherine's mind. From seeing the vision. She now understood a bit more of their zeal to unlock this treasure.

"Has Waya been here before?"

"No. I presume his angels told him about it. The war between heaven and hell is a conundrum, even to a veteran soldier like me. The spirits within both camps withhold information or action for generations then appear and strike decisively. They snap, are disinterested over massive problems then flare up, become jealous and petty from the slightest offense. Right now? I can feel the attention of both sides directed towards our ley-line. All we can do is seize the opportunity."

"Well, if Waya was able to solve this thing, how hard could it be? What have you tried?"

"Katherine. It's not that easy. Not in the slightest. It's a bit like, celestial beings see the world awash in color where we humans see the world only in numbers. Can you describe a color with numbers? You can assign it a place, but you do not get its feeling, its beauty, it's pure essence. Unless we think like the being who perished here, we cannot understand what it wants.

"Let me be clear, we have tried everything, everything to unlock this ley-line. We have built foundations to honor those lost in that riot. We have scheduled meetings and remembrances for the families, the victims, and the accused. We have laid to rest and honored every unmarked grave we have found within the city. Nothing has worked. We have spilt blood here, so much blood."

Katherine could feel what was about to be said. She knew in her bones what Joaquin was about to tell her and suddenly felt frozen in place, unable to do anything but listen.

"So many guilty men and women, killed here. So many innocent men and women, slaughtered here. We knew Patrick was a descendant of one of the defenders lost during the riot, Corporal Troutman. We knew he worked for Waya. We knew Waya thought he had a key. Serpitus was rash.

"This is the room where Patrick died."

"No." Katherine gasped.

Joaquin nodded sadly. "Sacrifice. Serpitus had me bring Patrick down here and tried to use his life to unlock this ley-line. I told him it wouldn't work, that Patrick was not the right kind of a sacrifice, but Serpitus would not listen.

"I am truly sorry. After Serpitus drank his fill, he used the rest of Patrick's life to paint this cannon red. And nothing happened. Christina's father died for nothing."

Katherine felt the floor meet her knees, felt her head fall into her hands. It was all too much. Too much.

She sobbed bitterly until Joaquin gently pulled her up and away from that awful place.

Part 3

In life there are an infinite number of possibilities for the future,

choices that can be made,
paths that may be taken,
words that could be said.

However, it is not in the abundance of options where life holds its awe.

The true beauty of life is found within the brief sparkle of each and every moment when possibility becomes reality,

action committed,
conviction followed through,
decision reached.

That is precisely where the wonder and mystery of the human spirit blooms.

TWENTY-ONE

KATHERINE SPENT EVERY POSSIBLE moment during the next two days on her phone, researching.

She started with Vamp Industries.

From what she could find, Vamp Industries had begun as a few different companies. One piece began in the 1850s in Germany by Karlos Von Brun after the German revolution. Schmerzfrei, a pharmaceutical company. Within a decade their products were highly regarded and by World War I, used by almost every hospital in the western hemisphere. Another founding company was created in 1883 in Brazil, a mining operation that also had some roots in coffee and sugar. Massive plantations, which quickly became unprofitable after slavery was abolished in 1888 but were turned around after some shrewd dealings with the royal government. The details were glossed over by the official company press release, but Katherine found from another source that the coerced labor had been prisoners. There was also a textile business established in Boston in the 1820s by Ulysses Smith. He led the transition of the dispirited regional market with a number of factories during the industrial revolution, boomed, then shrank as workers unionized, then boomed again.

Then, in the 1930s, these disparate pieces, along with a few dozen other companies began to be bought up by the conglomerate named Vamp Industries. The founder, Regulus Serpitus the VII was a mastermind of business, or so their website stated, and found synergies between industries where others saw incompatible differences. Today his company was on the S&P 500, just above GE and Honeywell in market value.

Katherine stared at the photos she found of Serpitus. He looked to be a hard man, with black peppered hair and a solid chin. She compared both images of the founding Serpitus in a few grainy shots to his supposed son and grandson. They looked identical. That wasn't hard evidence, it happened sometimes with families, fathers and sons looking like twins at similar ages. If it wasn't for what she knew, she would have left it at that. It was the gap in photo evidence that truly irked her detective side. There seemed to be less and less photos taken in the 60's, then a huge lack of anything on him till his death was mentioned in 2003. The only recent depiction of the founding Serpitus after the 60's was a painting hanging in their corporate lobby, him with white hair and wrinkles, what Serpitus could have looked like in 50 years if he had aged. When his 'son' took over, Regulus Serpitus the VIII, he appeared everywhere from 1983 till about 1995. Then he too disappeared from the photo record. That version of Serpitus was now retired, supposably, living in the countryside and Serpitus the IX currently held the corporate reigns.

She shifted her attention to Joaquin. He was the XIV, currently. Maybe he had started the patronymic lineage and Serpitus had copied it?

The first story Joaquin had provided Katherine about his past was plastered around the internet, him going to boarding school while his parents played, his father becoming a recluse but still remaining on the board, doing his duties from the shadows. She found no family photos when he was younger. According to the internet, there had been an unfortunate fire at the family's home in Brooklyn which had destroyed all paper records.

It all made sense. It was all very believable. Except, she knew where to pry and saw all the cracks.

Joaquin wasn't on any of the social media platforms, nor did he have much written about him outside of his corporate websites. He was mentioned in quite a few articles, quoted in hundreds of news stories, all business, and beyond that, was an online ghost. His raw genealogy was where things really fell apart. It was straight as an arrow, Joaquin Morales's up the tree until the first one recorded in the mid-1700s, with no father to him in records. Each Joaquin was married once, each couple having only one son. The imaginary wife always died young, sometimes due to the birth, sometimes a few years later. For eight recorded generations. That was a bit uninventive, Joaquin. You could have come up with something better! Each 'wife' had spotty trees of their own, families that weren't connected to any others in the databases and records incomplete as to their places of burial. Even the current version of his supposed mother's family disappeared when Katherine looked beyond her make-believe grandparents.

Either Joaquin was telling the absolute truth about him and Serpitus being vampires, or something else was going on. Both options left Katherine unsettled.

Extending out her net, Katherine had similar trouble researching Waya or Mr. Weiss. Waya was a respected leader among the Cherokee people, executive director for a thriving startup called Insight, business consulting. That had been their building in Denver. They had other buildings in Seattle, Boston, New York, Phoenix, Chicago, Los Angeles, Tampa, Prague, London, all headquartered in Charlotte. The company had been established in 2002 and had inroads with most major S&P 500 companies, including Vamp Industries. There was no mention of his private life on the internet. No kids, no family that she could find. Also, no social media. His family tree was complete and accounted for, all the way to before his people were forced off their land.

At least he was still human.

She found the most information on Mr. Weiss. He seemed to be the most normal, president emeritus for Liberty Bell Bank, partly retired after working there for forty years. One wife, three kids, five grandkids. She found a few dozen family photos posted on his own accounts, and thousands between his wife's and descendants. They looked happy. Vacations to Europe, laughter in the back yard, school drama, dating. Not the kind of grandfather she would expect to threaten single mothers in dark alleys. He had been telling the truth about his parents, or at least there was an article describing their journey out of Germany in the late '30s across the border with their young son, then their trip across the ocean to the beacon of hope, America. Mr. Weiss was a philanthropist, spoke at a considerable number of fundraising events and seemed to know everyone in the city, from the mayor to every major business owner, a few famous people and even one or two foreign royalty.

He was a very well-connected man.

Searches on vampires led her to all kinds of dark corners and forum threads, conspiracists, crazy people mostly. Any mention of golems sent her to stories about men made of clay, reanimated like Frankenstein. Folklore. Nothing recent. The Cherokee legends were fascinating, origin stories about the animals and the earth, the reason for this or that, but nothing about medicine men seeing the future. Gypsies sent her into a vast swath of areas, all of which led to nothing good, since she didn't even have a name to go with her searching. She tried Kaleem Truce, one of the names from the police's investigation and found nothing solid. There were a few who lived around the city but none that looked like an under-lord crime boss. Or an angelic messenger. Where the Gypsies a spawn of heaven or hell? Ley-lines were denounced as pseudoscience, with ideas from if you placed buildings in a certain way they would lead alien space craft to earth, to the ability to draw the earth's power away from its core.

Nothing but rumors and conjecture, insane speculators, and liars. Everyone could be trusted. Everyone told a different story. No one could be trusted.

Katherine still struggled to believe it all. Even with Joaquin and Waya telling her the same thing, even with Mr. Weiss all but confirming their story, even with her vision at the cannon. But really, how could any of this be true?

After two days of mulling and digging, Katherine decided she needed a second opinion.

Katherine sat cross-legged on her bed, Christina snoring softly in her pack-n-play. Shandra sat in the room's only chair, her mouth slightly open.

"I know, I know," Katherine waved her arms around as she finished spewing everything out, "I sound like a lunatic. I don't even believe myself. How could any of this be true?"

Shandra started slow, "Your amor, your billionaire, is a vampire."

"Yes."

"You met with some fortune teller in Denver, and Mr. Weiss leads some secret organization in the city?"

"Waya can supposedly see the future, or people's actions within the future, yes. And Mr. Weiss is part of this Golem organization. I don't know if he leads it or helps it out. They feel like the mob."

"Sure, sure, minor details. And based on what you pieced together from your monster boyfriend you think my brother's been following a gang of Gypsies as they fight against the vampires?"

Katherine nodded, "I think so. They're having a turf war or something, it all matches up."

"Should I be concerned for mi hermano? What superpowers do these Gypsies have?"

"I don't know. To either of those questions. Maybe?"

"Back to you, your ultimate question is you don't know who you should believe or follow. You want my advice. Do you follow the hot Spanish vampire who you can't stop thinking about, or the mind reading Native American who wants to bring your father back to life, or the Jewish Mobster who owns the city. Correct?"

"Yea, that's about right." Katherine's voice trailed off at the end, knowing she was even crazier than she knew she was. "I know, I know, It's insane. Sorry."

Shandra closed her eyes. Katherine braced for her best friend to laugh or agree that she was crazy. Tell Robert, tell Lester, tell even Ethan and Iris and everyone that she should be locked up. Instead, Shandra took a deep breath and asked a sensible question.

"What do you want to do?"

Katherine opened her mouth, ready to defend herself, then stopped. "Wait, you believe me?"

Shandra nodded. "Si. Should I not?"

"I…" Katherine shot across the bed and gave her friend a huge hug. "Thank you for believing me!"

"Hey, hey! I love you too!" Shandra patted Katherine on the back then pulled her gently away. "Look, my brother has been telling me crazy stories since I was twelve. He started it out as some cruel joke to scare his little sister. Killings, murders, things he's investigating that made no sense. Stuff they don't tell the public, stuff that doesn't make it on the news. This world is messed up. Insane. My brother can't sleep anymore, takes medication, goes to a therapist. This makes a lot more sense to me than believing humans are all sick in the head."

Katherine shook off some of the tension she had been holding onto for the past week.

"I still don't believe it all myself, not fully."

"Eh, details for later. For now, let's say it's true. What do you want to do?"

Katherine bit her lip. "I don't know. I want to help Joaquin. But I don't trust him, not fully. It's complicated. He's a bad guy, I can tell. I know he's done some really, really bad things, but I like him. But my feelings shouldn't matter. Not in this."

Shandra nodded. "Okay, but none of that's off brand for you. You always had a weak spot for those kinds of guys. Danger wrapped in mystery. What about Waya?"

"He was creepy, I felt like he could see through me."

"And do you want to help him?"

Katherine shook her head. "No. Maybe. I don't know. He says he can do these crazy things, things I really want. I want to see my dad again, I want out of this mess, this place in life where it feels everyone I love is either dead or hating me. It's too good to be true. But from what I can tell, he believes rewriting the past is as simple as a snap of his fingers, with my help, of course."

"Okay, what about Mr. Weiss? He seems nice and all?"

Katherine shook her head again. "No, he was creepy too, even before he dropped his mask. Like, he was that grandfather with a bad secret, you could feel all the wrong he had done, like a cloud around him, but you didn't know why you felt it. No, I don't want to help him."

"So, one man down, progress."

"I know." Katherine paused and thought. "I'm, conflicted. I don't want to help either of them. And I want what both of them are offering. Joaquin, he's, on the one hand, irresistible. He has this, this…"

Shandra smirked, "Attraction? You want him to have his way with you?"

Katherine blushed. "No. But yes."

"And the other side?"

"And on the other side, you're right. He's dangerous. He won't tell me everything. He thinks he knows everything. He is so confident, like he knows what I'm thinking. Like he can hear my thoughts. It's unnerving. Oh! Stupid men!"

"Right?" Shandra laughed, "Stupid men!"

Katherine laughed lightly with her friend, then quieted down. "I'm seeing him tomorrow."

"Oh?" Shandra smiled shyly. "You, have plans?"

Katherine glared, forcing her eyes to grow cold. "It's business. Nothing but business. Planning for our plan at Waya's art gallery. Planning to steal this key or something like that. I'm supposed to do everything Waya wants, so am I working for him? Why does Joaquin want me to play along? I feel a bit lost in webs I can't quite see and if I go the wrong way I'll step on a spider or something."

"What does Waya want you to do again?"

"Distract Joaquin at the gala. At ten. That's all."

Shandra's eyes glimmered. "Distract him, eh? Are you practicing, tomorrow night?"

Katherine threw a pillow at her best friend. "Stop that!"

Shandra's smile widened, feigning innocence, "Stop what?"

A knock came from the door upstairs. It was Ethan.

"Hey Katherine."

"Yea!" She yelled up at her brother.

"Something came for you."

"Can you bring it down?"

Ethan opened the door and descended, then extended out his hand with a long brown package affixed with a white envelope. "This came for you, from a courier."

Katherine took the bundle and pulled off the envelope. Inside was an invitation.

'Insight's Masked Gala, featuring the following rising artists.' The date was for Friday night, a week from today. Katherine's name was third on the list with ten others.

A week earlier than Waya had stated it would be. Katherine's heart raced.

A week away.

She ripped open the package. Inside was an asymmetrical black mask that would cover the wearer's eyes and left cheek, studded with hundreds of sequins. A dozen black feathers exploded from the top and black ribbon encircled it all. Katherine gasped at its delicate beauty.

She would need a black dress to match this. And shoes. And some jewelry. Was her artwork really being featured?

"What's that for?" Ethan asked, curious.

"My gala." Katherine whispered.

"Eeeek!" Shandra bounded off the bed and hugged Katherine, almost sending the mask flying. "I'm so happy for you!"

Ethan put his hand on her shoulder. "I am too."

Katherine stood between her best friend and her brother, unable to understand her own mix of emotions, and instead, took in the moment and enjoyed it to its fullest.

No matter the reason, she had made it.

Her dreams were coming true.

Twenty-two

"It's good to see you again, Ms. Mason." The receptionist to Joaquin's building smiled as Katherine stepped into the lobby. "Mr. Morales told us you would be returning."

Katherine smiled weakly in return. "Yes, um, same elevator as before?"

"Of course, this way."

As Katherine robotically followed the receptionist and entered Joaquin's private elevator, her mind continued to lurch about in a hundred directions. She had done this before, she had been here before, why was she making such a big deal about it? It was only dinner. Only a few hours to talk over the details for the gala that was less than a week away. Business.

Planning and plotting with a vampire, how to double-cross a man who could see the future.

A normal, everyday occurrence.

Gah! Why was her stomach still doing somersaults?

Joaquin was a creature of the night! Something strange and unknown, deadly. Vicious. Wonderful. His words, his mind. The way he smiled. No! No, she was there to focus on getting through this next week and helping him with his celestial war. A war in the streets of Philadelphia between mythical creatures. He was a twisted thing of hell, his words! She could not trust him. She shouldn't trust him. He had lied to her. He had assaulted her daughter, sort of. He drank blood! Which gave him powers! What did it really mean to be a vampire? 900 years old. What did he know? What had he lived through? He had to have so many stories, have seen so many things. And lovers, how many other women had he had? He was using her. No, she was helping him. This was her choice. She was strong, she was not at all enchanted by his deep blue eyes.

No. Not at all.

Why did he have to look at her like that all the time? It wasn't fair! Why did he have to talk like that all the time? That also wasn't fair! He had like 870 years on her, he was a much older man! They would never work out. Why did she want them to work out? They couldn't sleep together, he warned her. Why did she want to try anyway? He would kill her! Why did she keep thinking of him this way? He had money, power, everything. He had private jets, penthouses in the city, probably penthouses in multiple cities. Where else did he have a house? They could travel together, see the world together. He could tell her all of his stories, tell her the history of cathedrals and ruins in which he probably saw being built. They could walk down streets in Paris or Florence, hand in hand, him laughing, telling her about the king or queen he had met years ago, advised, tell her…

What was she doing? None of that would happen! She needed to snap out of this before –

The elevator doors opened, and she came face to face with Joaquin. He was wearing a dark blue suit tonight with a white shirt and black tie. He smiled lightly and extended out his hand.

"It's good to see you again, Katherine."

The blue from the suit made his eyes seem even deeper. Two pools that she could sink into and…

"Uh, huh." Katherine nodded and swallowed, stepping out of the elevator then almost tripping over herself. Joaquin caught her lightly in his arms.

"Are you alright?"

"I'm fine," Katherine pushed herself away from him, "Just fine."

She was not fine! She had it bad for this man! She couldn't even put together sentences anymore! He must think she was a total idiot!

Steadying herself on her high heels, Katherine turned slightly away from him and took in two deep breaths. Her vibrant orange dress showed off her shoulders and was cut much lower than she was used to wearing. She felt fully aware of how much she was showing tonight. It was a dress from before Iris was married and had her two boys. Something Katherine would never have worn before tonight, not for Patrick, not for anyone. Except Joaquin. She wanted him to see her in this. No, she needed to regain control. She needed to change the subject. She needed to start talking! She played with the double knotted silver necklace at her throat as she took one more breath and turned back towards Joaquin.

"I'm fine. Thank you. How are you?"

His smile grew, "Better now. Even though it's only been three days from last seeing your beauty, I say, that's far too long."

Katherine could feel the heat rising to her cheeks. She needed to get onto a safer subject! "Thank you. You, um, reading any interesting books?"

"Yes, in fact," he moved over to his couch and picked up a small book with two birds on the cover. "Almost finished 'This is How you Lose the Time War'. by Amal El-Mohtar and Max Gladstone."

"Oh, what's it about?"

"It's science fiction, fascinating, superbly written. It's about two combatants on opposite sides of a temporal war, writing letters to each other, taunting each other about how their side is going to win."

Yes, war was a much safer topic. "Nice. Who wins?"

"Not done yet."

"Right."

"But they fall in love."

"Oh?"

"These two enemies. From different worlds. They risk everything for love."

"Oh."

Even books weren't a safe subject with this man!

"Um, food?"

Joaquin's eyes tinkled, "Yes, food. That must be why you are so off. You're hungry."

Katherine nodded. "Yes. Famished."

"No other reason."

"Nope."

"Not thinking about betraying me or anything."

Katherine blinked, taken completely off guard. "Wait, what? Betray you?"

Joaquin nodded, folding his arms, his smile fading. "I understand. I can tell. You're going to join Waya's side. He promised you things I can't give you. Your father, your family. Fame through your art. Tell me the truth Katherine. I'd rather hear it from you directly then from the dagger you shove in my back."

Katherine felt lightheaded. She stepped over to the couch and sat down. "What are you talking about?"

Joaquin shook his head and remained standing. "You did not tell me about his offer when I asked. You were considering it. You've had some time to think. After Denver, after the Basilica. You've learned what I am, that I was part of Patrick's death. That I let it happen. You've now seen my true colors. You can't stand me."

"No! That's not it at all!"

"Is it not?" Joaquin opened his mouth to say something and instead stepped towards the windows and looked down on the city. The pause in conversation felt like a weight on Katherine's chest. She wanted to fill it in, to reassure him but did not know how.

Joaquin eventually continued, "This is why I don't do this, why I don't invite people in. Why I remain apart, alone. I seem to do nothing but hurt those I bring close to me. It's been almost a decade, a little over nine years since I last had dinner with someone, like the one we had in Denver. With someone I cared about. This time I thought, I thought maybe this time I could keep my secret hidden for a little while longer, enjoy your company, your presence for a little while longer before you learned. Before you hated me."

"I don't hate you." Katherine responded quietly, looking down at her knees. Should she move over to him? Should she tell him how she still felt?

Joaquin turned around, anger clear on his face, "How could you not? I'm evil, I'm the villain in this story. Lying to you, using my wealth to impress you, sending you in with Waya alone then asking you to remain on my side. But I see it now. I see that I am a fool."

In a sudden burst of insanity, Katherine stood up and crossed the distance between them, turned him towards her, took his face in her hands, and kissed him. At first his eyes went wide, then he fell into the moment.

Katherine let it go on far longer than she had planned but eventually pried herself away then lightly shoved him back.

She playfully glared at him, "That's how I feel about you."

Joaquin blinked, touched his lips, and for the first time she saw him unsure of himself. “I don’t understand.”

Men!

“What’s there not to understand?”

“You still want me? Even after you know what I am?”

“Yes! Why would I not?”

“Because I’m a vampire.”

“Because you were attacked and changed into something against your will?”

“Because of all the things I’ve done, all the people I’ve killed. Because of Patrick.”

Katherine hesitated on that one. “Sure, that’s not great. But I’m not that great either. There’s a difference between letting it happen and holding the knife yourself. I’m sure you’ve never killed anyone personally that didn’t deserve it.”

“Yes, I have. Plenty of people. I told you, I cannot control myself sometimes.”

Katherine bit her lower lip, “Okay, still not great. I haven’t seen you lose it around me. You seem to have control over whatever you’re worried about.”

“I do, until I don’t. It’s…”, he balled his hands into fists then released them. “It’s hard to describe. Have you ever been addicted to something? A drug or an activity? Something that has this pull on you, something that gnaws at your very soul?”

Could she consider him her drug? “Possibly. It’s like that for you?”

Joaquin nodded, “I have this hunger in me, always, this passion to feast. When I first turned, oh, if you saw me then, I was a wretched man.”

He turned, pulled away from her, and started to pace.

“I became a monster, truly, ran on instinct alone. Did whatever I wanted to do. I had already lost Elena, had no other reason to live except for revenge. And that was a near impossible dream. So, I fed my desires. I killed. I hunted. I thrived! In those days I could only move around at night, could only be outside on cloudy days and then for only so long. Serpitus set me free for a few years, after he knew I was stable, let me do what I wanted. I roamed the world, alone, hiding, running, feasting, sobbing, and going right back to it. For years!"

Katherine knew she knew she had no idea what he had gone through. She quietly sat back down on the couch and listened.

"Even now I am constantly fighting the urge. We, the lab, Vamp Industries has made great strides, great progress in singling out the proteins, the threads which lead to the Hunger. I have a medication which allows me to pretend to be human. But I am not. Even now I can feel it there, in the back of my mind, in the back of my throat, my Hunger, trapped in a box, waiting, waiting to get out."

He turned towards Katherine.

"It'll be impossible with you. Impossible for me to be with you. I've tried everything. Arousal awakens the demon, awakens the Hunger, lets lose its cage. Even with my drugs. I can wrestle with it in the moment, but then I would never be there with you, never be present in those moments with you. I'd always be holding back. You'll tell me you don't care, you might even convince me that it doesn't hurt. It will. My limitations. They erode. They poison. They destroy. Then, one day, one day you'll either walk out on me or I won't be able to stop myself. I can't do that, I can't have that. I can't."

Katherine was up again, this time embracing him. "It's okay. I'm not going anywhere."

He pulled her away and looked at her, his eyes swimming with tears. "I told myself I wouldn't do this again, told myself that I wouldn't fall for you. Katherine, you are beautiful. I can see how much you care, how much you love your family, your daughter. You are so unique, so brilliant. I have fallen for you, and I don't know how to stop wanting to see you."

Katherine could feel tears behind her eyes too. "Then don't stop."

"I am going to hurt you."

"No, you won't."

"You don't know me."

"I know enough of you. You are a good man."

Joaquin laughed bitterly. "I am neither good, nor a man."

Katherine changed her approach. "You saved my daughter, saved Christina from your boss. From Serpitus. That was good."

"A minor penitence, a drop of kindness within an ocean of malice and pain."

"You care about me."

"I want you for my own selfish reasons."

"Maybe I want you just as much for those very same reasons."

Katherine could feel herself growing hot again. His arms were wrapped around her waist, hers around his neck. They were inches apart from kissing again. She leaned in slowly only to have him pull away, out of her embrace once again.

"I'm sorry Katherine, we can't."

In a flash of annoyance, she looked around the room for something to throw at him. Everything looked more expensive than her life savings. Or too dangerous. Or both. Would she hurt him if she threw that fist-sized geode at his head?

"How about you let me take care of myself," Katherine crossed her arms below her breasts, "Let me make my own decisions about what I can handle."

Joaquin sighed. "Fine. But I can't sleep with you."

Katherine's nostrils flared. "You think that's all I want?"

"The hotel?"

"I was tipsy! You were enchanting! You took me on your private jet and made me laugh! What did you expect!"

He smirked. "And now? Am I any less enchanting?"

Yes, that massive crystal rock looked highly appealing! "Now you're being obnoxious. Thinking all I want to do is rip my clothes off and jump on top of you."

"My mistake." Joaquin held a twinkle in his eyes. "But if you did later, and I'm distant, gone, you now know why. It would be much better if you let me focus on your pleasure. Let you benefit fully from my centuries of experience."

Katherine had to turn away so he couldn't see her blush scarlet. This man!

"New subject! I'm here to talk about Waya and this gala next week. How we're going to outsmart someone who can see the future. We're not going to talk about you and I. No more about you and I, okay?"

"Are you sure?"

"Yes!"

Why was he able to both infuriate her and make her have crazy thoughts like, did he have a bed? If he didn't sleep, why would he need one? There were all these windows in this room, would everyone outside be able to see them? Did she care? Were there servants around? Did she care?

"Yes!" She repeated, splashing cold water on her own mind, "Let's get through the gala, let's get your ley-line open and after all that, after that craziness settles down we can figure us out."

"Okay." Joaquin nodded, smiling still, "We are professional partners until afterwards. Deal."

With the door now closed on those tantalizing ideas, she wanted nothing more at that moment than for him to throw caution to the winds, for him to pick her up and wrap her tight within his passion and love.

Instead, he did as he promised and moved on.

"Has Waya made anymore contact, sent anything else beyond the invitation and mask?"

Once Shandra had left last night, Katherine had sent Joaquin pictures of what she had received. "No, no phone calls, no messengers passing me secret death notes, nothing but what you already saw."

"Good. I've been using my resources to investigate the venue. No obvious problems yet uncovered. Staff are paid professionals that know nothing of Waya's plans, or even his name. They do their job, they get paid, doesn't matter by whom. I'll keep digging."

"What if you don't find anything? Am I still going? Are you still joining me?"

Joaquin nodded. "Yes. Waya has been a headache for far too long. If he wants me to dance a little before he makes his move, so be it. I can't catch a rabbit hiding in its burrow. I need him to hop around a bit first."

"And you're not afraid he'll catch you instead of the other way around?"

"No, I am not. But I am planning for the possibility. He has his visions, his angelic overlords to help him navigate around my defenses. I have my network and my allies. We know he wants the ley-line. He knows we want the key."

Katherine's gaze darkened. "You think you can trick someone who can see the future?"

"Attempt to, yes."

"How? And don't you think he'll know we're doing exactly that?"

"He will."

Katherine shook her head. "I don't get it."

Joaquin smiled, "Sometimes the obvious path forward is the best. Sometimes trickery is required. Sometimes you do what you know must not be done to do what must be done. Life is full of possibilities and is always surprising me. Even after all this time. Waya may know the future, or thinks he does. He is also human. He can get distracted, overcompensate, grow proud, forget, make mistakes. He has limitations and runs on assumptions and imperfect information. Even his angels don't know everything, can only see one thing at a time."

"That's great and all but isn't very helpful. Let's say he traps us in the gala and launches a full-scale attack on the Basilica. What's your plan?"

"The ley-line is his blind spot."

Katherine blinked, "Which means?"

"Waya's powers are limited. He can see the paths of people, but not those of the angels or demons. He sees no future within the room with the cannon, is as blind to any futures entering and leaving the space around our ley-line as I am. All we need to do is make sure I am in that room with him, with the key."

"How do you know that? Did he tell you? And if he's already there with the key, why wouldn't he use it immediately?"

"He won't." Joaquin stated simply.

"That's a huge hope."

"This is a huge moment. If we can be the ones to unlock the ley-line, wrench the key from his hands, the benefits far outweigh the risks."

"And since you've already thought of everything, how were you thinking I would distract you?"

"I was going to leave that up to you."

"That's not helpful."

Joaquin raised his hands, "Then let's think like Waya. Why do you think he chose to put a beautiful woman in my path? One in which has my full attention whenever she walks into the room? Makes me think of nothing else but her, makes me want to take a few risks?"

Katherine could feel her lips curve upward, "You'd like that, wouldn't you?"

"I am sometimes nothing more than a simple man, with simple desires."

"Stop that!" Katherine turned away again, feeling her body react to his words. "I told you we weren't going to talk about that till afterwards."

Joaquin laughed lightly and walked towards the dining room, then turned back towards Katherine.

"I'm being a bit playful, enjoying my time with you. Nothing more. You can decide how you want to distract me. I'll follow your lead. Dinner?"

"Great. Maybe I'll tie you up, sit on you for a while."

His eyes twinkled. "There could be worse things."

How was he able to twist her words into ideas like this? Why did he have this power over her thoughts? Why did she want to tie him up now? This was not fair!

Thankfully, or unfortunately, Katherine could not decide which, the evening shifted away from the chaotic energies swirling between herself and Joaquin and became something more friendly, more intimate. Over their dinner of eggplant parmesan, fried brussels sprouts with almonds, and wine, they shared stories from their past. Katherine spoke about her father, about how her mother left them when she was younger and the hardship they endured. She talked about her siblings, Ethan and his family, Laura off on the west coast doing whatever her heart wanted. Joaquin listened, asked questions, made her feel heard.

Joaquin chose stories almost at random from his life. The first time he came to the new world as a stowaway on a ship in the Caribbean sometime in the 1500s. The smell of the hold, the concern he held over a storm they barely limped through. Then a different story about his travels through modern day Mongolia, then the same area but earlier in time, during the rule of the Quin dynasty in the 1700s. How he had angered some locals with his request to only travel at night, which led to an unfortunate situation with the village elder who called him out as an evil spirit but after some quick talking eventually led to a very good price on silk. He laughed over his mistakes in Africa on the Ivory Coast and fell somber over his failures in Great Britain during America's Revolutionary War.

"What is it like to have lived for so long?" Katherine asked later that evening as she reclined with him on the couch, a fire their only source of light. "To have so many memories? Do you still remember them all?"

"It's lonely." He sipped on his wine, staring off into the distance of the past, "and still a bit hard to grasp, even for me. To think I have lived nearly twenty times longer than I should, and yet still haven't seen all there is to see, haven't read all there is to read. I would have gone insane long ago if I didn't have my passion for knowledge. I have seen many of my brethren flare out after a few hundred years, come to that point where they are done. They eventually take too many risks, push themselves too hard and earn their rest."

"And you don't, because of books?"

"Books are part of it, yes. Books and humanity's infinite creativity, the great wonder of life. For the surprise of tomorrow, for spending years alone, content, then meeting someone new, someone like you. I am looking forward to this gala for another reason. I want to see your art. I'm sure it's spectacular."

"Stop that." She smiled then sighed.

Happy.

Joaquin stared into his wine, contemplating.

"And I remain… for my revenge. If everything goes as I hope, I will finally be able to see Serpitus fall."

Katherine sat up a bit, "I was meaning to ask you about that. He's your boss? He was the one who turned you into what you are and killed your wife. Why do you work for him?"

"It's… complicated. Part of it is a way to stay close to him. The other part is the way the legions of hell have organized their hierarchy. To them, our situation is normal. Everything is about power, control. No one trusts anyone, yet we work together. Serpitus expects me to stab him in the back at all times, literally, and I expect the same from him. Keeps us both sharp. As long as I am useful, I am spared. The day I become a weight instead of a tool I will be disposed of."

"Has he tried to kill you before?"

Joaquin suddenly laughed, “Oh yes, many times! Sometimes for no other reason but to test that I am still fit to live. We respect each other while we wage our deadly rivalry. In our kingdom, only those who fight to survive, survive.”

“And have you tried the same? To attack him directly?”

Joaquin nodded. “I have, and I’ve lost. Many times. I can’t currently.”

Katherine was surprised at this, “Why not?”

“Because I’m currently near equal his power. A direct assault is too much of a risk. We vampires are a petty lot, view a lackey usurping their master as valiant, but an equal? Killing Serpitus outright now would be too much against the council’s honor. If I was to destroy him without provocation, I would be branded as a traitor. Instead of one problem, I would have the whole swarm on my head. My life would be on borrowed time.”

“Does that matter? If you succeeded? I thought you wanted to die.”

“I do, but not from suicide. I want to live! I want to be normal again, to be a man again, to feel the fulness of life again, unburdened, to take life’s sweetness for myself and drink deeply of its pleasures.”

He drained the rest of his wine.

“Killing Serpitus, even if I could succeed today, it would be a hollow victory. His name would remain untarnished, his legacy to my clan magnified, and mine? Erased. No. I don’t simply want the man to die. I want him to suffer. I want him to know he lost, to know he’s weak, to know he’s nothing. I want him to become a curse to all those who exhume his very memory. The example of a man annihilated beyond comprehension.”

Katherine breathed in, her heart beating faster. “That’s intense.”

“It is.” Joaquin nodded, to himself, to her. “It is. I need him to step far enough out of line with the council, injure his reputation beyond repair. Then I can act. His unprovoked attack against the Gypsies was a good step but wasn’t near enough by itself. The blowback hasn’t materialized. It will, soon. That is why right now is the perfect time. While he is distracted with his war against the Gypsies, he has left me in charge of these… minor… tasks. Defeating the fly that is Waya. Once he realizes his mistake, once Serpitus learns I wield the power of the ley-line it will be too late.”

Katherine could feel his passion, his hate. “If this ley-line can really do so much, wouldn’t you want to use it for something more than defeating Serpitus? You could help millions of people, billions of people. End world hunger. Erase war forever.”

Joaquin suddenly stood up, moving over to the fire. Katherine could feel his anger at her suggestion. She joined him anyway.

“You know what I have learned over the last few centuries?” Joaquin spoke, slowly, quietly, “I have learned that humanity in general is a rotten bunch of people. Men? They are corrupt. Women? Shrewd, scandalous, seditious, broken. Wars happen, over and over and over. Men pick petty squabbles and burn everything to the ground. Women manipulate from the shadows and stab others in the back. You think they deserve saving?”

“It seems like the right thing.” Katherine touched his shoulder. It was stiff.

He scoffed. “Humanity does not need saving. Humanity is a plague upon this world. And I am worse. I am death to the plague, the unjust justiciar chosen to witness centuries of our species’ depravity. Do you know why I’m rich? No, its not because I have better ideas or even because I have good ideas. No. It’s because I have the one thing that other men do not have. Time. Compound interest. One of the most powerful forces in this world. A force balanced by the fatality of man. Sure, you can donate your fortune to your kids, but what if you didn’t have to? I didn’t have to. I took what little I had and I waited. I waited until that little bit grew. And grew. And grew. It grew so large that I could begin to draw from it, from that bit of wealth and live. And it continued to grow. I eventually stopped counting, stopped caring. And it still grew.

“That’s humanity. We will grow more and more corrupt, more and more insidious no matter what we do. I have come to understand this fully. Men like Waya, men like Mr. Weiss, they are humanity’s true form, their darkest desires. Power, hatred, control. Why save them? Death is the only way they’ll stop.”

Katherine did not know how to respond to any of what Joaquin was saying.

“Me? I am simple. I know I am forsaken. And I want a simple thing before death claims me too. I want justice.”

"Is killing Serpitus the only thing that will make you happy?" Katherine asked in a small voice.

"No." He looked at her, truly looked at her. She could see the pain in his eyes. "No, it will not. Revenge is bitter. But it is what I must do. It is my destiny. My life will be complete either when I die, or when he dies. And in order to do that, I need to open this ley-line."

In that moment, Katherine knew she had made her decision. This man was hurting, deserved so much more than life had given him. While she couldn't fix his past or erase the shadow from his heart, she could help him in this.

"And to do that," Katherine smiled grimly, "We need to beat Waya at his own game."

Joaquin nodded, his expression hard and fatalistic, "We will."

"Hey," Ethan looked up from his laptop as Katherine stepped through the front door. "How was your evening?"

"Hey," Katherine's mind was still swirling with thoughts of Joaquin. "It was great. A little confusing, but we're working through it."

"That's good to hear." Ethan looked back to his laptop. "Christina is sleeping downstairs. She went down easily tonight. Iris is down there with her. You'll probably find her asleep on your bed."

Katherine took off her heels and threw herself on the couch next to her brother. "Thanks for watching her again. Again and again. I know it's been a lot recently. I've been a lot in general."

Ethan shrugged. "It's understandable. This seems to be your big break. Your first art show next week, meeting with clients, directing the world to your whims. Least we can do to help."

Katherine punched Ethan in the arm lightly. "Have I ever told you how much I love you?"

"Officially? As in during therapy? No, I do not have those words written down in my notes."

"What about unofficially?"

“A few times.” Ethan closed his laptop and smiled at Katherine. “Tonight was that good, huh.”

“It was.” Katherine grabbed a nearby pillow and hugged it, “It was. I don’t know, I don’t know what I’m doing here. This guy, Joaquin, he shouldn’t care about me at all. He’s got everything! Yet he thinks I’m fascinating. Am I fascinating?”

“As your brother, in that way? Absolutely not. As your brother, in the other way? Absolutely.”

“I’m a mess.”

Ethan nodded. “You are. And that’s what makes you lovable. You’re honest. You care. You’re real. You don’t hide behind a mask pretending to be perfect. You are you. It doesn’t take much for someone to be attracted by that.”

“He also needs me.”

“For your art? Sure. Everyone needs everyone else for something. Co-operation is what builds community and trust.”

Katherine hugged the pillow tighter. “I don’t know how it will go.”

“The show? Everyone will love your art.”

“They will? I know you don’t love it. You always said it looked like someone threw up paint onto the canvas.”

Ethan laughed, “It does! And I think it’s great, I think it’s great because it’s you. All your thoughts, your emotions on a canvas. If the art critics don’t see that? They’re phonies.”

Katherine could feel her brother’s love shining through his words. “You’ve never told me this before. What happened to my stubborn, stuck-up brother?”

“He realized he was wrong? Little sister, you have talent. Unrefined, maybe, a bit strange, sure, but talent. Art doesn’t have to make sense. I don’t have to get it all the time. People don’t have to make sense. And take my word on that last one! I talk to all sorts of people for a living. We are a complicated nest of conflicted wants, desires, hopes, and longings. We value the wrong things too highly, don’t take care of ourselves, and even the best of us makes a grand mess of everything!”

“We are a plague on this world.” Katherine repeated Joaquin’s words, feeling down once again.

“I wouldn’t go that far.” Ethan frowned with her. “Sure, we are messy, but we also are wonderful. We care, we love. We support each other when things get hard. We all have a great capacity for good in us.”

Katherine looked at her brother sideways. “And when did you become the optimist?”

“You caught me at a good moment. My case logs are filed for the day, the house is quiet, and neither of my boys killed anyone this week.”

“And last week?”

“Oh, last week they tried to tie those two stray cats together by the tails! I swear, why do you feed them? That just makes them multiply and come by more often.”

Katherine smiled. “I like to help. Helping others makes me happy.”

“Then keep feeding them,” Ethan stood up, yawning. “If it makes you happy, keep doing it. It’s late. I’m going to get some sleep.”

Katherine stood up and suddenly wrapped her arms around her brother’s side, pulling him in close. “I love you, big brother.”

“Hey, I love you too little sister!” He juggled his laptop, set it down on the coffee table, then returned the hug. “Always.”

“You’ve done so much for me,” She began to sob in his shirt, “You’ve been here for me when everyone else disappeared. You took me in when Patrick left me and Christina on the streets. You are so, so good to me. I don’t deserve you.”

“And I would do it all over again.” Ethan patted her back. “I know I haven’t been the most supportive of you lately, stress. Not a good reason. I know I can do better. You’re succeeding despite my headwinds. I’m proud of you.”

“Headwinds? You’ve helped so much!” She squeezed him tight.

Ethan eventually pulled her away. “No matter what, I’m here for you. Okay?”

She wiped away tears. “Okay.”

“But right now, I need some sleep. I’m glad you enjoyed your evening. Once you find Iris, send her up my way, okay?”

“Okay.”

Twenty-three

"I am absolutely coming to your gala tomorrow!" Shandra looked sternly at Katherine between the steady influx of customers. "Stop trying to talk me out of it!"

Katherine bit her lower lip, "I know, I know, but it could be dangerous."

"An art show, dangerous, ha!" Shandra flipped her hair over her shoulder. "Is your art that horrendous?"

"No, it's, you know, that stuff."

"Oh, right, that stuff. Well, if it will make you feel any better, I have convinced mi hermano to join me."

Katherine's eyes locked on her best friend. "You what?"

Shandra winked, "He'll protect me."

"But he's a cop!"

"Yes, you know this."

Katherine crossed her arms, "I don't know what that's going to change. I need to let Joaquin know. Your brother being there might mess everything up."

"Mess what up? You haven't told me what these secret organizations are going to do tomorrow night. Should I uninvite him?"

Katherine had her phone out, and dialed Joaquin's number. "No, no, it'll be fine. Probably. I think. I'll let Joaquin know. I'll let you know once I let him know."

Shandra looked at Katherine sideways. "You're acting more loco than normal."

It rang. "I don't know what's going to happen. That's the problem."

"Maybe you can ask him." Shandra pointed to Mr. Weiss who was crossing the street in front of the bakery. "Isn't he part of your secret societies?"

Katherine jumped and let out a high-pitched sound, spinning around and ending the call before Joaquin was on the line. "He didn't come yesterday. I thought he wasn't coming this week!"

"A day late I guess."

The door rang with the sound of a new customer. Shandra moved over to the register and smiled at Mr. Weiss and his two bodyguards. "It's good to see you, Mr. Weiss. The usual?"

"Yes, yes, a dozen croissants." He smiled warmly. "I missed my usual time yesterday, business. Business has been busy as of late. A lot of moving pieces that won't settle into their designated place. You understand, I'm sure."

Shandra nodded as if she did, moving over to the basket where the fresh ones were kept, "Of course. And croissants are one of the simple pleasures in life that ease worries."

"Exactly." Mr. Weiss smiled at Shandra then turned his attention towards Katherine. "Ms. Mason."

Katherine forced herself to turn around and look him in the eye. Forced herself not to run into the back and hide. "Mr. Weiss."

"Have you thought about our little chat the other day?"

"Some."

"Did you come to a decision? Can I count on you?"

Katherine swallowed, "I need more time to think."

"My dear, there is no more time to think. We have reached the end of our rope. I either tie you off, or I let you go, let you be eaten by the wolves."

"Wolves?" Shandra asked, moving the bag to the counter, "that sounds ominous."

"It's a figure of speech." Mr. Weiss smiled as he paid. "There are no wolves in this city, only bats. And a pack of bats is not the most terrifying of images. Little rats with wings. Pitiful things. There are also a few singing men and women, traveling folk with their heads in the clouds prancing around my city. And one small man trying to get a taste of power without an invitation. Does that sound about right?"

Katherine nodded slowly; her eyes still locked on his. "That sounds about right."

"Now, my dear, my time is limited. What is your answer."

"I…" Katherine swallowed again. "I can't."

Mr. Weiss straightened up slightly with the answer, his friendly demeanor evaporating. "I understand. No hard feelings with what happens next?" And he turned and left, his two bodyguards trailing behind him.

"That was, odd." Shandra leaned on the counter in front of Katherine, bewildered. "Maybe there is something happening that only you can see."

Katherine forced herself to breathe. "Hey, I thought you believed me about all of that, stuff?"

Shandra raised her hands. "I do! I do. Mi amor, I do."

"Then why say it like that?"

"Well, I was talking to Miguel and –"

"I told you not to tell anyone!" Katherine almost leapt on top of her friend.

"But he knows people and he hears things. I wanted to see if this conspiracy of yours had any legs. He laughed at me, thought it was the funniest thing he's heard in a while."

Katherine's eyes went dark, "This isn't a joke. This isn't funny."

"Well, I punched him for both you and me then." Shandra threw her fist into her imaginary brother's shoulder. "But no, he's heard all sorts of rumors, stories, people high or stoned on everything they put out on the street, seeing everything imaginable. He doesn't take stock in any of it. What he can see, what he can touch, and feel, is truth. That's how he stays alive among the evil, his words."

"You think I'm making this up? You think Joaquin is lying to me? That I went to Denver and was fed some story by a corporate suit with a weird fetish for muddling the minds of young women? Mr. Weiss there was not having his normal 'hi, how are you, my kids are amazing', kind of conversation!"

"He's an old man. Old men act weird."

Katherine growled in annoyance. "I thought you were my friend! I thought you were on my side with this!"

Shandra put her hands on Katherine's shoulders, "I am! And all those things did happen. I'm just leaving the door open for a more, reasonable possibility."

Katherine brushed her friend's hands off her shoulders and turned towards the front door, hoping someone would come in at that moment and buy something. Give her a reason to leave this conversation.

When no one did, Katherine sniffled, "I get it. It's fine."

Shandra was quiet, "You don't look fine."

Katherine turned back towards Shandra, steel covering up her face and doubts. "No, really, it's fine. We're done talking about it. Okay?"

After work, Katherine picked up Christina from Iris, who wanted to complain about how much Junior and Jack had been terrors that day, dumping a whole box of cereal on the floor, ripping apart their bookshelves three times. Katherine nodded and quickly made an escape to take her daughter to play. The day was hot, and the park less crowded than usual. She was glad for that, glad her maybe new mom friends weren't around. She didn't want to talk to anyone. She needed time to think.

Katherine smiled sadly as Christina tottered about on the stairs, across the small bridges, down the slides and back up again. Over and over, laughing, happy. After a bit of hovering, Katherine found a bench and let Christina explore on her own. It was good for kids to feel independent, to know they could do it all on their own. Christina was so independent, and big! How did she get so big already?

As Katherine thought about her daughter and the chaos that swirled around her, a feline friend stopped by. Lynx. The stray orange cat hopped up on the bench next to Katherine. At first, she was surprised, but she welcomed the company.

"Hey there Lynx, what are you doing a few blocks over here?" She asked the cat as he sniffed at her fingers then invited himself onto her lap. "You lonely too?"

As if he wanted to answer, the cat looked up at her with his big blue eyes then did two circles on her legs, eventually settling down into a ball. Katherine began to scratch the spot behind his ears, which caused him to purr.

"Yea, me too. Lonely and confused. I feel like I'm being pushed into something I don't understand. Or maybe walking into it willingly. Into something I wasn't looking for, expecting, wanting in my life. Yea, I don't know what I want. I thought I wanted Patrick, wanted to build a life with him. He left. He died. I thought I wanted to be an artist, but I haven't been able to paint in weeks. I keep staring at the canvas and nothing comes out. I want to be a good mother and I'm afraid I'm already ruining my daughter. She's so happy over there! Is she happy when I'm not around too? Is she happier with her cousins, with her aunt? And after all this time with her, taking care of her, weeks and months alone in that basement, I now have only one real friend left and she doesn't believe me. Do I believe me? I don't know. I have money now, more money than I've ever had, yet, I feel so, directionless.

"I don't know. I'm helping this man. Trying to help him at least. I still don't know where I fit into all of this. He makes me crazy, I can't get him out of my head, yet, yet I still have this thing, this small part of me, holding me back. I don't want to fall for him. Have I fallen for him? I don't know. Why am I so important to him? That's the problem! I overthink all of these things. And I'm worried about tomorrow. It feels like this huge cliff. Like, like anything can happen. You know?"

Lynx looked up at Katherine, yawned, and settled back down. She laughed.

"And I'm talking to a cat. I have a therapist for a brother and I'm talking to a cat. Why? Why am I like this? I know you don't understand. You couldn't. Your life is all about sleeping and playing with fake mice. Finding your next meal. Christina's life is easy too! She cares about food and books and sleeping and playing. Nothing else. She doesn't have all of these thoughts, these weights, these pressures all around her! Needing to be the best sister possible, needing to work hard, be on time, care for others, figure out life. Life! That'll come later. She'll grow up and have all these problems, well, hopefully not all these same problems! I want her life to be better, happier."

Lynx continued to purr. Christina slid down the slide and giggled, her little feet dangling in the air for a moment before she plopped herself onto the rubber ground, bobbled over to the stairs and started again. On the second step, she looked over to her mother and smiled with her massive toothy grin, laughed, bobbed up and down, then ran across the bridge.

Katherine took a deep breath. She smiled freely despite the storm in her mind. “This is good. My daughter is wonderful. This is happiness. I am happy, right now. I am happy. I have everything I need right here. I have Christina. I love her and she loves me. All we have to do is put one foot in front of the other. All we have to do is get through tomorrow.”

Katherine sighed and stared up at the sky, wishing she could fly away.

“Don’t tell anyone else Lynx, but I’m scared.”

Twenty-four

Katherine could tell something was wrong when she passed Haken Brothers Produce and began to see the reflection of police car lights bouncing around the buildings in the morning light.

The idea of someone being hurt was not a great way to start a day like today.

When she rounded the next corner and found three cop cars and an ambulance surrounding the bakery, she froze, then ran the remaining distance to work. After she weaved her way through the parked vehicles and cops milling about, she found both storefront windows shattered, the logo that she had stared at backwards for over a year, unreadable. Two of the cops shouted in her direction, telling her she couldn't be back here. She ignored them and headed left when she caught a glimpse of Robert.

"What happened?" She exclaimed to her boss.

Robert looked ten years older than when she had seen him yesterday, his hands wringing as he looked on towards his shop, helpless. "They aren't telling me much, won't let me go inside. I've been waiting for answers for over an hour. Two police officers interrogated me while they held me back, like I was the one responsible for this."

"Where's Lester?" Katherine looked around for the muscular baker. "Was he here when this happened? Did he see what happened?"

Robert's face lost more of its already diminished color. "They took him to a hospital before I arrived. Said he was in bad condition, but he would be just fine. I don't know any details about that either. They aren't telling me anything."

"What?" Katherine gasped. "Where did they take him?"

Robert shook his head, "I don't know."

He looked sorrowfully at Katherine, "What do I do now? This place, this was the only thing keeping me sane, the only rock I had left to hold onto. I can't just sit at home. I can't be there all the time, not with Margret's treatment."

"Margret? What's going on with your wife?"

Two cops stepped out of the bakery and headed straight towards Robert, cutting off their conversation. Katherine had flashbacks from a few months prior when she had returned home and they had told her about Patrick's death.

The older one, Kingly, took off his hat. "Sir, we have what we need. It's safe. We would like it if you would join us inside, identify if they took anything."

"Who did this? When did this happen? Why?" Robert asked.

"Call came in around 5:30, a disturbance in the area. From your employee, Lester Kintock. He said there were two guys trying to enter through the back, then milling around out front. He dropped the phone when they shattered your windows here. Dispatch heard the scuffle. When we arrived, we found him on the floor in the back. He's at Penn Medicine receiving treatment."

"What happened?" Katherine asked, "Is he alright?"

"Ma'am, please, we ask that you stay behind the police line."

"She's with me," Robert spoke up, "works for me. Is a friend."

"Still, even employees should stay clear of the area until we're done with our full assessment."

"What happened to Lester?" Katherine repeated, her hands on her hips, not moving anywhere.

"Stab wound," the younger cop, Jake, spoke, "single. Non-threatening. Still not great."

Katherine gasped. Robert groaned.

"Do you know why anyone would do this? Can you think of any threats you might have had recently?" the older police officer rolled the question into Robert before he could ask more about Lester.

Robert shook his head, "No. Everyone loves this place. I don't know why anyone would target us. Did they take anything? Is the safe okay?"

"We didn't see anything that was disturbed, there's a bit of a mess in the back, your employee was in the middle of baking. Smells good in there, that is, if you can ignore the tinge of blood."

Robert's face went completely pale at the comment. Katherine gasped again.

The older cop eyed Jake and his comment. "Ignore him. It's not that bad. Sir, can you join us inside?"

"Yes, yes," He did not move. "What am I going to do about this? My windows? My bakery."

"You had business insurance, correct?"

"Yes, of course."

"Then it would be best if you contact them. You'll have the police report soon, in a few days, and you can work with them on the damages. We see this stuff often enough, less so the stabbings with it, but businesses like yours bounce right back."

"Might even be good for business. Rally community support." The younger cop added.

Robert glared at him. "You think my employee being hurt and my business being attacked is good for it?"

Kingly gave his partner another side-eyed glare. "What my partner means to say is you won't be down for long."

"Who do you think did this?" Katherine asked.

"Could be random," the younger cop speculated, "could be part of the uptick in violence we've been seeing around the city. These kinds of things ride in waves."

"So, no ideas who did this?" Katherine asked one more time.

"Ma'am, please, behind the line?" Kingly asked again.

Katherine turned towards Robert. "I'm going to go check on Lester. Okay? Call me if you need anything. Okay?"

Robert nodded. "Yes, that's fine. I guess you can't really work today. Would be good if you visited him. Oh, and I should let Shandra know work is canceled for the time being. I can't pay you either, not if we're closed. I'm sorry."

Katherine grabbed his arm and squeezed in reassurance. "I'll call Shandra, and don't worry about the pay. I understand. You focus on this. Okay?"

Robert nodded again. "Okay."

Katherine called Shandra as she waited for her Uber to arrive. Shandra was in as much shock over the attack as Katherine felt, asking all the same questions. Who, why, when? Katherine answered the best she could, short, facts only. She wanted to speculate on the who further but resisted. She didn't know if the who could listen in on their conversation. Better to not talk over the phone.

"Robert also mentioned something about Margret, treatment. Do you know anything about that?"

"No." Shandra responded, "He only has good things to say about his wife."

Katherine frowned, "Odd."

While in transit she texted Joaquin.

Bakery was attacked.

She then added:

I'm okay.

She didn't want to say anything more, not without proof. Not without confirming a few things with Lester first.

Finding Lester was more of an adventure than Katherine had expected. Penn Medicine was a huge hospital with multiple buildings in various parts of the city. The police had not been specific as to exactly where Lester was taken. She went to the one closest to the bakery. After a twenty-minute conversation with the receptionist then security, she was gently asked to leave the building until she was sure her friend was there. No, they could not look up his information for her. No, there are laws against that, ma'am. On the sidewalk outside, Katherine called up Shandra again, who gave her Lester's number. She called him only to leave three messages.

How does one find someone hurt and in the hospital system? Did she know any doctors? Nurses? Did Lester have family that would know more? Why didn't she know anything about him?

Switching up approaches, she re-entered the hospital through a different entrance and instead of asking nicely to see her friend Lester, she created a bit of a scene.

Moving quickly up to the receptionist desk, breathing hard, her hair a bit disheveled, Katherine held back fake tears. “Is my boyfriend here? I’ve been running around the city, can’t find him, can’t find him!”

The sandy haired receptionist furrowed his eyebrows, “Ms., calm down. Let me see if I can help. What is his name?”

“I’ve been everywhere!” Katherine raised the drama a bit more than did what he asked, “Lester, Lester Kintock. He was stabbed. I don’t know why. Was taken somewhere this morning.”

The receptionist looked at his computer for a moment, then back up at her. “He’s at main campus.”

“Thank you!” Katherine smiled, “Do you know which room? Which floor?”

“I can’t give you that kind of information, but I can see he was admitted a few hours ago at Main.”

“Thank you.” Katherine smiled again and dashed out, both in excitement that that had actually worked, and so she was gone before any of the other, less helpful security guards could arrive.

As Katherine sat in her second Uber, Shandra called and confirmed that she had gotten ahold of Lester, and he was at the main campus. Katherine breathed a sigh of relief at hearing he was awake, and okay. She then asked Shandra to have Lester call her back, that she was on her way.

Once at main, Katherine then had the pleasure of a three-way conversation between the elderly receptionist and Lester on the phone.

“I’m in a room, west side. Windows.”

“Yes, Lester, what number?”

“I’m not sure, I can’t get up. They won’t let me.”

“Ma’am,” The receptionist interjected, “Have him call the nurse, have him get you on the list of visitors. Then I can tell you where he’s at.”

“Lester,” Katherine spoke into her phone, “Have the nurse put me on the visitor’s list.”

“Rodger.”

"Ma'am, you can sit over there." The receptionist pointed to a small waiting area.

Katherine's legs bobbed up and down as she waited, considering that maybe she should let Iris know that she wasn't at work anymore. In case she heard something. Hmm. What was the best way to tell her sister-in-law without having her worry?

"Hey, so um, I'm not at work. I'm at the hospital." She started.

"The hospital?" Iris asked, tense, "Are you okay?"

Katherine threw a palm into her forehead. "No, not like that. I'm here to visit Lester. He's our baker. He was attacked, hurt when the bakery was attacked."

"The bakery was attacked? Are you okay?"

Why was she so bad at this! "Yea, I'm fine. I know I'm not making any sense. I wanted to let you know I'm okay, I'm not at work, but across town. I'll be home once I'm done here. Okay?"

"Who attacked the bakery? Everyone loves Lavigne's!"

"I know, I don't know. Lester is calling me. And so is Shandra. Bye!"

She hung up on Iris before she had to deal with anymore questions or say anything else stupid.

"Um." Lester muttered, "What's your last name."

"Mason. Katherine Mason."

"Thanks. Mason."

Pause

"Okay. You're on the list."

How had they been working together for almost two years and neither knew each other's last names till one of them was stabbed? What kind of an awful person was she?

"Hey, I'm going up to Lester's now." Katherine told Shandra from the elevator.

"Okay, good." Shandra paused, "Robert's amor, his wife, she has cancer."

"Since when?" Katherine yelled, then apologized to the two ladies next to her. "How did we not know about this?"

"Six months? Robert apparently doesn't like to talk about it. I felt awful dragging it out of him on today of all days."

"I almost gave Iris a heart attack. You're not alone in putting your foot in your mouth today! Thanks for the update. Sorry, I'm at Lester's floor. I'll call you back in a bit."

Katherine popped her head into the hospital room then greeted Lester with a huge hug as he sat in bed. She had expected him to look as strung out as Robert had but he was sitting back, relaxed as if nothing had happened. For some reason, the scar on his face seemed more expected in this room, made him look more human.

"How are you?" Katherine asked as she stepped back, giving him space, "The police say you were stabbed."

"I was." He opened up the hospital gown and showed her a large patch near his belly button, near even uglier looking scars down his whole chest. "Small thing, switchblade I think. Didn't go in very far. I had worse in the desert."

"I can see that. Ow. Um, do you know who did this? Who attacked you?"

He shook his head. "Never seen them before. Two guys, generic looking. I heard some noise coming from the back door as if someone was trying to shim it open. Robert takes care of his place, so when that didn't work I think they went around to the front. I saw them wandering around for a bit. People don't stand like that in front of the shop that early in the morning. Then they started throwing bricks. First few bounced off the glass as I called 911, then they broke through and were inside."

"Why? What were they after?"

"I don't know, I didn't give them much chance to look around. I began to shout at them, hoping they'd be scared off. Didn't work. They came in the back after me. I got one clean in the face with a baking tray. But then my second swing went wide. Careless. That never would have happened ten years ago."

"What did they look like?" Katherine asked, "Were they big guys, huge shoulders like you? A bit like body builders or bouncers?"

"No, more average, unremarkable, street kids almost."

Katherine let out a breath that she had held since seeing the bakery. It had not been Mr. Weiss. Her refusal to work with him had not directly put Lester in the hospital. So then, who was it? Street kids? Was it the Gypsies? Were they trying to send a message to her too? On today of all days?

"Anything else you remember? Defining features to these two kids?"

Lester stilled. "Why?"

Katherine stiffened. "Why what?"

"Why do you care so much about these two kids? I told the cops all I know, and now you're coming in here too? Do you know who did this, what happened?"

"I... I care. I want to know why my friend is in the hospital. That's all."

Lester looked unconvinced. "That's all?"

She smiled, honestly. "That's all. Fine. Enough about that. You want some company? How long are they keeping you here?"

"Last I heard, till at least afternoon." He paused, considering her offer. "Sure, company would be nice."

"Great!" Katherine looked around the room for the best place to sit. "This will give us a chance for me to get to know you. Nothing better than a crime to bring people together!"

Katherine spent the rest of the morning chatting. A few calls came in while she was occupied, one from Iris, one from Shandra, and, her favorite, one direct from Joaquin. Even today she held her strict two-call policy. If she was with someone else, unless you called twice in a row, it wasn't important. Ignoring Joaquin for an hour also felt good, felt like she was a little in control.

When Katherine woke up that morning, her nerves had been humming with dreaded anticipation over the day to come. After finding the bakery in its ransacked condition and running around town to locate Lester, her nerves were now completely shot. She could feel the massive shadow looming at her back when she sat down across from her injured coworker, felt her limbs shaking with dread. But something unexpected happened while they talked. Sometime between the awkward start to the conversation and their warm goodbyes, she was able to forget for a moment about what was to come, forget about her gala for an hour and laugh.

She had no idea Lester was so funny! After breaking through the rust that was his gruff exterior, his, I'm not hurt, I'm okay, this is nothing, don't worry so much about me, they began to talk about work. About Robert and the early mornings alone with him. About Katherine's frustrations with how much he watched over everything like she was about to do something wrong. Like she was going to break everything.

Lester agreed. “Do you also think of Robert as a peacock?”

Katherine blinked, “A what?”

“You know, a peacock, those huge colorful birds, preening and strutting around like they own everything.”

“Maybe, a little?”

“Like this!” Lester threw out his elbows. “Did you use the right flour?” He craned his neck ever so slightly to imitate Robert’s gaze.

Katherine chuckled.

At this morsel of positive reinforcement, he continued.

“Did you let these rest long enough, twenty minutes until you bake them.” Lester stretched his neck a bit farther out.

Katherine added a giggle.

“Ah! Is that a flat croissant, in my bakery?” Peck peck, elbows out. “Why I never.”

At that one, Katherine spit out a laugh and the floodgates were opened.

They joked about the way Robert needed the display cases just so, no, the pastries are on the top shelf! They marveled over how he knew every customer’s name and made it a game to try to name as many as they could together. Katherine was impressed with how many Lester knew!

“Did he try to make you learn them all too?” Katherine asked in wonder.

“He did!”

“Why?”

Lester threw up his arms, “I don’t know, I don’t talk to any of them!”

They started to make up stories for each of them, since Robert always said you needed to know your customer! The woman with the cat handbag, she had twenty cats, they loved fresh baguettes. The man with the combover, Mr. Brown? Mr. Gray? Sure, he always came in after work on Mondays, but maybe one day his wife would have this craving for sourdough late that night. What would he do? Would he come in on Tuesday morning, just for that? He seemed like he would, he was that kind of a guy.

They agreed together that Robert was a great boss, who cared more than what was good for him. They were angry together at the destruction of their shop, then back to mutual agreement in the fact they would both help Robert double, no, triple their profits, and their number of customers once they reopened.

They weren't going to let a little thing like bricks and a stabbing beat them down.

"Did you know..." Katherine had just found out herself. Was it right to tell him? "Did you know about Robert's wife?"

Lester nodded. "Of course. Did you not?"

Katherine frowned. "He never mentioned it to me."

Lester sighed. "For how much Robert loves to get to know his customers, he has a hard time opening up."

"Don't we all?"

Katherine began first, talked about Christina and how it was like to be a single mother, how much worry she had for the future and worry over if she was doing the right things. Lester shared some about his time overseas. He mostly talked about his buddies, the guys who kept him sane while they lived in sand and more sand. Sand everywhere! In your boots, your socks, your eyelids. But Steve and Rob, Jon, and Mike had kept him sane.

"This one night, we were confined to base, and Rob got this crazy idea to fill up a few jumpsuits with sand, post them around the Humvees, see which one of the new recruits went apeshit over seeing these sandcrows posted all over our base. So we started filling up jumpsuits, naturally. The sand wasn't cooperating, would bunch in the feet and leak out the sides. And it's heavy too! Worst stuff in the world. Anyway, we get four of them stuffed and we set them up, they're awful looking, all lumpy with no heads. We go, Rob! What are we going to do about the heads! See, in the desert when the base is closed, you have a lot of time on your hands to do stupid shit like this, a lot of time. Rob grabbed a few helmets that wouldn't stay on, they looked stupid sitting on our lumpy sandcrow's shoulders without a head underneath them. Buckets didn't work. Propane tanks were too large. We thought about stealing a few watermelons, if they even had some, but that was too far past our abilities. But then, then Mike had this great idea to use more jumpsuits! Stuff the whole helmet with another suit and then, if you were drunk and squinting, and had only one good eye they looked exactly like a real Fuzzy!"

Lester was laughing, tears coming out of his eyes. Katherine laughed right alongside him.

"They were even worse looking once the sun came up! No one was scared! Most of the recruits called us sunbaked, fried in the head. We didn't care. The officers forced us to wear those jumpsuits for a week, after we got most of the sand out of them, that is. Since we only stuffed four of them full and it was Rob's idea, he was spared from the pain of the chafing."

"Why was Rob spared?" Katherine asked between her giggles.

"Because we were bored!" Lester exclaimed, "Nothing to do! The guy who came up with the best idea that didn't get us in trouble, well, too much trouble was king for the day. They were also the one who ate shit if we got written up."

Nurses came in twice to check Lester's bandages and stitches, one chiding Lester for laughing like that, he'd rip his stitches, but smiling at their mirth. The second one to discharge him early. Katherine gave her friend another hug, gentle around his wound, and walked out of the hospital next to him, revitalized by the unexpected happiness a visit to the hospital could bring.

Reality came crashing right down on Katherine as they stepped into the lobby.

"Oh," Lester said, throwing his leather jacket over his shoulder, "Those two guys, who jumped me. I didn't want to seem racist before. They were darker skinned, Native American almost. Both had their hair in braids, black hair. I haven't seen people like that around here much. Why they had made me a bit nervous. Standing outside, before the bricks came through the window. Stupid reason, I know."

And with that, Katherine knew exactly who would receive her wrath, in full.

TWENTY-FIVE

THERE WERE TWO MESSAGES on Katherine's phone.

The first was a long, rambling one from Shandra. She began with an update on the bakery, that nothing was stolen, which was really odd since the register had a few hundred in it. But things got stranger when her brother called and began asking her questions about her job like a cop, not wanting to let her know why he was acting so strangely and hung up without saying goodbye. Shandra could feel something was happening and she for sure was going to get Miguel to tell her what.

The second message was from Joaquin. It was simple, short:

'Hi, It's Joaquin, I know what happened. Call me when you have the chance. I'm glad you're safe.'

His voice alone sent her into a wave of emotions. He cared about her! Did he know it was Waya as well? Of course he could find out so fast. Had Lester's story from the police made it up to him that quickly? Or did he have other ways? Or maybe someone else was trying to make them both think it was Waya, make her not go to her gala tonight. Maybe it was Serpitus, trying to spook her and foil Joaquin's plans. Or someone else.

There were enemies behind every tree, shadows everywhere.

Why did one non-answer bring up thirty-seven more questions?

Putting all of that off to the side for now, no text messages from Iris, no messages from her earlier call either. Still, she should get home, she should be with her daughter for the rest of the day. She would be out late again tonight, out late at her gala. She should take advantage of the afternoon without work.

Her jaw tensed. She was going to help Joaquin end this whole thing tonight.

"Joaquin," She started first as the call went through, "Tell me what you know."

"Katherine, to verify, you're okay?"

"I am. And I know enough about what happened too. I'm not changing my mind. Unless you tell me the attack on Lavigne's was you, then I'll ask why. But otherwise, I don't care who it was. Your boss, Waya, the Gypsies or Golems or some other crazy cult out there you haven't mentioned yet. I am going to help you tonight. You have my word."

"That is good to hear." Joaquin's relief was clear in his voice. "It was Waya."

The confirmation didn't change her confusion, "Why? What does he gain from trying to scare me now?"

"I am not sure yet. I have my theories. Either way, he's in the city, for tonight. We've been tracking him since Wednesday. We have eyes on him and every known associate of his. When he springs his trap, we will be ready to steal the key unscathed."

"I trust you." Katherine responded.

"And I you. I'm putting myself in your good hands tonight. See you in a few hours?"

"Yea, tonight."

Katherine took another Uber home. As it drove she looked out on the city, worked to keep her breathing in check. Even with her steel conviction, reality felt like two walls closing in on her, the moment of truth rapidly approaching. She didn't know if she could survive anymore surprises like this morning's. If anything did have the gull to come, she was in a mood to kick and scream at it until it ran away from her in terror.

Among her fear, a stray thought bubbled up. Her dad had believed in her. He thought she had exactly what she had needed to succeed. An overwhelming desire to talk to him welled up in Katherine's heart. She hadn't missed him like this for years.

He had always known the right things to say.

The moment Katherine walked into her house, all three kids screams over which dessert they wanted shattered her thoughts.

"I want that cookie! I want that one!" Jack shouted from the kitchen.

"No, That's not fair!" Junior responded, "Not fair!"

"Aaaa!" Christina joined into the shrill sound, smiling, imitating her cousins.

"You'll get the one I give you!" Iris yelled over top of her boys.

"Not fair!" Junior continued.

"Hi." Katherine poked her head into the pandemonium.

Her sister-in-law looked up and visibly deflated. "It's never ending!"

Katherine gave her a sigh and a look of understanding. "Maybe I can eat all the cookies? I do like chocolate chip."

Jack looked at his aunt in horror then doubled his screams, "Don't let her eat them! I want that one!"

Both parents winced. "Alright, alright, enough of this! You'll get what you'll get."

Iris gave Jack his cookie of choice, sending Junior into more bouts of anger. When she handed him a different cookie, he threw it onto the ground, stomped on it, and wined. Iris sighed heavily and ignored him. As Iris handed one to Christina, who changed from her shouts of joy to giggles of happiness, Katherine moved the open bin from the counter where Junior was trying to sneak another one, to the top of the fridge. This sent him into another round of screams.

"Why did he get that one?"

"I want two!"

"Cookies mommy! Chok-latt!"

Ignoring the boys, Iris took three cookies for herself and headed towards the living room. She plopped on the couch, sighed, and took a large bite. Katherine followed, cookieless.

"Boys! That's enough!" Iris screamed as Katherine joined her in the living room, causing Katherine to wince. Iris's face then lit up. "That's right! You're not supposed to be here! The bakery was attacked? What happened?"

It was a quick story, punctuated by Iris dashing into the kitchen and pulling Junior off of a chair after the cookies tumbled all over the tile floor. Christina grabbed one of the half-broken ones and toddled over to her mother, offering it to her.

"Thanks baby girl." Katherine smiled, took the pieces from her daughter, and set it on Iris's pile. "Hey Iris, how about I take these three to the park, let you clean up? You'll have them all tonight. Give you a moment to breathe?"

Iris beamed up at Katherine from the floor. "That would be, amazing. Thank you! That's right, your gala, tonight! You don't have to, take the boys that is. I can join you."

Katherine waved off Iris, "Nope that is alright. I need the distraction, keep me from overthinking about tonight. They look to be at just the right level of insanity to combat my churning thoughts."

Katherine couldn't believe this was happening. It had to be a dream. It had to be.

She was standing in the middle of a high-end art gallery, white walls, her work displayed in all of its glory. Her work. Twelve of her best paintings, including the four she had painted after breaking up with Patrick, and of course, her favorite. The one she had wanted to show her father. Her rainbow-colored masterpiece, right in the center. Her heart felt so full when she walked into the room and they were all there. She never thought she would see her old friends again.

And there were people! So many people were looking at her work! Looking at what she did!

Despite the reasons, she had made it. This was really happening.

Katherine had arrived an hour before opening, going through the space with the gallery owner, Cassandra La'vue, and an unnamed assistant, confirming that everything was up to her standards. Was the lighting alright Ms. Mason? Do you like the order in which they were hung? Did we get the names right? We received these directions with the shipment. What, they're perfect? Okay, great.

It was more than a little unnerving to have her artwork labeled for her, but each name fully encapsulated her mood when she had been painting it. *'Dark Clouds at Dusk'* was done two months after her father passed away, all of her sorrow and pain thrown onto the canvas, the grays and blacks swirling and overtaking the lighter patches near the bottom. *'Life is a Beauty, Life is a Mystery'* was one she did between bouts of morning sickness, a swirl of greens filling the center with splashes of red and orange celebrations.

It shouldn't surprise her that a professional gallery would know how to do their jobs. Or was it Waya who had provided the descriptions? How much of her mind did he see?

That hard seed of worry over what the night would bring was quickly swallowed up with activity. Once the doors opened, Cassandra donned her angular green mask and pulled Katherine around for the first hour, introducing her to everyone she recognized. From a banker from Baltimore with a bulldog mask, to a few stockbrokers from New York each in a simple white piece over their eyes. Even a state senator with golden sequins covering his mask who seemed to be enjoying the evening with two slim females at his elbows. It was a whirlwind of names and faces and hellos. Waiters in black and white tuxedos moved around with plates of luxurious hors d'oeuvres and glasses of champagne as double-handed compliments passed in the air between rivals and friends. Katherine felt like she was swimming in a sea filled with only the best of people, a crowd she only knew had conceptually existed before tonight. She had no idea how she was supposed to interact with these perfect people other than to smile stupidly and be Cassandra's showpiece.

She wore a sheer black dress, cut high in the front and low in the back. A dress that showed off her legs with a slit on the left. A dress picked out by Joaquin. The light golden chain necklace and matching earrings were Iris's addition. With her high heels clicking on the wooden floor and her feathered mask that Waya had provided, she felt like a pigeon, strutting around awkwardly for others enjoyment.

But then, Joaquin arrived.

He was in his usual black suit, black shirt, and red tie but looked somehow sharper, crisper tonight. He wore a simple red mask made of cloth, almost like a silk bandana. Without any introduction he fell into Katherine's side, his presence somehow filling her with all the confidence she had been lacking, gallantly pulling her out of the art curator's talons.

He was instantly in his element among the crowd, flowing in and out of the invisible currents of the room.

And he made her smile, so much.

Unlike Cassandra, Joaquin talked with the people, not down to them. He introduced her to a professor with crazy gray hair and a wolf mask, the two of them smiling, Joaquin listening intently to the man's research into quantum particles, then Joaquin ever so gently playing up Katherine's work.

"You can see how the colors here sway, feel the emotion in the brush-strokes."

To a series of stiff businessmen that hadn't bothered to wear masks at all, Joaquin calmly wondered over the value of an investment such a piece would be, how art like this could show both their financial intuition and culture. To a few ladies in evening gowns and feathers that were two feet tall he complimented them on their attire then listened as they pulled Katherine's work apart as petty, uninspired. Katherine felt the urge to throw champagne into their faces.

"Maybe," He replied to the loudest one with a smile, "or maybe it takes a keener eye to appreciate this style of art. Maybe you don't have what it takes."

"Why, I never." The lady replied with a scoff, the group of them scampering off like ruffled chickens. Katherine was horrified at his direct rudeness, then began to giggle when he turned to her mischievously and shrugged.

"Is everything..." Katherine asked Joaquin when they had a moment of calm.

"Yes." His eyes were confident, relaxed. "My men are ready. All we need to do now is wait for him to make his move." He put a reassuring hand on her back. "You have done everything you need to do. Don't take on this burden as well. Let me handle it."

"Okay. I just feel like something bad is going to happen."

Joaquin squeezed her shoulder, "Worry is nothing more than the mind eating itself. Don't."

Katherine laughed, "Don't? Is it really that easy?"

Joaquin frowned, serious, "It is not. Controlling your own mind is the most difficult thing you can learn to do. It doesn't behave, it has its own thoughts, its own flow. Every person is a consciousness riding within the rapids of oneself. Worry is a whirlpool within those waters, dangerous and seductive. It pulls you in, makes you spin and drags you down. Sometimes you can't avoid it. The best option any of us have is to see it, to know it's there, and not move towards it."

"How are you so good at this?" Katherine asked, feeling exactly the way he was describing. "How are you so good at using words like this?"

"Years of practice." His lips twitched up slightly. "Now, shall we leave that whirlpool to its own devices and return to your moment of glory?"

"Yes."

They talked for a while with a couple who were known in the art world, critics, Joaquin whispered into Katherine's ear when their attention was diverted. Joaquin did no sort of subtle influencing with them when the conversation turned to Katherine's work, merely acting as a sounding board for their voiced options.

"I like this bit here." The sleek haired female in a purple mask said, pointing.

"Hmmmm." Joaquin replied.

"But this one, this one is forced." The pepper haired male in a reflective golden mask added.

"Uh huh." Joaquin neither agreed nor disagreed with a tilt of the head.

"Maybe she was going for the flair of the dramatic?" The female continued that train of thought. Katherine had not had a chance to introduce herself, which was probably for the better. The mask had its uses.

"Mmmm." Joaquin mused, his hand on his chin.

"You know what, I like her style. It's fresh." The man finished, nodding, the two of them moving on.

"Ahh." Joaquin smiled lightly to Katherine. Katherine beamed.

Moments later, Shandra nearly sent all eyes to Katherine's direction when she let out a less than silent squeal of joy.

"These are yours!" She hopped up and down a bit, her light blue mask matching her dress perfectly. "You did these!"

"I did!" Katherine held in a squeak of her own.

"And this, this must be Joaquin," Shandra dipped with a gentle curtsey, "A pleasure, caballero guapo."

Joaquin bowed with an equal amount of respect. “The pleasure is all mine, senora.”

Shandra grabbed Katherine’s arm. “Oh, I like him.” The two stared at Joaquin until Shandra remembered who else was with her. “Oh right, this is Miguel, my brother.”

“Nice to meet you both, Katherine, Joaquin.” Miguel was almost as tall as Joaquin and wore a plain black mask. “Shandra has told me all about you, well, more about Katherine then you sir.”

Joaquin smiled, “I understand, no offense taken. Katherine hasn’t taken me around yet to meet her friends. Again, this is a pleasure.”

“I want to see all of them!” Shandra pulled Katherine away from the men and straight towards her work. She gushed about how talented Katherine was, how there was no way she would keep working at the bakery after tonight, not after she was discovered like this. And who were all these people? These had to be the most important people in the whole city, there to see her work!

Joaquin eventually borrowed Katherine back from her best friend and strode through the rest of the gallery with her arm in arm.

“I’m glad Shandra could come share this with you.” Joaquin noted, “Makes it special.”

“It does. And what were you and Miguel talking about while us girls were having a bit of fun?”

“Oh, boring things. Unintresting, really.”

Katherine looked at him sideways, “You weren’t discussing work with him, were you?”

Joaquin’s eyes twinkled. “Insight comes from many sources. Even a man who won’t say anything interesting, has something interesting to say.”

They took some time and walked around the venue, viewing the other work being showcased that evening. They looked at a series of intricately woven tapestries, a collection of abstracts that were inspired from various parts of the city, and four small sculptures set in the center of an otherwise empty room. Each was a different color and material, Metal, glass, wood, and trash. Katherine and the young artist chatted for a moment about his inspiration for the piece, the way he saw the world full of unique elements, water, dirt, the sky, and humans, how we are separate, yet we combine together into something greater. Katherine could feel his enthusiasm, could see the passion in his eyes. She hated to say goodbye, but agreed they should stay in touch. Artists motivating other artists, brilliant minds spurring other brilliant minds to further greatness.

He had seen her work. She was the real thing.

It was all too much. Katherine wished she had made it this far on her own. If only she had achieved this without the spiders spinning their webs.

Anger and annoyance streaked through her otherwise elated mood.

Joaquin seemed to sense her internal shift. "Everyone needs someone. No matter how you got here, you're here. And believe me. You belong."

"I feel like I cheated. Like I'm riding coattails."

He took her back to her work and had her look at the wall in total.

"Did you paint these?"

"Yes." She answered slowly.

"Did you put your heart and soul into them."

"Yes."

"Then you are not riding anyone's coattails. These are brilliant! Every last one of them."

Katherine blushed, "You're just saying that."

Joaquin shook his head. "No, never. Opportunity is a fickle mistress. It's like lightning. You never know where it is going to strike, but you need to be ready when it does. You put in the hard work. You did your part. The rest was lightning. Ride it, enjoy it!"

Katherine pushed back, "I don't know. It still feels like I'm a fake."

"Trust me when I say, you are a true artist. Everyone can see it. Watch."

He took her over to a minor league pitcher and his bored looking date, opening the conversation by complimenting him on his game the other night. Masterful job for those five innings, and the one hit? They happen. Joaquin then turned towards the pitcher's plus one, asking her what she was thinking of the piece they were in front of.

"I don't know, I don't really see it." The blonde sighed then took a sip of her drink. "It looks like dripping paint."

Katherine's heart cracked a little at the comment.

"It's not that at all." Joaquin stood next to the blonde, cocking his head slightly to the left, "Here, look at it this way. And don't tell me what you see. What do you feel?"

"I don't know."

"Drink in the colors, don't look at the technique, or what you think it should be. What do you feel?"

"I guess, sad. I feel like the rain has washed away something."

"Exactly!" Joaquin smiled at the pitcher, the two of them sharing a look. Then back to his date. "You might feel like something has been lost, like something once beautiful has been ruined."

The blonde turned her head to the left, imitating Joaquin, "Yea, a bit."

"Ah, but that's the best part of it! The beauty has not been lost at all. It has been changed, streaked through with sorrow, and has become something more. Something real. Life isn't perfect, and that's wonderful. Did you know this piece was done by a master? An artist who understands the true depth of the heart and how to share their pure insights with others."

The blonde tipped her head to the other side, smiling. "Yea, I see that now. Life isn't perfect. And that is okay." She looked at her date. "Are they for sale? Can you buy this one for me?"

Katherine could not have loved this man anymore then right at that very moment.

"Let's get some air." Katherine pulled Joaquin up to the third story, past the bar, past the people and up to the rooftop garden.

She stepped out into the night and felt the light breeze stirring the evening air. There were a dozen trees and flowers of every color within the dim light of the space, the building set apart and sandwiched between other, taller structures. Her heart was a violent mix of emotions, swirling, conflicted, confused. Pure joy, fear, desire, unease, hope, and love, all wrestling with each other, all threatening to take over. Katherine moved over to the railing and looked out over the street, out over the city and sighed.

"I don't deserve any of this." She said to no one, to herself. To Joaquin. "I haven't done anything right in my life. I'm a screw up." She turned to Joaquin. "I don't belong in your world."

"Who told you that you were a screw up?" Joaquin asked, gently.

"Everyone. My brother, my sister. Patrick left me. My grandfather."

"Words have power. What we say to each other, what we say about ourselves has power. Words cover us, like paint, our souls a canvas for our internal monologue. Others voices add onto it too. Some words, evil words, repeat in our heads, make us go crazy. You can't change what other people have said. But you can change how you view yourself."

Katherine gave him a side-eye, "It's not that easy. Life isn't as easy as you keep making it seem."

He leaned on the rail next to her. "You are right, Katherine, life is not easy. Not in the slightest. It's exceptionally difficult. More difficult than you could ever imagine. And more amazing than you could ever dream. When you least expect it it catches you by surprise, makes you believe in the good of it again, makes you laugh and hope again."

He pulled her towards him, turning her toward him, his hands on her waist.

"I see the real you, Katherine. I see how much you care. How much you try. I see you pushing forward, even when it is hard. You are going to do great things, even greater than tonight, right here. You are absolutely amazing. All you need to do is see yourself exactly as I see you, the strong, beautiful woman that you are."

She had no other way to respond to that but to kiss him. She pulled herself as close to him as possible and kissed him deeply, with all of her love. He responded in kind, pulling her in his arms, nearly picking her up with his embrace, the two of them not caring about anything else but each other. They pulled their masks off, threw them on the ground so as not to get in the way.

Joaquin's watch buzzed. He pulled away from Katherine for a moment and looked. "It's ten."

The full weight of why she was there and what she had to do fell hard on her shoulders. No! She would not let anyone, not even Waya and his stupid games ruin this moment! She was going to make it her own.

She gave Joaquin a wicked grin. "And I'm supposed to distract you now?"

He nodded, "Yes. I think you've already succeeded in that."

"How… fully… should I distract you?"

Katherine looked around the garden and found a nitch that looked to be the perfect place for a bit of privacy. She pulled him along, her mind made up on exactly what she was about to do.

Once within the space behind the stairs, a wall on three sides, she fell into him again, kissing him with everything she had. She loved this man, him and his words. Him and his eyes, and his smile. Her hands wandered a bit, feeling his arms, his chest, and further down still.

Joaquin responded with an even greater desire, his hands moving along her body in kind. He touched her gently, took exactly what he wanted from her, wrapped his arms around her and let her know without words how he felt. Their hearts hammered together, their breath coming in gulps and gasps.

Joaquin eventually pulled back, shaking off a bit of their haze. "Katherine, I can't. I'm losing myself. We need to stop."

"I don't want to stop." She continued to entice him with her hands. "Are you distracted yet?"

"Yes, very much so. Katherine. I don't want to hurt you. I won't hurt you. This is dangerous."

"I know." She kissed him again. "I know." She kicked off her heels then grinned at him wickedly again.

"And as long as your mouth stays up there and you don't bite me, my mouth can go, somewhere else, and make sure you are, truly, fully, distracted."

When he didn't say no, she continued.

Stepping back into the gala felt like walking from one dream into another. Katherine struggled with slipping on her shoes again as they cooled down and worked to brush off the dirt from her knees. Her mask was a bit worse for wear, one of her feathers slightly less puffy than when they had started the evening. But none of that mattered. Joaquin was nearly floating next to her, a smile on his face that no one could wipe off. As they passed the bar, Katherine grabbed whatever was there and downed it in two gulps.

That was highly enjoyable. Unexpected! What did they just do? She was not like that normally! And she wouldn't change it, not for the world.

With their current mood, it took them both longer than they should have to realize something was wrong. The air in the building had changed, people whispering, stiff, a bit unsettled.

Joaquin looked over to one of the waiters, "Did something happen?"

"One of the art pieces downstairs was, attacked."

A ball of dread rolled over Katherine's mind. She dashed down the stairs, almost knocking over two people on her decent, Joaquin following in equally unflattering fashion. Once through the doorway to where her art was on display, she stopped, her mouth open in horror.

Sprayed across the entire wall in thick, black spray paint, directly over every single one of her pieces of art, were the words:

--- YOUR DAUGHTER IS THE KEY ---

TWENTY-SIX

KATHERINE'S MIND WAS NOT functioning properly. She was panicked, out on the sidewalk in front of the gala, trying to figure out which direction to run, going up, then down, then finding herself back in front of the gala, blinking. She pulled out her phone from her handbag, looked at it, and forgot why she had done so.

Christina was in danger.

This was not okay! Joaquin was supposed to protect her and her family. None of this was supposed to affect her, she was a pawn. She didn't matter. She did exactly what she was asked to do.

They were going to use her daughter.

They were going to kill her daughter.

Joaquin appeared suddenly and pulled her up the street, "They've moved against us, all over the city, attacked us in nearly every stronghold we own."

Katherine didn't care. She stopped him and grabbed his arm, "We have to get to Christina, now."

He shook her off, "Did you not hear me? They all attacked. All of them. Waya. The Golems, and the Gypsies. Everyone."

Katherine froze from this news. "I thought you said the Golems were neutral? Mr. Weiss was a glorified banker or something. That they never hurt anyone. That's what you said."

"Something changed." Joaquin looked as distressed as Katherine felt. "There had to be a signal jammer in the gala. I didn't get these calls or messages till I stepped out here, away from the building. Or they turned it off now that the ambush is underway. How did I miss this? How did I not think this could happen?!"

"Joaquin."

"Serpitus was fortified against the Gypsies, had that under control. They had been quieter these last few days. We thought they were planning something, but getting the Golems on their side? What did Waya promise to get them all on his side?"

Katherine stood up to her full height in front of Joaquin. "Joaquin, none of that matters. We need to protect your ley-line. We need to get to Christina."

The vampire nodded, returning to the current crisis and pulled her gently towards an SUV that magically appeared in the street. "Your daughter is a top priority, but not the only priority. I've lost contact with the men guarding your brother's house. I'm sorry, but I can only spare you Max. He will drive you home. Go find out what happened, make sure your daughter is safe."

He looked at his phone again, "Bloody Hell! I need to help clean up this mess!"

Katherine refused to get into the vehicle, her voice rising an octave. "You don't know if she's even safe? I could be running home to find nothing! I could be running into a trap! I thought you were protecting me!"

"I am."

"This does not sound like you're doing a very good job at it!" She screamed, multiple bystanders looking in their direction.

Joaquin raised his hands, "I had three men watching your house tonight. Some of my best men."

"Your best men." Katherine folded her arms. "And what, you think Max and me will be enough where three of your best men failed?"

She pulled out her phone and called Ethan.

"Max is the best, better than my best men." Joaquin responded as her phone rang.

No one picked up. She tried Iris. Nothing. She called Ethan again. Still nothing. She called Iris. Nothing again. She glared at her phone screen and resisted the urge to smash it into a million pieces.

"Katherine, I'm sorry, I have to go for now, there are dozens of other problems that need my immediate attention."

She grabbed his shoulder and nearly pulled him down, "Absolutely not. I am your main priority. I am all that matters to you right now. Me, and my daughter. You understand?"

Joaquin pulled her off of him, "The key, the ley-line doesn't matter if everything else is ash. I will be there to help as soon as I can."

"Don't you dare walk away!" She shouted at his back as he returned to his phone and briskly walked away.

"I need you!" She added, to no effect.

Fuck that man!

Katherine turned her ire on Max. "I need to protect my daughter. I need to find Christina. They might already have her. Can you get me home as quickly as possible?"

"Yes ma'am." Max nodded grimly, understanding the gravity of the situation.

The drive back home was agonizingly long. Katherine willed the car to move faster, urged the lights to remain green as they moved up the city. Once they arrived on her block, she didn't care about her own safety. She launched herself out of the moving SUV and stumbled up the sidewalk to her front door.

She had been expecting police cars, hundreds of them, droves of patrol officers with dogs searching for her daughter. Maybe even a helicopter or two in the sky. Instead, her street was quiet, uneventful. Like nothing had happened.

Katherine's keys dropped twice as she went to open the front door, cursing her shaking hands. She launched herself inside to find a very startled Iris and Ethan, cuddled up on their couch, in the middle of a movie. To them, Katherine probably looked a bit deranged, her hair tangled up a bit from her mask not cooperating as she had torn it off long ago, one of her heals broken from the dash across the sidewalk, her dress a bit worse for wear.

Katherine gulped in a breath, "Where is Christina?"

Ethan set their popcorn bowl on the coffee table. "She's downstairs, asleep. Why?"

For another time that evening, Katherine's mind could not catch up to the information it heard. "She's downstairs?"

"Yes." Her brother nodded. "What is going on? Why are you back so soon? We didn't expect you for a few more hours."

Katherine ignored the question, "Asleep?"

"Yes." He nodded again. "Katherine?"

Katherine dashed across the living room, destroying half a village and knocking over a train depot, but remained on her feet. "Ethan, Iris, I'll explain everything in a moment."

Without waiting for a reply, she turned on the light before entering into the kitchen, dodging a few trucks, and dashed down the steps to her room. Lying there peacefully in her pack-n-play was Christina. Katherine's heart nearly leapt out of her chest as she closed the distance and took her sleeping baby girl in her arms.

Her daughter squirmed a bit but did not wake up. Katherine closed her eyes and rocked her for a moment, keeping her close, never wanting to let her go.

"Hey, um, Katherine," Ethan spoke from the top of the stairs, his voice a bit unsteady. "A man is here, he says he's with you. He has a gun."

"It's just Max. I'll be right up."

Katherine set her daughter back down on her blankets and watched in the dim light as she curled up and sighed.

"Nothing bad is ever going to happen to you, baby girl, not while I'm here to protect you."

Katherine moved back upstairs, finding Ethan standing at the living room door, his arms crossed. Iris was still on the couch, concerned as well.

"I'm here to protect Katherine and your family." Max said sternly through the crack, "I need to make sure no one else is with you."

"It's just us, no one else," Ethan answered, making no move to open the door further.

As Katherine stepped forward to help the situation there was a pop, something outside. Max stiffened and fell to his knees. Before anyone inside knew what had happened, the front door slammed open, Ethan fell backwards, and Waya was stepping over Max's body.

"Ms. Mason," Waya entered the living room to Iris's screams. "You have my thanks."

Ethan scrambled to his feet but froze when Waya lifted his pistol.

"That's right, slowly, sit over there with your wife. And settle her down."

Katherine threw herself in front of the gun, her eyes on fire. "Get out."

"Ms. Mason, you performed marvelously." He spoke as if they were having a normal conversation. "Your actions have given my hunters space enough to let loose their arrows. I am here personally to see to one more item before you will never hear from me again."

"You can't have her!" Katherine cried out.

"Out." Ethan nearly shouted overtop of Katherine from his spot on the couch, causing Iris to jump. "Out or I'll call the cops."

Waya turned towards her brother, "Oh, they're a bit, busy tonight, I'm afraid. I wouldn't think a little domestic issue is high on their agenda."

"Why?" Ethan asked dumbly.

"Some nights have significance. Some nights change the very fabric of history. Tonight is one of those nights." Waya turned towards Katherine. "You know who I need."

"No."

"No?"

"No!" She repeated, stupidly shoving the man with a gun. "Get out!"

"Daddy, what's happening, who's yelling?" Jack was at the top of the stairs, rubbing his eyes, his racecar pajamas twisted up a bit around his middle.

Iris rushed up towards him, "Oh, Jack, this is nothing. Let's get you back to bed."

"Who is he?" Jack pointed towards Waya. "Why does he have a gun?"

"Someone your aunt knows. I'm not sure either. They're playing a game. He's just leaving. Let's get you to bed."

Jack pointed at Max, still crumpled up at the front door, "Is he dead?"

"I… I…" Iris had no good answer.

In the next moment, two hulking men appeared above Max's crumpled body. Two men Katherine instantly recognized. Mr. Weiss's bodyguards. Iris yelled again and disappeared with Jack. A crash came from the kitchen, the sound of wood splintering. Ethan used the moment of confusion to dash after his wife. Katherine turned around to come face-to-face with another bald bodyguard.

"Family went upstairs." Waya looked at one of the new arrivals, "Husband, wife, two sons. They can join us."

"Don't you dare!" Katherine threw her fists at one of the bodyguards, his arm feeling as hard as stone. Her flailing did nothing to stop his advance.

As Katherine was thrown like a rag doll onto the couch, the other two bodyguards followed the first upstairs while two more new arrivals took up posts at the living room's exits. One at the kitchen door, one at the front door. Within the span of a few blinks, Ethan, Iris, Jack and Junior joined Katherine on the couch, leaving little room left for anyone else in the relatively small space.

Ethan's nose was bleeding. Iris was frozen in shock, shaking and clutching her boys.

"Good. Keep them here." Waya smiled widely, holstered his pistol, then moved through the men and into the kitchen.

Katherine jumped up to follow, only to be tossed back down. She heard Cathrine cry and was tossed back down, hitting her elbow on the coffee table. When Waya returned with her daughter bundled in his arms, Katherine was back on her feet, angry.

"Ma'ma," Cathrine bawled, fear filling her face.

"Give me back my baby girl!" Katherine shouted, blocked from moving anywhere close by the living wall of muscle. Her next attempt to yell was cut short as a fist flew into her belly. She crumpled to her knees.

Waya looked down on her pitifully, "I know my methods are a bit crude, but I have no other choice."

"You are not … taking … Christina!" Katherine spat out, holding her middle as she tried to stand, only to have both of her shoulders held down by two different men. "Give her to me!"

"I promise you, when I am done, tonight will feel like a dream, maybe not even that. However, until then, I do not like to leave loose ends, even with the ones who have helped me. If you do not struggle, these men will make your deaths painless."

And with that, Waya stepped with a crying Christina out into the night.

Iris sobbed even louder after hearing Waya's instructions. Ethan's face had gone white.

"Why, why!" Katherine screamed, sobbing on the floor.

One of the men stepped back and pulled out a pistol. Ethan leapt off the couch and grabbed for a lamp, only to have his heroics stopped with a swing from one of their captors. Iris screamed as Ethan fell back, his wrist broken from the punch. When another of their executioners reached for Jack, Iris fell on top of her boys.

"They're just kids!"

Fists and boots were everywhere. Ethan received an elbow into his already mangled face, sending him unconscious to the ground. Jack yelled out for them not to hurt his father and tried to bite one of the attackers, only to be kicked away. Iris screamed yet again. Another of the men picked up Katherine by the hair and moved her to the front of the room, forcing her to her knees among the blocks and train tracks. She continued to sob, her tears landing on one of Junior's favorite trains. The green one with the happy, smiling face.

How had everything gone sideways so quickly? Where was Joaquin?

The man with the gun slowly moved in front of Katherine as Iris and the kids watched on in horror. Katherine could see the broken door in the kitchen through the man's legs. From somewhere outside, Lynx leapt onto the wreckage of the back door and dashed towards her. Oreo stood on the porch, curious.

Katherine found it bitterly funny that out of everything, her last thought would be about stray cats. That out of everything she was about to lose, she felt horrible that she would never be able to feed them again.

Then came the end. The loud bang.

Katherine could smell gunpowder, felt the impact of the shot ring through the air. She covered her head and rolled onto her side, waiting for the pain. But the only thing she felt were the toy blocks jabbing into her side. She opened her eyes and did not understand what she was seeing.

Lynx was on the gunman's back, but he wasn't a house cat anymore. He was the size of a tiger, with paws the size of dinner plates, claws that dug into the man's shoulder, and long, sharp teeth that sank deeply into his neck. The other four assassins had their guns out now, trying to aim at the feline attacker, two shots going into their comrade instead of the predator. Once the first man was down, Lynx lunged at two of the other men, sending them crashing into the corner desk.

Papers flew everywhere, Iris screamed some more. Ethan, now awake but in a half daze did his best to shield his boys and wife from the flying bits of wood and debris. The final two attackers joined in arms against the tiger, discarding their guns in the close quarters and pulled out knives. Lynx seemed to continue to grow, his mouth large enough now to fully crunch down on one of the attacker's heads, splitting it like a melon. He also continued to change shape, growing more powerful shoulders, a longer tail, and two sharp teeth. He looked like a sabretooth.

Katherine snapped to her senses and scrambled out of the way right before the pile of bodies and hair slammed into the corner wall by the door then onto the floor where she had been laying.

"Get out of here!" Katherine leapt over the coffee table and yanked up Ethan and Iris, more debris pelting them as the chaos continued. She pulled the four of them off the couch and shoved them up the stairs then dove out of the way as a man flew headfirst into the stair's landing.

She tried to follow her brother's family a second time but was grabbed by the ankle, flying hard into the floor. Katherine turned over and found a gun in her face, then both the man and the gun disappeared, the sabretooth roaring with all of its might. The man was able to throw two hard punches into the cat's side before his arm was ripped off. Katherine scrambled away again as the man seemed unaffected by his maiming and continued embedding his knife into the cat with his other arm.

There was much less blood than there should have been. As the fight continued, she could see the sabretooth was bleeding from a dozen places, but the men, headless and armless, fought on. Any gashes or loss of limbs revealed a monotone, dark brown interior under their flesh. Katherine stared on helplessly as the sabretooth ripped the five men apart, piece by piece. They only seemed to stop moving after their large barrel chests were cracked, and even at that, still twitched for a while.

The last man standing and the sabretooth fought on, dagger against tooth and claw, crushing the sofa then the television stand. Their battle spilled into the kitchen and only ended after the sabretooth pinned the massive man against the refrigerator and slashed him a dozen times in the front, shredding deeply into where his heart should be. The bald man held no expression, his glasses knocked off long ago, only staring blankly ahead as he fell to his knees, then straight on his face.

A moment of silence followed. The sabretooth breathed deeply as he licked his chops, his whole chest exposing his ribs in quick rhythm as he worked to settle his heart. His left ear was torn, his right eye swollen and matted with blood. Numerous parts of his hair were streaked red from his sustained injuries. He then turned towards Katherine and growled.

Katherine gasped and backed away slowly, tripping over something and landing back onto the ground.

"Good kitty!" She squeaked as Lynx stalked forward.

Katherine scooted until her back found wreckage. Lynx snarled, his teeth exposed, his lips quivering with hate. He stepped right over top of Katherine, put his face inches from hers, his eyes bright red. He then let out a roar. She felt his breath, hot on her face, felt her tears fly back across her cheeks. She trembled as the sabretooth closed his mouth, shaking his head as if he remembered something. The cat blinked, stepped back, pawed at the air in front of him, did two circles around the destroyed living room, then curled up into a ball on the floor.

They remained like that for over a minute, Katherine too afraid to move, the cat too exhausted to do anything but breathe.

Then, something rippled along the sabretooth's hair. He convulsed, like he was hacking up a hairball, his skin darkening, smoothing out. Katherine watched on as Lynx shrank, his two sharp teeth returning into his mouth, his ears disappearing into his hair.

What remained was a man in a tattered suit.

Joaquin.

Katherine rushed over to him, touching his face, gently moving her fingers over his swollen right eye. His left one was blue.

"How?" She somehow got out, her mind actively disbelieving that the last ten minutes had been real.

Joaquin smiled weakly. "I told you, I think bats are silly. A cat can sneak almost anywhere. Inconspicuous. One of my many talents."

Katherine stammered, so Joaquin continued. "Transmogrification. All vampires can do it, after we have had enough blood. Which is the main reason I couldn't come straight here with you. I had to make a detour for a few packs first."

Katherine had so many questions, "Why didn't you tell me earlier?"

"If I had, I couldn't have kept an eye on you. Make sure you were safe." Joaquin coughed, the back of his hand red.

She suddenly looked around the room, finding nothing but destruction and body parts, "You're hurt! I need to get you some help!"

He waved her off, "I'll be fine. I've had worse." He moved to sit up and groaned, "What we need to do is go after your daughter. We need to get her back."

Twenty-seven

"Car is out front," Joaquin stumbled across the living room with a bit of difficulty, not wanting to accept Katherine's help, but eventually letting her get his arms around her shoulders.

"What do we do about, about Max?" Katherine was numb as they moved up to his body. She was glad she couldn't quite see his face. She was also horrified to see him so still.

"Nothing now, we can't waste time." Joaquin bowed his head. "I'm sorry, my good friend."

Katherine's hatred for Waya was a raging inferno. He was going to pay!

"We have to go." Joaquin reiterated.

Katherine agreed with her feet.

They hobbled across the sidewalk. Katherine opened the SUV's door. Joaquin tumbled into the back seat and lay there, his eyes spinning, barely holding onto consciousness.

"Do you mind driving? I'm a bit, worse for wear back here."

"Yea, sure," Katherine jumped into the driver's seat and found the keys still in the ignition. She sped off, hoping it was the right direction.

"Left up here," Joaquin took two huge gulps then straightened up. He pulled something from his jacket. It looked like a small squeezy pouch of apple sauce, but red.

"I hope you don't mind." Joaquin murmured as he snapped the top off and sipped. Color quickly flooded back into his face.

"Is that?" Katherine looked back at him then back at the road, swerving. She knew in theory that he drank blood, but seeing it was completely different.

Joaquin took one more small sip and replaced the cap. His eyes had changed from blue to bright red. "Right up here. It is. Patrick's in fact. One of the last few we had left." His neck muscles tensed as he struggled against something.

Katherine didn't know where it came from, but she suddenly felt a massive spiky urge to leap out of the car and away from this, thing, in her back seat.

"Are you alright?"

Joaquin nodded slowly. His eyes were shut as he swallowed a few times, his hands opening and closing into fists. "It... this... helps me restore ... some of my strength... but it also... makes me... aggressive." Deep breath, "We can talk... but I will be focusing on remaining calm... for a bit. This is all... normal."

Katherine swallowed and focused on the road, focused on not crashing. This was anything but normal! She forced herself to ignore her deepest instincts.

After a few minutes of silence, Katherine voiced her immediate concerns. "When we arrive at the Basilica, what's the plan?"

"I don't know ... exactly. Get your daughter ... back. The Golems have never chosen a side... before tonight."

"Those men, they were Mr. Weiss's. They were Golems?"

Joaquin nodded.

"Who, what were they? They didn't bleed." Katherine then freaked out and almost clipped a truck, swerving back into her lane. "Ethan and Iris! The boys! We just left them with that mess!"

"They'll be fine." Joaquin gritted his teeth. "They're safer there... then with us."

"With a pile of dead bodies? I think not!"

"They were already breaking apart."

"Breaking apart? What was?"

"The Golems." Joaquin sucked in a breath through his teeth quickly as a ripple of something went through his body. "Have you ever heard of the Jewish folklore of the man who... the man who made a golem to serve him?"

"No, I don't think so."

"There are a few telling's, of men made from clay, automatons who serve their masters. A bit like Frankenstein, but not out of … human parts. That's a different group. Anyway… the golems are like that, manlike forms made from the immaterial, created to serve. Mr. Weiss and his group have the power… power from their angelic overlord to create perfect servants. The Golems."

"Those weren't men you killed?"

Joaquin shook his head, "No… more like puppets… or robots… or drones. Whatever you want to call them. They're not dumb, but they cannot think for … for themselves. They are given a task and they perform it without question. When they die… when they break, they dissipate, a bit like water, evaporating. Their form, their power… seeps out into nothingness."

Katherine parked right on the sidewalk in front of the Basilica and spilled out of the SUV, Joaquin at her heels. He was limping a bit but had regained most of his vigor. Katherine grabbed at the front door only to find it locked. A sign nearby noted that the church would be closed that night for a private event. She pulled at a few other knobs only to have the same problems, then bit off a scream.

Joaquin threw his shoulder into the wooden door, more for support than out of anger. He then took out a key. When Katherine went to grab it, he pulled it out of her reach.

"We don't know what we're walking into." Joaquin stated.

"I don't care. If there is a chance my daughter is in there, I'm going in." She grabbed for the key a second time, unsuccessfully.

"I won't be able to protect if it gets out of hand. I'm too weak."

"And instead, you want us to stand out here, powerless? Let Waya win? Where is the Joaquin I know that would do anything, make any sacrifice for the things he wants?"

"He's still here, along with the more cautious Joaquin."

"I need to save Christina. This isn't a debate. I need to."

Joaquin slowly nodded, "Looks like the reckless version of me is winning out tonight."

He smiled then unlocked the door.

"Thank you." Katherine meant it.

Once through, Katherine ran as fast as she could through the vestibule then down the main aisle, not caring this time about the sanctity of the space. She hooked a left and met another locked door, impatiently waiting for Joaquin yet again to unlock it.

Joaquin limped into the room, his eyes scanning everything, "I don't like this. It's too quiet."

"You'd rather get captured right away? Come on, I know she's here already. I can feel it."

Joaquin unlocked the next door, cracking it open a hair and examining the hallway beyond. "Stay behind me." He told Katherine then stepped forward, causing her to glare at his back.

She did not need him to babysit her.

She probably did. But still.

At each door, Joaquin scanned the next area before they moved forward, the back hallways of the church deathly quiet. At each door, Katherine was forced to stop moving towards her daughter, forced to stand still as she trembled inside. Joaquin was right, there should have been someone here to stop them. There should be resistance. This was too easy, too simple. Were they even here?

Katherine was able to breathe out her anxiety when they reached the door with the keypad. The keypad was smashed, the door slightly ajar.

"I can hear them. They're down there." Joaquin whispered.

"You can hear Christina?"

Katherine shoved past Joaquin and bounded down the spiral stairs. Joaquin shouted for her to stop, but she did not care. Once at the bottom, she found Waya and a single Golem in front of the vault door, waiting.

"Where is she!" Katherine yelled, throwing a wild punch at the man. He grabbed her wrist easily.

"Your daughter is upstairs. Unharmed." Waya shoved her back into Joaquin, who had just made it down the steps. "I'm glad you two could join us. Right on time."

Footfalls rang out from above. Eleven Golems spiraled downwards towards them, the first three holding assault rifles, the fourth holding Christina, the remaining enemies fitted with an arsenal of other impressive weaponry. Katherine launched herself towards her daughter, reaching out as Christina cried for her, only to be stopped by the living wall and a pair of rough hands. Only the first two Golems were able to join them in the space before the vault door, the remainder staying on the stairs.

"Ma'ma!" Christina reached out her hands, unable to escape the Golem's grasp. Katherine kicked and shoved at the men in her way to no avail.

She turned to Waya. "Give me my daughter!" She screamed, "You don't need her!"

"In fact, I do." Waya said simply, "She is the key."

"Waya." Joaquin nodded a greeting as if they were used to meeting under such circumstances.

"Joaquin." Waya nodded in return.

"How is Katherine's daughter the key?" Joaquin asked, more curious than concerned.

"Open this door and I will do one better. I will show you."

"Or we can do it in reverse. You can tell us now, then I'll open the door."

"You can't open it for him!" Katherine turned to Joaquin. "He's going to kill us once you do! He already tried to kill me once tonight!"

"If I wanted you dead right now, you would be dead." Waya stated to Katherine. He then turned to Joaquin.

"Your ley-line was created during the riots of 1844. Within those riots there were two warring parties, the Protestants and Catholics, two halves of the church, each attempting to eat the other whole."

"Christina isn't religious! She's never been to church!" Katherine laughed hysterically, "You can't sacrifice her here, won't work."

Waya ignored the interruption, "Also within the riots were the militia, by order of the governor. One of the militiamen stationed to protect the church was Patrick Troutman's ancestor."

"Christina won't work any better than her dad!" Katherine kept commenting, "They already tried with him, didn't work! Let her go!"

"Patrick's family line had been cursed, for a different reason, earlier on in their history," Waya continued, "Not important to your ley-line. What is important is that his ancestor met a terrible fate that day, leaving behind a pregnant widow. She raised her boy with the help of her family until he had a family of his own, and on, and on, until we reached Christina's father.

"On the night of Corporal Troutman's murder, his wife wept bitterly. Her husband had not cared for either side of the conflict, he was only there doing his duty. He served faithfully, and he was murdered. She cried out in her sorrow that night to the gods, to all the angels and demons for vengeance. She pleaded for a curse down upon her husband's murderer.

"A greater spirit listened, but not in the way she wished. For the spirits lost one of their own that day as well. So had a family on the protestant side of the conflict, one in which had a member also calling forth help from the beyond that night.

"Your ley-line is tangible proof of the totality of these losses. The greater spirits honored the sum grief felt within those twilight hours with their brethren's tombstone encapsulating this future kernel of their power. The spirits intertwined these two families within destiny, with the key requirement for them to set aside their differences and forgive one another.

"For the last hundred fifty years, Patrick's ancestors and the protestant family have been bitter enemies. While the aggressor's family prospered, expanded, spread out across the United States, the Troutman family remained a single thread, barely alive, but still alive. Whenever a Troutman tried to escape their curse, tried to move on past their cruel fate, the murderer's family was there, destroying them, keeping them down, defeating them at every turn.

"Christina is the first time since the riots that blood of the murderer's family, Katherine's family, and the Troutman's have produced an offspring. She is the living embodiment of 'the union of these bitter enemies.'"

"I see." Was all Joaquin said in response to the story.

Katherine tried to keep up. "You're going to kill my daughter because her distant relatives killed each other over a hundred years ago?"

Waya looked at her this time. "Yes."

Katherine suddenly laughed. "Oh, that's just perfect! You're telling me that I'm here, that I'm part of this whole mess of insanity because of some stupid coincidences? That I happened to be related to these people? That I happened to meet Patrick? That we happened to have a kid and you happened to learn about her?"

"No." Waya answered.

"No?" Katherine repeated.

"No." Waya shook his head, "We are here in this moment, Christina is here because I made sure she was born."

Katherine was incredulous, "You... what?"

"I made it happen. I spent years, nearly two decades, planning for tonight. I was given a vision by my gods, told of the ley-line held by the vampires within Philadelphia and the pieces that needed to be put into place.

"I sought out Patrick, befriended him, through college, let him fail a bit, then hired him. I gained his confidence, brought him into the fold through years of patience. After he became a believer in my way, I pointed him towards you, told him he was destined to serve our cause through a relationship with you. Once that was kindled, I told him he must have a child with you. He resisted at that point but eventually followed through. After he shared the news, I told him of your daughter's purpose, how she would serve us."

"No." Katherine raised her hands to her mouth. It couldn't be true. "No!"

Her meeting him at the Magic Gardens was coincidence. He was so charming. She had fallen in love with him. That was a lie? He pushed to have a kid, spent so many nights convincing her that her art career wouldn't suffer, that she would still be able to do everything even with a child. Even after she had said no for the hundredth time and she thought he would leave, he stuck with her, accepted her decision. Then Christina happened. It had been an accident. It had been an accident? He had convinced her to keep her, told her he would stay by her side. Then out of nowhere came his sudden change of heart.

No, it couldn't be.

Waya looked sadly at Katherine. "If it is any consolation, he chose you. There were two other available females within your family tree in which he could have created Christina through, two other options we could have used. Patrick liked you the best."

"Through Katherine and Patrick you created the key." Joaquin stated as Katherine's mouth hung open, "Then all you needed was to gain access to the ley-line."

"Correct. Even after Patrick's breakdown, he wanted to help. I planted him at Vamp industries, used him to find the location, uncover the security protocols, gain a bit of leverage within your systems, and otherwise cause havoc. Large companies like yours are very porous. Then, once we had enough, we attacked."

"You got your man killed. You made a mistake."

Waya nodded, "Patrick died for the cause. He knew it was a possibility. Once I open the ley-line I can bring him back."

"Why involve Katherine? It seems like you could have kidnapped Christina without wrapping her up into all of this."

"For... fun." Waya smiled slickly at Katherine, who charged at Waya, only to be stopped short by three different bodyguards.

Joaquin moved onto the next question, nodding back to the muscle still on the steps, "How did you get the Golems to help? What did you promise them?"

"The only thing they ever wanted. Information. You're not the only hook I had dangling out in the waters of Philly, simply the juiciest fish I wanted to catch."

"Well played."

Joaquin looked like he was impressed by Waya. Waya in turn brightened a little, the agreement between equals that the spoils go to the victor. Joaquin moved forward to unlock the door.

Katherine stared on in horror, going berserk in her own mind. Her whole life with Patrick was, a lie? It was all for some stupid cannon in the basement of a church? Christina was born to die? And how could Joaquin respect this man! He had manipulated the last five years of her life! They were going to kill her daughter and he was somehow okay with it?

"Stop!" Katherine shouted at Joaquin. "Stop! You can't let him win!"

Joaquin paused as his hand rested an inch above the reader. "Katherine, I know when I've lost."

He touched the pad and the large steel door clicked open.

"Stand down." Joaquin raised his hands as he opened the vault door, "Stand down, they're with me."

The two vampire guards on the other side of the vault looked confused for a moment, then did as they were asked. They set down their weapons and backed up to the opposite walls.

"Stop!" Katherine beat on the Golems, the men shoving her forward without reaction. "You can't do this!" She shouted at Waya then charged at him again.

Waya looked annoyed. "Restrain her."

"No!" She yelled as one of the Golems grabbed her by the arms. She fought but his grip was iron.

She shot Joaquin one more look of disgust. "Why are you helping him?"

Joaquin looked sadly at Katherine. Before opening the next door he turned towards Waya. "If this ley-line works as you say it does, I need your word that you will restore Christina's life with its power."

Waya bowed, "You have my word."

Joaquin opened the golden door.

"Stop!"

Katherine's mind wasn't working anymore. This was not happening. Joaquin could not be helping his rival. Her daughter was safe in bed. This was a dream. Yes. This was a very, very bad dream.

They stepped through the glass door and into the circular chamber.

No.

This was NOT a dream.

As they filed into the room, the Golems formed a semi-circle around the outside wall. Joaquin stood next to Katherine and her captor of his own free will. Waya stepped up to the cannon with the Golem holding Christina at his side. Katherine's daughter squirmed and wined, too afraid to cry.

Katherine repeated the words from the cannon's vision over and over.

'Innocent blood has been spilt.
Innocent blood must be spilt again.
Through the union of these bitter enemies
will my attention be stirred.
Only the one who offers a suitable
sacrifice shall claim my reward.'

Sacrifice.

Waya looked at Joaquin. “You have your knife with you, correct?”

“Yes.”

“May I have it?”

Joaquin pulled his silver dagger out from behind his jacket. The sapphires looked cold, like ice.

Sacrifice.

“Let me do it!” Katherine shouted wildly, trying to pull away from her captor. “Let me be the one to,” She swallowed, “sacrifice Christina.”

Waya looked over at her after taking hold of the dagger. “No. The one who offers the sacrifice is the one who claims the reward.”

Katherine continued to struggle, her eyes locked onto her precious daughter. “Then let me be the sacrifice!”

Waya scoffed. “That won’t work. You are only half of the puzzle. She is both.”

“You need blood?” She kept her mouth moving, kept going down this path without reservation. She would do anything to save her daughter’s life. “From both families, yes? Joaquin, you have Patrick’s blood. I have mine. We’ll give this thing both of our blood. Both of her parent’s blood.”

Waya’s eyes hardened. “That will not work.” He turned towards Christina.

“No!” Katherine thrashed and kicked. “Let me try!”

Waya paused and turned back towards Katherine. “Your death will mean nothing. Once you are lost, your daughter is next.”

Katherine was sobbing again, “If there is a chance, even the tiniest chance. Let me try. Let me take her place. And if it doesn’t’ work, fine. Fine! You can kill my baby girl and bring us both back to life with everyone else after you work your stupid magic.”

“I won’t.”

Katherine struggles doubled, “Let me try!”

“I won’t bring you back.” Waya clarified.

Katherine settled. “What?”

“If you do this, and your blood is not acceptable, I will not bring you back. I will restore Christina, I will restore Patrick, your father, his marriage.

Your family. But I will not bring you back to life. They will be happy, without you."

Katherine's mouth hung open. "Why?"

"Faith." Waya stated simply. "You must have faith. You must have faith that your daughter will not be ultimately harmed. You must have faith that it is within my power to protect her, though she may seem to be in grave peril. You require faith."

Katherine struggled against his words. None of this made any sense. There were no rules.

She turned to Joaquin. The look in his eyes told her nothing.

"Do what you think is best, what is in your heart." He said quietly, gently. "I cannot make this decision for you."

Katherine looked back at Christina. She remembered the first time she saw her daughter, held her daughter, that little bundle of happiness and sound, swaddled up and so precious. She remembered her first steps, her first words, her first everything. She was Katherine's everything.

She would protect her, even with her life.

Katherine looked back at Waya, a peace from her decision flooding through her veins. "I will take my daughter's place."

"You are making a mistake." Waya answered.

"For my baby girl, I am not. Now let me go."

Waya looked at the Golem behind her. The man's iron grip slackened, and Katherine fell to the floor. She stood up as gracefully as she could, her black dress ripped and matted with dirt and grime, her shoes lost long ago. She turned towards Joaquin.

"Patrick's blood."

He handed her the half empty pouch. "You don't have to do this."

"I do." She took it, turned away from Joaquin, and stepped in front of the cannon.

A final scream of doubt entered her mind. She had no idea what she was doing. She was crazy! Turning towards Christina, she cupped her daughter's cheek in her hand.

"I love you baby girl."

Christina reached out for her mother's embrace. The golem held her tight. Katherine wanted nothing but to take her in her arms and run. Instead, she shed a tear and turned away.

"Your knife, please." Katherine reached out her hand towards Waya.

Waya shook his head. "No. The one who makes the sacrifice claims the reward." He repeated.

"Fine." Katherine tried to look distinguished, tried to calm her own fears.

With shaky hands she unstopped the cap to the bag of blood and poured it over the cannon's tip. She then turned towards her executioner.

"I'm ready."

The last thing Katherine saw before the dagger plunged into her chest were Christina's beautiful eyes.

Twenty-eight

Katherine woke up with sand in her mouth. She turned over, groggy, and caught a face full of sun. Dazed, she threw an arm over her eyes and moaned.

As she lay there, motionless, she could hear the ocean, the sound of the waves churning in and out on the shore. She could smell the salt in the air, felt the spray gently caressing her skin.

Understanding and confusion were two high speed trains that collided within her mind.

Katherine sat up slowly, her head feeling like it was two sizes too big. Where was she? Had she died? Was this heaven? Was this hell? She touched her chest, touched her skin where she could remember the dagger biting into her heart. It was unbroken. Instead of her black dress, she wore a white tank top over a pink bikini top and khaki beach shorts. Her feet were bare.

Residing before her in all its majesty was the ocean, blue and unending. To her left and right was a beach as far as she could see, with pristine, undisturbed sand in both directions. She looked for signs of other life, both on the water and the shore and found nothing. Behind her was a rocky cliff that hugged the shore, the landmass maintaining a small section of sand between the cliff and the water as the shore snaked in and out. Could she scale the cliff? Maybe she could find a trail or another way up.

Once she made it to her feet, Katherine found a pair of flip-flops a few steps away. She put them on and began to walk, choosing her direction at random. The cliff to her left, the ocean to her right. The unbreakable rock to her left, the restless sea to her right.

As she moved, her thoughts began to break loose and churn, fragments floating up and around her like debris from a shipwreck.

Where was Christina? She needed to find her daughter. She had thought that thought before, before she was here, that she needed to find her daughter. Joaquin had helped her. Joaquin had helped Waya. Joaquin had tried to kill her, tried to bite off her head. He had? Was that a dream or reality? Waya had tried to kill her, tried to use those Golems to murder her. She had let Waya sacrifice her.

She wasn't a virgin. Waya had been right. She was a stupid sacrifice.

Had it worked? Was this her new life? There wasn't a beach like this anywhere near Philly! Still, she had no idea how any of this stuff worked. For all she knew, Waya had used the ley-line's power to make her a refugee on the beach in some foreign country. That idea made about as much sense as any of the other explanations that were buzzing through her mind.

Katherine continued to walk, unsure what she was looking for. Whatever it was, she felt like it was this way, somewhere up ahead, somewhere in front of her.

Eventually, she found something new. Or, rather, someone new. A small boy with moppy black hair working diligently on a massive sandcastle. The structure was almost as tall as Katherine, with a dozen towers, interlinking walls, roofs out of seashells, and a moat surrounding the fortress. When she came up upon the boy and his masterpiece, he was carving out windows with a small trowel, his tongue sticking out of the side of his mouth as he concentrated. Katherine watched on for a moment before speaking.

"Hi there." She waved, standing a few steps away from the boy. "Do you know where we are?"

"Yes." The youth replied, not looking towards her, his attention remaining on his castle.

"Um, okay." Katherine shuffled her feet a bit, "Where are we?"

"We are here." The boy answered simply.

"And where is here?" Katherine asked a second time.

At this the boy looked towards her, frowning. "We are on a beach. Look lady, no offense, but your questions are a bit distracting. Can't you see I'm trying to focus?"

"Sorry." Katherine murmured. She then looked up and down the shore, looking for where this boy might have come from. If he was here, wherever here was, his parents should be close by. Parents would mean a car at least, if not a town to begin to figure out this little mystery.

After Katherine stood there, silently, watching the boy sculpt for a few minutes, he set down his tools and looked up at her with a scowl.

"Are you going to gawk at me all day, or are you going to help?"

"Help?" Katherine blinked.

"Yes, join me. Two pairs of hands are better than one, even if you've never done this before. Have you ever done this before?"

Katherine could remember a single day, long ago on the beach with her family. Her mom was still there, still with them. Her dad had been happy, smiling through the sunshine and sea spray. It seemed like Ethan had brought a whole trunk-full of different buckets and shovels, ones for the walls, the towers, the moat. They had spent the morning trying to build a castle half as impressive as this kids, but every time they made a bit of progress something ruined it.

At first they had not used enough water, the sand collapsing on itself, not holding form. Once they figured out the right mixture, they had trouble stacking more than two buckets high without it collapsing. After Laura threw a bucket in frustration, their dad had come over and coached them along, showing them it was more about building up a solid base than a tall one. He was great, but he did, however, fail to tell them about how the ocean changed. The incoming tide destroyed their progress after another hour. Their third masterpiece was delayed by lunch, baking in the sun and losing its ability to be added onto without crumbling after their feast of peanut butter and jelly sandwiches and string cheese. Their parents nearly drug them away from their fourth and best construction site, with three towers nearly as tall as Katherine and a half-built wall. Sure, it was lopsided and had no detailing, the seashells half fallen off by the time they were packed up in the car, but it was theirs. They had made it with their own hands.

That had been a good day.

"Hello?" The boy waved his trowel in Katherine's direction. "Did I ask something hard to understand? Have you done this before?"

Katherine blinked back to the present. "Yes, a few times. They never looked quite as good as yours though. You sure you want me to help?"

The boy shrugged. "That's why you're here, isn't it?"

"I don't know why I'm here."

"Yes you do."

Katherine looked at the boy's eyes and thought she saw a whole constellation of stars shimmering within his pupils. An infinite depth of sight and knowledge. She shook her head and after looking again she saw nothing more than a youth with spaghetti arms and legs, a toothy smile, and ears too large for his head.

"Do you have another one of those trowels?"

The boy laughed. "You think I'm letting you do the fun part? Eh, no. Take those buckets there." He waved at half a dozen pails, "Fill them up with the sand just at the shoreline. Wet, but not too wet."

Katherine's stare flattened. "You want me to lug sand for you?"

He shrugged, "It's either that or you can leave me in peace. Your choice. The last guy who came through here had the same kind of attitude as you. Lazy, entitled."

"Last guy?"

"Doesn't matter. At least not right now." The youth pointed, "Bucket or keep walking."

Katherine muttered how this kid was getting on her nerves, giving her orders, but she chose to follow along. He directed her to pile up her sand a few yards away from his castle, create a new mound to be sculpted. They would link his castle to the new outbuilding via a skybridge. There would be a total of three of these expansions. The north one would be on a crazy rock island, jutting out of the sea. The west one, the one she was building, would be on the back of a giant turtle. And the east one? It would be floating on a cloud with nothing below it.

"Floating." Katherine wiped sweat from her forehead and threw down another bucket of sand. "How are you going to manage that?"

"With a cloud." The boy scowled, as if it was perfectly clear with his first explanation.

"Okay." Katherine trudged back to the ocean for another haul.

Once the first mound was large enough for the boy's satisfaction, Katherine began to pile up the north mound. As she worked, she kept an eye on the sun, waiting for it to begin to dip lower in the sky. She also began to worry about being out for so long without sunscreen. Or at least she had not remembered if she had put any on before waking up. She was going to be fried to a crisp with the length of day still remaining. She was also beginning to grow increasingly thirsty.

"Do you have any water?" She asked the boy after throwing another pile of sand down.

The boy cocked his head a bit and waved his arm out towards the ocean. "Water, all you could want right there."

"No, to drink."

He waved in arm in the exact same way a second time, saying nothing.

"I can't drink that."

"Why not?"

"Salt. And it tastes horrible. And it'll only get me more dehydrated. I need fresh water."

"No, you don't. Not here."

Katherine put her hands on her hips. "Yes I do. I've had plenty of salt water in my day. Almost drowned in it once. I can still remember coughing it up."

"Then don't go swimming in it. Just drink it."

At this, Katherine had had enough. "I can't, I already told you why. Look, I've been helping you with your castle for at least an hour now. Where are your parents? How did you get here? Where can I find a way to someone who can help?"

"You did."

"I did… what?"

The boy shrugged, "You did. You found someone who will help you. You simply have not been asking the right questions."

Katherine saw that same look in the boy's eyes as before, a whole constellation of stars. It was gone again after he stood up.

"And what questions should I be asking?"

"You could start with a typical one, like, oh, Hi, I'm Katherine, who are you?"

"Who are..." She paused, "Wait. How do you know my name?"

"See? Still not the right question." The boy acted like he was the one being infinitely patient with a small child. "Try again."

She did not like playing this game with a ten-year-old. "Fine. Who are you?"

"I know who I am. Who are you?" The boy smiled savagely in return.

Katherine swallowed back a scream. She stamped her foot and turned, began stalking away down the beach.

The boy followed, skipping along. "I have many names. Hmmm, I think the best one for you to call me is Philia."

Katherine stopped and turned towards the boy. "Are you joking?"

Philia paused as well, the constellations returning to his eyes. This time they remained. "No."

"You're named after my city?"

"No. The city is named after me."

Katherine sputtered. "You, you're ten. The city has been around for, hundreds of years."

The boy put his hands behind his back. "I appear to you in the least threatening form, for you, for your sake."

Katherine could feel a weight and a knowledge from this boy's gaze. She did not like it.

"Philia."

"Yes. It is derived from the ancient Greeks, who viewed love in four forms. Like a square, or a compass. Philia is that friendly, affectionate, bonding love of brothers. Philadelphia, the city of brotherly love. It's amazing the threads you can see once you know a bit about history. Each generation likes to think they are born into this wonderful world that is ripe for them to plunder and rape. Instead, they are born within a flow of time that has gone on before their arrival and will continue after their departure. There are many masters already here. I am one of the many who pull the strings, who shape that which you think is happenstance. I am the architect behind your whole city's heartbeat."

Katherine had no idea how to respond. Instead, she asked again. “Who are you?”

“I am Philia!” The kid smiled and started walking back to his sandcastle. Katherine followed. “You can think of me as your city’s guardian angel.”

“Are we, am I… in the ley-line? Did it work?” Katherine stared out at the sea. The sun was on the horizon, sending brilliant golden rays across the waves. She could have sworn two minutes ago it was over her head. When had that happened?

“The ley-line is not a place, but a door. You stepped through. We are within a space of my choosing, of your making. You may think of it as a dream non-dream. It is much more complicated than that, but we do not have the time for me to explain.“

“Why am I here?”

“*Only the one who offers a suitable sacrifice shall claim my reward.*” Philia quoted the line Waya had repeated a few times. “You offered your flesh, your life. You are the one who has reaped the boon of my attention. What would you like?”

“What would I like?” Katherine’s mind bent with the implications of the question. “What can I have?”

“Anything!” Philia hopped then dug his toes into the sand near his castle. “That is, anything within my power. While I rule over your city, I have a great many enemies that control the spaces beyond. And within. Layers within layers, a complex interweaving organism of moving parts, spirits unseen by mortals like you. The celestial hierarchy. Oh, and the demonic legions. They’re part of this soup too. It’s a good thing your offering was so delicious! Not like that other guy’s. Blech. So, as you can see, I’m in a good mood.”

“My offering?”

“Yes.” Philia stepped over to his sandcastle, moving his arms around it. As he waved his hands, the sand sharpened, minute details not possible within dry sand taking shape.

“There is a great deal of, humanity, in the world. Men and women struggling, failing, flailing, growing corrupted, compromising, dying, cheating, lying, destroying, killing. Men and women, with the best of intentions, becoming the worst creatures imaginable. One, small, grain of sand at a time."

Philia waved his hand dramatically and the whole castle collapsed, falling into a huge heap of nothingness.

"Men build their castles, flawed. Their castles fall. Their legacies shatter. And the next generation will try again, use the same sand. Or iron, copper, steel, gold, glass… all eventually tarnish, break, explode.

"Ah, but once in a great while humanity provides the best of yourselves. Selflessness, patience, love for no other reason but for the good of another, joy. Hope. You provided that. You chose to sacrifice your very life for your daughter, after you learned of the unholy plot in her birth, after you were warned that it might not work, that it could mean the end of you. Even though you had every reason thrown at you to stop, you gave yourself up. For her.

"That act, Katherine, to a being such as myself is pure ecstasy."

Out of the pile of sand Philia pulled a nugget of metal that shone as bright as the sun. He smiled at it as Katherine raised her hands to block its radiance. The stone's brilliance doubled in power then it flashed, vanishing.

"With your sacrifice, I have gained a great deal of influence within the ranks. With it, I will honor you with a sliver of my power. What do you want?"

It was a question Katherine had been asking herself for a while now, a question that seemed to have no answer. She opened her mouth twice and then closed it, no sound coming out.

This kind of an opportunity would never happen again.

What did she want?

Philia raised his arms above him, "Let me help you along. Look."

The sun disappeared and the expanse of the sky was filled with stars. More stars than Katherine had ever seen in her whole life. She spun, awestruck. From the edge of the ocean up and above her in every direction, millions of pinpricks of light shone. Within the stars, gigantic clouds of cosmic dust painted the otherwise black sky with color.

"I know you have been in conflict with yourself," Philia spoke, "feeling adrift, lost. You try and you fail, and you try, and you fail. You feel out of control, like your life is not your own. Let me pass you my compassion. Those feelings are absolutely normal. To struggle is what it means to be human. You, Katherine, are small. As insignificant to a single star in comparison with the cosmos. But you are unique, special. You struggle, and you try, and you fail, and you do not give up. You keep trying.

"The noble pursuit of a passion, of a goal against all odds, is just as powerful as love. You have that spark. Never let it go out. You have a strength of spirit that many do not have. Be proud of everything you have done so far.

"Life is best lived in the little moments. These are sometimes the ones with the most power.

"Ah, but you are still conflicted. Let me continue. What can I give to you? Do you wish to honor Waya? He came proudly to my feet looking for the power to change his whole people's history. A people maligned, taken advantage of, oppressed, and cast to the side of history. He wishes for his ancestors and his children to be the ones in control."

Within the stars an image of hundreds of crying mothers and children, broken fathers, and the soldiers over them all, weighing them down, appeared. The families walked in the snow, their heads down, all that they owned on their backs. As Philia spoke on, the images shifted to mirror his words.

"Waya wishes to change his people's fate. Ah, but such a grand task is outside of my power. Where I can adjust a dozen attacks against his people, a dozen dozen, the forces against him are still more powerful and the consequences hard to unravel. What is the end goal? Do I combat against the Devil that is American Imperialism and allow the Cherokee to retain their land? They would eventually lose their sovereign status as a nation, eventually choose to freely assimilate within the seductive American culture. Though their children's children live, their heritage would be forgotten. Discarded. Do I then fight against that Devil? Maintain lines of division? At a certain point the history that you know shatters. A war would break out between the Great Canadian Empire and the Cherokee Nation in the 1930s, leading to a great many lives lost. We can avoid that tragedy only by driving headlong into a political crisis within their radicalized nation of tribes, one in which eradicates Waya's whole family tree through forced sterilization and targeted assassinations by other evil men, now related to him, now of his culture and his skin tone, yet against him still. His people would remain, tainted by further evil and he, their unwanted savior, would cease to exist.

"Again, what is the goal? To provide what Waya desires is like straightening a crooked rope by pushing on the end. Each movement towards his supposed happiness for today produces greater and greater ripples, more bends, the result never quite providing his hopes for utopia. No matter which pieces we move, there will always be something wrong.

Philia sighed, "Or maybe you allow Joaquin to have his heart's desire?"

The images within the heavens of war and loss, pain and suffering were replaced with a great fire. At first it began small, then stars exploded, cascading from one to another in an unimaginable supernova.

"I could strike down the Demon Lord that protects Serpitus, allow your lover to realize his revenge. But it would be hollow, pointless. As all revenge becomes. Pain delivered out of pain delivered is a spiral into darkness. Eventually another would arrive, one of the many wronged by that monster, your Joaquin. He or she would strike out against Joaquin for their own revenge due to an unforgivable wrong he has committed against them. I could let the cycle continue ad infinitum.

"Hate upon hate, upon hate."

With a snap, the inferno above returned to a brilliant night sky.

"Or shall we focus on you? Recreate your family, carve them into your own flawed concept of perfection?"

As Philia spoke each of their names, he rose up out of the sand a copy of her family members, their faces frozen in terror.

"Provide for you the request in which has tempted you so? I could shift your parent's destiny, change your mother's heart to be content with what was, have her choose to remain with your father. I could then allow your father the insight into what was required to remain healthy, how to slow down and not overdo it. You would have the home you always wanted, the family dinners, the holidays, the phone calls when you needed an ear. Laura would be around, Ethan would be more caring, Patrick would praise you for your art, support you and love you unconditionally. You would be happy, that is, until you remembered that none of their actions were truly their choice, none of their love for you truly earned, but taken. Is love taken, manufactured, worth anything?

"In addition, what if I told you that with your parents at your side, you would not have had Christina? What if I told you that you would die childless? Is what you ask for worth that cost?"

"Why can't I have Christina and my parents too?" Katherine interrupted.

Philia picked up a pail and dumped out the sand. It suspended in mid-air, becoming a baby.

"Children, generations, destiny through the unborn is one of the thinnest and most fragile threads in all of Fate. One small change, a simple tweak to anything and the effects echo heavily. In your case, the correlation is shockingly simple. If your father was around, you would not have fallen for Patrick. I can force you to, but later on in life, after the possibility of Christina has past. While everything is possible for me to provide, not everything is possible at the same time.

"Life is cruel. Life is mysterious. Life is simple. There is always a give and take."

Philia smiled sadly as the sand people, including the baby collapsed. "One last time. What do you want?"

Katherine could feel her heart pull in a dozen directions. Nothing seemed right, nothing seemed like the perfect answer. She couldn't give up Christina. She would not help Waya. She agreed with Philia about Joaquin's lust for revenge. There didn't seem to be any perfect answers, even with unlimited power. What was the meaning of life? What was the goal?

Philia seemed to hear her thoughts. "No. Perfection is never the goal. Striving towards perfection is a noble pursuit, but you will never achieve it. Ever. You are human, flawed. You are absolutely beautiful in your flaws. A being such as I has no excuse not to reach perfection in every single one of my thoughts. You? When you strike that chord of perfection for a moment, for even an instant, joy unending."

When the length of silence seemed to stretch past what was proper, Katherine felt a single tear slide down her cheek.

"I don't know what I want."

Philia smiled warmly. “An honest answer. Mmmmm. I can feel your deepest desires. They are there, they are beneath your fears, your uncertainties. Dig, uncover them. With a hair more honesty with yourself, you will know exactly what you want.”

Katherine breathed deeply. He was right. She did. It was right there all along.

“Yes. There it is.”

Philia smiled with his toothy grin. He was a child in that moment. He was also an ancient presence with infinite wisdom.

“You’ve made a good choice. Here, take my hand. I will show you exactly what I will do for you in my name.”

Twenty-nine

For a second time that night, Katherine woke up with her face plastered onto the ground. This time, instead of sand, the first thing she noticed was the copper taste of blood on her lips. She slowly opened her eyes and didn't quite understand what she was seeing. Within the cannon's chamber underneath the Basilica sat Max. He was laughing as he rolled a ball back and forth with Christina. Joaquin sat nearby, his eyes closed, his breath coming in slow, deep draws.

No one else was there with them.

Katherine blinked twice, her head feeling like it had been squeezed through a sieve. "Max, you're alive?"

"Welcome back Ms. Mason," Max looked confused. "Um, yes? Am I not supposed to be?"

It had worked.

Upon hearing her voice, Joaquin's eyes opened weakly. He smiled. "Welcome back."

Katherine sat up slowly, "What happened?" She touched her chest, searching for a wound that she was sure to find. "Did Waya stab me?"

Joaquin nodded, "Yes, he did. Then the unexpected happened, or, expected if you have experience with ley-lines. There was a thundering flash and you and him burst apart. You landed there. I moved over to your side and to my surprise found his attack had not left a mark. Waya landed somewhere over there. You've been out for about fifteen minutes, give or take."

"They, Waya, left?" She stammered out.

"They did. There was a series of voices, after you collapsed, two male voices. I presume they were Waya's overlords because his face went white as the voices made clear their displeasure in his failures. As they finished their scathing critique, he rushed out of here with the Golems and left me with you and Max with your daughter. I am not sure if we'll ever see him again. The Thunder Boys are not known as the, forgiving type."

Katherine couldn't believe it had worked.

Joaquin's face clenched up and he took in a sharp gasp, "I'm still, a bit weak from my adventures tonight. How are you feeling?"

Instead of answering Joaquin, Katherine hobbled over to her daughter and sat hard onto the floor. She hungrily scooped Christina into her arms. "Hey there baby girl! I'm sorry if my friends or I scared you. None of this was planned. But we're safe. I'm not going anywhere. I'm here to protect you."

"I will assume, but still ask, Waya's rapid departure was your doing?"

Katherine looked at Joaquin and smiled, "Yea, you can blame me." Katherine then hugged Christina even tighter as she squirmed and murmured for her mom to stop squeezing her like that. "That's right! Your mommy found a way to help everyone."

Joaquin continued, "I had hoped… I risked a great deal on the assumption that from your actions, you would receive the boon instead of Waya. It was my only play. There was no way for me to seize it personally. I am sorry if I had seemed indifferent. I was anything but. You were amazing, your courage, your heart. Did you meet the Messenger? What did you ask for?"

"Thank you. And I did. I asked for a bunch of stuff."

Joaquin seemed less impressed than she expected, "Katherine, what exactly did you ask for?"

"I asked for help."

"Katherine," Joaquin said her name dangerously low, "Celestial beings can be tricky, taking your wishes and twisting them in unexpected ways. In addition, I dearly hope you didn't squander the moment. This is important. What did you ask for?"

"How is your fight going against the Golems and Gypsies?"

His jaw tensed, "I received word while you were out that the Golems have withdrawn. We were able to reach a stalemate with the Gypsies, of sorts. It's still fluid, but more stable than an hour ago." He paused, "Thank you."

Katherine smiled, proud of herself, "You're welcome."

"Katherine. Your exact request. Please." Joaquin asked one more time.

She didn't want him to fret too much, but being the one in control was nice for a change. "It wasn't as much a direct request, more of a feeling."

Joaquin's eyes darkened. "What kind of feeling?"

She shrugged, "Philia showed me a million possibilities, countless tweaks to our reality that he could provide. I could have changed the past, but I found that things would still be broken. I could have gained fame, fortune, love, power, but I knew if I didn't earn those things myself they would feel fake. Even bringing my father back would simply lead to losing him again, eventually. Sure, I could have made more memories with him, but I would have also lost some of the best parts of my life right now. There was no possible future where if my father was alive I would also have Christina. That hurt, but it also made sense. That day in the Magic Gardens, if my father was there, nothing Patrick could have done would have persuaded me to him. I would have never chosen this path if I still had him in my life.

"Did I want power, revenge, justice? I could have hurt anyone and everyone I have held a grudge against, changed any wrong done to me. It felt so, selfish, so… wrong. You and Waya were fighting over this gift for your own ends. I didn't want to do that. Then I found it. I found what I truly want.

"I want to help others.

"I know you might think us humans are all lost and broken. I don't. I think this life is hard, that we make awful decisions sometimes, we horribly hurt the people we love, but we also have the capacity to do amazing things! To love huge! So that's what I did. With Philia's gift I helped everyone I love, everyone who wants the best for me. I spread out his gift as far as I could, gave a little something special to everyone I knew, everyone who has ever touched my life in a positive way so that no one was left out."

"That is very noble of you." Max smiled, standing up. "I can see why this angel or demon chose you among a room full of, less then selfless people."

Joaquin looked hard at his employee. "While I do not disagree, helping those who help you is far from noble. Everyone does that."

"I also helped all those who want to hurt my family."

Joaquin was slow to turn back towards Katherine. He blinked.

"Why?"

"Let's call it, killing them with kindness. I'm not silly enough to hand my enemies a gun. But a bouquet with a bee? I asked Philia to give them exactly what they wanted, just as long as it pushed them away from my family and friends. Kept them too distracted on other things to ever bother me again."

Max's smile widened. "Smart. I like this one Joaquin. Are we going to keep her around?"

Katherine grinned back at Max then yawned in unison with Christina, "Tonight has been, a night. A night I will never forget. But it's time for it to end. Max," She almost choked up, him being alive again, then steadied her voice, "can you drive us home?"

Joaquin stumbled up to his feet, leaning hard against the wall. He nearly collapsed when he locked his knees. "I think… I think we should go back to my place. The Golems and I… we tore up your brother's home badly… if you don't remember."

Katherine stood up as well. She set her yawning daughter's head on her shoulder, enjoying her cuddles, her presence.

"You did, but it's not quite as torn up anymore. While there was quite a bit of the past I didn't feel right touching, I was okay adjusting a few details to your fight within my brother's home. Erased it, really. I even made it better than before. All the dust is gone! No kid needs that kind of trauma. Especially if their dad is a licensed therapist. Isn't that right Max."

Max nodded. "My daughter has nightmares from regular life. She's nine. There's no need for either boy to dream of sabertooths ripping up Golems."

"Even so," Joaquin continued, "I'm not sure it's safe for you there tonight."

"What, you don't trust that me and Mr. Angel can't tie up all the loose ends? Did you not get the memo? I'm the one calling the shots tonight. Max, since I'm still learning… everything, when it comes to vampires and the proper care for them when they are all, torn up… what does he need? Where do you bring him?"

"He has a set up in his penthouse where we can do a blood transfer. Best thing for him."

"Then that's our first stop."

"Katherine, I –"

"Think you can take care of yourself?" She cut him off. "Of course you think that. And I know better. Now stop arguing with me and let's go get you patched up."

Katherine had planned to head back home after dropping Joaquin off. She first insisted on following him all the way up with a sleeping Christina in her arms. Had to make sure Joaquin made it to his bed safely. If he had one. Maybe even tuck him in.

As Max continued to help the hobbling Joaquin towards one of the back rooms he pointed towards a door.

"There is a crib in that one, if you want to set Christina down."

"He has a crib? Why?"

"Toddler bed in there too. We weren't sure how Christina was comfortable sleeping."

Katherine peaked in. Sure enough, the pastel-colored room looked every bit like the pristine nursery. There was a rocker, changing table, dresser, toddler bed, three bookshelves filled with children's board books for easy access on the bottom and paper books on the top, and two baskets of toys.

"In case…" Joaquin whispered, "you ever needed a place to… lay low for a bit."

Katherine looked from the man who had died trying to save her life tonight, to the man who had put her heart in a blender and made everything in her life turn upside down.

"Thank you. Both of you.

"Now, no more talking. Save your energy for the last few steps, grampa. Once I get Christina comfortable, I'll help make you good as new."

Katherine set Christina down in the crib then kissed her on the head as she rolled over, fast asleep. "No more basements soon, baby girl."

She paused and soaked in the moment. This was exactly the kind of room she was going to give to her daughter. Maybe one with a tree outside the window instead of a drop to the city below, but everything else like this.

She still couldn't believe she could.

Katherine then wandered back to where she hoped Max had taken Joaquin. After poking her head into a study then an exercise room, she found the back bedroom. Joaquin was lying with his eyes closed on a black leather couch as Max connected a few tubes to his wrist.

"Hey, look at that, he does have a bed." Katherine moved over to the king-sized bed and sat down on the corner.

Max pressed a few buttons on a machine then stood up. "He'll be a few hours like this, blood slowly cycling back into his system. It's his, by the way, the blood. He lost a lot during that fight, nearly bled out. I still find his kind to be strange and amazing creatures. Any human in his condition would no longer be alive."

"Yea. We humans are fragile things." Katherine's memory of Max lying on the ground dampened her spirits. Philla had offered to help her forget, but she had wanted to remember. Wanted to keep her memories. Remember what almost became truth.

"Come," Max put his arm around her shoulders, "let's give him some space."

"Can I…" She bit her lower lip, "Can I stay for a little? Make sure he's stable and all of that? Christina is fine and I have nowhere to be… really."

"Of course." Max smiled and stepped away, "The staff have all gone for the night, so, if you need anything, give me a call."

He handed her his business card with the Vamp Industries logo.

"That's a special one, My personal number. I don't hand these out normally. Just in case."

Katherine nodded. "Just in case."

After Max left, Katherine lay down on her stomach on the bed, her chin propped in her hands as she watched over Joaquin. In the stillness she let her mind wander, let her memories of the past few months' insanity float wherever it wanted to go. In that space, in the silence, she found something new that flowed within her normally anxious internal monologue. A vein of calm. A flood of confidence and peace. She had saved them all. Had Philia given her that? Or was it an inner strength she had found herself? Something she had created through her own actions, through taking one leap of faith after another and finding that she was capable of handling each step?

Well, whatever it was, there were a few more steps to go. A few more notes to play. A few more brush strokes to paint to finish this masterpiece. A few more…

In Katherine's next thought, she jumped at the sight of an empty couch. Where did Joaquin go? She startled herself so badly she fell off the bed. It was after her groan that she realized it was morning. A stream of sunshine peaked out from behind the curtains as the smell of bacon wafted into the room.

Katherine rolled over and looked down at the black dress she was still in and cringed. It was torn, dirty, absolutely ruined. Standing up, one look in the mirror showed her make-up smeared, her hair a tangled mess. She couldn't walk out of here looking like this! Not in the morning!

Taking a risk, Katherine snuck into the hallway and checked on Christina. Finding her still asleep, she decided to steal some of Joaquin's clothes, dig through his drawers and find a shirt and a pair of pants that might stay up with a belt. For how much worse it would be, at least they would be clean. However, after walking into the bathroom she discovered Joaquin's forethought once again. On the corner of the sink sat a pile of clothes, her size, her style for a Saturday. Straight jeans and a bright green t-shirt. On top of it was a note. *'When you wake up, feel free to freshen up. The bathroom is fully stocked.'*

This man seemed to think of everything.

A shower reinvigorated Katherine's mood, the water washing off the last bit of grime. Peaking in on Christina again, Katherine smiled then moved into the kitchen. She found Joaquin at the counter, placing bacon onto two plates already filled with eggs, toast, and hash browns. He wore a simple button down with his sleeves rolled up past his elbows, black jeans. He looked relaxed and unburned, like a man who hadn't been inches from death only hours earlier.

"Good morning." He smiled as he set the hot pan back on the stove. "Breakfast?"

"Yes." She smiled openly at him, "I thought you didn't know how to cook."

"What gave you that impression? Coffee?"

"Yes please!"

"Anything in it?"

"Black is fine. You mentioned vampires don't need to eat. And you have all of your wait staff, chefs."

Joaquin slid both plates over to the other side of the counter, towards the benches. He set a steaming cup of coffee next to Katherine.

"Just because I don't need to, doesn't mean I don't still enjoy it."

"It looks amazing." She bit into the toast and almost moaned. "Is this from my bakery?" she asked with a full mouth.

"It is. Robert makes the best bread in the city. Bought it a day or two ago, before…"

Katherine nodded, knowing everything at Lavigne's was going to be okay, "Before yesterday."

After that first bite, Katherine found out she was famished. She dug into the plate of food without hesitation, stating her hunger before speaking another word. Joaquin was slightly more reserved, sitting next to her, smiling.

Those ten minutes, with the simplicity of it all, were perfect.

"How are you feeling?" Katherine eventually asked as she slowed down on her breakfast. "All healed up from last night?"

"Yes, much better." Joaquin took a sip of coffee. "I've taken more punishment before, but it doesn't get any easier. Pain, the pain is still there."

Katherine couldn't wait any longer. She dug into her pocket and pulled out a small bottle and placed it on the counter in front of Joaquin, a huge grin on her face. "I was going to give this to you last night, but the moment never felt right and now… anyway… For you."

Joaquin looked at the bottle. It was made from a deep red, almost black glass with golden foil and string holding the stopper on.

"What is this?"

Her smile widened. "Well, I wanted to help everyone. Last night, with Philia. Most of my helping was general, I only knew so much to help most people. But with some, with you, I knew exactly what I wanted to give you. The child, spirit, Philia, he said providing this was at the limits of his power, that there could be repercussions for him to meddle with a demon's design so directly, but he was in my debt. So… what is it? After you drink this you will be cured!"

Katherine couldn't read Joaquin's expression, so she kept talking. "With it you can be a human again! You can forget about all of your duties with Serpitus, you can be free. And you, you and I can…"

"I can't." Joaquin said, the words echoing in Katherine's mind.

She stared at him. "I'm sorry, you… can't? Can't what?"

"There is enough here for only one person, correct?"

"Probably, I wasn't given the full instructions, but I would assume so. I'd also assume you have to drink the whole thing."

"Then I can't, at least not yet."

Katherine stilled. This was not how this was supposed to go. "What do you mean, not yet?"

Joaquin looked pained as he spoke, "My job is not done. If I drink this, if I lose my powers, Serpitus will still be alive, still out there, laughing in my face. And even worse, if I take this as you propose I will lose my footing against him, abandon any opportunity I'll ever have to take him down."

"Or you could walk away from it all! This did not cost a little bit! This was the prize, the greatest reward for all of last night. Everything else, all the other tweaks Philia provided were crumbs next to this bottle. I knew how much the ley-line meant to you. I knew you wanted to use its power to break your curse. There it is. You've won."

"Thank you Katherine." Joaquin was stone still, his voice near to a whisper. "And I mean this sincerely, thank you. What you have given me, what this represents is the answer to countless long centuries of searching. It is a great step, but it is only a step."

"You have to drink it."

Joaquin stood up and turned away. "I will. Once Serpitus is dead."

Katherine stood up as well, "And when will that be?"

"I don't know."

The silence was heavy, palpable. Katherine swallowed away her sudden tears.

"Then we can't see each other. Not until you drink this."

Joaquin turned around suddenly and put his hands on her shoulders. "What are you talking about?"

She shook him off and began to pace. "I can't risk being around you, not as you are."

"What changed?"

Katherine set her jaw. "Last night, before last night, I thought I understood how your condition worked. You were able to live longer, were able to go without sleep, food. All benefits. You warned me about the other side, the rage, the inability to stop yourself. I ignored it. I did a stupid thing and ignored your warnings. And last night you… you scared me. You terrified me. You were that sabretooth, you ripped apart five men so easily, took them all down with such a rage! Then you turned on me."

"I remember. I did not hurt you. I did not touch you." Joaquin whispered.

"I know! I know, I know you stopped yourself, but I could see it in your eyes, see your anger, your hatred, your power. It scares me. I can still see it now. And then later last night, all the blood, and just in general! I thought I could handle that. I think I still could. But… I'm not scared for myself, it's my daughter. If I stay around you will Christina remain in danger? Will something like last night happen again? You are at war, your words, at war with the heavens and others like you. I can't actively pursue a path that could endanger her life. I can't willingly stay around such a dangerous whirlwind, for her sake. Even if I think I might be falling in love you."

She looked at him at the end, the tears coming, but staying strong, holding herself together as they streamed down her face.

Joaquin fell apart at the sight of her. He rushed over to her and pulled her into his embrace. "Oh Katherine."

"Then you'll drink it?" She spoke into his shoulder.

He pulled her back, his eyes also swimming. "I… I want to… I desperately want to, for you. I… I can't. Not yet."

Katherine shoved him away a second time, sniffling. She could hear Christina begin to stir. "Then… then… we should go."

"Katherine, I –"

She spun towards him and let go of all her rage. "Love means action! Love means sacrifice! Do you not get that? I have done everything you've asked, and I have asked you for nothing in return! Nothing! You have made me dance, pulled me into your world and made me crazy for you! Can't you see that? I literally went to heaven, or somewhere, I don't know where I was but I found you the solution. It's right here! Take it!"

"I will, I will Katherine. I promise you I will. But I cannot yet."

"You keep saying that. Why? Give me one good reason." Her nostrils flared, "And if you even mention your need for revenge, so help me!"

Joaquin's face was a picture of agony, "If I drink this now, as you ask, the moment Serpitus learns I am human once more he will either change me back or kill me."

"Why? You would no longer be a threat to him!"

"He's vain. He's petty. I've told you this. He causes pain for the fun of it."

"Like murdering your wife."

Joaquin sighed, heartbroken. "Exactly."

"He would use anyone, break anyone, in order to win?"

"Yes."

Katherine put her hands on her hips. "Then answer me one more question. Tell me the truth. In the past 900 years, has he ever used someone you loved, someone beyond Elena, to hurt you?"

When Joaquin did not respond, standing there, handsome beyond a dream, silent, sad, Katherine knew. She laughed bitterly, ungracefully wiped her nose on the back of her hand, then turned and went to her daughter.

"Katherine, wait." Joaquin asked as she came out of the hallway with Christina in her arms. "I can protect you. I can keep you safe."

"You keep saying that, yet my brother and their family almost died. Christina almost died. Max did die. The only reason they're safe is because of me. I protected them."

"Max died? When?"

"Joaquin, I hate to make this decision. It tears me apart to have to choose between my daughter's safety and having you in my life. But as a mother, I have to."

"Please, don't leave."

"I thought… I thought I could save you, thought I could somehow… it doesn't matter now. Philia was right. Life is about give and take. You can't have everything."

"We can work through this."

She shoved past him, "As long as you are a vampire, there is nothing more for us to discuss."

She was a rock now. Cracked, scarred. But she was strong. This would not break her. She would learn from this, and she would force herself to move on. For her daughter's sake.

"Katherine, please." Joaquin followed her to the elevator, his hands up, pleading, the elevator doors opening silently.

Katherine stepped on and turned back towards him. She should not have done that. The pain clear on his face crushed her heart. No. She held onto Christina even tighter.

"Call me if you change your mind. Until then, goodbye Joaquin."

After the doors closed, Joaquin stood there, staring at nothing for far too long.

Thirty

Katherine was beginning to think of her new place as home. Though she had the ability to live nearly anywhere, she liked the idea of staying in the city. She had considered staying near her brother's place, Christina still loved running around on the playground and Katherine had begun to really enjoy the moms she had met. But then this place closer to Center City had appeared on the market, right next to an ever bigger part, and it simply felt right. It had been a good choice.

And her new house wasn't anything modest either! A developer had taken a dilapidated section of the block and redeveloped it. Her house was a modern take on the neighborhood's architecture, a three-story corner unit with its own rooftop deck and full basement. Beyond the four bedrooms, two of which she was still deciding on their purpose, she had set up most of the third floor as a fully furnished art studio. With windows looking out on three sides, the natural light and open space was perfect for her to continue painting.

The story she told everyone who asked was that her art exhibition had been a resounding success. The spray paint attack had been part of the show. A bit Banksy. The lore of the night, of the atmosphere and the incident raised the demand for her twelve pieces high enough that she had been able to afford this house. And a few other things.

A lucky string of events.

The truth was that after talking to Philia on the beach and requesting nothing for herself, he wanted to impart something extra, something more for such a kind heart. He gave her 1%. A single percentage point stake of ownership in Vamp industries. With her stock options and leverage that she was still working through with the lawyers, she had millions. Scratch that, over a billion depending on the value of the stock that day. More money than she could have ever dreamed about.

Yes, the money was nice, but what she enjoyed most was now having the time with her daughter and the time for her art. The time for her to start up a philanthropy organization, to continue to help others. The time to be herself without worry. The time to laugh with Shandra and her new friends, be at peace with her family and share in their excitement and joy over their own turns of good fortune.

Beyond erasing the attack, both in memory and physical damages from Ethan and Iris's lives, Katherine had provided them with a simple change of perspective. A spark of hope. Iris had started working out, doing yoga and palates at a nearby gym with childcare. The daily break from her boys and the strengthening of her core helped her deal with their attitudes in a more constructive way. They weren't any quieter from the times Katherine had visited, but Iris seemed to handle it better. Ethan had found a new passion for his work, digging in and suggesting changes that eventually led to him being asked to join the partnership as an owner. They both looked happier, healthier and more relaxed, all from a little, well-placed nudge.

At first Katherine had wanted to erase the attack on Lavigne's bakery but chose to leave it alone as part of history. Once it reopened, the community did rally to Robert's aid, tripling his sales within the span of a month. When she had stopped by a week ago, Robert was considering opening another location across town. His wife's cancer had disappeared mysteriously, giving them both a new vigor for life.

For Lester, Katherine stilled his dreams. She provided for him a peace of mind over his trauma about the war. He claimed the minor attack had reset something in him, allowed him the healing he needed to move on in life. He was also able to reconnect with his buddies, put together a cycling club where they and others rode together every Saturday, rain or shine.

Shandra had been a bit harder to pin down a boon for her life. Katherine eventually landed on nothing new. Even if it seemed like a failure on her part or a slight to her best friend, Shandra already seemed happy, already had the right attitude and perspective. And with the resources Katherine now had at her disposal, she could enjoy giving Shandra gifts directly and sporadically for years.

Marge lost her love for alcohol. She quickly regained some of her senses, found her way out of her fog more often and even began to purge her home. No more fake flowers, they were out of style.

Mr. and Mrs. Preston received calls from their children. Katherine hadn't even known they had kids, three of them living in different parts of the country. They had been estranged due to silly arguments built up over the years. The Preston seniors were forgiven, and their relationships with their kids were able to begin anew.

Jerry was found on the streets and checked into rehab by his grandmother.

From the friends Katherine had in high school, up to the mothers that played with her daughter, she had worked with Philia to bestow some level of fortune on them all.

Then there were those on the other side of the coin.

A few weeks after the night at the church, she saw on the morning news that Mr. Weiss and a few of his underlings were being arrested on a multitude of fraud charges, ranging from racketeering to money laundering. When she had asked Philia to give him what he wanted, Philia had the wicked idea to give others like him that prize instead. Those in the Golem organization, those who disapproved of him lending out their strength to an outsider had much to gain for one of their rival's sudden legal problems. She imagined they were very happy with the outcome.

Even after three months she had not found out what had happened to Waya. His corporation continued on, doing what they did, consulting. She had called in a few times, anonymously, trying to delve for information, only to slam into a brick wall of bureaucracy and run arounds. Even though her curiosity wasn't stated, she decided to let it lie. Not knowing how his overlords delt with him would have to be good enough.

While talking with Philia, Katherine had been surprised to find the Gypsies never had an ill thought against her. As such, she let them be. Serpitus was also indifferent, though Philia was the one who had warned her about Joaquin's boss's future ire. The spirit's advice was to let those two groups burn each other to the ground rather than for her to intervene. She agreed.

Katherine looked out over the park from her art studio and sighed, a fleeting thought breaking her otherwise good mood. She had not heard from Joaquin since storming out on him. For the first week she had hoped to have his call come through at any moment, have his voice on the other line tell her he had been wrong. That she was worth the risk. The call never came. As the days stretched into weeks, her hope waned. It had been three months now, to the day. Three months since her life had changed and he had left her alone.

It still hurt.

A few times, late into the night she had almost called him, almost dialed his number just to hear his voice, just to tell him she had been stupid and he didn't need to give everything up for her. That they could make it work. A few of those nights had been absolutely impossible. But she eventually made it to the morning, and she eventually took another step forward in life. Safe. Both her and her daughter, safe. Without him. And today, this morning? This morning might be the first day in a long time that the idea of moving forward, without him, that it might be alright.

Not great... Not what she wanted, but alright.

She had Christina. She had her family. She had a whole life ahead of her.

She was going to make the best of it.

Yes. Life wasn't perfect, but it was going to be alright.

Joaquin sat at his desk and stared at the deep red bottle. For three months now he had carried it with him, kept it on his person at all times, remembering what it represented and the person who had given it to him.

Katherine.

For a few weeks now he had yearned to call her, to tell her he had been a fool. That she had been right. But he couldn't quite make it, couldn't quite dial her number, or show up at her new home unannounced. As the days went on, the urge only seemed to grow, and the difficulty only seemed to grow along with it.

He knew she wouldn't want to see him. He had been right. She could never love him, not as he was. Not with who he was. Not for all that he had done. Not for the threat he posed. For a few weeks he had been so close to changing for her, so close to throwing caution to the wind, drinking the bottle, and running away with her.

But then, the letter had arrived.

Joaquin did not need to read it, even though it sat open next to the red bottle. He had committed it to memory. As he let the words roll over his mind again, he stood up and looked out over the city, looked out over the humanity below him.

Katherine had been right. He had enemies lurking behind every corner. Until he walked away, he could be nothing but a danger to her and her daughter.

He had yet to decide what he would do.

Mr. Joaquin Morales,

I do not expect you to consider yourself indebted to me.

You are.

Under the Basilica, you may think you won. Consider it a hollow victory. You must know that I walked into that room fully aware that there was no way for me to claim my prize. I labored for nearly a decade, searched through every possible avenue and trail of Fate until I ultimately concluded that the past must remain, that my longing to find a remedy towards my people's injustice will remain unfulfilled. Hard work is never lost, it sometimes simply takes an unexpected form.

The past must remain. The future is open. The poison is provided. The choice is yours.

Christina was never the Key. It was always Katherine and her love. I knew this. No matter my attempts, she would always be the one to gain the reward. I knew this too. There was no way for me to convince her to take my side, so I pushed her towards you. It was so easy. She witlessly provided you with a way to destroy you completely. A way to break the back of the vampires forever.

Per my every design.

There are many trails in a man's life, many decisions and paths that can be followed, that can be explored. I have seen them all. You have but three in front of you now.

No matter which one you choose, the outcome will benefit me.

The first? You can drink the antidote and run into Katherine's arms. She will love you. You will be happy. Serpitus will flee Philly with you removed from his side. I will win.

The second? You can force or trick Serpitus to drink the antidote and kill him. You will lose Katherine forever, but you will have your justice, your revenge. Without Serpitus's strength, your fractured kingdom will fall. I will win.

The third? You do nothing with the bottle. You try instead to outsmart me. You try to outwit me. You cannot. You will die, having gained nothing. I will win.

I can see all paths for all men. The exciting part for me is the anticipation. Which will you set your feet down upon?

Your friend,

Waya Kipp

About the Author

Thomas G. Schubert is a licensed electrical engineer who works for an architectural & engineering firm in downtown Philadelphia. He currently lives in Lancaster County, PA with his wife, five kiddos, three cats, and one dog. He is an avid reader who believes that anything truly worth doing in life should be done well.

www.ingramcontent.com/pod-product-compliance
Lightning Source LLC
Chambersburg PA
CBHW030826310726
48980CB00006B/652/J
* 9 7 9 8 9 9 2 7 3 3 8 2 2 *